Age of Quintessence

Shadow Legacy

Vista Townsend

AGE OF QUINTESSENCE: SHADOW LEGACY

Print Edition 2016 ISBN 978-0-9906168-7-0

First Edition

Printed in the United States of America

Books By Vista Townsend

Science Fiction
Age of Quintessence series

Synthetic Genesis
Shadow Legacy
Vortex Crucible

Fantasy
Salt Legacy series

Masters of Souls

Historical Fiction

Jagged Road To Sainthood

Dedication

To all those who have lived in the shadow of another,

may your own brilliant light shine.

Prologue

Begin recording.

I'm filming this in the hopes of holding onto my sanity—what little I have left.

I was born Yashana Kalkar. Like my name which mean *victory now* and *challenge*, I am at war with myself, possessed by my hated enemy. Do you know what that is like? Of course not. No sane person would believe me.

So much twisted conflict, impossible paradoxes. I am both atheist and believer, celebrity and nobody, creator and destroyer, an adolescent full of fanciful dreams and an elder who has seen too much. I long for my first kiss yet remember passionate nights with my husband. How can I be both virgin and seasoned wife?

Who am I?

That, I wish I knew.

I bear the face of Layla Rangan, the creator of a clone race of legendary warriors called the quintessences. Because I inherited her talents, others wish to force me upon the path she paved.

But I refuse to live in the cursed shadow of her legacy. You wonder what it is like to be possessed? I can tell you. Worse, I will show you—for I live it every day.

End recording.

Part I

"Has this mind, so replete with ideas, imaginations fanciful and magnificent, which formed a world, whose existence depended on the life of its creator;—has the mind perished? Does it now only exist in my memory? No, it is not thus; your form so divinely wrought, and beaming with beauty, has decayed, but your spirit still visits and consoles your unhappy friend."

—From *Frankenstein* by Mary Shelley

Chapter One

Aware their boss was always watching, office workers keyed in data at terminals while chatting with clients through headsets. Thomas Macnab sat in his large office, watching his busy underlings from behind a glass wall. Pride highlighted his handsome face. Their hard work had earned him a third term as congressman for the Forty-fifth District of the planetary government for Stargleam. On the wall behind him hung degrees and plaques. On his desk was a picture of him accepting the position of president of the local chapter for the Coalition of Human Advancement.

Thomas swung his chair around to face the large windows looking out onto the city he ruled. Starhaven with its skyscrapers, temples, parks, schools, and apartments filled the horizon as far as the eye could see. *My city. My haven.* He smiled, lavishing the feeling of accomplishment. *My realm to manipulate.*

The office door opened, and Thomas turned in annoyance. Seeing his secretary, he barked. "I told you to always knock first. Better yet, send a message."

The dozens of harden spikes on his secretary's head quivered, revealing her deep agitation. Her species of stardancers were the original inhabitance of the planet, but centuries ago their low birthrate had slipped them into the minority where few now held positions of power. Yet somehow one had managed to be elected President of Stargleam due to his outgoing charismatic approach in finding common ground among the many sentient species who now called the planet home.

A mistake I plan to remedy soon, thought Thomas. *I may be human, but I can manipulate as good as the cursed edietheans who think they own the entire Basanti Empire.*

"Sorry, sir," said the golden-skin secretary, "but there are uninvited guests who just entered the lobby. I didn't think you wanted written warnings which might be traced."

"I'm busy. Tell security to kick out the intruders."

"They can't, sir." The many spikes on her head trembled so much that they seemed to dance, reflecting the name the original human colonists had given her species. "They come with Level One clearance sent by President Star'lan himself."

"It must be an investigation committee." Thomas frowned as he settled his athletic body back in his leather chair, giving the air of confidence. Why now after all these years? Had he been careless about something? *No, I have double and triple checked everything. There are no loose ends for them to find.* "Send them to my conference room. We have nothing to hide from them."

"Sir," the secretary's voice went up an octave. "They are quintessences."

For the first time Thomas's confidence faltered. "Are you sure?"

"There is no way to mistake them. They all look the same."

"Aid them in whatever they ask. We have nothing to hide." The decades of lying aided Thomas well in keeping his voice calm, hiding his sudden terror.

After his secretary left, Thomas quickly sent a general e-mail to all office workers informing them there were high level guests visiting. The message concluded with a common phrase, "May the gods of light always shine upon our golden kingdom." It was an ancient saying of the stardancers, used so often in greeting that it had become meaningless, but for Thomas, it was a code phrase which hinted to certain employees to begin wiping incriminating data files off the mainframe.

Thomas had barely hit the send button when he spotted the quintessences through his glass wall. Workers scurried out of the way as they stared in silence at six identical warriors, dressed in black, marching pass cubicles. The sober faces of the quintessences revealed no emotion, but workers whispered to each other in apprehension. Death drinker, mortis elixir, energy leech, walking horror, foeditas horribilis. Names varied between cultures, but every citizen of the Basanti Empire instantly recognized the clone soldiers whose faces were often displayed in news reports. Their species was relatively new, barely a hundred and fifty years old, but their abilities had already become mythical. The quintessences were truth seekers who brought order to chaos, salvation from destruction. But in turn, they left countless dead in their wake. Many were the admirers of the quintessences, but few desired to meet them face-to-face. Now they strolled through Congressman Macnab's domain.

Thomas waited until after his secretary had escorted them to the conference room before following, ignoring the nervous stares of his workers. Entering, he found the six quintessences seated along with a stardancer wearing a military uniform and a casually dressed human of Asian descent.

The golden stardancer with bronze spikes rose and handed Thomas a printed warrant. "I am Major La'beam. President Star'lan has asked for an investigation into your department. There have been repeated security leaks of sensitive information which we believe can be traced here."

"I assure you that we are very cautious with high-level information sent us. Every employee goes through intensive screening before being hired." Thomas kept his voice calm but forceful.

"Nevertheless, a spy has managed to pierce your ranks."

"Of course we will comply with your investigation, helping in any way we can. But is it not excess bringing in outsiders? Surely the quintessences have more important tasks than hunting moles. We can do that ourselves."

"You have not been successful so far. Captain Locke will head this investigation."

The captain stepped forward. Other than an extra stripe pinned on his black uniform above his name, Locke looked identical to his comrades. "We will need to interview every employee, from the highest ranking to the lowest. Starting immediately. We must also have unhindered access to all records."

"Granted. I will have my secretary send you an employee list. Anything else?"

"We need a room with no windows for our interrogations."

Thomas ignored the chill bumps he felt. "I will arrange it."

The congressman spent the rest of the morning in his office, monitoring communications. For lunch he had his secretary order out. Mid-afternoon a routine e-mail containing a code word informed him that the dangerous data files had been erased. He relaxed somewhat. His collaborators were too far down the employee list to be called today. At the end of the workday, they would simply go home and disappear, following protocols Thomas had come up with years ago. He had planned for everything—except for the quintessences. What were they to him? Just a weird science experiment designed to look human but have faster reflexes. *Good perhaps for battle, but dimwitted compared to my brilliance. They are merely soldiers, not politicians.*

He strolled out of his office and walked through the building towards the room being used by the quintessences. Standing guard by the closed door was the human Thomas had seen earlier at the meeting. Thomas casually chatted with the young Asian.

"How does their investigation fare?"

"Still ongoing."

"Discovered the mole yet?"

"No, but one case of embezzling, three taking illegal bribes, and half a dozen affairs. Nothing relating to the security leak."

Thomas laughed, thinking the man was joking. "Quite a sense of humor you have there."

The youth remained unsmiling. "Quintessences are very effective at what they do."

"You tell me." Thomas leaned closer, as if about to share a secret. "Just between you and me, I think the Galactic Senate wasted their trillions of credits manufacturing them. The laws of nature itself had to be broken for them to exist. A species which can't even reproduce except by scientists stirring their DNA in test tubes. What's the fun in that?"

"The process is a bit more complicated than that."

Seeing the youth's seriousness, Thomas wondered if he had misjudged the youth's loyalty. He had presumed the man was a low-level aide, perhaps fresh out of college, sent to monitor the quintessences then report back to his supervisor. "What's your name, son?"

"Ariyo." The youth mentioned no last name or title.

Down the hallway came four workers escorted by two quintessences. Thomas felt uneasiness as he looked over the ones waiting for questioning. They were maintenance workers near the bottom of the list. Surely the quintessences had not interviewed three hundred employees that quickly. They must be skipping around. But why? The door opened, and Thomas was surprised to see his secretary step out followed by Captain Locke. Why was she being questioned?

Seeing her boss, the secretary paled. "Sir, I will have those files you requested soon." She quickly hurried away.

Using anger to hide his nervousness, Thomas faced Captain Locke. "Why are you interviewing my secretary? I trust her completely."

"You will be glad to know then that she has committed no crimes, at least none relating to her job. She does buy smuggled caviar."

"Caviar? You are wasting my employees' valuable time investigating superficial charges. President Star'lan will not be impressed with a list of food smugglers."

"We pressed no charges against her, but we have arrested your press coordinator Rosin for embezzling."

Thomas did not try to hide his shocked expression. He would never have guessed that the man was capable of stealing money—from him. *The putrid sunsoaker. Lucky for him the quintessences found him before I did. Saves me the trouble of killing him and his family later.* "My thanks for rooting out such a pest."

"Who is next?" asked the captain, looking over the four tense employees standing nearby.

"The congressman was first in line," said Ariyo.

Thomas forced a laugh. "I was just stopping by to see how the investigation was going."

"We are questioning everyone, no matter rank." Captain Locke's dark, unnatural eyes locked on Thomas.

"Later." The politician glanced at his watch. "I have an important engagement in just a few minutes. My thanks again for freeing me from that leech." Keeping his pace steady, Thomas walked down the hall. He noticed Captain Locke and Ariyo exchange glances.

They know, whispered fear. *Of course not,* demanded reason. *They would have already arrested me.* Perhaps Pearson or Mayer had already been questioned, but surely neither would have broken down and babbled a confession. But why would his secretary confess to buying smuggled caviar or Rosin to embezzling? What interrogation techniques were being used by those *foeditas horribilis* behind closed doors? Imagining being trapped by the fiends in a locked room, their unnatural predatory eyes staring at him, boring into his secrets, caused the congressman to panic.

Back in his office, Thomas tried to calm himself. *I will go home, claiming to be sick. Keep watch from a distance for a few days. Maybe they will find another to blame without questioning me. If not, I will disappear before they can arrest me.* He had not been skimming off his election funds for years for nothing. He grabbed his briefcase and overcoat. Passing his secretary's desk, he informed her of his sudden illness, noticing she looked sickly herself.

He had almost reached the elevator before the young man working with the quintessences caught up with him. "Is your meeting over already?"

"Yes, but my old war injury is flaring up again, excruciating back pain."

"We will question you next, so you may then go home and rest."

"Doctor's appointment. When I get back, you may."

The elevator doors opened. Thomas stepped inside and punched the button for the first floor. The Asian slipped in between the closing doors. What was it about this youth that made him so impertinent?

"I insist that it be now."

"I am a congressman, not a child to be bossed about."

"If you have nothing to hide, then there is no reason to fear the interrogation."

"I fear nothing." Thomas's anger flared. "Not a snot-nose brat like you or those death dogs on the President's leash."

The elevator doors opened. The youth stepped in front of the politician, blocking his path. "You will come with me now."

"I think not." Thomas revealed the muzzle of a laser gun hidden under his jacket. "You will step out of my way, now."

"No." There was no fear in the youth's dark eyes.

"I will shoot you."

"Not here, where others can see. Surely you are too smart for that."

The doors shut behind the aide, blocking the congressman's escape route. Keeping the gun pointed at the man, Thomas moved to the elevator controls and punched the lowest basement floor. When the doors opened, Thomas gestured him out. "Walk down the hall, to your left."

They had only moved a short distance down the dimly lit corridor before Thomas stopped in front of a supply closet. "Inside, now."

"By doing this, you reveal your guilt."

"By the time you get out, I will be long gone."

Thomas shut and locked the door. He took the elevator up to the first floor then calmly strolled across the lobby. A friend stopped him, inviting Thomas to a dinner party next week. The congressman politely accepted then hurried outside. Hover vehicles zoomed by, forcing him to wait until the light changed to cross to the parking garage. *I should have taken the crossway*, he thought, glancing overhead at the bridge on the third floor connecting the capitol with the parking garage. *I'm too jumpy, not thinking clearly.*

He glimpsed two quintessences running across the crosswalk, straight towards him. *Idiot. You didn't think to take that fool's telecom.* Fearing they would reach him before he could gain the safety of his car, Thomas began running down the sidewalk, looking for a taxi in the rushing traffic. Seeing one in the distance, he increased his speed while gesturing for it to stop. Behind him there was a loud thud followed by a second thump. Looking over his shoulder, he saw the two quintessences rising from crouches after having leaped from the parking garage three floors up, their dark eyes glaring at him.

Thomas panicked. He wildly fired several shots at them then ran towards the taxi. The driver saw the laser beams and refused to stop. The politician yelled a curse and keep running, thankful he had kept in shape after his discharge from the military. Pondering if he should double back to his car, he turned a corner and entered the parking garage. Suddenly he skidded to a stop. The Asian youth stood directly in front of him

"What the…how did you get out so quickly?" Not waiting for an answer, Thomas pointed and fired.

The youth tried to dodge, but the beam burnt into his shoulder. Ariyo fell to the ground. As Thomas ran pass, the youth swung out a foot, knocking the older man down. Thomas regained his footing, but too slowly. He was losing too much time. Seeing the two quintessences rounding the corner, he pointed the gun at the youth sitting on the floor.

"Come a step closer, and I kill him."

The pursers stopped and watched him silently, their expressions stoic.

"Now back off."

Ariyo slowly stood, his hand covering the burnt flesh of his shoulder. "Lesson One when dealing with hostile quintessences—kill first or be killed."

"Shut up. You're coming with me to my car."

"If you surrender now we will not kill you. But that offer will only last for a few seconds."

"I'm the one with the gun. I decide who lives or dies. Walk."

As they moved pass parked vehicles, Thomas kept his gun pointed at Ariyo, but he kept glancing back at the two quintessences who remained motionless. Suddenly Ariyo dodged to the side, agile despite his injury. Thomas fired one shot which went wide before Ariyo gave a high kick, knocking the gun from Thomas's hand. Then Ariyo whirled behind Thomas and bit him where neck and skull joined.

The congressman's body trembled briefly then then his limp body slid to the concrete floor. Ariyo glanced at his now healed shoulder. The only evidence left of the injury was the blackened fibers around the hole in his shirt.

He greeted his two comrades walking up. "We will need to arrest Person in accounting and Mayer in records. And my brother Rinji needs to be freed from the basement."

"I will inform the captain," said the nearest one.

The lips of the second one curled into a ghost of a smile. "If I had any say-so, I would vote that your model never leaves beta testing. They never guess what you are until it is too late."

11

"But why would I want to be limited to only forty-nine brothers when you have tens of thousands?" jested Ariyo, stepping around the dead politician.

"An unknown face is best for infiltration."

The youth pulled out his telecom. "President Star'lan, the leak has been fixed. The head was Congressman Macnab. Yes, we will have more than enough evidence to go public. No, there will be no need for a lawyer for Macnab. He resisted arrest and has been executed."

Chapter Two

The shuttle shook as it passed through the stratosphere. Yashana Kalkar gasped as she looked out the window, seeing the planet of her birth hanging in the blackness of space. Mansoor was as beautiful from a distance as it was close-up with its silvery mushroom shaped skyscrapers and huge tracts of parkland. Homesickness struck the thirteen year old, but she quickly pushed it away. She had wished for this day for over three years, ever since a representative had visited her home and invited her to attend Luncaster University, the most elite school in the empire. All expenses paid by a scholarship.

Her mother had flat out refused, saying Yashana was too young. Pleading and crying had not softened her mother although her father had agreed early on. Yashana spent months pointing out that the gifted classes she took at school were too easy and she needed to be around other prodigies like herself. But her mom continued to hold her back, not understanding why her offspring could not enjoy staying a child for a while longer. Even when Yashana had graduated high school at the age of eleven, her mother had insisted she attend a local junior college. When Yashana completed all the required courses of her double major, her mother finally, reluctantly, let her youngest daughter go.

"Looks much cooler than in the vids," said a boy buckled in beside Yashana.

She glanced at the brown haired youth who looked about her age. "It's my first time off world."

"Mine too. I'm going to Luncaster University."

Yashana stared in astonishment. "I am too. What a strange coincidence."

"Not likely a coincidence. If you got the same scholarship I did, then the person buying our tickets naturally booked them together."

"Oh." Trying to appear sophisticated, Yashana said, "I was invited to attend three years ago, but my mom refused. I hate being a minor. Adults think they know everything."

The boy looked away, troubled. "I didn't come when first asked because my mom was sick. Then after she died, I was worried about my dad being alone."

"Uh, sorry."

"It's alright. My grandmother moved in. Dad's more cheerful and insisted I head out to become a man, though I'm in no hurry. Men have to pay bills."

The girl laughed while brushing a long strand of black hair away from her face. "I guess there are some nice things about being young. I'm Yashana."

"Ethan. Maybe our rooms on the spaceliner will be near each other."

"I hope so. It will be nice having a friend for the trip."

A short time later the shuttle docked with the liner. The teenagers grabbed their carry-on bags. Pulling out their tickets, they were delighted to discover their cabins were indeed beside each other. They found their rooms, unpacked, and then explored the ship. As they ate in the elegant dining room, Ethan pointed at a security camera barely visible in a corner.

"That's from the C series. Outdated. I would think on a spaceliner like this, they would have updated their system as least a decade ago."

"You know a lot about technology?"

"Tons. I can tell you every major breakthrough for the last millennium, the inventors and companies involved, and how each invention impacted society."

"I'm just happy the lights work when I flip them on."

"Sorry, I didn't mean to brag. I'll try to avoid boring you."

"It's alright. I've had to dumb down my conversation for years because no one understood me, not even my teachers. I'm into science, especially bioengineering, though many fields interest me."

Ethan smiled. "It's a relief to finally be around another like me."

"Agreed. My mom never could understand why I insisted on going to Luncaster."

The teenagers spent hours talking. As Ethan relaxed, he admitted to using computers to pull pranks on fellow students and teachers. "They always suspected me, but I rarely got caught. I'm an expert at covering my tracks. I pranked my dad too. Well, prank may not be the right word. I programmed his computer to call him 'Super Dad' and his car to flash messages like 'You're the best dad in the world.' He was really depressed after Mom died, so I did anything I could to cheer him up."

"You're a saint compared to me," admitted Yashana. "I fought with my older sisters and fussed with my parents, especially my mom. I resented that she would not let me go to Luncaster. I know she was just trying to protect me, but I was really mean sometimes."

"She'll forgive you. Parents are good at that sort of thing. Want to go check out the pool?"

A week later the spaceliner dropped into orbit above the planet Xi'an. The excited youths sat beside each other in the shuttle taken them planetside, their faces eagerly peering out the window. As they hit the stratosphere, flaming vapors blocked the view and the ship trembled. Pale-faced, Yashana held her armrest in a death grip. Ethan joked, pretending to be calm, but he also held tightly to his seat. As they descended lower, the view cleared and the shaking stopped. Yashana relaxed and watched a blue ocean rush pass. As they slowed for the approach, land appeared, covered by thick forests and huge plains. Suddenly the wilderness was broken by a vast complex of buildings, training fields, and hangers.

"That must be Essence Institute," pointed out Ethan. "Even from this high up I can recognize Richton Tower. The building is massive. Its architect won a Zelzer Award."

Yashana shuddered. "It's home to the foeditas horribilis."

"I wouldn't call them *horrifying foulness* to their faces."

"No worries there. There is no way I'll go to Essence." The complex had already disappeared from view. The city of New Hope with its tidy roads and monorails now loomed below.

"It would be fantastic to view their security system. It was originally designed by Richard Cambridge. He won a Zelzer too. Not for that, of course, but for his DNA software. Still hard for me to believe he was only seventeen when he started Cambridge Software which is now the most influential computer company in the galaxy."

"Do you have the life story of every Zelzer winner memorized?"

"Only for the last two hundred years. Do you know that Layla Rangan won a Zelzer the same year as Cambridge? She still holds the record for being the youngest winner at age twenty-seven."

"For designing the death drinkers when she was thirteen. That I did know."

The sprawling city of Luncaster came into view, and soon they could make out tiny hover cars and people walking below. After the shuttle landed at the nearby space port, they grabbed their luggage. In the busy lobby they found a man holding a large sign with their first names written on it. They walked up and nervously, but excitedly introduced themselves.

"Good to meet you." The elderly human smiled at them. He was dressed in a casual brown suit, his hair combed to cover his balding top. "I'm Professor Duken. Most likely I will be one of your teachers. You are the last to arrive this morning. Got your things? Good, follow me."

Yashana and Ethan, along with half a dozen other students, followed the professor who walked partly scooped, using a cane for support. The professor led them to a large hover van. Yashana noticed that she and Ethan were the youngest in the group. Normally no one younger than fourteen could attend the university, but exceptions were given for species who matured faster or for especially gifted individuals. The one requirement which never changed was that every candidate for Luncaster University had to be a proven genius before they ever set foot, fin, or tentacle on the campus.

The van soon reached the university. Yashana admired the sleek, natural architectural of the buildings surrounded by trees, gardens, fountains, and flowery courtyards. She wondered if its designer had also won a Zelzer and was about to ask Ethan when the van stopped.

"All females out," said the professor. "This is your dorm."

For a moment Yashana was reluctant to leave Ethan. "Call me later when you get settled?"

"Sure. Maybe we can eat lunch together."

Yashana wheeled her suitcase down the sidewalk to a large, glass covered-building which reflected blue sky and green trees. She waited with the others at the registration desk. Finally she was given a packet which included her room number and her assigned e-tablet which was already synced with the college's security network. After checking a map, she took an elevator up to the third floor. Outside her new room, she paused and took a deep breath. She placed her thumb on a small sensor then waited until the lock clicked. Slowly she opened the door.

The room had two desks, two small closets, and two beds, one already covered with a black bedspread. A large lizard looked up from unpacking. Both girls stared at each other.

Yashana was caught off guard. On Mansoor, almost all sentients were mammals. She had never been near an intelligent reptile before. "Hi, uh…I am your new roommate. Yashana."

"Greetings. I am Gauge of the Blackrock Tribe." The reptile returned to her unpacking.

Yashana dragged her suitcase to the unmade bed and pulled out her belongings, feeling awkward in the silence. What did one say to a talking lizard? From sideway glances, she watched Gauge hang plain, unfashionable clothing in her closet. Instead of hair, the reptile had several bony ridges on her head and down the back of her neck. The tip of her broad tail twitched as she worked. Fingers ended in claws. Her thick, scaly skin was dark brown on her back, but her face and limbs were lighter. She was nearly a foot taller than Yashana and most likely several years older, that is, if she matured at roughly the same speed as humans.

Finished with unpacking, Gauge worked on syncing her e-tablet with the electronic billboard on the wall. As she typed in her class schedule, the calendar on the billboard automatically updated.

"I'm from Mansoor."

"Zon." The reptile did not look up.

"I've never heard of that planet."

"Few have. It is located on the outer edge of the galaxy. We only developed light speed two centuries ago."

"Uh…what is Zon like?"

"Nothing like Xi'on. Not green. No oceans. Little water above ground."

"I have read that deserts are pretty."

Gauge stopped typing and looked at her roommate. "Zon is not a desert. My world is just….different than here. Yes, it is beautiful, at least to us." She spoke with a heavy accent, pausing at times to consider which word to use next.

"Would you be offended if I asked which species you are?"

"No. You may call me a zonner. What we call ourselves is too difficult for you to pronounce in Standard."

Yashana's telecom beeped. As she texted back an answer to Ethan, she said to her roommate, "Gauge, would you like to eat lunch with me and a friend?"

Gauge's lips parted in a polite smile, revealing small, sharp teeth. "Yes, I would like that."

They met Ethan in front of the cafeteria. Like Yashana, he was at first unsure how to interact with a sentient reptile, but he greeted Gauge politely. As they ate, the conversation remained forced until Ethan learned that zonners have only developed space travel recently. Eagerly he quizzed Gauge about her planet's technology. She shared what little she knew.

"Forgive me, but I know not how our warp drives work. I could give you addresses of several of my clansmen who are engineers. They could tell you much."

"I would enjoy that." Ethan took a bite of his burger. "Wow, it's amazing I'm actually sitting here talking with you."

"I am glad you enjoy the conversation, but I am not that entertaining."

"I mean, your species' technology evolved completely untainted from other cultures. Do you know how rare that is? True innovation almost never happens anymore. Yes, we are constantly making technical advances, but it's usually only small steps built on top of concepts that are centuries or millenniums old. The most exciting breakthroughs are when we step away from what we know into the unknown."

"You flatter my race, but you will find we are far underdeveloped compared to most civilizations. We did not even know life existed on other planets until after we developed light speed and ran into a mining ship. It was decades before the first anthropologist visited our planet and shared with us what the rest of the galaxy was like. That is when we learned that over ten thousand years ago the edietheans were the first species to travel to the stars. Empires rose and fell as various sentient species fought to colonizing the most planets and hoard the most resources. Eventually many species united under the Basanti Empire. And the most brutal conflict of all, the Great War, was fought until no galactic power was left except for Basanti. All this my world missed for we were too remote and primitive to be noticed."

"Perhaps you're lucky," said Yashana. "Your people never died in wars."

"Ah, but war we do know. Clans fought each other since our beginning. We were so proud, so arrogant. Our shock was profound when we discovered that not only were there great civilizations on other worlds, but we were the least of them all. We desired to take our place among them, so we united under one government and applied to the Galactic Senate for nationhood." Gauge paused to cut a piece off her tenderloin. Her plate contained only meat. "So far, the Senate will only give us developing status."

"You're not even citizens of the empire?" Ethan was shocked. "I thought if a culture had light speed technology then acceptance was automatic."

"There are many requirements besides that. We are considered children next to you. One of our weaknesses is education. We must raise our level much higher. That is why I am here. Each clan raises money to send one of their own off world. After we master a topic we are to return and teach our people. Where once clans fought for land, now we compete for knowledge. I am the first zonner to be accepted at Luncaster. I bring much honor to Blackrock by being here."

"Your whole tribe raised money for you?" Yashana glanced at Ethan, feeling guilty that their scholarships had been given so easily.

"Yes, they began saving long before I was born. The greatest moment in my life was when I was chosen. And my worst fear is that I will fail them."

"You won't," said Yashana. "It's normal to be nervous. I was nervous about coming here."

Ethan added, "I was too until I meet Yashana. Friends help each other. We can be study partners, at least when we have the same classes."

Gauge gave a toothy grin. "I thought I would find no comrades among warm-blooders. I am relieved to find I am wrong."

Chapter Three

The large student union bustled with activity. Adolescents of many species studied on couches arranged in clusters. The fish-like squamigers used translators on their helmets since mammals could not understand their water language. They preferred being study partners with ophthalmias who never left their slim mobile tanks of salt water.

Faculty and pupils stood in line to buy meals from vendors or ate at tables scattered about the large forum. Newsfeed constantly changed on the huge screens hanging from the ceiling in the middle of the chamber.

"Your alarm is going off again," said Gauge, looking up from reading a textbook of early Basanti history on her e-tablet.

Yashana frowned as she turned off the alarm. "Oh, I set it yesterday to remind myself to check growth rates of bacteria for my project. Unfortunately, this morning I found my sample dead, again. My partner is going to kill me."

"I'm surprised he hasn't already. That makes the third time." Ethan grinned, his brown eyes almost the same shade as his shaggy hair in need of a cutting. "Good thing you never killed our computer projects when we were freshman."

"That was because you were there to swoop in to save me at the last minute from killing a virtual plant or animal." Yashana, now fourteen, tucked a long strand of black hair behind her ear and continued studying for a genetics exam. "Too bad we don't have the same major. I could use your help."

"I keep to the virtual world. Real life is too unpredictable."

"That is strange." Looking up at the nearest vid, Gauge partly rose from the couch she lounged across. Zonners could sit like humans, but when given the opportunity, they preferred stretching prone.

The others looked towards the large screen. Instead of showing newsfeed, the vid displayed a cartoonish figure of the university's dean quoting whimsical poetry in a high-pitch, girlish voice. Below the cartoon a ticker said, "Brought to you by ~ Data Phantom." Students laughed along with several teachers, but other professors looked offended. The video only lasted a few minutes then flicked back to the news.

"How immature," said Ethan. "Data Phantom. What type of name is that?"

"Think you can do better?" asked a neodite, turning around on a couch behind Gauge. His smooth skin was currently blueish, but it had the tendency to change shades based on his emotions. His thick, lavender hair was styled into a pompadour, and cut short around his squarish ears.

"Don't tell me that was your handy work, Thorus. I could make political cartoons more realistically than that when I was eight."

"Then why haven't you shown off your skills lately?" As a senior, Thorus made it his business to know every hacker at the school. Little in the tech realm went unnoticed by him.

"I'm too mature."

Thorus snorted. "Where you not the one who reset the clocks in the entire school so that we all woke up at midnight for first period?"

"I never claimed it was me."

"Right. It was the Prankster Brainster. What type of stupid name is that?"

"No worse than Data Phantom."

"From your...I mean Prankster's...absence, I reason that you can't break the new security codes."

"There is no code yet written that I can't hack."

Gauge sighed loudly. "If you two wish to argue, please do so elsewhere instead of over my couch. I am trying to study."

The neodite turned back around, and there was silence for a while. Suddenly Thorus held up his e-tablet, grinned wickedly, and touched his screen. Immediately the fire alarm sounded and red lights flared. Students and workers, annoyed, looked for smoke as they headed out of the building.

"Geek warfare is so irritating," complained Yashana as they walked towards the nearest exit of the student union.

"Two hacks in the same day. He will get caught for sure." Ethan led his friends away from the crowd gathering outside the building.

"They should increase the penalty for hackers—like expulsion," said Gauge.

"What? You want me kicked out?"

"No, but I do prefer my sleep."

"I made sure that the clock episode was not on a major test day."

Yashana rolled her eyes. "What is it about geeks and pranks?"

Ethan stopped walking. "It's a way to become immortalized. The best pranks are still talked about decades or centuries later. Our legacy is passed on to future generations of students."

"Immortality is not that important."

"Don't you want to be remembered?"

"I just want to pass my test tomorrow."

Yashana forgot about the conversation, but Ethan did not. A month later he excitedly greeted her after third period.

"Come, I've got something to show you."

"What about lunch?"

"This is more exciting."

"Than food?"

Yashana followed him down the hallway, passing students heading in the opposite direction towards the cafeteria. They left the building and stopped in a deserted courtyard surrounded by a thick hedge.

Gauge waited by a fountain which spewed water in five directions into a deep basin. "I received your message. Why are we missing lunch?"

Ethan sat his e-tablet down on the marble bench beside the zonner. "Because this is a historical moment in the history of geekhood. I wanted to share it with my two best friends."

"It better be really spectacular because I'm hungry," complained Yashana.

"I'm about to perform the greatest hack in recorded history."

"You're not going to turn on all the sprinklers are you? I don't feel like getting wet today."

"Child's play." Ethan took a deep breath then smiled dramatically. "I'm about to hack into the most secure system in the galaxy—Essence Institute."

"That is a military facility," said Gauge. "The penalty would be severe."

"I've covered my tracks too well. I can't be caught. Even if they did, they will just thank me for finding flaws in their system."

"How are you going to get in?" asked Yashana. "I mean, is not their system well protected to keep people like you out?"

"To keep it in simple terms for you, I'm going through the backdoor. Computer programmers create them for maintenance and emergency use. Cambridge Software upkeeps Essence's security. I found their hidden door weeks ago then wrote a brilliant little program which knocks, tries a new password, and runs away. Then it does so again but from another direction, randomly using dozens of different routers so it can't be traced. It was only a matter of time before I found the right combination."

He pulled up a program on his e-tablet. "Now watch this."

Ethan touched a command and a red box popped up. "Access denied."

"No, no, no!" he yelled. "I kept the program active too long, but the code won't be changed yet. I need another computer." He looked around, desperate.

"You're not using mine," said Yashana. "I don't want the energy leeches coming after me."

"I told you I'm untraceable. I've never been caught at Luncaster."

"You may use mine." Gauge passed her e-tablet over.

Ethan smiled his thanks, logged onto the network then zoomed through a dozen anonymous proxies, hiding his identify. Finally he stopped at Essence's backdoor and typed in the password the other computer had found. He gave a loud whoop when the code was accepted and a plain page appeared, showing a few links.

"We're inside Essence's mainframe right now. Top that, Data Phantom."

"Does not look like anything to me," said Gauge.

"Ah, looks are deceptive. I have enormous power in my hands right now. If we had time, I could show you all the inner secrets of Essence. But there are technicians looking out for security breaks, so I have to be quick."

Pages of information, blueprints, and forms flew by in a blur. Ethan occasionally paused and had the computer take a snapshot of the screen. Personal records popped up. Ethan hit a button for entering new staff then typed in the name Prankster Brainster.

"What job should I give him?"

"How about jester?" suggested Yashana.

By the time Ethan had finished filling out the form with silly data, all three were laughing hard. Ethan took another snapshot then exited out of the system.

"I'm sending the pictures to one of my dummy e-mail accounts. Later I will send it to all the geeks as proof that Prankster Brainster is the best hacker in the universe."

They were still laughing as they hurried to their classes. That night after dinner, they went to the student union to study. Ethan chose a seat adjacent to where Thorus and his buddies worked on a computer project. Half an hour later, Ethan sent an e-mail showing several pictures of the hack to every student majoring in technology. Then he waited patiently until one of his neighbors checked his e-mail. Soon all the tech students were studying the pictures, debating if they were real.

"Got to be fake," said Thorus. "There's no way anyone can hack into Essence."

Keeping a blank face, Ethan peered over the back of his couch and said, "Obviously someone did."

"But how?"

"A Prankster never reveals his secrets."

"Does the Prankster have witnesses?"

"Yes, two. But they must remain anonymous."

"I'll certify it's real if the Prankster reveals how he did it."

"Meet me after curfew in the snack room."

Ethan turned back around to face his friends, grinning boldly as he relished the feeling of success.

Chapter Four

Yashana quickly finished writing her conclusion paragraph about the benefits of using viruses as tools in genetic engineering. Her fingers moved easily over the sleek surface of her e-tablet.

"Time is up," announced the professor at the front of the classroom. "You will submit your essays now. Remember your mid-term is Friday."

Yashana hit the send button and a window popped up, asking for ID verification. She typed in her password then placed her thumb over a square. The window turned green, recognizing her fingerprint. The built in camera automatically snapped her picture and sent it along with her test. The extra security that the college used to prevent cheating was annoying and time consuming. *If there weren't students like Ethan and Thorus who keep trying to outsmart the system, the college wouldn't have to be so strict,* she reminded herself.

Tucking her e-tablet into her handbag, Yashana left the classroom and headed to the nearest courtyard where she and Gauge often hung out between classes. Many of the benches were already filled with students, but Gauge had not arrived. Yashana sat on a bench by a fountain where water drizzled from the leaves of a bronze tree in remembrance of the historic Tree of Serenity where the first Emperor of Basanti had signed a treaty with his defeated enemies, uniting his planet under one government, not knowing that two thousand years later his empire would control the entire galaxy.

Yashana read a textbook on her e-tablet, occasionally glancing up, expecting to see Gauge. She became concerned when the next class started and her friend was still missing. Just before the professor started his lecture, Yashana quickly sent a text message, asking Gauge where she was. When class was over, she still had received no response. As she headed to lunch, she noticed that clusters of students seemed tense as they chatted. At the cafeteria, she met up with Ethan.

"Gauge is missing."

"I'm sure she is around here somewhere." Ethan placed a slice of bumbleberry pie on his tray as they walked away from the food line.

"She didn't answer my message."

"Maybe she's in the middle of a group project meeting."

They had barely sat down before Thorus left his table and joined them. His blue skin had purplish splotches, revealing his stress. "Energy leeches are here."

"Impossible. They never come here," said Ethan.

"They must have tracked yesterday's hack." Thorus leaned across the table and whispered, "They arrested Gauge."

"Are you sure?" Ethan's face paled.

"Two hours ago my roommate saw them escorting her from the History Department."

"I was careful. I covered my tracks."

"Foeditas horribilis have Gage?" Yashana felt sick at her stomach. "Why did they arrest her and not you?"

"I used her computer, remember. But how did they know? I should have been untraceable."

Thorus kept his voice low. "Did you wipe her computer's memory clean?"

"Of course. Like I said, I'm care…." Suddenly Ethan's eyes widen. "The pictures. I didn't erase the originals. They are still on her hard drive." He smacked a fist against his forehead. "How could I have been so stupid?"

"The real question is how they traced it to her e-tablet in the first place. Obviously, no geek told on you or you would have been arrested instead of her."

Yashana fought against panic. "Why did the leeches arrest her instead of school security? Those monsters will kill her."

The neodite leaned closer. "The hack was into their own system. That makes it personal for them." Pity filled the senior's eyes. "There is nothing that can be done for her now. But you still may have time to erase any evidence left on your computer."

Yashana became angry. "What do you mean nothing can be done? She's innocent. Ethan, you have to tell them."

"Ethan's confession won't be enough to save her," said Thorus. "The evidence on her e-tablet will convict her no matter if she keeps silent or names Ethan as a collaborator. Either way, they will view her as guilty. The leeches may be on their way right now to arrest you. That's why you need to clean up your trail quickly."

Ethan placed his head in his hands, groaning. "It was a prank. Just a prank. I have to tell them it was me. She's innocent."

"It's noble you want to help her, but you're talking about confessing to a galactic level crime—hacking into a military base. They aren't simply going to give you detention."

Angrily Ethan shot back, "What do you think they are going to do to Gauge? Her tribe's honor is tied to her education, and I stole that from her—from them. The only ones who will miss me are my father and grandmother."

"I will miss you." Yashana placed a comforting hand on his arm.

"Thanks." Ethan closed his eyes for a moment. Then he stood, steel determination on his face. "I'm going to the dean and tell everything."

Yashana rose. "I'll go with you. I was there too."

Thorus shook his head in denial but looked at them with respect. "I'll pray to my people's god that you don't become a meal for the foeditas horribilis."

Silent and tense, Ethan and Yashana walked across the campus to the administration building, passing students chatting, laughing, or studying—what their own lives had been like just half an hour ago. After entering the lobby, Ethan asked the secretary for a meeting with the dean, explaining he had information about the hack. A few minutes later he and Yashana were ushered up to the third floor.

Dean Wellesz, a human in her fifties, sat behind her desk. Her office was tidy. Books lined up evenly on shelves, and cabinets displayed digital labels for the files they contained. With a stern face, she greeted the teenagers. "Have a seat. I am informed you know something about a hack which took place yesterday."

"Yes, I was…" Ethan took a deep breath. "It was my fault. I did it, not Gauge."

"They found evidence on her computer."

"She is a history major. I am a tech genius. I just used her computer. I didn't mean to get her in trouble. It was just a prank, a joke."

Wellesz leaned back in her chair and studied Ethan. "Do you realize what you have just confessed to me? You are claiming that you broke into an imperial military facility as a joke."

"A joke, that's all."

"They classify it as an act of terrorism."

"A terrorist. Me?" Ethan forced a laugh. "I'm just a fourteen-year-old geek."

The dean sighed. "It is a pity what happened to your friend. She will be missed."

"They have to let her go now." Yashana spoke for the first time.

Wellesz looked at her. "She was your roommate, I believe. Your loyalty is commendable, but you cannot help her. Gauge has confessed that she was involved, and there was evidence on her computer. Go back to your classes and forgot what you have told me."

Ethan looked at Yashana in confusion then said, "But I confessed."

"One life is ruined today. I do not wish to lose another."

Yashana leaned forward. "What about Gauge? Her tribe is counting on her."

"There is nothing you or I can do for your friend. The charges against her will not be dropped..." She looked Ethan in the eyes. "...if you are also arrested. She willingly allowed her computer to be used. Put this down as a painful lesson which you are never to repeat."

"But...they can't. She's innocent."

"Zonners are not citizens of the empire. The quintessences may hold her as long as they wish without trial. She will simply disappear."

"That's unfair."

Wellesz turned her monitor around so the teenagers could see the pictures Ethan had taken of the hack. "This e-mail was sent to me yesterday by a tech professor." With a click, the dean pulled up a hidden data tag which had been attached to a photo. "We have the date and serial number of the computer used."

"Serial number?" Ethan looked like he might faint. "I've never heard of that being attached to a photo before."

"It is one of our security measures to counteract cheating. Every student's e-tablet automatically attaches a data tag to every picture, telling us which computer it came from. It was easy for the quintessences to use this info to track down Gauge."

"Why did she confess? She should have told them it was me."

"She is protecting you like you are trying to protect her. Honor her sacrifice. Go back to class and forget all of this. Make something wonderful of your life in remembrance of her."

Ethan and Yashana left the building in a daze. They had not walked far before Ethan began trembling. He turned off the path and ran, finally ducking behind a large bush near a dumpster. Yashana caught up with him and silently sat on the ground beside him as he sobbed. She felt awkward, having never seen him cry before. She placed a hand on his back, offering what comfort she could.

"My fault. Mine. My pride. My vanity. She should not bear the consequences of my sins. I have destroyed her. Slaughtered the hopes of her people."

"Maybe they will realize it was just a prank and let her go soon. All you did was create a dummy employee. You didn't do anything malicious."

Ethan looked up, his eyes red. "Have you ever heard of the foeditas horribilis being merciful to the guilty? You know the stories. They will keep them in prison at Essence, feeding on them day after day. Mercy would be killing them immediately. But the leeches won't. They drink the prisoners' life force over and over until they beg for death."

"Those stories are fictional. The news has never reported that." Yashana looked away, shuddering at the mental image of Gauge being feed upon by shadowy figures.

"The government controls the media. Do you want that fate for Gauge?"

"No, but what can we do?"

"I don't know. But I can't live with this guilt. I can't."

"Don't talk like that, ever. Do you hear me, Ethan? The dean is right in that you should live a good life to honor Gauge."

"How can I ever look my dad in the eyes again knowing what I have done? I cannot, will not bear this weight. I must make things right."

"You already tried confessing."

"Then…then I will free Gauge."

"How? They probably already have her locked in their prison."

"If I hacked in once, I can do it again." He stood up, brushing away the last of his tears. "The code will have already been changed, but my program can discover the new one."

"Didn't that take you weeks the first time?"

Ethan led the way back to the paved path. "If I only use one computer. But if I use many and cut down on the number of random routers to hide behind, maybe, just maybe, I could break through tonight."

"I want her freed as much as you, but what good will hacking in a second time do? You will be arrested, and they still won't free her."

"Don't you see? Once in, I have the power to do anything. That includes opening her cell door. I can turn off the alarms, and she could walk out, completely free. Then we will hide her, raise money somehow to fly her back to Zon. They can't touch her there because it's out of galactic jurisdiction."

"You're talking wildly. It won't work."

"I have to try. I don't care if I'm caught. I just can't live with myself if I do nothing."

"How will she know that you are helping her? She won't know that the alarms are off or the door unlocked."

"Then I will have to walk in and tell her."

"This is crazy." Yashana stepped in front of Ethan, forcing him to stop walking. "You can't be running around a maximal level prison and trying to hack at the same time."

"Watch me. The Prankster Brainster still has never been caught." He moved around her and continued walking. As they neared the tech department, Ethan texted a message. A few minutes later Thorus met them. As Ethan shared his plan, the neodite looked doubtful.

"You don't have to help me. I can do this without anyone."

"Not if you are to be successful." Thorus lowered his voice. "I can provide the computers you need. I have access to the basement where broken hardware is stored. Some can still access the network. Meet me there in roughly half an hour, but don't come together. We must avoid attention."

Nearly an hour later, Yashana walked into the large, shadowy basement of the Technology Department where several were already hard at work. Ethan was copying his hacking program into an old desktop while Thorus searched through the countless shelves of hardware for any computer capable of going online.

"What can I do to help?" asked Yashana.

"Guard the door." Thorus pushed aside a dusty printer and picked up an e-tablet with a cracked screen. "I have a few more friends who are coming to help. They'll give the codeword Data Brainster."

Over the next several hours, half a dozen geeks drifted in to help. They joked as they worked, but tension was tangible, all aware that if caught, their school career could end—or worst, their lives. By evening, three dozen computers constantly bombarded the backdoor of Essence's security network. Now came the long wait. Several students left while others discussed what should be done if the code was found.

"This is my problem," said Ethan. "I'm going in alone."

"You can't run around their base and hack effectively at the same time. It's a two person job." Purple stress marks were visible on Thorus's skin.

"No one else is getting into trouble because of me."

"I'll go," said Yashana. "She's my roommate."

"I don't want you arrested too."

"Look, I was present at the first hack, even gave you suggestions on what to type. I carry part of the blame too. I may not be able to navigate a network like you, but I can memorize a map. I'll go in."

Ethan tried to argue her out of it but eventually agreed.

Thorus left the basement for a while then returned with equipment. "These earbuds will allow you to talk to each other unmonitored. At least for a while. And this GPS I'll sync with Ethan's computer so he can track your location. You will have to be quick. The moment they realize that there's an intruder, they will attempt to close down all outside communications. Then you will be on your own."

"Makes me feel like a spy."

"If you get caught, that is what they will accuse you of," said the senior. "This is no longer a game."

"I know." Yashana swallowed, trying not to show her fear.

The hours moved too slowly. Yashana fell asleep on the hard floor, using her handbag as a pillow. It was nearly three in the morning when Ethan woke her.

"We found it."

Yashana sat up. "We're good to go then?"

"Yes, but you don't have to do this. This is my burden to bear."

"Some burdens are too heavy to carry alone. Like you, I can't leave Gauge to be feasted on by those leeches."

Thorus looked up from his e-tablet. "I'll send a fake distress call to distract guards at the east gate. Hurry. I've already called a taxi for you."

Yashana rose from the floor, feeling stiff and cold. She followed Ethan out of the basement and into the chilly night. Only two building separated them from the college's east gate. Carefully they walked, avoiding the few security guards on patrol. Near the east gate, they skirted sprinklers watering flower beds then exited through the large arched gateway. The guardhouse was empty. They walked to the next street corner where a taxi was just pulling up. Hurriedly they got in and rode to the nearest monorail station. Ethan paid the driver.

Only a few people moved about the station at this late hour. Ethan bought tickets, and they caught the next train heading to the city of New Hope. Their car was empty, but they spoke little, each lost in their own thoughts. Yashana was torn between disappointing her parents and her

31

loyalty to Gauge. *You were right, Mom. I am too immature for college. Forgive me for what I'm about to do.*

When they reached the border of New Hope, Ethan broke the silence. "Did you know that Richard Cambridge designed this city?"

"Cambridge, the software developer?"

"Yeah, the one that won a Zelzer. He wasn't just satisfied with writing codes. He wanted to improve lives, so he created a program that helped him design the perfect city when New Hope was only a trailer park for construction workers building Essence. He was considered a visionary and humanitarian. He remained mayor for over thirty years until he retired. New Hope has always remained at the top of the list for *Best Cities in the Empire.*"

"Um....so it's a nice place to live."

Ethan swallowed, trying to control his emotions. "I'm nothing like him. I'm just a computer nerd who wants to see how far I can push technology. I haven't been thinking about how what I do affects others. I've only been thinking about myself, wanting the glory."

"Enough of this guilt." Yashana brushed back her long hair to place the earbud. "We're both selfish and spoiled. Gauge is the saint. Perhaps tonight we can redeem ourselves."

The train stopped, and they exited the monorail station in a residential area. Several streets away rose a thick concrete wall overshadowing the tidy homes near it. The seventy-feet-tall concrete barrier separated Essence Institute from the city where most of its workers lived. The wall's top edge was made from electric barb wires monitored by sensors. Guard towers were posted every five hundred feet.

"Who would want to live by that?" wondered Yashana.

"This city has one of the lowest crimes rates in the galaxy."

"Well, we're about to change that."

Chapter Five

Yashana shivered in the chilly darkness beside Ethan who double checked the equipment. They hid in the shadows between a tall hedge and a flowering bush in someone's front yard. Across the street rose the giant, barren wall. A hundred feet away was a small tunnel barely big enough for a van to drive through. Most workers at Essence used the monorail for transportation into the institute, but several tunnels allowed access for supply trucks and other vehicles.

"Are you sure this tunnel is abandoned?"

"Yes, since that new highway was built on the other side of town, they rarely need to leave the institute from this direction. Shouldn't be any guards, but there will still be alarms. Don't try to open the gate until I tell you." Ethan logged onto the network with the cracked e-tablet he had borrowed from the basement. "You can still back out."

"So can you."

"No, I can't."

"Then neither can I."

Yashana casually walked across the street and strolled along the sidewalk, feeling eerie to be inches from the massive wall. When she reached the tunnel, she ducked inside and treaded carefully through the darkness, using a small flashlight as guidance. She kept to the sidewalk which ran parallel to the old street. She stopped by an empty guard house. Beside it a metal fence blocked the rest of the passage.

"I'm at the first service gate."

She waited several minutes until Ethan said though the earpiece, "I'm in. Both gates should be turned off now."

The teenager pulled on the handle and the small gate slid open. "No alarm sounded."

"Good. That means the electricity should be off on the next one."

"Better, or you will be rushing me to the hospital."

Yashana continued through the gloom to a second fence. Gingerly she reached out and touched its metal surface with one finger. Nothing happened. She found its service gate and went through. Dim moonlight ahead outlined the exit of the tunnel. She hid in the shadow of the archway and peered out. Nearby were maintenance buildings, several broken vehicles, and old equipment. Beyond lay the prison, if the old map Ethan had downloaded hours earlier was correct.

Keeping to the shadows, Yashana moved through the maintenance area, heeding Ethan's directions in her ear. Finally she peeked around a corner and saw a beautiful oval building, its glass walls reflecting streetlight.

"Your directions are wrong. It's an office building."

"No, it's the prison. I'm looking at the blueprints from their mainframe right now."

"It's too small to house thousands of prisoners."

"Remember, this is Essence. Nothing is as it seems. Head to the back. I'm unlocking a door for you."

"I think you're wrong," mumbled Yashana, walking through a wooded area to approach the building from behind. She followed a sidewalk bordered by flowers which led her to double doors. Standing in the entranceway, she noted a camera pointed at her and the security lock on the door. "Do you have it yet?"

"Give me a moment. It's asking for an access code."

"I don't have time for you to search for codes."

"Be patience. It's only a ten digit one."

"Is that camera off?"

"I think so."

"You think?" Yashana felt vulnerable standing exposed in the entranceway. What if Ethan could not break this code? How long should she stand here, just waiting? At any moment the hack could be discovered and his line cut. Then she would have to rush back, not knowing if the electric fencing would be off. In the distance she heard footsteps coming down the sidewalk. She flattened herself against the wall, panicking.

"Ethan, open the door now."

"I'm hurrying as fast as I can."

The footsteps were nearing. Yashana grabbed the door handle and pulled. It would not budge. Fearing someone would walk around the corner any second, she looked around desperately, but there was no place to hide. She pulled on the door again. Seeing a thumb scanner, she placed her finger on it. The red light on the security lock turned green. She yanked open the door and rushed inside an unlit lobby. Ducking behind a couch, she pressed her body against the wall, her heart pounding. Peeking up, she glimpsed a guard passing the entranceway, continuing on his patrol.

"That was a close one."

"You're in?"

"Yes. Thanks for waiting to the last second."

"I still haven't assessed the prison system."

"You must have without realizing it. Where next?"

"You need to find a stairway. The prisoners are kept in subterranean levels."

"A dungeon?"

"You tell me. You're the one there. Should be stairs at the end of a hallway on your right."

"Perhaps I'll find a torture chamber." Despite the jokes, Yashana felt terrified as she moved along the dark hallway, passing office doors and paintings of generic landscape. The end of the hall was blocked by another security door. "Have you unlocked it yet?"

"I've told you, I don't have access."

Yashana pressed her thumb on the scanner and the light turned green. "Then how did I just get in again?"

"Perhaps Thorus's god is looking out for you. You may need to offer a sacrifice later."

"Hopefully it doesn't require a blood sacrifice."

She headed downstairs, treading as quietly as possible. The stairs seemed endless. She passed several landings but Ethan instructed her to go deeper, much deeper.

"What do they have under here? A nuclear bomb shelter?"

"Actually, I think so."

"How much further?"

"Next landing. Through a double set of doors. Security is tight." Ethan's voice sounded tense. "Hope that neodite god is still looking out for you."

Like before, the first door opened to Yashana's touch. She walked into a plain, dimly lit room. The walls hummed and a blue beam of light scanned Yashana's body. The teenager almost bolted in fear, but she forced herself to remain still. The humming stopped and the far door automatically slid open. *What have I gotten myself into?*

She stepped into a vast, dimly lit chamber. Row upon row of double stacked cells seemed endless as they vanished into the gloom.

"Fifth row, bottom level, cell one five eight."

Tensely Yashana crept down the correct row, staring at the cell occupants behind force fields, hoping they were asleep. The night cycle lights only barely revealed the outline of the sleeping prisoners. Reaching cell one five eight, Yashana peered closely in the darkness, making sure it was Gauge before she placed her hand on the scanner. The door slid open.

She knelt by the cot and whispered, "Gauge, wake up."

The sleepy zonner was slow to awake. "I dream."

"No. I've come to rescue you. Ethan too. He's monitoring security."

"You will get in trouble. Leave me."

"I haven't come this far to abandon you. Come on."

"Hide. A guard comes."

Yashana ducked down under the cot then remembered the cell door was open. Too late to close it. Footsteps were close, almost above their heads. They became louder, closer, then faded away.

"Another guard will patrol on the other walkway soon. He will see the door," said Gauge.

"Then we should leave now."

Yashana closed the door after they exited. They crept down the aisle, keeping to the shadows cast by the overhead walkway. They managed to dodge the next guard on patrol and enter the scanning room. Both felt uneasy as the walls hummed and the blue beam scanned them. Suddenly lights began flashing red in the room, the doors remaining locked. Text scrolled across a screen above a data pad, "Unauthorized exit."

"Ethan, we've been discovered. You have better override the system now."

"I got through the first code, but now it wants a second, longer one. Their security is well designed."

"Stop admiring their system and get this door open."

Gauge walked over to the data pad and randomly punched keys. "Maybe we can enter a code here."

Yashana yelled into the earpiece, "Give me a code, now!"

Ethan rattled off a series of numbers, and Yashana punched them in. Nothing happened. Frustrated, Yashana hit the hand scanner. Text on the scrollbar changed to, "Do you wish to authorize prisoner transfer?"

"Yes!" screamed Yashana at the same time she punched the command.

The exit door slid open. Up the endless stairs they ran. Yashana was soon panting, barely able to breathe, but Gauge's reptilian body easily took the climb. Yashana stopped to catch her breath. In between gasps, she gave Gauge directions of where to go once out of the building.

"You will be with me," said the zonner.

"I…will…try. If…I fall…behind…leave me."

Running footsteps below announced that guards approached. Both teenagers bolted up the stairs. They had just passed a landing when its door opened and two quintessences rushed out. Yashana barely had time to scream, "Don't stop!" before a stun blast hit her, causing her body to go limp.

Yashana woke, dazed, slowly realizing she lay on the floor of a small holding cell. An energy field flickered in place of a door. She winced as she sat up, feeling the bruises she must have received when falling on the stairs. Across from her were more cells, all empty. She moved near the shimmering field and peered down the corridor. Near the far wall stood a silent quintessence guard.

Yashana shivered, fighting against panic. *Will they execute me immediately or feed on me slowly for weeks? Calm down. Gauge is not here. Maybe she got away. Or placed back in her official cell.* Hours crawled by, providing no relieve for Yashana's torturous thoughts. Eventually she fell into a light doze.

"Up. You are to come with me."

The teenager opened her eyes. A quintessence stood just a few feet away where the energy field had been. Alarmed, Yashana jumped up. Had he come to eat her?

"This way." The death drinker turned and walked away.

Knowing nothing else to do, Yashana followed fearfully. Two other guards closed in behind her as they walked out of the cellblock and down a hallway. They stopped in front of an elevator. *Would have been nice if Ethan had me to use the elevator instead of the stairs.* Yashana expected the elevator to drop down to the maximum security level; instead, it rose to ground floor. The doors opened to reveal a large forum brightly lit with morning sunshine. Humans, quintessences, and other sentients walked passed without glancing at Yashana or her escorts.

The teenager was led out of the oval building to a small security hover car. A quintessence sat on each side of Yashana as the vehicle zoomed pass glass-covered buildings, broad plazas, and flowery terraces. The architecture reminded Yashana of Luncaster University, natural and inviting, but her college lacked monorails or landing pads for spacecraft. The hover car headed towards Richton Tower, an immense structure whose core rose up fifty floors then mushroomed into a glass covered dome. The vehicle stopped. Yashana was led through a maze of hallways to another elevator which stopped on the forty-fifth floor.

She was ushered into an executive office then the guards withdrew. For a moment Yashana thought she was alone as she surveyed the huge room. The outer wall was concave and made completely from glass. Along an inner wall were dozens of shelves holding artifacts from many cultures. One end of the room contained several couches and chairs centered around a huge video screen. At the end furthest from the door was a broad, oval shaped desk. Only then did Yashana realize that she was being watched by a quintessence sitting behind the desk.

He did not speak but gestured her forward. She moved slowly across the chamber, trying vainly to feel brave. Strange wood carvings on shelves held her attention briefly, but too soon she stood in front of the marble desk. A plaque read, "Alexander Rangan, Director." The quintessence was the oldest Yashana had yet seen, black hair specked with gray, tan skin bearing a few wrinkles. Still, his frame was muscular, his dark eyes cold and piercing.

"You may sit."

Yashana sat in one of the black padded chairs, feeling lost in their bulkiness. The director studied her for a long time then rose and walked around the desk. The teenager wanted to bolt but remained still.

The quintessence sat on the edge of his desk and finally spoke. "Why did you break in?"

"To free a friend. She was innocent."

"So you prove her innocence by committing another crime?"

"We were saving her from you, leech."

"Save your name calling until out of my presence. I would speak very carefully if I were you. We quintessences do not tolerate lies. Who sent you?"

"No one."

"Why did you hack into our system?"

"I didn't." The director's dark eyes narrowed, and Yashana flinched. "A friend of mine hacked in as a prank, a joke. Everything just got blown out of proportion after that. We meant no harm."

"You broke multiple galactic laws yet meant no harm?"

"Yes…sir. It was just an adolescent prank. You know, we do those sometimes."

"I congratulate you on being part of the only successful prison break in Essence's history."

"She made it?" Yashana felt a leap of hope.

"Yes, she enjoyed fifteen minutes of freedom before the New Hope police arrested her and Ethan Covey, both students at Luncaster University."

"Arrested?" Horror filled Yashana. It had all been for nothing. She could endure her own fate as long as she knew her friends were safe.

"They are being held in New Hope's jail at this moment. Your hacker friend forgot to turn the GPS off on the computer he used. Our technicians, who had been monitoring him from the moment he entered our system, easily backtracked his route and located his IP address."

Yashana turned her despair into anger. "Your technicians aren't that good. I walked right into your prison."

"We allowed you inside to see what you wanted. The hacker never had access to our prison security."

"Then your technicians were the ones opening those doors for me?"

"No. But neither did your friend."

"Then how…"

"Because you are dead."

Yashana's mind reeled. Was he threatening her or joking? "Do you plan to kill me now?"

"Not yet. There are too many unanswered questions. Going back to the beginning, who sent you?"

"I just told you. No one sent me."

"Are you part of any terrorist organization?"

"No. I'm just fourteen."

"I have met terrorists younger than you. Have you been approached by any organization, offered any benefits, received money for any reason?"

"I get an allowance from my parents. I got a scholarship to go to Luncaster. That's it."

"Who sponsored the scholarship?"

"Uh, the Palakkad Foundation, I think."

"Are you adopted?"

"What type of question is that?"

"Answer it, please."

"No, my mom said she was in labor three hours with me, not nearly as long as she was with my older sisters."

"Did your parents use a genetics company to create you?"

"No…yes. My sisters and I were engineered. It's pretty common for the upper-class to do that on Mansoor, but they used my parents' eggs and sperm."

"Which company?"

"I don't know. I wasn't born when my parents decided that. Why are you asking me these questions?"

Alexander studied her for a long moment then picked up from his desk a digital picture frame which slowly rotated through photos. He touched the forward button several times then turned the frame around for Yashana to see. A teenager, perhaps eighteen, laughed while someone out of view of the camera made silly hand signs behind her head. Except for age, the youth looked remarkably like Yashana. Same Indian face, long black hair, and brown eyes.

"That is Layla Rangan, creator of my race. And my wife."

"I don't understand."

"You are her clone. A perfect match. We ran the test three times."

"That's impossible. Sentient cloning is illegal." The room seemed to be spinning as Yashana struggled with reality suddenly turned upside down.

"It is also illegal to break into maximum-level prisons, but that does not stop some who believe they are above the law."

"We never said we were above the law. Ethan tried to confess, but Dean Wellesz said he should just forget it. But we couldn't abandon Gauge."

"Your dean knew Ethan was the hacker and asked him to remain silent?"

"I shouldn't have said that."

"Come." Alexander led her across the room to the huge vid. "Stand against the wall, out of camera view."

Yashana obeyed as the director sat on a leather couch directly in front of the vid. Using a remote, he navigated through menus and called the dean. Soon, Wellesz's face appeared on the screen.

"Director Rangan, what may I do for you?"

"I am calling to inform you that three of your students are now in custody."

"Three?" The woman's face paled. "Who?"

"Ethan Covey and Yashana Kalkar broke the zonner out of our prison. Kalkar is currently in our custody, the other two in New Hope Jail."

"There must be some mistake. Ethan and Yashana are two of our brightest students. They would never be involved in something like that."

"Perhaps their actions resulted from the frustration of being told by a superior to withhold information in an ongoing investigation."

Wellesz eyes widened, but she spoke calmly. "The children may have misunderstood me. I would never hinder an investigation. I voluntarily sent you those pictures and the computer serial number."

"Yes, you were quite helpful in arresting the zonner, but now we must deal with the other two. Breaking into a military base is a galactic level offense. As you are aware, the punishment is death."

The dean smiled woodenly. "They are just adolescents, sir. Prone to childish mistakes. Surely you can overlook this."

"You did not offer that argument when we arrested the zonner."

"She was not a citizen."

"Surely as an educator, you care about all your students, no matter their status."

"Of course. But the media will care nothing about a zonner. If two human children are executed, it will stir up much trouble for you."

"Do you think we care what the media reports? Our job is to enforce the law. Again, you are placing greater value on the humans than the zonner. That is not professional."

Wellesz's eyes flared in anger. "Are you challenging my integrity? I have been dean for ten years, working hard to educate the finest minds in the galaxy. That is not an easy task."

"I imply no insult but offer a deal. Taking into account that all three are minors, I am considering suggesting to the police chief that they receive community service."

"That sounds fair."

"A New Hope judge will set the conditions for Covey and Gauge, but Kalkar is in my custody. She will be required to serve one thousand hours at Essence over the next two years."

"Too much. It will interfere with her studies."

"I can always execute her, thus ending that problem."

"One thousand hours will be fine."

Alexander ended the transmission and turned to Yashana. "Do you agree with my judgment?"

The teenager's mind whirled with questions and fears. Every time she had heard the director mention *execution* or *death*, her heart had pounded in fear. "Gauge can go back to school?"

"Yes."

"Then it is fair."

"Does your religion see any day as holy?"

"I have not really thought about religion."

"Then you will work Saturdays and Sundays until your time is completed, starting this weekend. One more thing, it would be best if you keep the knowledge that you are a clone to yourself. You may return to your school now."

Yashana took several steps towards the door before turning around. "May I ask one question, sir?" Seeing Alexander nod, she said, "Why did the prison doors open for me?"

"Because my wife's top security level was never revoked after her death. The computer thought you were her. My technicians have already remedied that oversight. No more doors will mysteriously open for you."

A guard escorted Yashana to a monorail station. By the time she made it back to her dorm room, she was mentally and physical exhausted, her mind a whirl of thoughts. How could she be a clone?

Half an hour later, Gauge entered the room and eagerly embraced her in a tight hug. "I thought I would never see you again."

"I did too. Are you alright? Did they hurt you?"

"No. Yesterday after my arrest the quintessences told me I was to be deported back to Zon. Now I am told I can stay in school, but I will have to work for a community somehow. I am grateful for the change but don't understand why."

Yashana explained most of what she had experienced. After texting Ethan, she collapsed into bed, sleeping through the afternoon. In the early hours before dawn, she awoke and was unable to sleep again as thoughts of how close she had come to losing her best friends and her own life overwhelmed her. She finally forced herself to focus on what terrified her the most.

She was a clone. What did that mean? How was she supposed to feel? No longer was she a unique human but a copy of another who came before her. *How am I alive?* Her existence was unlawful. She was certain her parents had never known. Someone had swapped the sperm and eggs donated by her parents for the DNA of a stranger. And not just any stranger, but a long dead famous geneticist. Was someone trying to resurrect Layla Rangan from the dead? Who? Not Layla's husband. The director had been surprise by Yashana's existence.

Nothing made sense. There had to be a reason someone went to so much trouble to bring Layla back. *Am I even myself?* The teenager sat up in bed, confused. *Am I Layla or Yashana?* She looked around the small dorm room.

Her area was cluttered and disordered, Gauge's section immaculate with everything in its proper place. In the bed across from hers, Gauge slept peacefully. Yashana envied her. When the zonner awoke, she would still be Gauge of Blackrock, not magically morphed into somebody else.

Yashana went over the few facts she had memorized about Layla for a test. Creator of the quintessences. Zelzer winner. Founder and director of Essence Institute. Had married the first born of her creations. That seemed a bit weird. Was that like marrying one's own son? Layla was one of five hundred genetically engineered geniuses called *Homo sapiens profectus.*

Yashana's heart rate increased. The ediethean DNA used to enhance the intellect of the profectus had been a dramatic enough change to classify them as a subspecies.

I'm not even human, at least pure human. I am alone, separate from the human race. Sleep remained as allusive as her identity.

Chapter Six

The metal staff whirled quickly in Ariyo's hands. He stuck at his opponent then dodged a counterblow. He leaped back and circled, looking for weaknesses in his rival. The C1 model, design to appear as a Caucasian human, was broader and brawnier but a faction slower than Ariyo's slimmer body. Ariyo feigned to the right then twisted sideways, his bō smacking the ribs of the C1. His rival swirled away and swung, the tip of his staff grazing Ariyo's shoulder. If they had been practicing with iron tips, the blade would have cut through fabric and skin.

Ariyo pressed the attack, swinging and striking. The C1 smoothly parried each move. Dropping to the mat, Ariyo rolled under his rival's swinging bō, knocking the legs out from under his opponent. Ariyo was quicker to his feet. He quickly brought his staff up, its rubber tip hitting the C1's throat.

"A kill." Ariyo kept the bō pressed against the other's neck.

"Agreed," said the C1. Both quintessences broke apart and politely bowed to each other. "Another round?"

"I must decline. I have a meeting."

While the C1 sought another rival among the bystanders, Ariyo stepped down from the matted platform and walked to the side of the room. He placed his bō on a rack beside other staffs. Across the huge gym, dozens of bō competition were in full swing. Most contests were only between pairs, but a few consisted of up to six quintessences attacking each other simultaneously. And they were not using rubber tips. Only the most skilled dared such a challenge. Many bystanders gathered around the largest battles. Quintessences watched the contests with few comments, but other sentients cheered for their favorites. The Bōjutsu Gym was a popular hangout for scientists and custodians on break or quintessences relaxing after work.

Ariyo paused to watch a contest between a ME2 model, who looked like an athletic Middle Eastern, and a determined blue-skin neodite. While bōjutsu classes were offered free of charge to workers at Essence, only the boldest dared facing off with a quintessence. Glancing at his watch, Ariyo moved through a large energetic crowd surrounding an intense match between five quintessences. *In two or three decades perhaps I will be skilled enough for such a match,* thought Ariyo.

Exiting the gym, Ariyo increased his pace down the airy, glass-roofed corridor. Arched doorways opened to other gyms, each dedicated to a different sport. The hallway led to the huge indoor plaza, the Grand Forum for Richton Tower. Ariyo marched pass eateries and vendors, ignoring the hundreds of sentients relaxing, chatting, or tapping on e-tablets. He found an express elevator, punched in his access code, and rode up to the forty-fifth floor.

As Ariyo walked down the hall, he wondered why he had been summoned. Normally Commander Hancock chose the missions for the AS1 models then sent them a text message informing them where to meet a squad captain who would brief them on mission details. But this morning one of the Five from the first born generation of quintessences had summoned him. Either Ariyo had earned high honor or committed an atrocious act. He reviewed his recent missions. There were weakness he still needed to improve, but he was certain he had not broken the Code, a crime punishable by death.

Ariyo knocked on Director Rangan's door then entered. The elderly quintessence stood across the chamber, surveying Essence through the glass wall. Ariyo marched up and saluted.

Alexander returned the salute. "At ease. I have been reviewing the mission logs for your model. The highest success rate for any your age. And the highest kill rate for non-war conflicts."

"Have we acted inappropriately?"

"The opposite. Your model's unique skills has allowed you to blend in well with humans, a talent you have effectively used many times. That is why I am considering using you for a difficult task, a mission dealing not with hunting down criminals but building relationships. Did you hear on our news channel about the prison break?"

"Yes, sir. A prisoner escaped but was caught soon after."

"We have never had a successful prison escape before. Three teenagers from Luncaster University were involved. One of them, a fourteen-year-old female, will be serving one thousand hours of community service here. I want you to be her handler. She will report to you when she arrives, when on break, and when she leaves. You will choose her chores and be aware of all her activities."

45

"How is this a difficult assignment?" Ariyo kept his face blank but felt disappointment to be given a babysitting job.

Alexander turned on the huge screen and pulled up a picture of Yashana. "Notice anything about her?"

"Other than she seems a bit young to have a criminal record, no."

With a click, Alexander displayed another picture beside Yashana taken from a magazine cover showing a smiling teenager holding an infant. "*Galactic Times*, one hundred and seventy years ago. The first photo of me and my future wife. What do you notice now?"

"They look like the same person."

"Yashana is a clone of Layla."

"How is this possible?"

"I would like to know myself. I have investigators looking into the matter, but that is not your concern. Yashana is your mission." Alexander looked at a digital picture frame on the wall which showed a twentyish Layla working in a lab. "I already know her better than she knows herself. She is about to undergo a difficult adolescence. She will need a friend and a mentor."

"I will do as you ask, but my missions have never dealt with teenagers before. What advice do you have for me?"

"This mission will be your most difficult because it will require new skills for you to develop. You must balance firmness with friendship, discipline with kindness. Adolescent humans can be irrational and cruel, hiding a host of insecurities. You will need to guide her, overlooking her faults. I wish for her to follow in the footsteps of Layla, becoming a geneticist at Essence. But she must make that decision of her own freewill."

Ariyo saluted. "I will do my best, sir."

As Ariyo left, he wondered how handling one teenager would be harder than facing a dozen enemies shooting at him at once.

Chapter Seven

"You have one minute," said a professor slowly walking through the aisles of desks.

Yashana panicked and randomly keyed answers on her mid-term genetics test.

"Please submit your answers now."

The fourteen year old tapped in her access code and then pressed her thumb to the screen. *Another test failed,* she thought bitterly. She really had tried studying for mid-terms, but she had missed all the reviews on Wednesday due to her arrest. Neither did it help that she was having trouble sleeping.

She walked to a courtyard and met Gauge who was much more cheerful. They began walking towards the cafeteria.

"I am sure you did not fail," said the zonner. "Just not earn top score."

"I can barely concentrate. And then I have to start working tomorrow at Essence."

"Maybe the work will be interesting."

Ethan pushed his way in between them. "At least you don't have to appear in front of a judge tomorrow. I feel like a criminal."

"You are one. Bona fide police record and mug shot," teased Yashana.

"It's improved my geek status. I'm notorious. The only hacker who has been in the Essence system—not once but twice."

"And how did your family take it?"

The boy winced. "Not well. My father wanted to take me out of Luncaster. Dean Wellesz managed to talk him out of it. How about yours?"

"Not much better. I'm grounded the entire month of summer break. House arrest."

"It is nice you have a break," said Gauge. "Like always, I take extra classes during that time. My planet is too far away and the flight too expensive."

"At least it allows you to double major."

They chose an empty table in the cafeteria, but soon it was crowded with students all asking about the jailbreak. Gauge and Yashana preferred to keep the details to themselves, but Ethan soaked in the attention, giving a long, elaborate narrative. The technology majors asked about the hacking program Ethan had written, how he had found the backdoor, and what the Essence system was like. Yashana felt bothered by how much he shared.

As students headed to their next class, she pulled him aside. "Don't you think you're giving away too much information? If they break in and get arrested, it will be your fault."

Ethan laughed. "Relax. Before I was released from jail, I had to meet with Essence's chief technician and give him all the details. His staff, of course, will rewrite the programming. No one's going to get in again, at least not that way."

"I still don't think you should brag so much."

"Why not? I've won. No one will ever top Prankster Brainster's record. I will be remembered forever. A hundred years from now geeks at Luncaster and across the galaxy will still speak with awe when they say my name."

"All you have done is inspire others to perform crimes worse than yours. Do you realize how close you came to losing Gauge...and me? We could have been killed by those leeches. We're only here now because Director Rangan decided to be merciful."

"I'm doing it again." Ethan's face fell. "Sorry. It's my nature to gloat."

"You are my friend. You don't need to ever hack another system or write a program to impress me. You have a caring heart under your arrogance. Be your real self, not the Prankster Brainster."

The youth sighed. "You sure know how to cut down one's ego. I know friendship is more important than accomplishments...or crimes. How about after class I treat you and Gauge to ice cream?"

Yashana smiled. "I would like that."

The next morning Yashana wished she never had to get out of bed. She lay there, letting the alarm keep buzzing until Gauge finally complained. Reluctantly she dressed, ate breakfast with her friends, and then faced the inevitable. She took a hover bus to the monorail station. The twenty mile ride by train flew by in barely fifteen minutes. At the boundary of Essence, she switched trains. This one moved slower, stopping often. When she heard a mechanical voice say, "East Richton Tower," she exited the car.

To leave the station, Yashana had to pass through a turnstile then a short, narrow tunnel. She had barely entered the tunnel before both gates automatically shut and red lights flashed. *What have I done now?* Two quintessences rushed up and pointed guns at her through the grating.

She held her empty hands up. "I'm supposed to be here. It's my first day of work."

The guards reset the machine then guided her at gunpoint to a small security room where they locked her in a holding cell. She stood there, staring at the shimming energy field trapping her, feeling both angry and worried. *I've done nothing wrong this time.* Surely it would be all straightened out as soon as they called the director. Still, it was embarrassing to be arrested again— especially on her first day of work.

A short time later, a guard turned off the energy field. As the teenager stepped out of the cell, a young Asian man greeted her.

"Hello, Yashana. I am Ariyo. I will be your handler. The directions sent to you said to get off at West Richton Tower."

"I did."

"No, you got off at *East* Richton Tower. I was waiting for you at the correct station."

"Oh, sorry."

"This way." As he led her out of the station, he handed her an ID badge. "You are to wear this at all times when at Essence. It contains a microchip that allows your movements to be tracked. Anyone moving about the facility without a microchip will trigger security alarms."

Yashana clipped the badge onto her blouse. "You're not wearing one."

"Some workers prefer wearing the chip in jewelry, watches, or bands. At birth, quintessences are implanted with the chip."

"Doesn't sound nice for the babies." Noticing he wore no jewelry, she wondered if his chip was in his high-tech e-band.

"They don't remember the brief pain."

The monorail station was connected by a glass-roof crosswalk to a huge indoor plaza bustling with hundreds of workers. Customers stood in line at booths to buy breakfast in the food court. Tables and benches were elegantly arranged around trees and flowers growing indoors. Multiple passages led off in various directions.

"Is this a mall?"

"No. The Grand Forum. You will meet me each morning at this entrance. During lunch, we will eat here."

He led her through the plaza, passing an arched doorway to a museum. Along the wall were historical pictures with nameplates underneath. A fifteen foot picture of Layla caused Yashana to pause. The elder director was smiling, looking confidently over the thousands who passed her each day. *Is that what I will look like when I'm old?* Yashana shuddered, feeling the eyes from the larger-than-life portrait staring at her.

"By looking into the pass, you can see your future."

Ariyo's voice caused Yashana to jump. "I don't want to see my future."

The man studied her for a long moment before saying, "This way." They walked down more well-lit corridors leading deeper into the massive building. Finally they entered the Fetus Department. They passed through a break room for employees and a locker room where scientists donned white jumpers. Near a small office a brown haired man in his forties greeted them.

"Welcome. This must be the intern you spoke with me about. I am Doctor Anthony Cashman." He smiled at Yashana. "Heard you are studying genetics at Luncaster. An excellent major. Perhaps you will work here full time after graduation. We have had many do so over the years."

"I haven't thought that far ahead."

"Always good to plan for the future."

Ariyo cut in. "I will leave you with Doctor Cashman now. At lunch where are you to meet me?"

"The food court." Yashana answered politely but felt resentful. She was not about to forget where to go—this time.

After Ariyo left, Doctor Cashman chatted good-naturally as he went over safety rules. "Our embryos are grown in a clean room to prevent pathogen contamination. They are very vulnerable to viruses at this age."

He handed her a white jumper and boots to wear. After her long hair was hidden under a hair net, she followed him into a small chamber. Both doors sealed and the lights flashed as sonic waves flooded the room. When the far door opened, they stepped out into a vast chamber. Row upon row of incubators held fetuses growing in artificial placentas inside glass canisters. Scientists and maintenance workers moved about, recording data and monitoring equipment.

"This room houses five thousand embryos in various stages. We produce a total of twenty thousand infants a year. Next door is another chamber just like this one."

Before he left, Cashman introduced her to the cleaning supervisor, a female stardancer with ritual marking tattooed on her orange skin. She opened a door to a supply closet. "Like our other interns, you will begin with the basics—cleanliness." She pulled out a fancy vacuum. "This sonic sweeper kills pathogens while sucking up debris."

For the rest of the morning, Yashana pushed the sonic vacuum down endless aisles. Too often, the stardancer called her back to resweep an area. The fetuses were far more interesting to watch than staring at the boring concrete floor. Through the thin placentas, Yashana caught glimpses of fetuses kicking or moving tiny hands. *It's hard to believe these cute babies will grow up to be foeditas horribilis.* From her studies, Yashana knew all the fetuses were male, a safety measure to ensure population control.

Yashana turned down another aisle were dozens of scientists birthed fetuses who had reached six-months. Yashana watched in fascination as fluids were drained from the canisters then the struggling infants were freed from their slimy placentas. After cleaning the newborns, workers wrapped them in blankets and placed them four to a cart. Caregivers from the Infant Department wheeled the newborns away.

A throat cleared behind Yashana. The teenager looked sheepishly at her supervisor. "Sorry. I have never seen anything born before, at least not in real life."

"Births happen every day here. Back to cleaning."

For lunch many of the workers ate in the breakroom, so Yashana headed out on her own to find the food court. She became lost several times and repeatedly had to ask directions from strangers.

When she finally found Ariyo, he was leaning against a wall near the food court. "You are late."

"Got lost. This place is too big."

"What would you like to eat?"

"Uh…" Yashana looked at the nearby vendors. "Pizza, I guess."

After buying their meals, they sat near a flower bed. Yashana ate slowly, studying the quite man across from her. She resented having to report to him like she was a child. She preferred exploring the area during the hour-long break. There was much to see.

"Why are you called my handler? Sounds like I'm a pet in need of training."

"Perhaps you are."

"I'm no one's pet," she shot back angrily. "When I finish my thousand hours, I'm never coming back here."

"Some scientists claim they would sell their souls to work at Essence."

"I'm not religious so soul selling is out of my expertise." Yashana sucked soda loudly through her straw, hoping to irritate him.

Ariyo remained placid. "Interesting that you chose the same major as her."

Yashana froze. *He knows I'm a clone.* She placed the cup on the table. "So? I happen to like genetics. Lots of rich kids on Mansoor are genetically tweaked."

"But few of them choose genetics majors. And none of them are profectus."

The teenager winced at the term. "Do you have to say that out loud?"

"I chose this table because it is isolated. Talking about who you are can help you accept it."

"Who said I have a problem?" She crossed her arms and glared at him. "You know nothing about me."

"I know you are a one-of-a-kind clone working in a cloning factory."

"I don't think the galaxy needs a hundred or a thousand copies of me running around."

"I think our security system can handle the challenge, arresting you as many times as needed."

Hours later as Yashana rode the train back to college, she reflected on her job. It was not nearly as bad as she feared. The menial labor was boring, yet she felt enthralled walking among thousands of unborn synthetic sentients—but she would never admit that to Ariyo. *Seeing the birthing was cool.* Still, the muscles in her back and limbs ached. At home her parents forced chores upon her, but nothing this strenuous. *My sisters would think it is funny to see me sweeping for eight hours straight.* Worst of all, she had to do it all over again tomorrow.

She met Ethan and Gauge for dinner at the college cafeteria. Their court hearing had gone relatively well.

"We have a thousand hours as park janitors," complained Ethan.

"It will be fascinating to learn how to grow flowers," said Gauge. "We have none on my planet."

"No flowers?" Yashana could not imagine such a world. "Then how do your plants reproduce?"

"Various ways like runners and bulbs. Or implanting in animals and growing out of their dead bodies." Seeing the shocked expression of her friends, Gauge smiled. "My world is very different. Dangerous and beautiful at the same time."

Ethan shuddered. "Remind me not to go on vacation to Zon. So, Yashana, how was your first day?"

"Boring. I swept all day when I needed to be writing a research paper."

"That's what I will hate the most, I think. Picking up trash and digging in dirt, wasting my time when I have real work to do."

"Perhaps," said Gauge, "It would do you good to be away from computers for a while."

"Maybe I can build a robot to do the work for me. And get a grade for it in my robotics class."

Gauge rolled her slanted eyes at him, an expression she had picked up since coming to Luncaster. Yashana threw a dirty napkin at him.

Over the next month, Yashana and her friends struggled with juggling the demands of intense classes and the physical labor of community service. Long after curfew, they poured over textbooks, pounded out research papers, and tackled projects. She hated keeping the secret of her DNA from her best friends. Sometimes she almost slipped and told them, but then she feared they would not look at her the same. Would they still see the friend they laughed with or the legendary Layla reborn? Grades slowly slipping and lack of sleep irritated Yashana, but she tried not to take it out on her friends. Instead, she saved the anger and frustration for Ariyo. She hated reporting to him, hated eating lunch with him, hated putting up with his probing questions. And she especially hated passing under the giant portrait of Layla Rangan which mocked her on every visit.

After one annoying day where she had to resweep the same aisle three times, Yashana made it to the food court a few minutes early. Seeing Ariyo already eating, she plopped down in the chair across from him.

"I am really getting tired of that sundancer. She has it out for me."

The man looked up from his burrito. "Which sundancer would that be?"

"My supervisor. Who else would it be?"

"I think you have mistaken me for another."

Yashana stared at him. "What do you mean, Ariyo?"

"I'm not Ariyo. My name is Rinji."

"But your…." The teenager trailed off, noticed for the first time that his clothing was not the same as what Ariyo had worn that morning.

Another Asian man sat down, carrying a hamburger. Besides a different color shirt, he looked identical to Rinji. "Hello. You must be Ariyo's special assignment. I am Tadeo."

"I…uh…where is Ariyo?"

The first one touched the screen of his e-band, pulling up a map. "He's entering from the west side as we speak."

"Um…thanks."

Yashana walked away but glanced over her shoulder at the twins who had resumed their meal. Surely they were not quintessences. The leeches' faces were flashed in the news all the time. There were several models but none had ever been Asian. But what other explanation was there? She doubted Ariyo's mother had given birth to triplets who all happened to grow up to work as Essence. Being quintessence, he would not even have a mother or a father. Almost all the quintessences she had seen wore military uniforms with their names and ID numbers prominently visible. Ariyo and his brothers looked so normal, dressing in casual clothing with no name tags.

Come to think of it, Ariyo's eyes did look a bit peculiar, but she had presumed it was an oddity like being born with a big nose. While his dark eyes were normal size, they seemed too intense, too round, too something she could not quite define.

She met Ariyo near the crosswalk coming from the monorail station. He took one look at her face and asked, "What happened?"

"Why didn't you tell me you were an energy leech?"

"Are we on the level of name calling now? Should I call you a talking ape?"

"No, I'm sorry. But you never told me."

"You never asked."

"It's not polite to ask someone their species."

"Impoliteness seems to be one of your favorite traits. Shall we eat now?"

Yashana glared at him but remained silent as they bought food. Ariyo chose the table were his two brothers ate. Yashana hesitated but sat beside him, feeling uncomfortable being near triplets. How much did they know about her?

"How do you like Essence?" asked Rinji.

"It's different." Yashana kept her eyes downcast on her salad.

"Your shocked expression was amusing when you found out I was not Ariyo."

"I didn't think quintessences had a sense of humor."

"We do, though what is funny to us may not be to you. For example, on our last mission I posed as a VIP visiting a company we were investigating. To show me the facility, they had to enter my ID into their computer system. While I was being given a tour, Tadeo sneaked in and had free reign to explore their secrets. We enjoy the irony that we can move among humans undetected."

"You think it's funny deceiving humans?"

Riniji smiled. "Like I said, you will find our humor different than yours."

"I find much about you different. Like your model smiles and frowns, unlike the other leeches...I mean quintessences...who act like emotionless robots."

Tadeo explained, "It seems that way because you have not lived among us. Why shout when a raised eyebrow conveys the same information? You are right that our model is more expressive. It allows us to interact with humans better."

"Why have I never heard of your model before?"

"Because we are in beta stage. There are only fifty of us. It will remain that way until we are given full status. Then many more copies will be made."

"Do you like being a copy of someone else?"

Ariyo cut in, "Quintessences are classified as a collective hive society. We function as both individuals and as a group. Having kinsman who share our DNA creates a strong link between us." He paused, struggling to find words to explain. "You have a family. Both a nuclear family and an extended family. It is the same with us, but with three levels. Birthmates, brothers, and brethren."

Tadeo added, "We use the term *brethren* to refer to all quintessences. Our *brothers* are those who share the same model. *Birthmates* grow up together."

"At birth we are usually divided into groups of one hundred who eat, play, study, and train together. After graduation, depending on our models, birthmates may all be sent together to a battlefront or divided into smaller units who will work together throughout their bonded years. The connection of birthmates is so strong that many choose to stay together their entire lives, even after completing their bondage."

"I thought no quintessences has died yet from old age."

"None have. But we still die. The C models have the highest death rate because of their exceptional combat skills. They are often stationed on battlefronts."

"They also have the highest kill rate," pointed out Riniji, "but our model has the highest non-combat kill rate."

Yashana looked at the three young men. "You have killed?"

"Many times," said Tadeo. "Every single one of us."

The teenager glanced at Ariyo, feeling more uncomfortable. *I sit beside mortis elixir, the miraculous drinker of death.*

Ariyo sensed her uneasiness. "You are in no danger. We do not kill for sport. That would break the Code."

"The Code? What's that?"

As one, the triplets recited, "All quintessences shall place the welfare of their brethren above themselves. Each must live an exemplary life, obeying superiors, avoiding vices, protecting the weak." Their voices had the same identical pitch, pausing and rising in unison, causing chill bumps to run down Yashana's arm.

Rinji smiled. "After that comes a long list of do's and don'ts which we memorize as soon as we learn to talk."

"It's a very strict list," said Tadeo. "Killing for sport is considered a vice. Commit a vice, you appear before the Synod and most likely will be executed. So you see, you are quite safe—unless you are a criminal."

Yahsana flinched. Just because she had been arrested did not make her a hardened criminal. Besides, she was paying the penalty for the break-in. Still she continued to feel uneasy sitting beside the triplets.

Chapter Eight

Yashana swung her feet impatiently, wondering why she had been summoned to Director Rangan's office only to sit outside while some important meeting was being held inside. The door occasionally opened for aides going back and forth on errands. Ariyo sat calmly nearby, seemly with no concern. *At least this is better than sweeping,* Yashana told herself. After six weeks of floor duty, Yashana felt like screaming every time she picked up that hideous sonic vacuum. *The job is so boring. What a waste of my genius genes.*

Each time the office door opened, Yashana caught glimpses of officials sitting on couches around the huge vid. She knew none of them, but guessed they were high-ranking because she heard titles like *senator* and *ambassador* mentioned. The door swung open again, and Yashana peered through. On the screen was a picture of a middle-age human morphing into an image of Ethan. Yashana gasped. Why would they be discussing Ethan? Did they believe he was involved in new crimes? But surely not. She would have been the first to know. Ethan always shared his secrets with her, and she was certain he had been avoiding hacking since the arrest.

Shortly after, an aide called her. Ariyo walked into the office with her and stood silently near a wall. Yashana was asked to stand in front of the vid which displayed a large image of a teenage Layla. A dozen dignitaries studied her intensely, their eyes flickering between her face and the photo of Layla. They talked among themselves about her eyes, her skin, her field of study, her personality. Yashana hated being exposed like this, hated them staring at her, hated that they now carried the knowledge she was a clone.

Finally, Alexander said, "Is there any doubt?"

A greenish-red male wearing an embroidered robe said, "You have certainly proven the evidence. What troubles me is how deep this runs. How many are involved?"

"That is still under investigation, Senior At'lic. For now, this must be kept away from the media. Do we have your full cooperation?"

Promises were given and the meeting ended. As the officials left, Yashana remained still, feeling angry and vulnerable. Only one dignitary remained, a grey-skinned ediethean whose white hair was streaked with red. Instead of leaving, she walked over to Yashana and gave a curt bow.

"You honor Layla. She would have liked you."

"I am nothing like her."

The elderly ediethean smiled. "Ah, but you are very much like her. You have the same fire as she. I am Ambassador Roobaroo. Layla and I were classmates at Luncaster and lifelong friends. If not for her applying political pressure, I would still be in prison today."

Alexander walked over, his dark eyes as piercing as ever. "Ambassador Roobaroo is a terrorist who I arrested over a century ago."

"*Was* is the correct term. I have served my time. I regret there were lives lost, but my cause was honorable."

"That is what most terrorists believe."

The ediethean leaned towards Yashana and whispered confidentially, "He is concerned I will be a negative influence on you." She straightened up her slim body. "Do you have questions about Layla? I can tell you almost anything."

Yashana decided she liked the ambassador. "Was Layla ever arrested?"

Roobaroo opened her mouth to speak, but Alexander cut in. "No, she was a law abiding citizen. She always worked from within the law."

The ambassador glared at the director. "Except when she rewrote the laws. First with rewriting nature itself, doing feats with genes that geneticists thought impossible—while still only thirteen. At twenty-four she had her first face-off with the Emperor and Senate, beginning a pattern she repeated the rest of her life. Ah, she was both fire and ice, a loyal friend and a dangerous enemy. What the history books do not tell is that most of what she did, she did for love."

"Or curiosity," said Alexander.

Roobaroo ignored his interruption. "Unlike me, whose ongoing controversial actions force politicians to face major social changes within their own nations."

"Social upheavals, you mean."

"Call it what you wish, but many lives have been improved because of my sacrifices. Yashana, wherever your path may take you, seek a righteous cause then fight for it with your entire soul. Many people sleep their way through life. But Layla was not one of them. And neither are you, I believe."

"Ambassador, the pilot of your ship is waiting."

"Could you possibly give a more polite brush off, Alexander? You know I am right."

Yashana thought about Ethan's picture she had seen on the vid earlier. She doubted the director would answer her questions, but maybe this woman would. "Before you go, could you tell me why my friend's picture was on the vid?"

Alexander answered first. "We were discussing the break-in."

Roobaroo glanced between Alexander and Yashana. "You should tell her."

"She knows all she needs to."

"This is her life, not yours. The fate of her species. She deserves to know what has been done to them. If you do not tell her, I will."

The elderly quintessence stared at the ediethean for a long moment. "Those who defy my orders are arrested."

"Yes, I know. Everyone bends to your beck and call, except for the few of us who are actually older than you. Besides, you already arrested me once. Do it again, and the ghost of Layla may come back to haunt you."

"Perhaps she already does," murmured Alexander, briefly looking away. He picked up the remote and flipped through pictures on the vid until finding Ethan's smiling face. At least it seemed to be Ethan, but the hair was styled differently and he seemed older. "This photo appeared in *Galactic Times* one hundred and seventy years ago. Part of a side article discussing Richard Cambridge designing the software which was used to create my species."

Yashana stared, comprehension coming slowly. "Ethan is a clone? Of Cambridge? That's...that's...impossible." She slowly sank into the nearest chair. "Who...why?"

"The who and where we know, but not the why. Both your parents and Ethan's parents sent eggs and sperm to Boninc Genetics Foundation. But instead of mixing the traits that the parents ordered, someone sent frozen embryos of profectus back. Investigation into BGF records revealed Doctor Larson oversaw both cases. Unfortunately, the doctor retired five years ago and the forwarding address was fake. His current whereabouts are unknown."

"Show her the rest," prompted Roobaroo.

Alexander flipped to a picture of a grinning young woman holding a Zelzer Award. "Diane Richton, chief architect for Essence."

Yashana stared, stunned. "I've seen her. She graduated the year I came. I think her name is Mary."

"We have pulled the records of every student for the last fifty years at Luncaster, finding a total of twenty profectus who have attended. All within the last two decades, and all linked to Doctor Larson. But we do not think the doctor acted alone. Many would have to be involved to pull off something this elaborate and precise. The profectus chosen for cloning were the top in their field, their achievements far reaching."

"How would someone get their DNA?"

"BGF was the company that first engineered the profectus and where Layla created us. Officially the profectus DNA was supposed to have been destroyed when the project was cancelled, but someone has obviously kept a copy of it."

The room spun and Yashana placed her head in her hands to steady herself. It was excruciating bearing the weight of being a clone of a celebrity, to be a shadow of someone who came before. Now Ethan, her best friend, was a clone. He did not deserve to be haunted by Cambridge's ghost. "You are not telling them, are you?"

"No. I think you understand why."

"Because no one should live constantly being compared to…to whatever you call the originals we are cloned from. The other profectus should never be told. I wish I had never heard of Layla."

Roobaroo placed a comforting hand on Yashana's back. "You are part of a rare super species, the results of trying to advance humans to the level of my own race. The ones who created you broke the law, but that does not change the fact that your race is one of the smartest in the galaxy, capable of creating great wonders or hideous wrongs. The power of your race is tremendous. That is why I think all profectus should be informed of their identity. If not told, they may make very grave errors."

Alexander turned off the vid. "Sentients make mistakes all the time. In this case, I believe the profectus should not know. A superior species they may be, but they still carry the same faults as humans who think too individually. Cloning frightens them."

"They have a right to know their own genes."

"This is an order I will enforce, Ambassador. Do not push me."

The elder ediethean sighed. "Layla often complained you were stubborn."

"She could be quite obstinate herself."

Roobaroo gave Yashana another pat then left. Ariyo, who had stood silently by the wall throughout the conversation, came forward and gently said, "It's time to return to work."

Yashana looked up, her face hidden by long hair. "I don't feel like working. May I go home?"

Ariyo glanced at the director who nodded then he said. "Yes, I'll walk you to the station."

Back at Luncaster, Yashana said little to her friends. She sat on a couch in the student union, watching Ethan testing a robotic dog he had built for class. A small crowd gathered around, laughing as the animal awkwardly tried to fetch thrown objects. Even Gauge found it amusing tossing paper balls for it. Thorus took over the controls and made the robot sit up, but it was unbalanced and topped over. Ethan rushed forward and placed the animal back on its metal paws.

He is happy. He should never know that his greatest feats are only because he is a copy of another, someone greater. He only hacked into Essence because his other self designed the system. He must never bear the horror of being a shadow. Never.

Yashana was depressed over the following days. Her friends noticed and tried to cheer her up, but she kept the cause of her darkness hidden. No one needed to carry her burden but herself.

Final exams drew near, but Yashana had difficulty concentrating. She rarely spoke when eating lunch with Ariyo.

"You have barely touched your lunch."

Yashana did not bother looking up at Ariyo. "I'm not hungry."

"I noticed your grades are low. You are in danger of failing nanobiomaterials."

"Doesn't matter. I'm going to be grounded anyway when I get home. Spend the whole break under house arrest. My parents don't trust me anymore. My sisters will be elsewhere hanging out with their friends while I rot in my room. Which is perhaps a good thing since we fight when together."

Ariyo studied her for a long time then tapped out a message on his high-tech e-band. "I just informed your supervisor you have a special assignment for the rest of today."

Surprised, Yashana said, "Does it still count towards my community service?"

"Yes. Come."

They tossed their trash into a recycler then walked out of Richton Tower. They strolled west, passing a quadrangle where young quintessences, who looked like twelve-year-old boys, practiced bōjutsu. Their young, agile bodies swirled in unison, their staffs a blur as they copied the example of their instructor.

Ariya paused to watch the preteens. "Do you know they are only five years old?"

"I have read that you become adults when only seven."

"At the end of seven years. Then we spend the next fifty years serving the Basanti Empire, paying for the cost of our existence. Only then can we become citizens for the government we bleed for. That is one of the gifts that Layla fought hard for us to keep. When the Senate realized how long our life expectance was, they tried to raise the bond years to a hundred."

"Layla is really important to you."

"Far more than I can explain to you. As our creator, we revere her. We pass on her stories from generation to generation. She is in the thoughts of every single one of us. Our DNA is her fingerprints. Like all sentients, she had flaws. We pass down these stories also, at her request. She wanted us to care enough for other sentients that we would be willing to die to protect them. And many of us do. A tenth of the brethren never complete our bond years. In some ways, you could say Layla will never really die as long as quintessences live."

Yashana felt the heavy weight of her predecessor. *Who am I when compared with a creator of a new race?*

They could have taken a train or bus, but Ariyo preferred to walk. As the tour continued, Yashana noticed that few buildings had straight lines in their designs. Many were glass-covered, reflecting the natural beauty of nearby flowery terraces and courtyards. Near the edge of a huge parade ground Ariyo pointed to a large crescent-shaped structure.

"Sebok Barrack. My childhood home. The name is misleading. Each barrack functions as an independent community housing five thousand young quintessences, and contains a school, cafeteria, and other living areas."

The teenager peered at the huge building, wondering what it was like growing up with so many siblings and no parents. "How many quintessences are at Essence?"

"One hundred and forty thousand children, not counting the adults who work here. We graduate twenty thousand a year. As property of the empire, they are sent out across the galaxy and rarely have the opportunity to return until their bond years are completed."

"You and your brothers live here."

"The advantage of being a beta model. Researchers record everything we do, scrutinize all mission logs, write papers about us, attempt to discover our unique skills and flaws, see if we are worthy to belong to the family."

"What happens if you are found unworthy?"

"Our model will be discontinued. If flaws are perceived as too critical, then our entire line will be culled."

"By cull, you mean…"

"Termination. Death. We don't get a pink slip and told to find a new job. Until our bond years are completed, we are just property of the government."

"I'm sorry. It should not be that way." Yashana felt awkward, remembering the many times she had disappointed her parents. If she had to live under the same strict rules of the quintessences, she would have been culled long ago.

"It is simply the way of life for us. This is the building I wanted you to see." He gestured toward a giant, ball shaped structure. "This is our Recreation Center. Even quintessences need downtime."

As they entered, nearby quintessences stared at Yashana then shifted their eyes to Ariyo. He gave a curt nod then ignored them. Everywhere were games. Countless video consoles, table games, simulators, and holograms. Quintessences of all ages moved about, playing or watching peers compete.

"There are only quintessences here," noted Yashana.

Ariyo smiled. "For us that is an amusing story. When this building was first opened, anyone could come. But certain employees, especially two of our founding fathers, spent too much time here and their wives asked Layla to ban all non-quintessences. The two men, Derrick and Zylar, tried to organize an employee strike, but their wives threatened to never share a bed with them again."

"I'm not going to be arrested for being here am I?"

"I have already seen to that. You are safe today."

They wandered about, exploring the many floors. Despite being a gigantic arcade, the atmosphere was relatively subdued. Small groups gathered around popular games, but no one yelled or egged on opponents. One section had simulators of aircraft and tanks which tilted according to what happened on the screens. Another area consisted of hologram battlefronts. Yashana watched the stern adolescence faces of six year olds firing at waves of incoming soldiers. The effects were extremely realistic, showing dying opponents twisting in agony, blood dripping from wounds.

Loud explosions ripped the ground apart, sending debris and body parts flying.

Yashana looked away, troubled. "These are more than games."

"Yes. This is really a training facility—the real reason Layla banned non-quintessences. That hologram game was programmed using war footage. Those were real men you saw dying."

"Why are children allowed to play such games?"

"Because for us, it is not a game but our future reality. The lives of quintessences are harsh. We are asked to perform tasks and endure hardships which would eat away the souls of most sentients. We handle that which others prefer never to see or think about. This is the purpose we were created for."

They moved to a quieter area and watched half-grown four year olds playing shuffleboard. An especially good block or win brought a ghost of a smile to the players' faces—the most expression Yashana had seen on any model besides the AS's. In just a few years these children may die in a war.

"Why did you bring me here?"

"Outsiders rarely understand us. To the Galactic Senate, we are pawns to be sacrificed. To planetary leaders, we are tools to restore order and root out corruptions. To scientists, we are a fascinating experiment. To common citizens, we are feared and avoided, seen as a necessary evil. To Layla, we were people. You deserve an opportunity to see who we really are."

"Why? I'm just a fourteen year old who can't pass nanobiomaterials. I'm sure Layla never failed a class her entire sainted life."

"Despite your feelings, you have inherited her legacy."

"I am not your mystical creator. I'm only here because I have to be. When I finish my hours, I'm out of here."

Ariyo sighed. "It is hard for me to understand your anger. We see our clones as our brothers. But you hate your sister clone."

"Layla, my sister? She may have been a great person, but I feel trapped by her. She is a ghost which haunts me, and I'm sick of hearing about her."

"Does the source of your anger relate to your sisters on Mansoor?"

"What do they have to do with anything?

"You often argue with them. Why?"

"Because…because…they irritate me. They mocked me since I was a child, making fun of me because I used words they couldn't understand. I was younger but in a higher grade than them. I was an embarrassment they didn't want their friends to know about. I guess you could say none of us wanted to live in the shadow of another."

"Quintessences do not have sibling rival."

"Lucky you. Thousands of brothers and no fights."

"We save that for the battlefront."

Part II

"Learn from me, if not by my precepts, at least by my example, how dangerous is the acquirement of knowledge and how much happier that man is who believes his native town to be the world, than he who aspires to become greater than his nature will allow."

—From *Frankenstein* by Mary Shelley

Chapter Nine

Yashana sighed, wishing the last shuttle would arrive so they could leave the spaceport. She was eager to begin her senior year at Luncaster, despite she would be required to write the dreaded dissertation before she could earn her Ph.D. Over the entire break, she had pondered which topic to choose.

Leaning forward, she cut off Ethan's conversation with another student. "Have you chosen yours yet?"

Instantly he knew what she referred too. "Yep. The components of robotic autonomous system. My research will help me improve Rover's control and speech. Maybe I'll start a robotics animal company."

"You do know robotic animals have been around for centuries."

"But mine will be so realistic you won't be able to tell the difference."

"Will yours be able to have puppies?"

"Okay, maybe not that realistic, but mine will interact realistically with their owners, be trainable, have personalities. They will never die or poop. The perfect pet. So, what's your topic?"

"No idea."

"You still don't know? It's not like you went anywhere all break."

Yashana sighed. "My parents finally ungrounded me, seeing as I am a senior—maybe because they know all I do is sat around and read. We have a family joke that this is the Year of the Senior. My oldest sister is a senior at Mansoor University, and my other sister is a senior in high school."

"If you were ungrounded, why didn't you call me so we could do something together?"

"You're still on my parents ban list. They blame you for my arrest."

"Granted, it was my fault. Good thing they don't know we chatted all summer by net. Got to love those anonymous proxies."

The chauffeur driving them to college called out, "That's the last arrival. Grab your belongings."

As Yashana stood up, she noticed Ethan had hit his growth spurt and was now four inches taller than her. His brown hair was in need of a trim, but he cared little about fashion. She followed the other students to a hover van and chatted easily with Ethan during the ride to the university. Her first glimpse of Luncaster in a month brought a stab of joy. This would be a year of transition, when she would finally leave adolescence behind and be recognized as an adult. People with Ph.D's were not told who to see or where to go. She would be seventeen by then, ready to have her first real job, first apartment, first car—if she could just get over the hurdle of writing that dreaded dissertation.

Gauge was not in the dorm room when Yashana arrived. As she unpacked, her cluttered mess was a strong contrast to Gauge's tidy half of the room. She opened her closet to hang up clothes, pausing to study she reflection in the mirror. She had been a late bloomer, but her body had finally developed feminine curves. Still, she was plain looking. *Or Layla was. Perhaps that's why she was twenty-seven before she married. I won't wait that long.* Yet Yashana was in no hurry. She had a Ph.D to earn and a career to begin.

She had almost finished updating her electronic billboard on the wall above her desk when Gauge entered. After a happy exchange of greeting, Yashana learned Gauge had a part-time job.

"How do you have time for that?"

"Since I do not travel home during breaks, I finished my community service weeks ago. They were so pleased with my work that they asked me to continue, but with pay. How could I refuse? I enjoy the outdoors and meet so many people at the park. They are as curious about me as I am of them. I was invited to several luncheons and even meet the mayor's wife. When she heard I was a political social major at Luncaster, she asked me to be a member of a youth committee sponsoring community service."

"How ironic."

"Yes, I get paid for my work, and I can use the experience as research for my dissertation."

"The most exciting things I did was visit the library and the mall with my sisters. We actually got along—most of the time. I guess we are finally maturing."

"What topic have you chosen?"

"Uh, I made a possible list." Yashana pulled up a file on her e-tablet, and Gauge scanned the list

"Fifty-eight topics. Very random. Musculoskeletal reanimation, viruses versus nanos, generational diseases, carnivorous plants. Aren't these a bit extensive?"

"I was actually thinking about your planet with the last one. An entire ecosystem where plants kill animals in order to reproduce."

"Little research has been published about our environment. You would need to fly to Zon to conduct first-hand observation."

"Perhaps I'll save that until after graduation." Yashana sighed. "This is so hard. Dissertations often open the door for our first jobs. I'm trying to find a topic no one has done before, something significant."

"What about your work at Essence? Why not choose a topic which relates to quintessences? You could do firsthand research."

"I want nothing to do with those foeditas horribilis. Nothing."

Yashana's deep venom puzzled Gauge. "Why do you dislike them? I thought they were considered the zenith of genetics."

"Oh, they are the proud banner that the Basanti Empire waves. Look at us. We're the best in the universe. We rewrote natural laws, skipping evolution, to create the perfect warrior race. Bow to our superiority. Worship us or we'll send a squadron of mortis elixirs to your planet."

"You should not mock the empire. Even before the quintessences were created, Basanti had two thousand years of stable growth in economics, technology, medicine, and science. Its strength lies in its unity of so many cultures sharing their knowledge. The entire embodiment of my world's accomplishments is ash when compared to one ediethean village."

"That is where you are wrong. Your people are dazzled by Basanti's power, but your culture is just as important as the almighty edietheans. You should not change who you are to try to equal them."

"Why would we want to look like an ediethean?" Gauge gave a toothy smile. "We are happy with our appearance. But we would like to understand terraforming to make more planets in our solar system livable. How is this wrong?"

Yashana looked away, unable to explain she had really been criticizing the creation of her own race, the profectus. "It's not. I was just running my mouth. Ready for dinner?"

During the first week, all Yashana's professors pushed the dissertation, reminding students they needed to have their topics approved soon and not delay beginning their research. On Wednesday Yashana was required to meet with her adviser. After lunch she entered Doctor Duken's small, cluttered office. On the wall were pictures of well-known genetic engineered animals.

"Have a seat," said the elderly human, tossing a folder onto a large stack of files. "You would think with all the e-files we send, we would never need real paper again." The man leaned back in his chair and folded his hands together. "What topic have you chosen?"

"I haven't yet, but I have a list of ideas. Maybe you can give me some suggestions." Yashana handed over her e-tablet.

The professor's lips pressed into a frown as he surveyed her list. "Several of these topics do not even relate to your major. Have you really given this serious thought?"

"It is all I have thought about over the summer. I was trying to find a topic no one has done before."

"I suggest keeping to your field of study, focusing on what interests you. As I have repeatedly said in class, the dissertation often sets the path that your career will follow. Do you really plan to get a job working with carnivorous plants?"

"No, I guess not."

Doctor Duken glanced at his computer screen. "I see you're interning at Essence, a rare accomplishment that only a few of our students achieve each year. You are working at the finest genetics institution in the galaxy, yet you listed nothing relating to the quintessences."

"I was trying to avoid them."

"Why?" The professor's firm brown eyes peered at her.

Yashana shifted uncomfortable in her seat. "I just don't like them. Surely there is something else I can do."

"The topics you listed here are not worthy of the talent you have shown in my classes. In your case, I think you are avoiding that which you should be doing. Perhaps it is your destiny."

Anger rose in the teenager. "My destiny has nothing to do with those leeches."

"You have free choice of your topic, of course, but if you take too much time in deciding, it may delay your graduation by a year." Doctor Duken handed back her e-tablet, giving her a grandfatherly smile. "I have learned that when you face your fears, the object of your fear loses its control over you."

Chapter Ten

Saturday came too quickly for Yashana. Gauge would be working with a dozen teenage volunteers from a local school to renovate a run-down playground, Ethan headed to the city park to continue his community service, and Yashana returned to the realm of her enemy. As she passed once again under the shadow of Layla's huge portrait, she clenched her fists, wishing to rip down the picture with her bare hands. Ariyo greeted her, informing her this term she would be working in the Research Department. She had been rotated after each school break, much to her relief. Last term she was a nursemaid in the Infant Department and before that sanitized toys in the Toddler Department. Nothing exciting, but it did give her insight into different areas of the institute.

Ariyo led her deep into the heart of the complex, at last arriving at the high security entrance to the Research Department. They passed several quintessence guards and entered a small room where a bright light scanned them. The computer recognized them and the far door slid open. Beyond lay more corridors, offices, and work rooms. Scientists in lab coats barely gave them a glance as they moved down the hallway. They entered a large laboratory where a dozen sentients bustled about.

Ariyo walked up to a human who was lecturing a youth for spilling the sticky contents of a beaker. "Doctor Golnick, this is Yashana, the intern I spoke with you about."

The man spared only a brief glance at Yashana. "Yes, she will be in the washroom. Dan'ukva, make yourself useful and show her where to go."

A purplish sea laven with rough, bumpy skin tossed his cleaning cloth into the dirty bin, grabbed the half empty beaker with a webbed hand, and led Yashana down several hallways to the washroom. Along one wall were several large sinks built into a long, metal table. Everywhere were trays stacked with glass tubes, culture dishes, tools, hoses, and other dirty objects of all sizes. In the center of the room hot vapors escaped from the flaps covering the ends of a bulky washing machine.

"The work is endless," complained Dan'ukva, placing the beaker he carried on a table. He was young, most likely a recent college graduate. "And I have been doing it all by myself for the last month, after my partner got promoted. It's good to finally get some help."

"I only work on the weekends."

The sea laven frowned. "At least that is better than nothing."

He taught her how to place the various dirty objects in trays which were sent through the huge machine whose double purpose was not only to wash but its high temperature killed pathogens. Cleaned equipment was sorted then placed on carts which Dan'ukva pushed out of the room to take back to the labs. Some of the dirty objects were too large to go through the machine and had to be washed by hand in a sink. For hours, Yashana sweated in the hot, humid room, trying to juggle between stacking and unstacking, keeping an eye on the washing cycle, and scrubbing the dried remains of experiments at the sinks. Occasionally a glass dish slipped from her rubber gloves and shattered on the concrete floor. The first time it happened, she picked up the broken glass with her hands and several shards cut through the rubber, piercing her hand. Dan'ukva walked in, noticed the bleeding, and silently pointed her to a wall dispenser of disinfectant cream. He then grabbed a broom and swept up the remaining glass.

By the time the lunch break arrived, Yashana was exhausted. Ariyo met her at the food court, but Yashana had little interest in food. She quickly drank all her soda and went for a refill.

As she sat down again, she complained, "This is the worst job ever. Do you pick them to torture me?"

"I just pick the department. Your supervisor chooses the position."

"I want to transfer back to Infant Department. Dirty diapers were only smelly, not dangerous." She held up her hand, showing off two bandages.

"You cannot transfer. There is much for you to learn in the Research Department."

"I've already mastered how to clean a canister of boiled acid beetles. How in the universe does that relate to quintessences? Do the researchers just come up with this stuff to have an excuse to stay busy so they can get a paycheck?"

"I am certain there was a valid reason. You have barely eaten."

"I'm too hot and grossed out. I may never eat again." Yashana finished off her second drink. "Really, can I get a transfer?"

"No, you have only worked there four hours."

"Can I get a transfer after forty hours?"

"No." Ariyo calmly ate his hamburger while Yashana scowled at him.

"You're irritating."

"And you are not?"

"Isn't there some law against the abuse of minors?"

"Washing dishes is not classified as abuse."

"I'll never make any of my kids wash dishes."

"Then you plan to wash all their dishes for them?"

Yashana gave an exaggerated sigh then tossed her uneaten meal in the trash. When Ariyo suggested they go for a walk, Yashana complained she was too tired. As they sat in silence, waiting for the lunch hour to end, the teenager pondered dissertation topics. With her full load of classes and physical demanding job on the weekends, she began to worry that she would be unable to conduct the research needed before the end of the school term. She needed an easy topic, one that involved air condition and getting out of the washroom.

Yashana leaned forward, suddenly excited. "I've finally decided on my dissertation topic. It deals with quintessences."

Ariyo remained silent as he finished off his drink.

"Don't you want to hear my topic?"

"If you wish to share it."

"I will study gaming habits of quintessences, looking for relationships between models and type of games played."

"How do you plan to conduct your research?"

"At the Recreation Center. All I have to do is keep a tally of which models play which games." Yashana noticed Ariyo's frown was deepening, so she talked faster to keep him from interrupting. "It will take hours and hours of observation. The information could be useful in choosing which games to buy in the future. I could do it in place of wash duty so it wouldn't take up any of your extra time."

"No."

"Don't you want me to graduate?"

"Yes. To do so, you will need a serious topic."

"Gaming habits is a serious topic."

"I doubt your evaluation team will think so."

"If I got my advisor to agree, would you go along with it?"

"My opinion does not matter. As you know, the Recreation Center is off limits to non-quintessences."

"You got me in before."

"That was a onetime deal for which I attained Director Rangan's permission."

"Then I will ask him."

"He will require you to give a formal petition, speaking in front of the Five."

"I can do that."

Ariyo leaned forward. "You do not realize the seriousness of your request. There are many who have entered their chamber and never left again—alive."

Yashana forced a laugh. "It's just a request for research, not a criminal trial."

"Never take the Five lightly. The weight of their combined power is nearly as influential as the Emperor himself."

"What's with the scare tactic? I thought your job was to encourage me to become a better worker and student. Don't you want to see me succeed?"

"I will help you with the petition but do not expect it to be approved. Nor will you be getting out of your washroom duty, which starts in five minutes."

Yashana hurried across the complex, determined to make her plan work. If she could get her community service hours and research hours combined, it would save her a great deal of trouble. Four hours and two broken breakers later, Yashana had a plan mapped out in her head. Back at Luncaster University, she ate a light supper then typed out a proposal, using the biggest terms her thesaurus could find to prove the study of gaming habits were important. Sunday at work she broke only one dish, and managed to earn a few compliments from Dan'ukva. Seeing how overworked he was, she felt a bit guilty trying to transfer so soon. Guilt, though, did not stop her on Monday with meeting with her advisor, seeking permission for her topic. He was not impressed after reading over her proposal but did agree that if the Five approved her request, he would support her topic.

Wednesday afternoon Ariyo came to the college to help her prepare. They sat on a couch in the bustling student union, reading over the proposal. Gauge sprawled out, taking up an entire couch across from them, while typing a paper. Ethan sat on the floor with the inner workings of his robotic dog scattered on a coffee table. As he worked with a screwdriver to fix wiring, he kept a wary eye on the quintessence. Yashana had warned her friends in advance that Ariyo was not human.

"You need to simplify your wording," suggested Ariyo. "What does 'quantitative collection of summative variables' mean?"

"That I will be collecting lots of data and sorting it."

"Why not say that then?"

"It's not fancy enough, of course."

"If the Five cannot understand your terminology, they will not approve your request."

"They supervise the largest scientific institute in the galaxy. I'm sure they know what I'm talking about."

"They are quintessences. Fancy words do not impress us."

"Just because you can't understand, doesn't mean they won't."

"Do it your way. You are just setting yourself up to fail." Ariyo stood up.

"You're not leaving? We're only on page three."

"Why did you bother asking for my opinion when you refuse to heed my advice?"

"I'm sorry," Yashana quickly said. "I really do need you. I'm listening. I must simplify my wording."

Ethan scowled, hoping the quintessence was really leaving. "How simple should she go? Can they understand baby talk?"

Yashana forced a laugh, "Ethan's joking. He is still upset about Gauge's arrest."

"And his own, I presume." Ariyo looked disapprovingly at the youth but sat back down.

Yashana made notes about areas that needed revising, which covered most of the proposal. Afterwards, she invited Ariyo to eat with her friends in the cafeteria. Gauge helped Yashana in keeping the conversation polite, but Ethan sulked in silence, occasionally spewing double meaning statements insulting the quintessence. Ariyo ignored the rudeness.

After Ariyo left, Ethan burst out, "Why did you have to invite him for dinner?"

"It was the polite thing to do," answered Yashana.

"Why be polite to a leech?"

Guage answered, "Because your life may be in their hands again one day. Why are you so upset? It was I, not you, who spent a day in their prison."

"I will never forgive them for what they did to you."

"I was not harmed. And we did break the law."

"I did, not you. But they went after you."

Yashana cut in, "Is this some hidden guilt trip you are dealing with?"

Ethan angrily shot back, "Guilt? Have I not repeatedly admitted my wrong? This is not about me. He is a *foeditas horribilis*, the horrifying foulness. And you two sat across from him chatting about cuisine."

"We were being polite."

"Will you still be polite when he feeds on you to kill you?"

"He would not do that to me."

"They were designed to be the ultimate killer, the predator of criminals. Which we are."

"Thanks to your recklessness."

Ethan walked off in a huff, refusing to talk with Yashana for several days. She ignored his silence as she rewrote her proposal, attempting to use clearer wording. The weekend was filled with another sixteen hours laboring in the steamy washroom.

Monday evening, dressed in her best dress suite, she entered the Chamber of Five. Though Ariyo was beside her, Yashana was very nervous as she stood in front of the five elderly quintessences, each identical face as expressionless as the next. In front of each Five rose thin pedestals that held a computer screen and keyboard. Everything was painted white in the simple, round room. There were no chairs. Yashana felt as if she had entered a large, surreal bubble.

Yashana walked to the center of the room and begin her prepared speech while the Five glanced at her proposal on their screens. After she finished, they questioned her.

"How is this topic related to your major?" asked the one whose nametag read *Mason*. "It seems more appropriate for a social or psychology student."

"Their genes will be involved as I will be comparing the different models."

"As a geneticist, should you not be looking directly at DNA, not behavior?" said Caleb.

"A geneticist must see the whole picture, not just the code. We must understand the consequences of the codes we write. No one has evaluated how DNA affects which games quintessences choose. As you can see in my proposal, this data can be used in many ways."

"You hold a criminal record yet are asking access to a forbidden area for non-quintessences. Do you have an agenda beyond just pure research?" Gabriel's eyes bore into the teenager.

"Uh, no."

Ariyo's warning whispered through Yashana's memory. *Many who have entered their chamber never leave again—alive.*

Heeding his advice, she tried to be as honest as possible. "Accept that I need to complete this research in order to graduate."

The questions continued for several more minutes, each attacking Yashana from unexpected directions, catching her unprepared. The interview ended suddenly, and Yashana was sent outside for the Five to debate.

As she shakily sat on a bench in the anti-chamber, Ariyo said, "You spoke better than I expected."

"They are very direct with their questioning."

"The Five are always this way."

Only a few minutes passed before they were summoned back in. Yashana tried to appear relaxed as she waited, but her palms sweated terribly.

As director, Alexander gave the verdict. "Your proposal has been accepted if you can work within the conditions we set. You will never enter the Recreation Center without being escorted by Ariyo. The hours you spend researching will not count towards your community service hours. Everything you write must first be read by Ariyo then by Tiah Vay, head of our Psychology Department, before it is sent to your professors. Any information considered confidential will not be published, even if it affects your grade. Do you agree with this arrangement?"

Yashana glanced at Ariyo before saying, "Yes, I agree."

It was not until they were in the elevator that Yashana relaxed, grinning boldly. "We did it."

"You did."

"Still, I could not have done so without your advice. Thanks."

Ariyo allowed himself to smile. "You are welcome."

While they ate dinner at the food court, they discussed plans. It was decided that each weekend Yashana would spend mornings working in the washroom and afternoons at the Recreation Center.

"I wish they would have combined my hours. It means I won't finish my sentence until my last semester at school. Gauge has already finished hers, and Ethan has less than two months."

"Just be glad they allowed you at all."

"What was with all that confidential information talk? My topic isn't controversial."

"A safety measure. It is a duty of department chairmen to oversee all published research coming out of Essence."

"Have you met Tiah Vay? What style writing does he prefer?"

"I have met *her* too many times. Her writing style I know nothing about as I have never read her work. Quintessences have a natural dislike for psychologists. Do be cautious around her. She is married to Jacob."

"You mean Jacob of the Five?" Seeing Ariyo nod, she went on. "You just said quintessences don't like psychologists. Why would he marry her?"

Ariyo took the last bite of his burger. "The next time you are feeling suicidal, you can ask him."

Chapter Eleven

"I see you were very busy last month." Tiah Vay glanced at her e-tablet. "In just four weeks you had thirty-six kills and seventeen arrests. Is there a particular reason your kill rate was so high?"

"They resisted arrest." Ariyo keep his demeanor calm, his face blank.

The furnishings of Tiah's office were chosen to create a peaceful, relaxing astrosphere. In one corner water fell in an endless cycle down a series of miniature waterfalls into a tiny pool surrounded by flowers. Plants bloomed in windows. A vine climbed high up a wall, nearly touching the ceiling. Tiah sat across from Ariyo in a thick cushioned chair. Perhaps the room worked magic on many subjects and they opened up, spilling their inter-most secrets to the psychologist. Quintessences were not fooled by such deceptions.

"Eleven at one time?"

"I politely asked them to toss down their weapons. They chose to shoot."

The neodite's striking figure, long purple hair highlighted in lavender, and friendly manners may have caused many tongues to tell all, but quintessences were not impressed by beauty. Well, not enough to bare their souls.

"Your report says you suffered two laser burns, one bullet in your leg, and several cuts from grazing bullets. With that much firepower going on, I'm surprised you survived long enough to heal."

"I dodge well."

"Why were you alone? What happened to your team?"

"They were in another part of the building. I was following a hunch."

"Perhaps you should have told several of your team members about your hunch and brought them with you."

"They were busy with other problems at that time."

Tiah switched tactics. "Congratulations, Ariyo, on breaking the record for most kills in a single day for a non-warfare mission. Eighteen total. And you hold the highest monthly kill record. Should I also mention you also earned the highest monthly injury record?"

Ariyo answered with silence.

"How does that make you feel?"

"I am satisfied with completing my missions."

"No pride in your accomplishments?"

"Quintessences do not gloat."

At this point other psychologists working at Essence would have dropped the line of questioning and moved to another topic. Tiah was not like other psychologists.

"Could you not have found a more peaceful way of handling the missions?"

"I did ask them to surrender. You read all my mission logs. Have I ever broken the Code?"

"No, but perhaps if you were not so rash to rush into a dogfight, you could have a higher arrest record than kill record."

"I did what was called for at the time. All the missions were classified Level Five. They cannot be accomplished without some bloodshed."

"Interesting that you volunteered for every one. Why only Level Five? Are you deliberately seeking situations leading to butchery?" Tiah kept a professional tone, but Ariyo knew the questions held a hidden agenda.

It was always like this with Tiah. A cat and mouse game. Tiah probing, the quintessence dodging. The curse of being a beta model. While other models went about their normal lives, rarely, if ever, seeing a psychologist, beta models had to endure a host of evaluations from numerous departments. Only after decades of testing might models be commissioned and their DNA included in the regular cycle for new fetuses. Stakes were high for the AS model, for no new models had been commissioned in over forty years. They may be the first and last of their kind.

"Well?" Tiah looked at Ariyo with a face as expressionless as a quintessence, expecting an answer, reminding Ariyo how much she had changed from the naïve newbie fresh out of college ten years ago.

Back then, she had been just another irritating evaluator asking silly questions from a list that Ariyo knew by rote. Every month he was required to answer them despite his responses never changed. She had been a bit different from the other psychologists, over friendly, her excitement for her new job still not worn off after three months. Occasionally she asked off topic questions about the daily lives of quintessences, but Ariyo and his brothers told her little. Then one day she broke the pattern.

That day Ariyo had flown through the questionnaire, not waiting until Tiah finished speaking before giving his curt answers. Tiah's frustration of the uselessness of it all was evident. As Tiah reached over and turned off the recorder. Ariyo stood up, ready to leave.

"Just one more question. During the epulo bite, what information do you seek when you have not been given specific directions?"

Ariyo stared at her, shocked, wondering if he should kill her immediately or report her to a commander first. What really went on during the epulo bite was forbidden knowledge to outsiders and never spoken aloud. Let the galaxy think it was only a defense tactic used for healing and killing. The truth was far more potent.

Seeing Ariyo's dark look, Tiah gave a reassuring smile. "It's all right. The recorder is off. See? Jacob gave me permission to ask such questions."

"Why would he do that?"

"We are…seeing each other." She blushed, the smooth skin on her face turning pinkish. Quickly she pushed her emotions back, and her skin returned to a deep blue. "Well, what is your answer?"

"I can give no response." Ariyo walked out, ignoring her call to come back.

He had almost reached the bōjutsu gym, when he received a summons to meet Jacob immediately. That meeting had been the worst of his life—so far. Ariyo was forced to stand silently before his elder while being lectured like he was a careless child. Jacob never raised his voice. There was no need. Breaking the Code by disobeying a direct command of a superior carried the punishment of death. Ariyo's defense was he had not believed she really had the backing of the Five. Though Ariyo's offence was forgiven that time, he was ordered back to Tiah's office to answer any questions she wished to ask.

Ariyo warned his brothers that Tiah had become an insider who they must be wary of. Barely three weeks later Jacob married Tiah and appointed her the head of the beta branch inside the Psychology Department. Anger ran rampant as some co-workers resented Tiah's sudden rise in power. At first Tiah attempted to smooth hurt feelings, trying to be buddies with those who hated her. She had to endure many painful lessons before learning some situations could only be solved by leaders being tough. Eventually she fired or transferred those who opposed her and revamped the entire beta evaluation program. Gone were the silly questionnaire and recorders. Her college textbooks had not prepared her for psychoanalyzing quintessences, but marriage to Jacob did. Overtime she gained the respect of her co-workers. When the head of the Psychology Department announced his retirement two years ago, it was a panel of her peers who recommended her as the new chairperson.

"Well," said Tiah again. "Why do you only choose Level Five missions during the month you were away from Essence."

"I am simply fulfilling my duty."

"You are being evasive, Ariyo. I am here to help you, but you must work with me."

"You have my answer."

"It is not enough. I can have another quintessence pry the answer out of you for me, but I prefer this way. You choose."

Ariyo liked her better before she learned to bully. "I am attempting to make up for my months of no action when babysitting Yashana while my brothers bleed for the empire."

"So it is guilt then that dives you?"

"Why would I feel guilt when I have committed no crimes?"

"The Five consider Yashana very important. Do you disagree with them?" Tiah tapped notes into her e-tablet as she spoke.

"I never said she was unimportant. My model, by design, prefers action, not inactivity. Is this a fault design?"

"Of course not. All quintessences are this way. But you must also have balance. Many of your elders have found themselves in administration jobs where they must spend long hours doing paperwork, among other mundane tasks. They manage that without going stir crazy." She typed a final note on her e-table then dismissed him.

As Ariyo headed towards the food court to meet Yashana, he went over the interview, irate that Tiah has probed so deeply yet again. Could she not be satisfied that he was an expert combatant? He broke records and she claimed it was because of guilt. Fortunately, she could not perform the epulo or she would discover his anger and frustrations he successfully kept buried—most of the time. Quintessences must never let emotions control them; instead, they must control emotions. It was only during the heat of dangerous missions or intense sports competitions that he could release his pent up feelings. Then he felt truly alive, adrenaline pumping through his body, his trained muscles reacting on instinct. His brothers led adventurous lives, traveling across the galaxy while he spent the weekends babysitting a teenager and the rest of the week either pushing his skills in the gyms or Recreation Center. And he was failing. Trying to change the mind of a stubborn teenager was far more difficult than surviving a gunfight. There he simply killed his opponents.

Lunch with Yashana was typical. She complained about her job, how hot it was, how researchers were so messy, how terrible the cleaning fluids smelled. Ariyo's attempts to turn the conversation into discussing positive aspects of Essence were always meet with objections. Then off they went to the Recreation Center. Yashana would position herself near a wall for a while, marking tally marks on forms in her e-tablet as she watched quintessences moving among the games. After a while she would suddenly, without warning, head to another room. Ariyo made sure to always move in front of her, peering into the next chamber before she arrived, blocking her path briefly if necessary.

So far he had kept her from seeing that which would lead to dangerous questions. There were no cameras in the Recreation Center for a reason. The building was a safe zone where quintessences regularly bit each other, swapping information and stories. It was as natural to them as to some species who greeted friends with a handshake and a chat. The young quintessences had been warned to avoid doing so around Yashana and not to ask why she looked like Layla.

After Yashana left, Ariyo received a message on his e-band. He navigated through the vast complex to the Infant Department, took a side passageway, and entered a small observation room which overlooked a huge nursery where five thousand infant quintessences lay in small cribs. Both sentient and robotic nursemaids moved along the aisles, tending the babies. Alexander Rangan was in a deep discussion with the department chairman.

Ariyo waited patiently near the door, watching robotic nursemaids roll down aisles, changing diapers, and feeding infants. The upper body of the robots were humanoid shaped and covered with skin-like rubber. Their blank faces, except for eye sensors, only served the purpose of aesthetic. A sundancer held a crying baby, rocking him till he quieted. The robots kept to a strict feeding and cleaning schedule, giving no time for comforting upset infants. That was left to the sentients, most taking their job as caregivers quite seriously.

Even Yashana, thought Ariyo. Last year he had secretly watched her many times through this window. At first she had been awkward and nervous around the babies, but over time she gained confidence, even occasionally singing lullabies to them.

The chairman left and Alexander turned his attention to Ariyo. "Tiah's report about your evaluation this morning was grave."

"I answered as truthful as possible."

"Perhaps so. She recommends that you only be allowed on Level Two missions for a while. We approved her request."

"Have I let you down in any way?"

"No. Your performances in the field are becoming legendary. Too much so. Ones such as you have a habit of dying young, and you have your most important mission yet to complete. How goes your subject?"

"The same. Upon graduation, she plans to have nothing further to do with Essence."

"Your time is short in changing her mind."

"What else can I do?"

"Stay patient. The critical time comes when she passes from adolescence into adulthood. That is when she will be most vulnerable. Tiah believes you do not see the importance of this mission, leading to resentment. I will remind you that though we have some of the greatest scientists working in our laboratories, no new models have been successfully designed without input from Layla. During the last few decades of her life, she continued to design, but her mind was declining, and all her work was rejected by her own department using the standards she had implemented years earlier. It was a bitter disappointment for her."

The elder quintessence became silent for a long moment as his mind drifted into the past. "Accepting one's own morality is difficult. In the end, she found acceptance far better than I. After her death, researchers played around with her designs, putting some of them into production. Most never made it past Stage D. You are the last design she created that was accepted by the Research Department, but even then they believed her design flawed. Decades went by before your DNA was moved to Stage C, and only then because there was nothing else left of Layla's work that remained untested."

"We have never been told this version of our creation story."

"I am sure it is unpleasant to be told you almost never existed. I only tell you this now so you may understand why the stakes are so high for Yashana to work here at Essence. She solves logic problems using the same methods as Layla and has the same brilliant gift for writing the code of life, even if she has not accepted that yet. Without her here, your model may be the last to reach Beta Stage. Our program will continue as before with our scientists changing small things like hair color, but to create a brand new individual is far more complicated. Layla dreamed of our species becoming a proper civilization made up of many models with different skills helping the whole becoming stronger. I take your model's success or failure very personally."

"My brothers and I will do whatever you ask of us to our fullest capability."

"What is your capability? As a beta, neither you nor anyone else knows that yet. You are still so young, untested in many areas."

"Which tests should we prepare for?"

Alexander looked out the window at the infants. "For one, you have not been tested in love."

"I do not understand. It is twenty years before we complete our bondage. The Code forbids sexual relations before that time. We will never break the Code."

"You can love but cannot act upon it. The best action, of course, is to avoid love until your service is completed. Saves much stress. What I meant was that we do not know how well you can resist temptation for you have never been tempted. Half a century ago, we almost commissioned the ME6 models before their bondage was complete, but first one then nearly a dozen broke the Code. So many that we discontinued the model completely."

"We will not act dishonorably."

"No one plans to. Code violations take place during moments of weakness when a quintessence places his own desires above his brethren."

Ariyo felt distressed. Did the Five think he and his brothers were flawed, untrustworthy, only fit for extinction? "How may we prove ourselves?"

"By keeping your emotions under control and not getting killed in battle. Your model's greatest strength is your greatest weakness. The AS1 are more expressive than other models, allowing you to interact better with other sentients, but you are more likely to react on your emotions than the rest of us. Many in the Psychology Department believe your model should be cut."

"Tiah is wrong. As we mature, we will become better."

"Tiah is one of your few supporters. She believes you will reach the balance you need. I believe that too but not all of the Five agree."

Ariyo stood rigidly at attention. "We will accomplish all that is asked."

"Good. Keep your focus on Yashana. Listen to her carefully. Push her as needed. Take whatever measures you need to, except using the epulo. She must choose freely or later she will become resentful and leave."

"Yes, sir." Ariyo saluted, his earlier frustrations replaced by determination.

Chapter Twelve

Yashana opened the door to her dorm room as quietly as possible and wheeled her suitcase in, keeping the lights off. She was relieved to be back from the month long break spent with her family but exhausted from the delays and late arrival. All she wanted was to sleep. Leaving her luggage by her closet, she treaded across the messy floor towards her bed. She slipped on something in the darkness and crashed to the floor.

Instantly Gauge was awake, sitting up in bed. "Who is there? Yashana, why are you sitting on the floor?"

"I didn't want to wake you and fell."

"I wanted to greet you when you arrived. How was your trip?"

"Okay on Mansoor. Only one real fight with my sisters, but we made up later. The flight back was horrible. Because of a big storm, our shuttle landed in a different city. Eight hours we had to sit in its spaceport. At least I had some time to work on my dissertation, but not much. Ethan's stupid dog kept drawing crowds of kids who all wanted to play with it. How was your break?"

"Today is my Day of Passage."

"Oh, I forgot about that." Yashana struggled to remember what Gauge had said about it months ago. The event was supposed to be very important, something to do with reflection, speaking, and twentieth birthday.

Gaugue's eyesight was good in the dark, letting her see Yashana's pondering look. "This is the eighth day since my birthday. Traditionally our youth meet with our family and tribe elders. There we speak about important life lessons we have learned which will shape our future. As my family is not here, I had hoped you and Ethan would substitute."

"Sure. It would be my honor, but Ethan is probably already asleep."

"It is after curfew anyway."

"That would not stop Ethan, if he could stay awake. He would just hack the security cameras, calling it a noble deed." Both girls giggled, then Yashana said, "What am I supposed to do?"

"What you are already doing, sitting and listening."

Gauge lit a small candle and placed in on the floor in front of her friend. She kneeled on the carpet, wrapping her scaly tail around her body, and sung in her native tongue. Yashana could not understand the words of the ancient tune, but its mystery drew her in along with the flickering candle light casting strange shadows around the dark room. Chill bumps ran down her arms, and she wondered what it was like to grow up on a primitive world, completely alien from everything she knew.

After the last notes faded, Gauge spoke in a singsong voice. "Blackrock, I give you my life, my story, my song. For you I traveled far away to the land of the warm-blooders. For you, I lived among them, learning their ways, taking their knowledge, gaining their wisdom. What is the greatest lesson of all which I bear? That they are not so different from us. Hopes, dreams, values. Among them walk both good and evil, givers and takers, oath keepers and oath breakers. Some we can trust, some we cannot. My people, there is a place upon them for us. One day we can rise to be their equals without giving up what it means to be zonners. This is my song. This is the purpose of my life. May my story be passed to generations yet to come."

For a while both girls sat in silence, watching the wax dripping down the side of the candle. Finally Yashana said, "That was beautiful. More profound than the cake and presents I get on my birthdays."

"When I go back, I will sing this song to them, but in our tongue. When I first came here, I was terrified. But you and Ethan were so friendly, so helpful and curious. It was through you I was able to reach out to others, making many friends. When I go back to Zon, I will carry part of you with me, sharing you with my people. My tribe will know your name, calling you comrade."

"Now you're embarrassing me."

"This is our last semester at Luncaster. I believe we should speak what is on our hearts."

"You're making me feel sentimental, yet we still have five months before graduation. Perhaps longer for me as I may never finish my dissertation."

"You will do fine."

"Since your song is kind of like a life vow, can I make one too?" Yashana sat up straight. "I am going to appreciate each day, living life to the fullest. How is that?"

"Does that mean you will complain less?"

"Ah, sure." Ceremoniously, Yashana held her right hand up. "I promise to be more positive."

Yashana's new outlook on life was sorely tested the next day. Her professors seemed to have doubled the workload in every class, not giving seniors a respite. At lunch, Ethan was depressed because over the break his roommate Ben had bought a robotic dog which could do far more than his own.

"I worked three years, three long years, on mine and it was outperformed by a toy." Ethan stared miserably at his mechanical pet he had placed on the lunch table. "All that work for nothing."

"You always made top marks on your grades relating to him, and the kids at the spaceport loved him." Yashana reached for the salt but stopped. "Rover, fetch salt."

The dog's mechanical head turned to her and its tailed wagged. It looked across the table, tongue hanging out, ignoring the shaker a few inches away.

"It doesn't know what salt is. Neither can its mouth handle the shape of the shaker. The lips are too rigid. So many problems."

Gauge asked, "Could your roommate's dog have picked up the shaker?"

"No, but its AI is smart enough to figure out it could push it." Ethan sighed in frustration. "Ben had two job interviews over break and has a video interview set up for next week. I haven't even begun applying for jobs yet."

"Don't feel bad," said Yashana. "I haven't either. We have plenty of time."

"No, we don't. Five months will go by like…" Ethan snapped his fingers. Rover barked. "I wasn't talking to you, pile of scrap metal."

"I am certain you will both find jobs," Gauge comforted.

"How lucky you are having your job lined up before you even came here. With my police record, I may be the first to graduate from Luncaster without a job."

Yashana remembered her vow from the night before. "Stop being so negative. We're in the same place. You don't have to stay in robotics. You are a genus coder. Plenty of companies would want you to keep them safe from cyberattacks."

"Or they may fear to hire me. Who wants a juvenile delinquent running around in their security network? You're already working at Essence, and they're begging you to stay, at least that leech you hang around does."

"As you know, I am serving a sentence, not working by choice. As soon as I graduate, I'm out of here."

"Where to?" asked Gauge.

Yashana hesitated, uncertain. She had been so busy running from Layla's shadow that her destination had never matter. "I don't know. Just far away."

Hearing the phrase *away*, Rover began walking towards the end of the table. Ethan grabbed the dog just before it fell off the edge. "I sometimes think about moving back to Mansoor to be closer to my dad. There are plenty of companies there. It's just that I feel I will disappear, becoming just another hired hand. I want to do something important with my life. Not just vanish into obscurity. Do you know what I mean?"

Yashana swirled the potatoes on her plate with a fork, feeling uncomfortable. "Not really." The less people recognized her face, the better.

"I want to have the Big Idea which future generations will remember me for. Maybe that sounds arrogant, but it's deep inside me. I want to do something spectacular."

"More spectacular than hacking into Essence Institute?" asked Gauge.

"Something legal that the entire galaxy will appreciated, not just geeks. You have the noble cause of helping your entire species, and you will be in the position to do so. Is it wrong for me to want to be more than a nerd sitting in an office cubicle the rest of my life?"

"No," said Yashana. "There is nothing wrong in wanting to be someone special. It's built into your genes. I believe both of you are destined to do great things."

"What do you want to achieve?" asked the zonner.

"Me? Survive college is all. And get a job, though I don't know how I will find the time."

"I'll help," volunteered Ethan. "Give me a list of the criteria you are looking for and I will do the research, making a list of the best places. All you will have to do is fill out the applications."

"You don't have to do that for me."

"It's my fault that you lost your weekends. This is my way of trying to make up for that. After all, that is what friends are for." At the mention of *friends*, Rover tried to stand on its back feet in Ethan's lap, its wagging metal tail sending a plate crashing to the floor. "Stupid dog, I wasn't calling you a friend."

"Aw, you will hurt its feelings," chided Yashana.

"Robots don't have feelings."

"Still, it is your creation. Be nice to it."

Saturday Yashana met Ariyo in the Grand Forum at Essence. His text message had said to wait for him by the picture of Layla. For nearly ten minutes, Yashana stood under the shadow of the giant director, silently cursing Ariyo for choosing that spot. She worried every time someone glanced her way. Would anyone guess she was a clone? No, they only saw an Indian girl standing by a wall of old photos. Nothing more. What would it be like when she became older, her face more resembling the renowned director?

She will haunt me my entire life, thought Yashana. *Maybe I'll dye my hair purple. Perhaps pink. Keep it cut short. Or shave it all off. Get a nose ring. Anything not to look like her.*

When Ariyo finally showed up, she behaved politely, despite her feelings. "Which department am I working in this term?"

"First, we are going to visit the museum." He gestured at the arched doorway behind them.

"I prefer to wash dishes than go in there."

"This is not an option."

He led her through the arch doorway. Having toured many famous museums on Mansoor, Yashana considered Essence's as petite, consisting of several large chambers broken by dividers into smaller areas. They walked among collections of historical memorabilia, passing interactive displays. Only a few other patrons wandered about.

Yashana paused in front of a bulking machine behind glass. "So that is what the early nanotech DNA builder looked like. It's uglier than that dishwasher I used last year."

"At least it worked. Without it, my species would never have existed."

"And I would be a proper student spending her weekends studying."

"You probably would not have existed either."

"Excuse me, profectus existed years before quintessences did."

"Whoever cloned you only did so because of Layla's achievements. If she had not created the quintessences you would never had been born."

"Need I remind you that there are twenty profectus clones? Layla could have done something else to make her famous."

"Come, you need to see this." Ariyo led her to one of the interactive holograms which showed a transparent Layla. Ariyo pressed a button and a long list of achievements began scrolling by the phantom Layla.

"I've taken tests on her. I've already memorized all this."

Ariyo pressed a different button and Layla was replaced by the glowing face resembling an older Ethan. Yashana flinched and took a step back, staring at the middle-age face of Richard. Despite the age difference, both had the same eyes, nose, and semi-messy hairstyles. *Ethan must never step foot in this museum,* vowed Yashana. *He must never have to go through this identity crisis which I struggle with. Then again, he may get a kick out of sharing his DNA with a famous software programmer and mayor. Probably use the publicity to launch his Big Idea, whatever that will be.*

"Richard Cambridge, founder and mayor of New Hope, CEO of Cambridge Software." Ariyo flipped pictures. "Diana Richton, chief architect of Essence Institute, winner of many design awards." He continued onward, showing picture after picture of profectus.

"I don't need to see all five hundred of them."

"Not five hundred. Only twenty are in this database. Do you know what they all have in common?"

Yashana felt a sicken dread. "Quintessences?"

"Yes. Every one of them contributed in some way to my species, from designing the prototypes of weapons and aircraft we use today to supporting us in galactic politics."

"There were plenty of profectus who had nothing to do with your kind. My race made huge advancements in many fields."

"In the short time before they became extinct."

"Dormant, not extinct. Our original designers just overlooked the fact that the ediethean DNA they used to give us super intelligence were attached to recessive genes. As few profectus married another, there were only several born in a second generation. The ediethean gene is still out there, but the chance of a profectus being born naturally is nearly impossible."

"Leading someone to break the law to bring you back. Interesting that the twenty they chose to clone are the same ones in this database. Perhaps the culprit visited this exact spot, looking at this same hologram."

"And perhaps not. He could have pulled the data up from any computer. I don't care about all this. I exist. That is enough. Now what is my job this term?"

Instead of answering, Ariyo led her out of the museum and through the huge building, finally stopping in front of the Research Department.

Yashana frowned. "I did this last term. I thought my job was always rotated."

"It is, but you will still be working in the same department. Last time the supervisor chose your position. This time I did."

They went through the security scan then down several hallways until finding Doctor Golnick pouring over files in his office.

"Good morning," greeted Ariyo, "Yashana is ready for her now position."

The chairperson looked up, frowning for a moment as if he had never seen her before. "Ah, yes. A lab assistant on Project AF." Ariyo left and Golnick led Yashana to a large room were nearly a dozen researchers bustled among the high-tech equipment. "Frank, here is your new assistant. Now maybe you will get the prototype back on schedule."

Yashana quickly said, "I'm only here on weekend mornings."

Frank glanced at her, the human's frown revealing he was unimpressed. "We're always in need of someone to run errands. Golnick, as we discussed, it may be years before we are ready for Stage C."

"And as I told you, we need to go ahead and run some primary trials. If we wait until you are satisfied that you have the perfect DNA, it will never happen."

Yashana stood, feeling awkward and forgotten as the men debated several minutes. Finally Frank turned his full attention on her. "You'll clean and run errands. Don't mess with any equipment you have not been trained on. My lab is not a child's playground."

"I am about to graduate with a Ph.D in genetics."

"Ah, you're one of those from Luncaster. I won't deal with any arrogant backtalk. You will do as told. Is that clear?"

"Yes, sir."

"Zoe'ul, give her something useful to do."

With a webbed hand, a light purple sea laven beckoned Yashana over to a cart from the washing room. Zoe'ul, like all of her species, had no hair but bony ridgelines on her head. "I will show you where the clean equipment goes. It was not so long ago that I was new here."

"Last term I was the one washing these breakers." Yashana began helping to empty washed equipment from the cart.

"I know. Dan'ukva told me about you. Said you were a hard worker. You took my place in the washroom. Place those on the top shelf there."

"Oh, you are the one that Dan'ukva sometimes talked about. Are you seeing each other?"

Zoe'ul laughed, revealing sharp fangs. "He wishes to be my lifemate. But so does Bi'ak who already works in this lab. I am undecided yet."

"Must be nice having several choices." The culture dishes Yashana was stacking on a high shelf wobbled dangerously, and she struggled to straighten them.

"Not really. The more options available, the longer it takes to examine all the variables, the same problem we have with our project, except we have millions of variables to deal with."

"What is Project AF?"

"To create an African quintessence model. Layla Rangan dreamed there would be models reflecting every major racial group of humans. Unfortunately, all her AF work was rejected before her death. Her designs were too flawed. The problem with her growing old. But we continue her vision. Researchers have worked for decades creating new designs. We're close, I believe."

"Frank doesn't seem to believe so."

"Computer simulations predict the results will be unstable. Golnick wishes for us to at least begin attempting to grow cells. I agree with Golnick. We will learn much from the mistakes we make."

There was a crash as a stack of culture dishes fell onto a counter from the shelf above, several cracking. "Oh, no," groaned Yashana.

Zoe'ul smiled. "Perfect example. From your failure, you will learn to stack correctly."

"Do I have to pay for those?"

Zoe'ul patiently explained how the lab was run, giving tips to avoid angering their temperamental supervisor. Yashana found the work fascinating, far better than any job she had yet been assigned—causing her to distrust Ariyo more.

For most of lunch, Yashana and Ariyo ate silently. Finally the teenager asked, "Why did you choose this assignment for me?"

"I thought you would find it more interesting than washing."

"Why must you constantly flaunt Layla in my face?"

"Why do you hate her?"

"Why are you answering my question with a question?" Yashana glared at Ariyo.

"Why should I not?" The quintessence continued eating placidly.

"Because it irritates me! You enjoy this, don't you? How much can the profectus clone take until she has a mental breakdown? You may be happy with being a copy of another, dutifully following orders, but I'm an individual. I refuse to be forced along any path but the one I choose."

"By listening to those who came before you, the wrong paths can be avoided."

"Well, I learned today that sometimes we have to be allowed to make mistakes before we can discover the best path."

"What if the one who came before you already discovered the path of your destiny?"

"Her destiny. Not mine."

Ariyo put down his fork and looked Yashana in the eyes. "You will avoid much trouble if you embrace your destiny instead of running from it."

"My destiny is to find the quickest path to the Recreation Center so I can complete my work." Yashana tossed her napkin on her empty plate. "Are you ready?"

"The question is are you?" Ariyo stood and walked to the recycler to toss his trash.

Chapter Thirteen

The first month of the term flew by in a blur of work for Yashana. Between classes, studying, and work at Essence, Yashana spent as much time as possible with her friends. Keeping his promise, Ethan gave her a list of possible companies to apply to, shyly pointing out that many of them were located on planets where he was also applying. She sent in applications to each then focused on class projects and her dissertation. When weeks went by without a response, Ethan became concerned, but Yashana was too busy to notice.

One day Ethan asked Yashana and Gauge to meet him in one of the study rooms in the library. Groups of students often reserved the rooms to work on projects or prepare for tests.

As Yashana sat across the table from Ethan, she noticed his worried expression. "What's wrong?"

Ethan glanced between Yashana and Gauge. "Something unethical."

"Have you been hacking again?" asked Gauge.

"Yes, but that wasn't what I was referring to. Yashana, how many companies have responded to your inquiries?"

"None, but it takes time."

"I've applied the same time as you and already received six messages and had two video interviews. You should have received at least a few letters of interest. Luncaster graduates are highly sought after. I became concerned and hacked into your school records just to see what potential employers were being sent about you." Ethan turned his e-tablet around so they could see the snapshot he took of her file. Boldly across the top were the words *Juvenile Delinquent—Crime: Terrorist*. "I checked my own file and Gauge's. Our records are clean, despite our arrests."

Yashana stared, mouth open in astonishment. "It's…it's…like someone wants to scare away employers."

"Exactly. Someone is trying to purposely prevent you from being hired."

"Why? Who would do that?" asked Gauge, peering closely at the screen.

"Use logic. Who would benefit the most if no one hires Yashana?"

"Essence Institute." Anger raged through Yashana. "They would expect me to turn to them in despair when I couldn't get a job anywhere else. This is going too far. I'm not going to keep playing their games." Yashana stood up and headed for the door.

"Where are you going?" asked Gauge, concerned.

"To tell them they may get a thousand hours of my life, but not my whole life. I will decide my fate, not those leeches."

On the train ride to Essence, Yashana allowed her anger to boil into a raging thunderstorm. Who did the quintessences think they were? As a citizen of the empire, she had the right to work where she wished. Once she reached the institute, she boldly marched to Alexander's office and demanded the secretary allow her to see the director.

"Director Rangan is currently not in," informed the sundancer, glancing up from a monitor.

"Where is he? I am one of his special cases and need to see him at once."

Several of the secretary's spikes twirled in contemplation. "He is escorting Ambassador Roobaroo to her ship at Pad Five."

"Thank you very much."

Yashana hurried back to the elevator. In the Grand Forum, she paused at a large map on the wall to find the space pads. Not too far away. She hurried through bustling crowds, searching as she walked, refusing to let her anger die down and fear replace her boldness. A glass canopy covered the outdoor path which led to the landing platforms. She passed a group exiting a ship on Pad One. Yashana skirted around patrolling guards who glanced at her. The path split and she turned towards Pad Five. Finally she spotted her nemesis in conversation with the ambassador.

Boldly Yashana marched up. "How dare you tamper with my file!"

Alexander stopped in mid-sentence to look at her. "What reason do you have for interrupting me?"

"You're interrupting my life! I've done everything you asked till now. Swept your floors, changed smelly diapers, and washed gross dishes. But this is the limit. Clean up my file now!"

The elderly quintessence kept his face stoic. "Your rudeness is unnecessary. As for files, you need to be more specific."

"More specific? You know what I'm talking about. You had my school records fixed so no one will hire me and I would be forced to work here."

Roobaroo said, "Surely, Alexander, you have not stooped to blackmailing a teenager."

"I assure you, Ambassador, I have not ordered her files altered in any way."

Yashana placed hands on hips. "Yes, you did. Perhaps it was Ariyo or someone else who did the dirty work, but I demand you fix it."

"Demand?" Alexander gave her a stern look.

"I petition that you clean up my file so I may work where I wish. You have no right to force me to toil here."

"Yashana, I know you better than you know yourself, and I would never force you to work here."

"Then fix my file."

"I did not change it."

Desperate for help, the teenager glanced at the ambassador.

Roobaroo stepped closer to the quintessence, her long grayish-red hair almost touching his shoulder. "Is it possible someone misinterpreted your intentions and altered her file without informing you?"

"I do not believe so, but I will have the case investigated."

The ediethean gave Yashana her contact card. "If you do not hear from him soon, send me a message."

The teenager smiled her thanks and tucked the card into a pocket, giving Alexander a final scowl. Roobaroo and her escorts began walking across Pad Five.

Roobaroo chatted, "Alexander, I appreciate your time today and will research more about what we discussed. Now I must be off. One of my granddaughters is to be wed in a few days. You, of course, are invited. It is a high profile event as the groom is a governor's son."

"And great-grandson to a High Council member of your home world. You know we quintessences are disliked by your council."

"The very reason why you should come. Flaunt your presence. They loath the very idea that my genes will intermingle with their bloodline, but it is the delight of my life's accomplishments. No longer can they maintain the purity of the castes for those of us who live in diaspora. The High Council's power is slowly eroding, one marriage at a time."

"I will consider coming. Perhaps bring several of my brothers."

"Excellent. The more of you, the greater the High Council's silent rage in front of the cameras. Delicious to me."

Having reached the edge of the pad, Yashana stopped near a security guard. Roobaroo gave a brief bow to Yashana. "Remember to call me if your problem is not fixed."

"I will. Thanks."

As Alexander escorted the ambassador up the ramp of her private space yacht, their deep conversation continued. Yashana walked away, touching the card reassuringly. She would key the contact information into her e-tablet as soon as she got back to college. Hearing the engines of the space craft, Yashana glanced back. The ambassador had already vanished inside, and Alexander had begun walking back towards the sidewalk at the edge of the pad.

Boom. The rising spacecraft became a fireball. The blast ripped outward, sending debris flying, shattering the glass canopy over the walkway. Yashana's body was thrown to the ground. She lay stunned on the sidewalk, her mind uncomprehending, staring at the shredded metal frame above her that had once protected pedestrians from rain. Dazed, she slowly sat up, barely noticing the glass fragments falling off her body and blood dipped from shallow cuts. Nearby lay a quintessence guard, his arms twitching. Yashana stared at a long, twisted rod rising out of his chest. Some logical part of the teenager's mind knew she was watching his finally death throes, but shock cut her off from feeling anything. A high pitch alarm sounded in the distance.

A large glass pane fell from overhead, and Yashana moved out onto the launch pad to avoid more. Heat from the burning wreckage of the yacht assaulted her. Among the debris field lay Alexander, his body blackened, blood oozing from deep burns. Yashana watched him try to rise then fall again. Automatically she walked towards him, ignoring the heat. As she neared, he locked eyes with her, trying to speak, but no words came. Still acting only on instinct, Yashana dropped to her knees beside him, recalling that quintessences could sometimes heal from near death if they fed quickly.

Just minutes earlier she had hated the director, but now she only thought to save him. She brushed her long hair away from her neck then bent so the back of her neck touched his lips. For a moment nothing happened. Then a prick of pain was followed by the consciousness of another mind touching her own.

You must not, came the thoughts of the other.

You're dying, answered Yashana, briefly wondering how they could communicate. *I don't mind. Really.*

I will not take your life to save my own.

Yashana felt the other's mind begin to fade. *Come back.*

You are so much like her. Through the link came the intense intertwined emotions of love and lost. *More than you realize. I had such hopes for you.*

100

I'm sorry you lost your wife.

Take the memories I have of her. Take everything. May it aid you.

A heavy mental wave as powerful as a tsunami smashed through Yashana's mind, and she became lost in the vortex of a lifetime of memories pouring into her mind within the fraction of seconds. She cried out in pain, but it continued to come. Even as the link weakened, the memories poured forth, Alexander desperate to protect his wife's essence before death annihilated all. The pain increased, becoming unbearable. Yashana screamed over and over until blackness claimed her.

Chapter Fourteen

Ariyo studied the pale teenager sleeping in the hospital bed, his own mind swirling in confusion. One of the Five dead. After all the hardships and dangers the director had overcome fighting across countless planets, he had been murdered in his own homeland. Ariyo grieved deeply along with all his brethren for the first born of the quintessences, the husband of their creator. Rescue workers still fought flames on the launch pad, the final death count unknown.

Ariyo had been target practicing outside with his brother Rinji when the very air vibrated and the ground shook under their feet, knocking over several of their targets. They both looked back towards Richton Tower, seeing smoke rising beyond it. An alarm sounded somewhere. Ariyo's instinct was to run towards the fire, but if thousands of others did the same, it would only create mass confusion. Ariyo and Rinji stood with other quintessences gathering quietly, watching rescue vehicles rushing down streets towards the bellowing smoke. Every few minutes the quintessences checked their e-bands for news or commands.

The first message came within several minutes, asking for those not on rescue duty to stay clear of the disaster but to keep alert, reporting anything odd. Nearly half an hour passed before an official message was sent, claiming the spacecraft of Ambassador Roobaroo had blown up, presumably killing all on board, along with three on the ground including Alexander Rangan. Ariyo felt coldness roll over him. He looked at his brother, seeing his own shock mirrored in his twin's face. No words could express their deep grief. A Five gone. The first generation of quintessences had seemed as permanent as the sun itself, leading the brethren from being just pawns of the Galactic Senate to becoming a powerful civilization with their own homeland.

Names of known causalities scrolled by on his e-band. When Ariyo saw Yashana's name, he felt as if the universe itself had collapsed. He had failed the Five, not fulfilling the one request that the elder had personally asked of him. His hope returned when another message claimed she was alive and being sent to the medical ward. Ariyo glanced at his brother. Rinji knew him so well that the glance was all that was needed to explain where Ariyo was going.

Ariyo sprinted across the huge campus. The monorail had been closed after the explosion, forcing Ariyo to take the entire route by foot. He passed large crowds of sentients. Most stood about talking, some crying, others angry, debating who the director's murderer was. The quintessences, though, were mostly quiet. In a plaza a hundred young quintessences stared silently at the smoke, bō's still held in limp hands from their interrupted practice. Vehicles had stopped in the middle of streets, the drivers standing among the crowds. Ariyo reached Richton Tower and entered through the Grand Forum. The huge, deserted chamber echoed his steps. Ariyo raced down hallways, ignoring the pain in his side, warning he was pushing his body too far. When he finally reached the medical ward, guards prevented him from entering until he flashed the high security badge Alexander had given him for dealing with Yashana. A vital gift today.

Now Ariyo sat across from the unconscious teenager, watching, hoping that the director's dream had not died with him. A slightly chubby human nurse with a nametag labeled "Michelle" studied the monitor near the bed.

"Any changes?" asked Ariyo.

"No. She sleeps. Wait, she is coming out again." The girl stirred on the bed, muttering, eyes fluttering open but seeing nothing. "She may need to be sedated again."

"Why? Is it not good that she awakes?"

"She was screaming when they first brought her in. Would not stop until we put her under."

"You said her injuries were minor."

"The ones we can see are." Michelle glanced at the teenager then lowered her voice. "He died feeding on her. It may have caused brain damage."

"Brain damage?"

"We don't know right now. We have never had to deal with a case like this before. Do you know her well?"

"We work together."

"Can you notify her family? They should be here for her."

"They are off planet, but I will notify her friends."

He barely finished a text message to Gauge, when Yashana's eyes opened again. She looked about the room, searching for something. Ariyo stepped near the bed.

"You are in the medical ward, Yashana."

"Fire. Roobaroo. She's…she's…" The teen clenched her hands into fists. "Pain. Why does it hurt?"

"What hurts?"

"My head. Make it stop."

The nurse reached towards the monitor and tapped in a command to increase the anesthetic. "You need rest, honey."

"The pain. Alexander, he was laying there. Where is he?"

Michelle motherly patted Yashana's hand. "You were very brave trying to save him."

"He did something to me. Trying…to…save…her." The teenager clasped her sheets, grinding her teeth. "The pain. Help. Please."

"I will put you back to sleep, dear."

"Not yet," said Ariyo. "Yashana, what did he do to you."

"My mind. It explodes."

The nurse tapped a command on the monitor's screen. "You will sleep now."

Instead, Yashana's back arched as she screamed in pain.

"Just relax. The medicine will kick in soon."

The teenager panted and twisted on the bed. Ariyo and Michelle each grabbed an arm, holding her down until her body went limp.

"She will sleep for a few minutes at least. Will you watch her while I speak with the doctor?"

"Of course."

Ariyo waited until the nurse departed then locked the door behind her. He gently rolled Yashana onto her side and bit the area where head and neck connected, linking their brains together through the epulo. Over the course of many missions, he had peered into the mind of countless sentients, but none as bizarre and fragmented as Yashana's. Order was missing. Millions of jagged memories were randomly scattered as if the mind had exploded inward, a life's collection of memories suddenly shaken loose. Confused, Ariyo warily treaded through the chaos. Yashana's body may have been affected by the spacecraft's explosion, but it could not account for this type of mental damage.

As Ariyo brushed pass one fragment, he saw an image of a child giggling as she painted a turtle purple. Another fragment was a teenager attempting to keep her balance while hoverskating. A tree blowing in the wind as children, all with identical faces, played under its shadow. Laser guns firing at targets. A young man fiddling with a bulky machine growing fetuses. Lovers intertwined in passion. Ariyo stopped and went back to the last memory, focusing on faces. Layla and Alexander. How could that be? Somehow Yashana had the private memories of Layla drifting through her mind.

Though the epulo, quintessences often passed along messages or stories, but always they were aware of where the memories came from, never confusing it with their own private thoughts. And it was only a few memories at a time, not millions. Somehow as Alexander lay dying he had transferred his dead wife's memories to Yashana. Yet that made no sense to Ariyo. They were not memories of someone looking at another's thoughts, but Layla's own emotions and reactions. The only way Alexander could have gotten those memories would be if he had ripped them directly out of his wife's mind. According to the Code, that was only permitted when probing a criminal marked for execution or in special circumstances such as when one was in the field and needed a mental map of a building but lacked the time to memorize it. Simply tear the memory from the goon and make it one's own. The host was permanently damaged, never recalling the stolen memory again. Why would Alexander do this to his wife? And not just a few memories but all her memories? No husband who loved his wife would ever do this.

Unless…perhaps the wife was dying and he was trying to save some part of her. The Code did not address this issue. Many quintessences had outlived their wives, but as far as Ariyo knew, none had literally ripped out a wife's entire mind. It would require much time to complete the process, and take up far too much room inside the quintessence own mind. Without even asking the elders, Ariyo was certain it would be forbidden. Yet Alexander, the first of all quintessences, had done so. And now those memories were scattered about, disorganized, inside Layla's clone.

Ariyo probed deeper, fearful that Yashana's mind was damaged beyond repair. He would go to the elders with what he knew, but he doubted even they could corral the millions of fragmented memories that was destroying Yashana's sanity. As he began to pull out of her mind, he brushed pass something unnatural. He paused to examine the huge, tightly packed collection of memories. A ziphema here? Ziphema were zipped memories, compacted into a small area that could be quickly passed between quintessences. The receiver could unzip the memory and explore it, just as if he had been looking into the host's mind. The technique allowed original memories to be passed to other quintessences without the need to rip a memory.

No other known species in the universe could create or maneuver ziphema. Why was there one in Yashana's mind? She could not access it or even be aware of its existence. And it was larger than any Ariyo had seen before, far more immense than even the Canon, the collection of memories selected by the elders to be passed to every four year old after they had begun learning the epulo. For the rest of their lives the youngsters would carry the sacred memories of Layla and the Five, explaining how the quintessences came into existence and important lessons explaining why the Code must always be followed. Any quintessence could open a ziphema, but it took decades of practice to master creating them.

Now there was a massive one in Yashana's mind, slowly killing her. This was the source of Yashana's pain. No human mind, even one enhanced by the ediethean gene, could handle it. Ariyo probed the surface, seeking to know its source. Alexander. Why would the legendary director place it here, knowing the teenager could never use it? Perhaps as Alexander lay dying, he reacted on instinct, not rationalizing that he would be endangering Yashana's life.

It had to be removed immediately. Gently Ariyo's consciousness surrounded the ziphema, drawing it into himself. The ziphema was more fragile than Ariyo expected and cracks began appearing on its surface, threatening to spew loose memories into Yashana's already chaotic brain. Ariyo tighten his hold, refusing to let anything slip away. Slowly, slowly it became his own. Finally he pulled back from Yashana's mind.

He stood and blinked, seeing the hospital room again. Yashana lay peacefully in the bed, asleep. Banging came from the door as the nurse tried to gain entrance. Ariyo walked towards the door to open it. A deep exhaustion fell on him and the cracks around the ziphema widened. The quintessence reached the door, but instead of opening it, he leaned against it, barely aware of where he was. Memories, thousands of them, were spewing out of the ziphema into his mind. It was not supposed to be this way. Ziphema were usually compartmentalized inside a quintessence's mind where they could be opened and examined whenever the owner wished. But ziphema were never this size or this fragile, having made the passage through three minds in just a few hours.

"Open this door now! If you don't, I'll have security break it open."

Banging aroused Ariyo enough to turn the lock. The ziphema exploded, sending millions of memories racing through his mind. Ariyo's body fell unconscious to the floor.

Wakefulness came slowly. He lay on a hospital bed, bright sunlight visible through a window. Across from him sat an AS quintessence watching him closely.

"Ariyo, why am I here?"

The youth looked puzzled. "You are Ariyo. I am your brother Rinji. You fainted after locking yourself in a room with your ward. What happened?"

"I...I do not remember." Swirls of disconnected memories danced through his mind, ideas almost forming then fading again. "Something... strange."

"A fainting quintessence is strange. You have slept over twenty hours. Are you hungry?"

"Hungry? Maybe." Ariyo wobbled as he stood. Rinji was quickly by his side.

"Perhaps you should rest longer."

"There is something I am supposed to do...or report."

"What is that?"

Ariyo tried to focus on the thought, but it danced away, an elusive phantom. "I do not know."

"A good meal will help."

Rinji led his brother out of the room and down the hallway of the Medical Ward. As they pass an open door, Ariyo saw a teenager asleep on a bed, a brown-hair boy and a reptile sitting in chairs near her. Their faces stirred recollection. There was something important relating to them, but the idea again escaped from him.

"Where do you think you are going?" A stern nurse, arms folded, blocked the hallway.

"We are going to dinner," said Rinji.

"Not on my watch. He has not been released by a doctor."

"Since when have quintessence needed doctors?"

"When they began fainting in my ward." Michelle walked closer to Ariyo. "Why did you lock me away from my patient?"

"I...thought I could help."

"By stopping me from reaching her? If you had not fainted, I would have had you court-martialed."

"He has learned his lesson," said Rinji. "Now may we go, your highness?"

Michelle frowned but moved out of the way, muttered under her breath about arrogant cowboys. Ariyo and Rinji walked to the food court. After

107

buying their meals, they sat with Tadeo. Ariyo ate in silence, barely noticing the conversation between his brothers.

"Since when did you begin eating *idly*?" asked Tadeo. "We decided when we were three that we did not like it."

Ariyo glanced at the spicy mix of parboiled rice and lentils on his plate. "I do not know."

Though the rest of the meal, Tadeo and Rinji kept glancing at their twin. Ariyo was vaguely aware of their concern, but all he wanted was sleep. He continually fought against deep exhaustion pulling him into forgetfulness. After the meal, they walked to their barracks. Ariyo collapsed on his bunk bed, unaware of his brothers pulling off his shoes and covering him with a blanket. In sleep, his mind began the natural process of storing and sorting recent memories.

Chapter Fifteen

Yashana rolled over in bed, her hand reaching out, expecting to touch warm skin but only finding the edge of her dorm bed. She felt disappointment but did not know why.

"If you do not get up soon," said Gauge, "you will not have time to eat breakfast before our first class."

The teenager sat up, groggily, feeling drained and weak. She winced from a light headache as she stood.

"Are you alright?" asked Gauge.

"I'm just tired, that's all."

"You slept for three straight days at Essence. They said if you were not feeling well, to report back."

"I need no more of their tests. They said I was fine."

"No, they said they could find nothing wrong with you."

"Same thing."

Yashana dressed, and they headed to breakfast. She barely spoke as they ate. The headache grew stronger, but nothing near as bad as before. Drowsiness pulled at her, tempting her into its comforting embrace. She nodded off several times, her head almost touching her plate before she snapped awake again. Ethan and Gauge tossed concerned glances her direction and tried to pull her into their conversation, but she was unresponsive.

As they exited the cafeteria for class, Yashana said, "I'm skipping first period. I need a little more sleep."

"I think you should go back to Essence." Ethan worriedly moved closer in case she fainted.

"I thought you hated Essence."

"I do. But their medical staff was very professional. I will ride the train with you."

"No, you already missed enough classes babysitting me the last few days. I'm fine. Just tired is all. See you at lunch."

Yashana walked away, not telling them about the pounding headache. Back in her dorm room, she fell into a deep sleep the moment her head touched her pillow. When Gauge tried to wake her for lunch, Yashana stirred only enough to mumble that she was not hungry. Hours later, she vaguely heard her telecom ringing. Gauge picked it up.

"No, she still sleeps. Has all day." Gauge paused, listening to the caller. "Alright. I will have her there."

Yashana rolled over, facing the wall, trying to ignore Gauge ordering her to get up. "Leave me alone."

"No. Ariyo is coming to pick you up. If you do not go to him, he will come here."

"Boys aren't allowed in our rooms."

"That will not stop a quintessence. He will carry you out if needed."

To avoid that embarrassment, Yashana sat up and allowed Gauge to put her shoes and jacket on. They walked to a nearby parking lot. Yashana sat on a bench in the shade, quickly falling asleep again.

"Wake up. He is here." Gauge shook her friend gently.

Yashana stood, dazed. Ariyo guided her to a hover car. As he buckled her in, he reassured Gauge that her roommate would be fine. As Ariyo cranked up the car, Yashana gave a brief goodbye wave to the zonner.

"Since when did you get a car?"

"I borrowed it. I did not believe you could handle a train today."

"I'm fine. Just let me sleep."

Yashana closed her eyes. Seemingly only a second later, Ariyo had her door open and was unbuckling her. He guided her into Richton Tower, using an entrance which avoided the Grand Forum. An elevator took them to the twelfth floor.

Walking increased Yashana's alertness. "This is not the medical ward."

"No, we needed a quieter place. Stay here a moment."

Ariyo left her standing in a hallway. She barely had time to find a chair before he returned. Taking her by an arm, he directed her passed a receptionist's desk, now empty.

Seeing large words on the wall above the desk, Yashana said, "You brought me to the Psychology Department?"

"Relax. You are not seeing a doctor. Almost everyone has gone home."

"Why are we here?"

"Because I need a place we will not be disturbed." They entered an evaluation room, simply furnished with a couch and a few chairs. Ariyo locked the door behind them. "Lay on the couch."

"Why should I?"

"Because you are sick and cannot think clearly."

"I am alert enough to know that we are not supposed to be here. If you want me to cooperate, then explain yourself."

Ariyo moved close. "I will explain but you will not understand. Two ziphema were placed in your mind by Alexander as he died. I removed one, but the other shattered. Unless I can bring order to that chaos, you will probably either die or go insane."

"You're right. You speak nonsense."

"You sleep because your mind is trying to heal itself, but human brains were not created to handle this."

"I'm not human but a profectus, remember."

"Profectus are only a subspecies of humans. The only difference is that ediethean gene gives you a brain able to hold more complex thoughts, and perhaps that gene is what is keeping you alive at this moment."

"Why would the director but a zip whatever in me if it could kill."

"He was dying and not thinking rationally. He was trying to save that which was most important to him, to all quintessences. The memories which make up the history of our race." Ariyo grasped both her arms and gently moved her to the couch then he knelt in front of her. "Alexander is sorry for what he has put you through. If he had been thinking clearly, he never would have placed your life in danger. And he deeply regrets what you are about to face."

"How do you know what he thinks? What am I facing?"

"Lie down now."

Yashana wanted to keep questioning him, but already heavy sleepiness pulled at her. She stretched out on the couch. Ariyo waited until sleep claimed the teenager then rolled her till her back faced him. Still kneeling, he brushed her long, black hair away from her neck. He bit with the epulo, linking to her mind.

Random chaos. Just as he feared. Yashana's mind was unable to organize the fragments into patterns, so he was going to have to do it—at least begin the process. A lifetime of memories meant millions, if not billions, of collected ideas which normally organize into schemas that the brain could access at a moment's notice. Ariyo threw out a mental net, pulling dozens of fragments to him. Each he examined then placed within schemas already in Yashana's mind. Ariyo worked slowly at first, for the process took time to learn. As he grew more confident, his pace increased. Not all memories he manipulated may have been placed in the proper schemas, but he hoped that once he had begun the process, Yashana's mind would continue, reorganizing itself as needed. Brains of both animals and sentients did this subconsciously every time they slept. Yashana's just needed extra help.

Ariyo worked through the rest of the evening and late into the night, but he only shifted roughly ten thousands fragments. Barely a drop in her vast storage of memories. Exhausted, he napped in a chair, sleeping longer than he had planned. Sunlight streamed through a window when he woke her. Dazed, she sat up, looking around the room but not really seeing it. Ariyo took her by an arm and guided her out into the hallway. The receptionist was just turning on her computer and looked puzzlingly at them as they passed. The elevator doors slid open, and Tiah Vay stepped out, surprised to see them.

The psychologist frowned as she noticed the quintessence holding the teenager's arm. "Ariyo, I do not recollect that we have a meeting today."

"We do not. I am just leaving." He stepped around Tiah, ignoring the chairwoman's stern look, and pushed an elevator button. "Good day."

As the elevator dropped to the first floor, Yashana's body slumped against him. He gently shook her, arousing her enough to walk to the hover car. She slept the whole way back to Luncaster University. Gauge met them in the parking lot.

"What is wrong with her?" asked the zonner, helping Yashana out of the car.

"Her mind needs rest, but she will be fine. Keep an eye on her. Call me if she acts strangely. All she will want to do is sleep, perhaps for many days. Try to get her to eat occasionally."

"I will." Gauge glanced at Yashana, barely conscious. "Are the doctors sure she will be alright?"

"The problem has been fixed. With rest, she will be a new person."

Chapter Sixteen

Across the vast parade ground thirty thousand quintessences stood at attention, their grim faces looking towards a broad platform containing eleven coffins, only two of which actually held bodies. Thousands of other sentients sat on bleachers or stood in clumps along the edge of the field. Camera drones flew about, recording the historical funeral, only the second time such an event had been held at Essence Institute. The parade ground could not hold all who wanted to attend, and many quintessences and employees watched the live news feed on vids around the campus.

A passing camera caught the angry expressions of several High Council members sitting on a bench. For ten thousand years of ediethean history, their races had been kept separate, marriage forbidden between the castes. Roobaroo, born of the highest caste, had broken that taboo by marrying two levels below her, an act punished by death on their home world of Edieth. Prison time had increased her popularity among edietheans living in diaspora outside the High Council's jurisdiction, leading others to follow her example of marrying outside caste.

The eldest daughter of Roobaroo spoke, praising her mother's many accomplishments, her calm voice only breaking twice. She ended the speech with a statement wishing for the unity of all edietheans. As she walked back to her seat, many non-quintessences clapped politely, unaware how loaded her statement was. As a child growing up in exile, she had only known her parents from a distance as they served out their prison sentences. She had taken their grievances as her own, becoming an outspoken opponent to the High Council. Like her parents, she had become a respected leader of edietheans living in diaspora.

A new speaker walked to the microphone. Caleb of the Five spoke about his brother's life. The elder displayed no emotion as he talked, gave no promises of unity or swore revenge for the murders. He simply listed Alexander's achievements in chronological order. The watching quintessences were frozen statues, bodies rigid, faces stoic. Outsiders may believe the silent quintessences felt little grief, but reality was opposite. They were overwhelmed with pain from the loss of the firstborn of their kind. Always firmly in command of their species' destiny had been Layla and her husband. No longer. Others of the Five and the Synod were still there to guide them, but Alexander's death was a sharp reminder that the elders were not immortal. The universe beyond Essence was hostile, the quintessences seen as puppets of the Galactic Senate, pawns to be sacrificed as needed for the good of politics. Layla and Alexander had been a bridge, a protective hedge, who worked closely with the Senate, but always keeping the welfare of the quintessences first.

Strange to watch one's own funeral, thought Ariyo surrounded by his forty-nine birthmates watching the vid in the lobby of their barracks. His brothers stood as rigid as the quintessences at the parade ground. None spoke.

On the screen, an ediethean priest dressed in ceremonial robes stood in front of the coffins. The granddaughter of Roobaroo, dressed in a traditional wedding shawl, moved slowly through the throng of thousands, arm in arm with her fiancé. Many of the edietheans in the crowd began singing, the voices of the castes united. None of the High Council joined in, not even the grandfather of the groom. The council members were only in attendance at the funeral because they had already committed to the wedding when it was to be held on the planet Alz Haven.

Roobaroo, you would have loved the irony, Ariyo said to himself. *Few outside your race would have noticed the wedding, but now it is being broadcasted to all known worlds. Thanks to your death…and mine.*

As the wedding ended, camera shots showed sentients in the crowd, some weeping even though they were not edietheans. A wedding at a funeral stirred vivid emotions. As a reporter spoke with bystanders, several expressed outrage about the murders, upset that an attack had taken place at the quintessences' home after all they had done for the empire. Others threw out wild theories of who was responsible. Any guess aimed at the edietheans' High Council was censored, yet public opinion swung strongly that way.

The AS models began to disperse, and Ariyo joined a group heading to the Recreation Center for virtual target practice, their pent up emotions needing releasing. They had almost reached the building when Ariyo's e-band beeped, informing him of an incoming message. He glanced at it then excused himself, telling his brothers he had a meeting. A short time later he walked into Tiah Vay's plant-filled office.

"Sit," commanded the psychologist, anger in her voice. "I placed great faith in you, Ariyo, claiming in my reports that your model could handle emotions."

"What event has led you to doubt me, Tiah?"

The chairwoman flinched, not liking his use of her first name. "You slept with Yashana. I have occasionally had to deal with this before, but to flaunt it in my own department?"

"You misunderstand."

"I have the log. That is why we have that microchip implanted in you at birth. Your whereabouts can always be traced at Essence. You spent the whole night with her in one of my offices." Tiah's blue skin was splotched with purple, revealing her anger.

"I am aware of that."

"Then why were you so stupid to do it in my department, of all places?" Her purple splotches became outlined in red as her rage built.

"I am innocent of what you accuse me of."

"Ariyo, the data says you both were right beside each other on a couch almost the whole night."

"Statistics can be misleading. Only Yashana was on the couch. I was on the floor beside her."

"Doing what exactly?"

"Not what you think. I was using the epulo. She was sick, I was helping her."

"We have the medical ward for that."

"They could not help with her problem. I could."

"Which was what?"

"At this time I prefer to keep that to myself."

Tiah sighed, the red disappearing from her skin but the splotches remained. "I want to believe you, but I am required to report all suspicious activity of this nature to the Synod for investigation."

"I would prefer you did not. Yashana is still ill and needs me. They will order me to keep away from her until they have time to question me, but with the funerals and selecting a new director, it could be many days."

"You should have thought about that before you spent the night with her."

"I was saving her life."

"Why did you not report your plan to your supervisor before taking action?"

"Alexander was my direct supervisor in this matter, and he was dead. I had no one else to consult."

"Either way, you will stay away from Yashana until the Synod has a verdict."

Ariyo stood up. "I apologize, but I cannot obey you."

Tiah also stood, red reappearing among the splotches. "Do you have a death wish?"

"No, I wish to keep Yashana alive. Only I am skilled enough in helping her right now."

"You are a youngling who thinks too highly of himself. And I am your superior."

"No, I outrank you."

The psychologist stared at him in shock. "I am a department head. You are a beta model still serving your bond years. And right now I am considering adding *insanity* to my report right beside *sexual misconduct*."

"You would be wrong on both accounts." Ariyo sat down again, studying the endless waterfall for a long moment. "I will explain to you the truth, and then you will erase all copies of your report."

"You do not command me." But she sat down, showing her willingness to at least listen.

"Actually, you have obeyed me many times. I am Alexander."

Despite her anger, Tiah laughed. "A joke will not save you."

"I am not joking. Hear me out before you judge. As I…Alexander…lay dying, he passed two ziphema to Yashana. But not just any ziphema. These each carried the entire essence of a being, every memory, every thought."

"Impossible. No quintessence is capable of creating something like that."

"Who was the first of all quintessences to discover our species ability to create ziphema? And who taught his brothers this ability?"

Tiah frowned, splotches slowly fading as she became absorbed in the story. "Alexander Rangan."

"He never told anyone how he made the first, not even his brothers. As his wife lay dying, driven by instinct to save at least a part of her, he ripped her thoughts, all of them, from her mind in a matter of seconds. He compacted them then pulled them into himself. She became the first ziphema. He was too lost in grief to understand what he had done. Later, when he realized he had stolen his wife's essence, he was too ashamed to tell his brothers. Overtime he learned he could peek into the ziphema, exploring her memories, his wife's presence always with him. He experimented, discovering how to create new ziphema from his own thoughts, original memories compressed without the need to rip. He taught his brothers then passed on the knowledge to all quintessences."

"Was that when the Canon was created?"

"Yes, but no one realized that the memories of Layla he selected for it came directly from her ziphema. When Alexander found himself dying, his instinct was to protect her ziphema, passing it to Yashana, not realizing how fragile it was after he had opened it so many times. It barely survived the passage, exploding almost immediately when it reached her mind. He was unaware of this, too busy trying to preserve the history of his species by creating a new ziphema of himself and passing it also to Yashana. Dying, he reacted on the instinctive need to protect that which was most important to him, not rationalizing that Yashana's mind was incapable of handling the ziphema, almost killing her."

"This is the reason why you spent last night with her?" Tiah's skin had returned to its normal deep blue.

"Yes, I was trying to help her mind organize the memories."

"You do realize she probably will go insane trying to deal with memories of two others."

"Only one. Alexander's ziphema remained intact until after I pulled it from her. Now his essence is mine."

Tiah leaned forward, violet hair falling around her face. "What do you mean by *his essence?*"

"What it sounds like. All his memories are mine now. Every decision he made, every mission, every person he met. They are a part of me, as real as Ariyo's memories."

The psychologist leaned back in her seat, reflecting on his story. "Spilt-personality is a disorder which afflicts some species. It is difficult to cure."

"You misunderstand. There are not two individuals inside me. Alexander and Ariyo are now one, united in action and thought. No separation exists."

"I will have to tell my husband what you told me, and he will inform the other Five."

"I know. I had wanted to wait until I understood things better, until after Yashana was out of danger."

"Her mind will not be able to handle this as well as yours."

"That is my worry also."

Chapter Seventeen

As Yashana drifted through layers of sleep, her hand reached out, searching for someone. When it found only the edge of her bed, she awoke, feeling vaguely disappointed. Disoriented, she took in her surroundings. A dorm room. Her half messy and chaotic, the other side neat and organized.

That looks normal, thought Yashana, as she climbed out of bed and treaded over the clutter to her closet. A reflection in a mirror caught her attention, holding her mesmerized by the youthful Indian face staring back at her. *That is me yet somehow wrong.*

A large reptile walked into the room, scaly skin glistening from a recent shower. Yashana stared, slowing recalling as if from a dream that the lizard was her roommate.

"You are finally awake. You have slept five days." Gauge began dressing.

"Five days? Would I not be dead from dehydration?"

"You woke enough to eat, even took a few showers, but you moved like one in a dream. Do you remember any of it?"

"Vaguely, I guess. I must be behind on class work."

"You have missed over a week, including three days spent in the medical ward."

"I was in a hospital?" Yashana struggled to remember more. Flashes of faces, a bloody quintessence with metal sticking out of his chest, fire raining from the sky, a sense of loss. "There was an explosion. Someone died."

"Eleven was the final count, including the director of Essence and an ambassador."

"Director? But I'm here."

"You spoke nonsense as you sleepwalked. Do you yet sleep?"

"I'm fully awake." Yashana opened her closet and flipped through her clothes. Not finding what she wanted, she searched a second time then dug through the dirty clothes on the floor. "Did you borrow my red blouse, the one with the silver glitter on the collar?"

"Why would I wear your clothes? They are too small for me." The zonner tilted her head, thinking. "I do not remember you ever wearing a glittery shirt."

"Of course I have, many times. It is my favorite. Blaaze gave it to me as a birthday present."

"No, you have not worn such a shirt. Who is Blaaze?"

"He is my brother."

The zonner's snout twitched in puzzlement. "You have no brother but two sisters who you often fight with."

"Oh." The teenager turned away and grabbed a sleeveless shirt and shorts from the closet.

Gauge looked at her strangely. "It is winter. Perhaps a warmer outfit would be more appropriate."

"Good idea." Yashana put on pants and a sweater.

"After classes are finished today, maybe you should go back to Essence for a check-up."

"I told you I am fine. I have too much to do."

"Like finishing your dissertation."

"I have not finished that yet?"

"No, your research is still ongoing, but you must finish it soon to graduate."

Yashana looked blank. Seeing Gauge's concerned look, she smiled and grabbed her backpack. As they walked across campus, Yashana felt as if she was trapped in a strange, surreal dream. This was Luncaster University where she had spent many years of her life. Familiar buildings surrounded her, yet the landscape was somehow different. The wrong plants spouted from snowy beds, trees grew where she remembered clearings, sidewalks led in unexpected directions, and the cafeteria was furnished differently.

They sat by a familiar boy, but his name remained elusive to Yashana until Gauge mentioned it in conversation. She pretended all was normal, but their concerned glances hinted she was failing. Ethan had to guide her to her first class. Yashana tried to take notes on her e-table, but it was organized wrong, running programs vaguely familiar yet icons in strange locations. Frustrated, she gave up and just listened. The professor droned on about nanite molecule construction. Yashana sighed. She already knew all of this.

"In this case," said Professor Duken, "the molecules will attract each other."

"You are wrong," said Yashana. Everyone in class turned to see who dared challenged their instructor.

"Please explain, Miss Kalkar."

"According to research, they would repeal because of the effects of the artificial magnetize field used to hold them."

"Which research are you referring to?"

"Derrick Cashman, of course. His work is well-known."

"Doctor Cashman did make several important advancements in improving nano construction, but his work is now outdated. The magnetize fields we use today no longer reverse orientation. I appreciate you are reading classical studies, but you must also keep up with the latest advancements."

A couple of students snickered. Yashana stared at her e-tablet, angry. *I never cared about how nanites worked, but I know Derrick's theory is correct. When his work was first published in a textbook, he gloated about it for months. How could he be outdated?*

After class, Professor Duken stopped Yashana. "I am glad to see you back in class. All your teachers have been worried about you. Are you over you illness?"

"Not quite."

"If you need an extension for your mid-terms, I can provide that." The professor appeared genuinely concerned. "How is the research for your dissertation coming along?"

"Uh, well." The teenager silently wondered, *What is my topic?*

"Your panel, including I, look forward to reading the finished piece. It is a rare opportunity for one of our students to have such high access to quintessences."

"I will try to make you proud, sir."

Second period was confusing to Yashana, but she kept silent when told information which conflicted with what she knew. How could scientific theories change that quickly? On her e-tablet, she pulled up the date and stared at its claim of 2215 B.E. *Impossible. How can it be the twenty-second century of the Basanti Empire? This is the twenty-first century. I'm sure of that.* The feeling of surrealism returned. *Perhaps all this is a dream. I sleep. That lizard said I had been doing so for days.*

After class ended, Gauge and Ethan met her in the hallway for lunch. As Yashana sat at a table, Ethan stared at her selection of food.

"*Idly* and *sushi*. What a strange combination."

"I could not decide between them so I got both."

"I understand the fish choice, but not the lentils. You hated when your mom made you eat your older sister's version of it, and you vowed never to eat it again."

"Well, I am eating it today. Do you have a problem with that?"

"It's not my vow you are breaking." Ethan and Gauge shared a glance.

Yashana ate in silence, pondering the lapse of memory. Had she really made such a silly vow about a sister who seemed more of a ghost than a real person? *I don't even remember what my mother looks like.* Worry destroyed her appetite.

"What is the topic of my dissertation?"

"Gaming habits of quintessences," answered Gauge.

"Gaming habits? Why would I pick so stupid a topic? It does not even relate to genetics."

"You thought it was an easier topic to research than musculoskeletal reanimation or carnivorous plants."

"What?" Yashana tossed down her chopsticks. "Am I Frankenstein trying to bring back the dead?"

"Those are the topics you listed."

"I have had enough of this. You keep telling me I did this and I did that, but I have no memory of any of this. I do not even know who either of you are."

Gauge looked at her, stunned. "We are your friends. I have been your roommate for four years."

"You tell me this but I have never seen you before today. You could be lying to me. Even the calendars are deceitful. Twenty-second century, my foot."

Ethan leaned over and whispered to Gauge, "Give me your telecom. I'm calling him."

"You do not like him," the zonner broad tail twitched in worry.

"I know, but she's having a mental breakdown. He promised to help her."

As Gauge passed over her device, Yashana frowned. "Who are you calling?"

"Ariyo, a friend who can help you," smoothed Gauge. "He has been very concerned, calling every day."

Ethan talked briefly into the telecom then hung up. "He said to meet him in the parking lot in twenty minutes."

"I am not going anywhere with another stranger." Yashana crossed her arms and glared at them.

"I don't trust quintessences either," said Ethan, "but he seems to understand what is wrong with you better than anyone else."

"Ariyo is quintessence?" Yashana relaxed slightly. "He will be from Essence Institute. That is where I want to go."

"Now I know you are bonkers. You hate Essence and especially quintessences."

"Why would I hate…never mind. Where is the parking lot?"

They put up their trays and left the cafeteria. Outside snow sparkled in the bright sunshine. Several students tossed snowballs at each other. A bot cleared ice from a sidewalk. It was the university Yashana remembered, accept that the students wore strange fashions and the bot was a model she had never seen before. Nothing made sense. Near the parking lot, Yashana sat on a bench, silent and tense, while Ethan and Gauge whispered uneasily.

Catching a bit of their conversation, Yashana asked, "What did you say happened to Alexander?"

"He died," answered Ethan, "in that explosion that hit you."

"You lie. Alexander is fine. He is waiting for me at Essence."

Gauge sat on the bench beside her. "No, he died along with ten others last week. You were almost the twelfth."

"I do not believe you. My Alexander can survive anything. He once was blown out of a six-story building and lived."

"Quintessences are not invincible." Ethan pulled out his e-tablet and pulled up an article from *Galactic Times*. "Look, here is the article. Director Alexander Rangan, Ambassador Roobaroo, and nine others killed in an explosion caused by a bomb placed on the ambassador's ship."

"Roobaroo is dead too?" Yashana pulled the e-tablet out of Ethan's hands and skimmed through the article. "How can this be? It says he was one-hundred and seventy-three."

"The reporters wanted to put you in the article too, but the Five asked them not to mention you because you didn't need the publicity right now."

A tear sled down Yashana's cheek. "It cannot be true. It cannot."

Gauge placed a clawed hand on the profectus's arm. "You acted heroically, rushing to save the director's life, offering to allow him to feed on you."

"That sounds like what I would do if Alexander was dying."

Ethan grimaced. "If I was there, I would have allowed him to die, especially after he doctored your student records."

"Why would he do that?"

"To trap you at Essence."

"You did not know him, and you especially do not know me. Essence is my home, our home." Yashana broke down into tears.

Ethan looked perplexed. "He was just a quintessence. There must be a million copies of him."

"You are not helping," chided Gauge.

"He's a foeditas horribilis. She never cared about them before. Hey, don't drop my e-tablet." Ethan snatched his computer from Yashana's limp hands.

A hover car pulled up, driven by an Asian youth. Gauge stood up and opened the passenger door. Ethan frowned but nodded a welcome to the driver.

Yashana tried to contain her sobs, "Where is Ariyo?"

"That is Ariyo," answered Gauge.

"He is not quintessence. I am not going anywhere with him."

"I am quintessence," said the youth, climbing out of the car.

"No. I know every model, and you certainly are not one."

The man smiled and bent down in front of Yashana. "You do indeed know every model. So you should recognize me."

"Quintessences do not smile."

"They can, but it is rare except for my model. Surely you have not forgotten AS 193?"

The teenager tilted her head, pondering. "That was just a design, a pattern on a screen, the last accepted by the Research Department. They rejected everything else."

"Good, your memory is functioning." Ariyo brushed damp hair away from her tear-stained face and leaned closer, whispering, "Despite what you felt then, they never rejected you personally, Layla. They hold you in high esteem to this very day."

The seventeen year old stared at him. "Who are you?"

Only a few intimate friends knew about the dark years of depression she experienced when design after design had been rejected by her own Research Department.

"A life-long friend who knows your greatest achievements and darkest nightmares. I will explain everything to you at Essence." He stood, gently

123

pulling her up from the bench and led her to the car. Loudly he said, "She is on her way to a full recovery."

Ethan scowled. "Do you tell us that, leech, to avoid a lawsuit? She doesn't even remember who we are. If it wasn't for your tyrant director constantly trying to control her, Yashana would be fine."

Gauge placed a hand on Ethan's arm. "He is just trying to help."

"Or cover up whatever they did." Ethan stepped nearer, looking eye to eye with Ariyo, unconcerned the other was a trained killer. "If you do not fix whatever is broken in her, I will go to her parents and the media with all I know."

"I am as concerned as you," said Ariyo calmly. "And I sincerely believe she will be herself again soon."

Ariyo climbed into the driver's seat. Within the city, he kept to the speed limit, but on the highway, he floored the pedal, zipping around slower traffic. Yashana watched the scenery blur pass.

"Do I dream? Nothing feels real."

"You are as awake as I am."

"Then Alexander and Roobaroo are truly dead?"

"They both died in the explosion."

Tears trickled down the teenager's cheeks, and she remained silent the rest of the trip. Reaching Richton Tower, Ariyo led her through a side entrance and took an elevator to the twelfth floor.

"I do not need a shrink," complained Yashana.

"There is privacy here."

Ariyo spoke briefly to the receptionist then led the teenager to Tiah Vay's office. Yashana hesitated going in, but Tiah's friendly handshake relaxed her. As Ariyo locked the door, Yashana stared at the flowers and waterfall.

"The plants are from my home world," explained Tiah, sitting in a cushioned chair. "Most patients find in calming."

"I am not your patient."

"Take a seat on the couch," said Ariyo. "I need to see how your mind is healing." The teenager glanced between the psychologist and the quintessence. "It is alright. Tiah is married to Jacob. There are few secrets left she does not know."

"Jacob married? He and Mason joked that they would die old bachelors."

"Much has changed since you last walked on this planet."

"This is a dream. No quintessence would marry a shrink."

"Jacob did," said Tiah. "Please sit so Ariyo may explain what has happened to you."

Yashana moved to the couch. Sitting beside her, Ariyo gently took her shoulders and turned her back to him. As he brushed her long hair away, she glanced at the neodite calmly watching, feeling uneasy. Epulo bites were usually not done in front of other non-quintessences. There was the familiar prick then another consciousness touched the teenager's mind, probing through her thoughts.

She suddenly found herself in a long neglected courtyard, beautiful in its wildness. Moss-covered statues of ancient gods were scattered among flowers overrunning their beds. Hedges had grown into lush trees. Yashana looked expectantly towards the center of the garden and was not disappointed. Beside a huge cracked fountain stood the one she had been searching for from the moment she had awoken this morning. Her soulmate. He appeared as she last remembered, muscular and broad-shouldered.

He smiled and beckoned to her. As she neared, she studied his well-built body which she had designed, the arms which had often held her, and the lips that had passionately kissed her so many times. His eyes held her, quickening her heartbeat. She wanted to run to him, to embrace him. Instead, she stopped several feet away.

"You are not Alexander, but Ariyo taking his form from my memories." She had experienced the epulo many times, and knew that the host could manipulate feelings and emotions.

"I am Alexander, beloved. I was dead but now am alive."

"That is impossible."

"Are you sure? Are you not dead also, Layla? Did you not remember signing that form, forbidding the doctors to resuscitate you, forcing me to watch you die?"

"I was old. My body wore out. Death eventually claims us all."

"Yet here we are."

"How is this possible?"

"Take my hand and I will show you."

Layla knew they did not need to touch, but she wanted the excuse. Memories danced around them, scenes morphing into new images, events playing out in front of them, as Alexander explained the creation and transfer of the ziphema. Through the link he allowed her to feel his emotions of love and rapture, of harmony after half a century's separation, and of concern about her present mental state.

He finally broke the link, and Layla found herself back in a teenage body sitting in a flowery office. The Asian man whose arms touched her contained the essence of her husband.

"Welcome back," said Tiah. "How is the healing coming?"

"Well," said Ariyo, pulling away from Yashana. "Like I hoped, Layla's memories are settling within."

Tiah looked to Yashana. "Do you know who you are?"

The teenager hesitated, looking between the two. "I am Layla inside a clone of my body."

The psychology glanced at Ariyo. "Has she blended like you?"

"There has been no blending. Only Layla's personality is active."

"She is in grave danger then of developing split-personality."

Layla cut in, "What is wrong with me controlling my own body?"

The psychiatrist answered, "It is not your body, but belongs to a teenage girl who has the same right to exist as you do."

Ariyo said, "I have achieved a balance, blending the memories of both Alexander and Ariyo. You must do the same."

"What if I do not want her memories?"

Tiah leaned forward. "You face insanity. Two beings cannot possess the same mind. They will war with each other."

The old woman trapped in the body of a teenage studied the one who held her husband's memories. "You do want me, do you not? Layla, your wife?"

"Of course. But you need to be whole. You are more than just Layla now."

"I feel that I am me, not some stranger. I remember my whole life, my family, my work, you. The Five. Building Essence. I do not want to lose all that. It is my life."

"I have not lost my identity. I remember quite clearly being married to you. As vividly as I remember being Yashana's handler."

The psychiatrist tried to reassure her. "Her memories are also in your mind. You need to learn how to access them, letting them become a part of your life. As you live Yashana's life, those memories will be vital."

"Live her life? I have my own. I am director of Essence and have more models to complete."

"Layla, to the universe, you are just another college student about to begin her career. Caleb was just appointed the director, and he is not about to give that position up. But you can continue your life's work by taking a job in the Research Department."

"As a newbie? I ran this whole institute."

"In time, perhaps you will again," said Ariyo.

Chapter Eighteen

Layla tried to take over Yashana's life, a daunting challenge. She blundered through each surreal day, relying on her childhood memories outdated by nearly two centuries. Everything was different, from the layout of the campus to the technology available. Mistakes she made were blamed on her recent illness. Ethan and Gauge patiently, but worriedly, explained missing concepts and refrained from laughing at her strange questions. Ethan familiarized her with new software, and Gauge helped her learn the faces of people she was supposed to already know.

The extra help was still not enough. Ethan and Gauge shared no classes with her and could not fill in the gaps of her knowledge that a senior majoring in genetics was supposed to know. Layla failed her first test in nano bioengineering. As she read the questions, she panicked. Nanites had been used for many centuries in constructing DNA of cloned animals at genetic companies like BGF. Layla herself had used them when creating the quintessences, but she never had to understand how they worked. She designed new DNA patterns then Derrick and his staff used the nanites to turn a computerized map into living flesh. The basic concepts she understood, but not the technical details.

As she floundered through the test, she attempted to dip into Yashana's memories. Surely buried someplace in the teenage mind were the answers. Bits and pieces Layla found, but they slipped away like water in a leaky cup, concepts too fragile to hold together.

This is so stupid, thought Layla in frustration. *I created a brand new species and never needed to know this. Why is it a required subject now?*

Because of you, came the mocking voice of a teenager. *If your leeches had not been so popular, attracting tons of voracious students hoping to get elite jobs at Essence after graduating here, the class would never had been offered.*

Go away. Layla mentally shoved the voice away. As it faded, so went all memories learned from the class. During the brief contact, Layla could feel the rage of the other.

The experience frightened Layla. Yashana was still there, a separate consciousness who hated her, lurking about, waiting to take over the brain they shared. Layla pretended nothing had happened, telling herself that access to Yashana's memories was unneeded, but with mid-terms coming up and the teen's mediocre grades, Layla faced the reality of failing the entire semester. Every few days Ariyo drove her to Essence where he probed her mind in Tiah Vay's office, checking on its healing. Both he and the psychologist warned her that she must bridge the breach between Yashana and herself. To Layla, it was not simply a gap but a battlefront between two sworn enemies.

Nearly two weeks went by before Layla attempted to work a shift at Essence. Nostalgic emotions overwhelmed her as she entered the Research Department. Her fingerprints were everywhere, from planning the floor layout, the number of laboratories, type of equipment, protocols, and security measures. It was as much a home to her as the penthouse Alexander and her had shared. Deeply she breathed the familiar scents of chemicals and cleaning liquids. As she walked down familiar hallways, passing busy scientists, it was as if time had stopped while she was gone—except she recognized none of the faces of the workers, and some of the equipment was completely new to her.

"Welcome back," said a friendly sea laven with light purple skin whose name badge read *Zoe'ul.* "We have wondered when you would return. Your heroism has been much talked about around here."

"Heroism?"

"When you so bravely tried to save Director Rangan. We are all still in shock over his death."

"You're back," said Bi'ak, walking in with several boxes of new glass tubes. Being male, the sea laven's ridgelines were twice as tall as Zoe'ul's. "Sterilize all of these and try not to break any this time."

For the rest of the morning, Layla cleaned, stacked, and ran errands for the staff in the lab. After being the boss for so many decades, it was difficult adjusting to being on the bottom. Zoe'ul chatted easily with her, but the others were cold and informal, only noticing her when a new chore needed to be done. If any thought the teenager was a hero, they refrained from showing it.

For lunch, Layla and Ariyo ate outdoors, sitting at a table across from a bubbling fountain in a small, isolated courtyard which attracted few visitors. The tranquility of vines swaying in the warm breeze hinted of the coming spring. Layla relaxed. This was how life should be, Alexander and her sharing a meal together.

"How was work?" asked the quintessence who talked like her husband but had a different face.

"Strange. I am use to giving orders, not taking them."

"You will get use to it with time."

"I hope not. I am ready for my own lab to start where I left off."

"A new graduate with her own lab would raise too many questions. You must be content with small steps."

"Would becoming Research Chairperson in five years be moving too fast?"

Ariyo laughed. "Wait eight years like Jacob's wife."

Layla grinned. "I have never seen you laugh in public before. Or any quintessence. When you talk I see Alexander in you, but you are more expressive."

"It's one of the traits…or faults of the AS model, depending on how you view it. Useful for interacting with other sentients who presume we are human."

"I enjoy seeing you laugh. You could go on doing so for weeks and I would never get bored."

"Good, since seeing each other is the only contact we will have for the next twenty years until my bond years are completed."

Layla frowned, stirring her coffee. "Twenty years is a long time to wait, especially for a human."

"I have waited far longer than that already for you. Surely you will have the patience to wait two decades so we may be husband and wife in not just spirit but flesh? I promise that when our time of celibacy is over, I will spend endless hours toiling to make up for all your suffering."

His bold stare caused Layla to blush as a thrill of excitement ran through her. *What am I, a virgin?* she chided herself. They had been married for ninety-three years. During those last few decades, she had become old and frail, only a husk of a woman. Yet he never turned away from her, never considered adultery though he remained healthy and strong, taking on the responsibilities of running Essence while she slowly faded. He had been patient then, as she must be now.

Layla raised her eyes and boldly met his glaze. "When your bond years are up, the gift which I will hearty bestow to you will be my youthful body.

May you find enough pleasure with it to erase the memory of those forlorn days sleeping beside my old, wasted one."

Ariyo leaned closer. "I treasure the memories of you as an elder as much as I do of your youth. What I promised you in your past life still holds true. I will stand by you no matter your age or when you become debilitated. Simply having your love is enough."

Layla smiled, wishing the bond years already completed, so she could hold his hand without arousing questions from passersby. During the afternoon they stood side by side at the Recreation Center, Layla making notes in her e-tablet, Ariyo watching silently, neither of their minds on the research.

As mid-terms neared, Layla reached deeper into Yashana's memories to prepare for the tests. The teenager's consciousness slipped through mental cracks, randomly breaking into Layla's thoughts. Layla tried to hide the duality, but she knew Ariyo was aware of it and shared that knowledge with Tiah, which meant the entire Synod with its fifty-four members had full knowledge. Within the quintessence culture, it was hard to keep secrets, especially if you were on the bottom rung. That position was difficult for Layla to accept. She wanted to meet with the elders just to talk, to share the experiences of their lives during her absence, yet her requests sent through Ariyo were politely denied. Ariyo told her to not take it personally, as they were still dealing with the impact of Alexander's death and adjusting to a new director, but Layla felt there was more to it than that. She had created, raised, and lived among the quintessences who later became the Synod. She had considered them her friends, her family. Now they avoided her. How could she not take it personally?

Layla managed to pass mid-terms, but the effort of wrestling data from Yashana's memories took a heavy toll. The voice of Yashana came more often, whispering insults as Layla went about the everyday life of the teenager. Nightmares haunted her sleep of being pursued by an ominous presence. When it finally caught up with her, it bore her resemblance, laughing mocking as it reached out for her. Sometimes she awoke before it touched her. Other times it entered her mind, taking over her body, controlling her like a puppet. Telling herself it was just a dream, Layla would fight to awake, straining towards consciousness as the presence pulled her downward, smothering her mind until all thoughts faded into obliteration.

To make up for lost time, Layla planned to spend the entire spring break at Essence, at least that was what she told Ethan and Gauge. What she really

131

wanted was an excuse to spend more time with Ariyo. Unfortunately, that meant long mornings in the Research Department. By Tuesday she had grew impatient and cranky as she was sent to the washroom yet again to hurry up Dan'ukva with lab supplies then back to Lab Five to put up the clean equipment.

Layla stacked beakers in a cabinet over Bi'akin, who ignored her as he typed data into a computer. A cartoonish image of a dark-skinned quintessence appeared on the screen. Then the words "DNA not compatible" flashed across the picture.

Bi'akin sighed and said to no one in particular. "AF Design 2178 is out."

The teen peered closer at the screen, a beaker still in hand. "How are you overcoming the hair problem?"

The sea laven noticed her for the first time and frowned. "Don't you have work to do?"

"Doing it right now." Layla put the last beaker in the cabinet. "The hair dilemma was one of the major hand-ups that I...Layla never overcame. In the original ME model, she used hair from a desert rodent, but it does not have the texture needed for realistic African *Homo sapiens* hair"

"I'm too busy to tutor infants right now."

Layla headed to the back of the lab and sought out Zoe'ul who was bent over a microscope. The teenager waited patiently until the sea laven looked up from her work. "I was wondering, how is the hair dilemma being handled?"

"That is one of several major hurdles we are working on. As you know, the coakyatte DNA used for quintessence hair lacks the texture we need. One theory was to use completely new DNA from another creature, but the argument against that is the model will no longer be pure quintessence, but a subspecies. The other theory was to edit pieces of the coakyatta DNA until we can produce hair of the right consistence. For decades both theories had been explored. Only recently have we come close. Dr. Frank has actually grown coakyatta hair cells which meet our needs, but when the DNA is added to the AF designs, the computer predicts an enzyme conflict."

This is so boring, complained Yashana's voice. *Who cares if there is yet another foeditas horribilis model? Get back to washing dishes. It's always amusing watching you break something.*

Layla ignored the voice. "Can I see the DNA map?"

"Sorry, but interns are not really allowed to do that. Not even my clearance level is high enough for me to see the whole genome. There is the concern that a spy might copy the data."

"Of course, I understand."

Layla waited until everyone left for lunch, then she tried to use Bi'akin's computer. A box popped up asking for a password. Layla entered code words that, as director, had allowed her to access any file at Essence, but none worked. Frustrated, she randomly typed phrases.

Oh, now this is more fun than seeing you accidently run into your boss with that cart. Too bad you don't know any hackers. But I do. Ethan is the best in the universe, but he would never help you with this.

"I do not need him," mumbled Layla out loud.

"Who do you not need?" asked Ariyo, his sudden appearance startling Layla. "You are late for lunch."

"Uh, Bi'akin. This is his computer, but I do not need him to access it. You will do just fine." Layla stood and gestured for Ariyo to take her place.

"Why are we trying to break into his files?"

"To see the AF designs. It is for the betterment of science."

"You mean so you can satisfy your curiosity." Ariyo sat and began typing. "Caleb has already changed the director's password."

"But there are others. As one of the Five, you still have access to many secrets."

"I am no longer considered a Five, just a beta model who should not know how to do this." Ariyo pressed enter and a complete genome appeared on the screen.

"Thanks," beamed Layla, taking over the chair. She zoomed in, searching through thousands of genes, pausing occasionally to click in the note sections to read comments and reports of researchers. "They really have come a long way. Even have the skin tone correct."

"You need to wrap it up. They will be back soon."

"But I have not even found the hair gene yet. I need more time."

"Perhaps in a few days we can do this again."

"I may be able to fix the enzyme conflict. I will not know until I can have a closer look at it."

Ariyo glanced towards the hallway from which came the sound of a distant door opening. "You are out of time."

"There was a virtual lab built just after I semi-retired. We could upload this information, and I work on it in there."

"We both are not supposed to have clearance to do that."

"Please, Alexander. I can do this. Was this not the whole purpose of why Ariyo was assigned to monitor Yashana? The Synod wanted her at Essence to create new models. I can do it now, without needing ten or twenty years to climb up the career ladder. Just give me the chance." She used her most pleading look, knowing he would melt before it.

Ariyo sighed. "Alright, but not so you can jump start your career. I do it so we may welcome more brothers to strengthen my family. And I would enjoy sharing my beta status with another model."

His fingers moved rapidly across the keyboard as he entered more codes and uploaded a copy of the genome to a private file. They had barely finished when several workers entered. Ariyo hit a command which pulled up the screensaver.

"Still here?" asked Zoe'ul, pausing in her conversation with Bi'akin

Layla smiled friendly. "He had to fill out an evaluation form and needed to see what I had accomplished."

Make sure he reports that you hacked into top level files and stole a quintessence genome, mocked Yashana. *A crime punishable by death. Is there any crime in the code that does not carry a death sentence? I guess that doesn't worry you since you are already dead. But if you get me killed, I swear, I will haunt you forever through whichever hell you believe in.*

The virtual lab was located near the back of the Research Department. When they arrived, Layla was surprised to discover that there was not one, but four of them. Virtual reality rooms were very expensive. Layla smiled, remembering her staff's hype when the first had been installed so long ago. Arguments had broken out on who could use it when. It took months before the novelty had worn off enough that employees began using it for real work instead of play. Nor did it help matters that Layla, then in her seventies, had been the primary offender in hogging its use, often tinkering with it late into the night.

A panel by the first door flashed, "In use." Moving to the fourth door, Ariyo punched in codes then downloaded the genome. The door slid open and they walked into an unlit circular room. The chamber momentarily became pitch-black when the door automatically shut behind them. Several glowing icons appeared in the air at the center of the room. Ariyo stood near the wall as Layla walked forward and poked a finger at one of the icons. A menu appeared. She navigated slowly through it, finding the file of the genome. Suddenly the entire chamber filled with thousands of virtual genes hovering in the air, each displaying excerpts of notes researchers had attached to them. The vivid holograms moved fluidly as Layla surfed through them.

"It is so beautiful, nothing like the old system." Layla felt overwhelmed. "It is the closest we can get to truly touching DNA with our own hands. Makes one feel almost like a god."

"It would probably be best if you refrained from developing a god complex while you are still dealing with possession."

Layla winced. "Save your jokes, Alexander. I am not that conceited."

Are you sure? asked Yashana. *You did come back from the dead. I think it's gone to your...my head.*

Layla touched a gene. Immediately it enlarged, filling up most of the room. She walked about, studying the DNA coding. "This is slow going. How do you make a segment move without me having to walk to it?"

"I know little of how the program works as I have never needed to use it."

"Can you find someone who can explain it to me?"

"No. You are not even supposed to be here."

"How about Zoe'ul. Tell her it is for some top secret project." When Ariyo answered with silence, Layla turned to flattery. "You are an expert manipulator, able to protect the interest of the quintessences while allowing the Galactic Senate to believe they are in control. Handling one sea laven should be easy for you."

"As I remember, you were just as manipulate as I was."

"I learned from the best—you." Layla made a pleading face, eyes begging. "Please, Alexander."

"You have already used your quota for that today." Still, he turned and left the room. Several minutes later he returned with a sea laven, but not Zoe'ul.

Dan'ukva entered, smelling of bleach. "Zoe'ul said you were working on some top secret project and recommended that I help you." He glanced at the virtual helix crossing the room. "What exactly are you doing?"

"It would probably be best if you did not know so you can claim innocence. Do you know much about using virtual reality?"

The sea laven laughed, fangs glistering in the dim light. "We had several dozen VR 4000's in my elementary school. My dissertation was about using VR to build antiviruses. I would be ashamed to represent my species at Essence if I didn't know how to use them."

"Why do they have you working in the washroom?"

"Everyone starts in the washroom, including you." Dan'ukva walked to a small shelf nearly invisible in the darkness and picked up a wired hat. "You will found that this speeds up your interaction quite a bit. It monitors your brain waves and works with the sensors in the room which watch your eyes." He put the metal cap on. "You look at what you want and it obeys, at least with simple tasks. More complex commands require specific gestures." He demonstrated by having the giant DNA twirl while he rubbed two fingers together. "Easy once you memorize all the gestures which vary between programs."

For several hours Dan'ukva tutored Layla. By the time he left, she could navigate quickly through the genes, zooming and rotating objects as needed. She pulled up the hair gene, examining its base pairs. Ariyo quietly stood near the door, watching her study double helixes, comparing different patterns, and reading researchers' notes. The data was meaningless to the quintessence, but he enjoyed observing the lithe body of the teenager dancing through the code of life, her mouth laughing in delight as twisted ladders swirled around her. This was Layla Rangan's playground, the one place she felt completely herself, embracing the destiny which always had been hers—coder of life.

The door opened and the department chairman entered, looking grumpy. "Who is running this at such a late hour?" Doctor Golnick stared at the teenager too absorbed in her work to notice him. "You don't have clearance to be here!"

Ariyo stepped in front of the heavyset man. "I gave her permission."

"Who do you think you are? I am chairman, not you. No one can use the VR without my personal permission. How do you even get access?"

"Alexander gave me permission before he died."

"To a beta? You're lying. Now clear out of here. I don't appreciate the extra work you are causing me because now I must file a complaint with the Synod."

"They will simply override you and allow Yashana to continue. Save yourself the trouble and do not bother."

The man crossed his arms, indignantly. "My word carries much weight with the Synod. If there is some project going on, I should have already been notified. Unless you can prove your authorization, I will file the complaint."

Ariyo changed tactics. "You are right, Doctor Golnick. You should have been notified. You have proved yourself time and again a trusted professional, a true friend to the quintessences. Because this is such a sensitive case, we have kept tight control of information, but I believe you can be trusted. What I am about to tell you carries the highest level of security. If you leak this information, it will not only cost your job, but most likely your life. Do you still wish to know?"

The middle-age man frowned. "You cannot intimidate me, youngster. I would not have been appointed chairman if I didn't know when to keep my mouth closed. Will the Synod back up your story?"

"You may go tomorrow and verify with them everything I say, but tell no one else." Ariyo gestured towards the teenager. "Who does she remind you of?"

The supervisor peered at the teenager flipping through virtual records of older experiments, examining why each failed. "She is just a girl."

"Look more carefully. With your heart, not just your eyes. You have seen photos of her before."

Layla showed no awareness of being watched as she opened a glowing file and vibrant chromosomes filled the air. The doctor took a few steps closer, cocking his eyebrows in concentration. Suddenly his mouth opened in astonishment.

"God's mercy." He looked back at Ariyo then at Layla. "How can this be?"

"An unknown person or group decided to clone Layla Rangan. The case in under investigation, the particulars you do not have clearance for. You only need to know that the Synod placed her here to see if she has the same talents as her predecessor."

"Does she...can she do it?"

"That is what we are here to find out. She is examining the AF genome to find ways to improve it. The results I will send you to analyze. If you believe it meets your department's standards, you may pass it on to your colleagues. What you must not do is credit her with the results. Her identity must be kept hidden for now."

Golnick swallowed nervously. "Frank has worked several decades on this project. He will not accept a new version of his genome suddenly showing up. It will raise many questions."

"I know. That is why you must first judge if her version is worthy. If so, the Synod will probably allow Frank's team to know who Yashana is, and then give them public credit if the project succeeds."

The chairman sighed. "Frank is finicky, but if she can really fix the glitches, he would be open-minded enough to test it." He looked at the teen zooming in on nucleotides. "I hope for everyone sake she does succeed. God knows how long we have worked on this project. What does she need?"

"Solitude. And access to files."

"I can increase her security level. But how do you expect to hide her identity? People will begin noticing her resemblance to Layla."

"You have seen her many times in the hallways yet not once guessed she was more than an intern. People see what they want to see."

As the man turned to leave, Layla called to him without looking up from her work. "I highly suggest, Doctor Golnick, that you promote Dan'ukva to Project AF. He is being wasted in the washroom."

The chairman paused, studying the teenager, an eerie feeling creeping over him that he was looking at Layla Rangan reborn. "I will look into it."

It was nearly midnight before Ariyo convinced Layla she needed to eat and sleep. He drove her back to the college then picked her up early the next morning. Layla spent the rest of spring break working on the AF genome, ignoring homework and friends. Having dealt with the older Layla's many obsessions with projects, Ariyo stepped into the role of supporter, fetching Dan'ukva to answer questions about software or Zoe'ul to explain info on the AF model. When she tried to skip meals, he coerced her, threatening to turn off the VR. She usually complied, but when the weekend arrived, she pushed harder, knowing once classes resumed, she would no longer have spare time for the project. She worked throughout Saturday night, took a brief nap on a couch in a lounge, and then was back in the VR lab. Mid-afternoon, Layla sent to Golnick a copy of her edited genome that, in theory, no longer contained the enzyme conflict.

Ariyo drove her back to college using the hover car which was still registered in Alexander's name. Layla sleepwalked towards her dorm, barely aware of a crowd of students gathered to watch robotic animals racing each other. She felt annoyance when the sidewalk was suddenly blocked by cheering students. As she forced her way through, applause broke out as a metal dog crossed the finish line first. Ethan held Rover up high as his peers congratulated him. Catching a glimpse of Layla, he hurried to her side, grinning proudly.

"I worked all spring break, but I finally got Rover running nearly as fast as a whippet." Seeing Layla's bland expression, he added, "Well, maybe not that fast but enough to win. Have you finally finished your prison sentence?"

"Just about." Layla walked faster, wishing Ethan would find someone else to talk with but he kept pace with her. Soon the crowd was left behind.

"I got two job offers but haven't accepted either yet. I was waiting to hear what offers came your way. Did your school records get fixed?"

"Yes, but I have no need to keep looking. I accepted the job at Essence."

You have, I haven't, complained Yashana in Layla's mind. *And I never will.*

"What?" Ethan stopped, reaching out to grab Layla's arm. "How could you? We talked about getting jobs on the same planet, maybe even in the same city. Why would you work for those leeches?"

Layla replied calmly, "It is a good job which fits me well."

"You hate the foeditas horribilis."

"People change."

"Especially you." Ethan looked betrayed. "Since that explosion, you have become a completely different person. What did they do to you? Is it blackmail? I can help you. Just tell me what they have done."

"No one forced me. This is by my own choice."

"I don't understand. You would not choose this path freely."

"I grew up. I have an elite job many would sell their souls for. Why should I go anywhere else?"

"Because I thought…we were…" Ethan suddenly turned and walked away.

You're hurting him, cried Yashana. *Don't do this.*

Layla answered, *He had to learn sooner or later that there was no future for us.*

It's bad enough that you took over my body, messed up my grades even worse than me, and treated my friends like dirt. But to destroy my future? Enough of your possession, demon. Yashana fought, pushing hard against Layla's consciousness, exhausted from lack of sleep.

Yashana gained control and ran after her friend. "Ethan, wait. I'm sorry."

The youth with the face of Richard Cambridge turned to Yashana, anger in his eyes. "I'm the one who is sorry—that I'm not good enough for you. I can only offer a boring, mundane life, stuck in an office job the rest of my life, nothing compared to your precious mortis elixir. Enjoy consuming their elixir, that is if they don't consume you first."

A tear ran down Yashana's cheek as raw emotions tore through her. Over the years she had taken Ethen's friendship for granted. He was like a rock that she had believed would always be there. Now that she was endanger of losing him, she realized how intensely she cared for him. "You are my best friend. I'm really, really sorry I haven't been myself. I can't explain why to you, just forgive me, please."

Ethan stared at her, his expression wavering. "What happened between us? We were always together and then you started hanging out with Ariyo. Always him." His eyes opened as insight smashed his innocence. "You love him, don't you?"

"I...I...it is complicated."

"Right, because he still has his bond years to complete. You prefer to love a monster than me. He is a slave who can give you nothing. Of course, I have nothing to offer either, except..." He glanced at the robotic dog tucked under his arm and laughed bitterly. "How could I have deluded myself in thinking you felt something for a geek like me?"

"My friendship is genuine. I don't want to lose that, even when I act weird."

The youth looked away, his untidy hair tossed about in the wind. "Friends. Right."

He turned and walked towards his dorm, leaving Yashana crying in the shadow of a tree. She almost ran after him, wanting to shout the truth of the depth of her feelings. But already she felt the presence of the other trying to regain control.

The battle for supremacy raged as she walked to her dorm room. Gauge saw her tearstained face and questioned her. Yashana said that she and Ethan had a fight. Then she curled up in bed, crying herself to sleep.

Chapter Nineteen

"Tell me of Yashana's virtues," said Tiah Viay, sitting on a couch across from her patient.

"Virtues? She has none." Layla stared pass the psychologist's head, watching water splashing in its endless trek, recycled over and over, falling pointlessly on fake rocks.

She hated these meetings. So many tasks needed doing, yet here she was stuck in Tiah's office. It irked her that Ariyo kept reporting to Tiah the ongoing war in her mind. Perhaps that was why Tiah had asked Ariyo to remain out in the hall today. Layla felt that mental problems should be kept private, not discussed among the entire Synod, which was what Tiah did with the information she gleaned from Layla. Whatever happened to doctor-patient confidentiality?

"Surely, Layla, you can find one good trait about Yashana."

"I am tired of these games." Layla pretended to speak like Tiah. "Be understanding of Yashana. Find what you have in common. You must bond." The old woman in the teenage body sighed. "We are nothing alike. She is an aimless juvenile delinquent with mediocre grades whose only life goal was not to be me. By the time I was her age, I had already created a new species, revolutionized the field of genetic, and appeared in *Galactic Times*. Ha, I even had my own car which I brought with earnings from a real job."

"And you were a recluse who hid yourself from people." Tiah keep her voice calm, despite her patient's anger.

"Which allowed me to achieve so much."

"I have noticed many similarities between you two. Same college, same major, even born on the same planet."

"That was set up by whoever cloned this body."

"Still, you share many experiences. You need to seek common ground, compromise, end the conflict between your two consciousnesses."

"We care about different men. How do you expect us to compromise on that? Polygamy? I know it's legal on some planets, but neither Alexander nor Ethan would go for that."

Tiah sighed. "You need to take my suggestions seriously. We want you to find peace between yourselves."

"No, you and the Synod want a Layla who can magically cook up new models every few years. That's what they wanted long before I was bombarded with her memories."

"Am I talking to Yashana now?" Tiah was quick to spot the difference in voice tone.

"For a brief moment." Yashana stood up and walked to a window, absently staring at a potted fern. "She is stronger than I because she has more life experiences, more memories. But I will never allow her to know peace. She stole my life."

"Not on purpose."

"She has already lived one life. It's unfair for her to claim a second. I want her out of my head. You have no idea what a nightmare this is for me."

"I wish to help you both. You need to find common ground."

"Please, we are both sick of hearing you say that. There can be no peace, no compromise. Either she or I must die." Gloom was in the youth's voice. "Unfortunately, I am the one everyone around here wishes would disappear."

"That is not true. Both Ariyo and I wish you to blend, becoming one person."

"Impossible." The teenager's expression changed, becoming harder, and she walked back to the chair. "I have a chemical analysis to run. Can we wrap this up?"

"Soon, Layla. You still have not answered my question. Give me one positive trait about Yashana."

"She avoided too much junk food and has a healthy body. Now a question for you. How did you persuade Jacob to marry a psychologist? Your exotic looks were not enough to attract him, despite his age."

Faint splotches appeared on Tiah's skin, revealing her sensitivity to the topic. "He pursued me. That is all you need to know. Our next session will be in three days."

Enjoying irritating the shrink, Layla kept her grin to herself until out of the office. She headed to the Research Department, passing scientists barely noticing her. How much longer would that last? Frank's team kept a tight lid on her identity, but sooner or later somebody else would recognize her similarities to the first director of Essence. Layla preferred that, ready to stop hiding and reclaim her legacy. School would be out in a month. Her community service hours were already completed, and she had enough research hours to complete her dissertation. Still she came, wanting to spend as much time as possible with Ariyo and to see if the AF Design 2199 would be successful.

The dozen workers of Lab Five were gathered around the screen of an electrical molecular microscope which showed a close up of a cell and long lists of incoming data. Layla moved into the group, standing beside Dan'ukva, who was enjoying his new promotion. As the final statistics appeared, everyone leaned closer, each trying to see the final results. Layla's view was blocked by Bi'akin's head.

"Cell count is over one hundred and fifty. We made it to blastocyst," said Frank, among cheers.

"Is it stable though?" said Zoe'ul, trying to peer pass those in front of her.

"Proteins, amino acids, and enzymes are all behaving normally. No chromosome fragmentation. All is well so far," said Bi'akin. "This may really be it."

"Of course it is," grinned Dan'ukva, glancing at Layla. "Now that we have our champion reborn."

The teenager smiled modestly. "All I did was tweak what was already there."

"Your techniques were brilliant," said Frank who rarely gave compliments. "It may have been another decade before we hit on the right pattern. Your mind can comprehend all the intricate components, understanding how they fit together better than any computer program." There was awe in the supervisor's voice. "In all my years I have never seen any who possesses your talent."

Most were still staring at the screen and missed the teenager wince at the word *possesses*. Layla stepped away from the group and moved about the large lab, looking for something to do. Seeing a cart from the washroom, she began stacking clean dishes. Zoe'ul came over to help.

The sea laven's face looked radiant. Over the bare ridgelines on her head, she wore a circlet from which hung colorful, jeweled charms. "You did well."

"So did the entire team. They found solutions to problems that I missed the first time." Seeing the sea laven's puzzled look, Layla quickly amended, "if I had been working here for a long time."

"Do you notice anything different about me today?" Zoe'ul tilted her head so the charms jingled against each other.

"Uh, you have a new necklace, though I guess it's not really a necklace since you are wearing it on your head."

"It's my ancestral Tiara of Joining. Last night Dan'ukva and I became lifemates." With a webbed hand, she took off the circlet and pointed to a gold fish embedded with a green stone. "This is my birthstone, presented by my father to my mother on the day of my birth. Last night she added my stone to the Tiara of Joining. And the red one linked to mine was attached by Dan'ukva's mother."

"Congratulations, Zoe'ul." Layla felt a stab of jealous. Twenty years was an eternity to wait. "Should you be on your honeymoon now?"

"My name is now Zoe'ulva. Honeymoons are not in sea laven culture, but in a few months we do plan to spend our vacation days exploring the water caves of Moondream Island."

"Enjoy yourselves. I believe you chose your lifemate well." Layla was happy for them but felt a lingering sadness for herself. Her parents and brother were long dead, along with almost everyone she had known from her past life. She still had a few acquaintances upon the long-lived ediethean, mainly relatives to Roobaroo, but she could not walk up to one and say, "Hey, I'm Layla Rangan reborn." The elders of the quintessences were the last contact she had with her past, yet they avoided her.

The melancholy feeling had not vanished as she ate lunch with Ariyo in the quiet courtyard nor when she stood by his side in the Recreation Center, making useless tally marks on her e-tablet.

"This dissertation is so stupid. What was she thinking when selecting it? Writing it will be like trying to eat soup with chop sticks. Completely pointless."

Ariyo glanced at young quintessences playing arcade games nearby. "This is not the place to talk about such things."

Looking around the area, he spied a janitor's closet. He led Layla into the small room. Mops and brooms hung from pegs. Shelves were neatly stacked with cleaning supplies.

"You need to listen to what Tiah tells you instead of automatically dismissing it."

"I thought you were on my side. Then again you are telling her everything that happens in my mind. It's none of her or the Synod's business. It's her fault that the Synod will have nothing to do with me."

"No, it is not."

"Then why do they avoid me like I have a plague? Do not tell me that it is because they are still dealing with your death. They are the only family I have left."

"Yashana has family."

Angrily Layla took a few steps back, bumping against the wall. A mop handle hit against her shoulder. "I do not want to hear anything about her. Stop changing the subject and answer my question."

"It would be best if you dropped that for now."

"Alexander, you know me better than that. I will persist until I finally learn the truth."

The quintessence sighed and stepped closer. "You are too stubborn for your own good. It is destroying you. The elders do not wish to see you because it is too painful for them."

"How can it be painful? I am the one suffering here, not them."

"They limit their contact with me also. You and I bear the treasured memories of the founders of my species, but also harbor their greatest secrets. The Synod is concerned about what will happen if we become unbalanced."

"I thought you were fine, saying all that stuff about being one with yourself."

"My blending is complete, but I still represent the unknown. They are uncertain how I will respond to you."

"To me? I know I am struggling at the moment, but as soon as I get rid of this Yashana thing, I will be back to my old self, and we can reclaim the lives we once had."

"That is your problem. You cannot accept that your old life is gone. To the universe, Layla Rangan is dead. Her position, her power now belongs to Caleb. I accept that I am now just a beta, not a director, who must obey the orders of my superiors. You are in denial, pushing away the other part of yourself."

Layla become annoyed. "Now you will tell me that if I don't find common ground with her, it will lead to insanity or death. Tiah has told me this before."

"You still do not listen. The Synod is concerned that a bearer of their secrets may be insane. As a former director of Essence, you should remember what that implies."

Layla went quiet, her face paling. "They will order my execution."

"They already have. If your grip with sanity slips too much or Yashana begins spouting secrets to outsiders, you both die."

Layla's heartbeat quickened, and she tried to move further back, but there was only the wall and swinging mops. "They cannot do that to me. I am their creator. I did so much for them. I gave them Essence as a homeland. How could they betray me like this?"

Ariyo placed his strong hands on her shoulders to calm her. "Do you think they wished to issue such an order? That is why they avoid meeting with you. Your death will be harder for them to endure than when old age took you peacefully in the night. They care greatly about you and fear losing you so soon. Torment will never end for the one who actually performs the execution." He looked away, unable to go on.

Layla swallowed. "You volunteered, didn't you?" His silence confirmed the truth. "Oh, Alexander."

"I could not allow another to touch you, to drain life from you. It is my fault you are in this predicament. It is my responsibility to bear the weight of failure." Ariyo touched a tear running down her cheek.

"No, Alexander. Doing so will destroy you." Layla clung to him, crying. "I promise to win this battle."

Ariyo wrapped his arms around her. "As long as you perceive it as war, you will lose."

Gently he ran his fingers through her long hair, wondering, fearing that their wedding day would never be. The teenager laid her head against his chest, listening to his heartbeat, feeling protected in his arms. Her tears stopped. Out of a lifetime of habit, she kissed him gently on the lips. Immediately Ariyo pulled away.

Layla felt hurt. "Is it wrong for a husband and wife to comfort each other?"

"No, but Ariyo and Yashana are not married. You know the Code."

"Screw the empire and screw the Code."

A cold mask replaced the tenderness that had been on Ariyo's face. "Layla, you are one of the founders of the Code. The very one who added the line that forbid sexual activity for bonded quintessences."

"As you know, I did so to prevent them from becoming lustful monsters, not as a wedge between husband and wife." She leaned back against his chest. "You are my husband."

"We are married in our hearts, but the universe does not perceive us that way."

146

"I do not care what the universe thinks."

Layla wrapped her arms around Ariyo's neck and kissed him firmly. When he tried to pull away, she held him tighter, refusing to let go. She pressed harder, felt him yielding. His restraint slipped and he kissed back, passionately, pushing her body against the wall, mop handles bumping against them. For a few glorious minutes, rules and governments lost their power. There only existed the other to touch, to kiss, just like in the days of old. But when Layla began unfastening Ariyo's belt, he stopped her.

"We cannot do this." Ariyo took several steps back.

"You are my husband."

"No, Yashana is unmarried. And only seventeen. There are several laws which forbid this."

"I do not care." Layla stepped closer, but Ariyo held palms up and shook his head. Angrily she sputtered, "Will you always be a slave to the empire, letting them control every aspect of your life?"

"You shame yourself." Ariyo took a deep breath to calm himself. "As I shame myself. Laws are made to prevent societies from collapsing. That is why we wrote the Code so long ago. Are we so mighty that we force others to obey it but not ourselves? As directors, we both signed execution orders for bonded quintessences who gave in to lust. I know the sleepless nights that burden has cost you, cost me. Weight that Caleb will bear when he signs the death order for me." Ariyo moved to the door.

"We kissed. That was all. Caleb will not have you killed…if this is reported at all. Some light punishment is all."

Ariyo wrapped his fingers around the doorknob but did not turn it. "The Five became stricter with the Code after your death."

"Our case is different. We are…have been married. Your brothers will not kill you, especially knowing it really would lead to my insanity. "

"Go home. Make peace with Yashana while you still can."

Ariyo opened the door, and Layla followed him out. Several seven-year-old quintessences gathered around a shooting game glanced at the emerging couple then at each other, their bland faces hiding their thoughts. Nearly adults, they would soon graduate and receive their first posts. Already they had been trained to report any strange behavior of another quintessence to a superior. Ariyo firmly met their inquisitive stares, hiding the guilt he felt.

This is Essence, mocked Yashana's voice. *All secrets eventually find their way to the Synod. Your precious Alexander will be killed because of your selfishness. And you claimed to be the more mature one of us.*

147

Shut up! shouted Layla. *The Five would never kill Alexander.*

They already plan to kill you, their mighty creator. I can murder you with just my mouth. Hey, reporter, let me tell you what really happens at Essence. The foeditas horribilis don't just suck the life force from their victims but steal their memories. And they can manipulate thoughts, making you change your mind without you ever realizing. Senators, they are far more dangerous than you thought. Are you really sure you want to use government funds to keep producing them?

Layla ignored the voice in her head as she silently walked beside Ariyo, passing youths playing games. Several paused to quietly watch them. Others focused on screens or holograms, competing with each other for the highest scores.

Outside the building, Ariyo said, "I think you know your way home." He left her and headed in the opposite direction, needing time to think.

Walking slowly, Layla wandered towards Richton Tower, far more worried about Alexander than herself. Would he wait to confess until he was summoned for the next mind probe or voluntarily turn himself in? He always had a strict sense of duty. *I must head him off, take the blame before he does.*

Layla sat on a bench and pulled out her e-tablet. Carefully she wrote a short, formal message to the Five, asking to meet immediately with them about an urgent matter. She bypassed the normal channels that such messages were usually relayed, instead sending a separate copy to each of the Five's private addresses. Then she wandered among the plazas and courtyards, waiting, absently watching young quintessences train. Over an hour passed before she received an answer. She hurried to Richton Tower.

Soon she stood before the entrance to the Chamber of Five, a dreaded place she rarely visited when she had been director of Essence. There the Five decided the fate of both quintessences and other sentients who had broken regulations. At least the quintessences were already aware that death was one of the possible punishments. The other sentients usually thought the worst that could happen was being fired. Usually they were right, but sometimes they were deadly wrong.

Taking a deep breath, Layla walked into the bare, circular chamber. Four elderly faces, each identical to her dead husband, watched her with stern eyes.

"What is the cause you believe to be so urgent?" said Caleb, standing by the middle pedestal which supported a computer screen and keyboard.

Layla felt a stab of both grief and anger. She had created the Five, changed their diapers, watch them grow up to become leaders of a new species. They were like family to her yet now they treated her like a stranger.

"I am here to request that Ariyo be allowed to marry me before his bond years are completed."

"Why do you waste your time? You know the answer will be no."

"You wish to have a sane Layla who can expand your species. I also wish to keep my sanity. I need Alexander for that."

From the left, Mason spoke, "Do you feel you are endanger of losing your sanity?"

"I will if you kill Alexander."

"Why would we do that?"

Fear gripped Layla, but she forced herself to say, "Because I kissed him today. We are married, at least we feel like it. He kept to the Code and walked away. If you deem any punishment deserved, I ask you to place it on me and spare him. It was my fault. I am but a weak human." Heart pounding, she slowly looked each elder in the eyes, waiting.

Gabriel was the first to speak. "You wish to die in his place?"

"If you believe that to be the punishment for a wife kissing her husband."

Mason said, "You were never a weak human, profectus. You are trying to force our hand, but I will call your bluff. You believe yourself immune from a death sentence."

"On the contrary, I know you have already decided to kill me if I lose control of myself. I am trying to find a path in which we all win. Being near Alexander helps keep me sane. The saner I am, the more brethren I can design for you. Granting Ariyo marriage will insure my healing."

"Your reasoning is faulty." Jacob stepped from behind the computer pedestal. "My wife believes you will not heal until there is a blending with Yashana. Marriage is just a strategy to not deal with your problems. You must face and accept her."

"I face her every day, and I am sick of it." Layla fought to control her frustration. "You are married, Jacob. You understand the need to have someone there for you, to comfort the other after a rough day. Caleb and Gabriel, if your wives suddenly appeared from the dead, would you turn a cold shoulder to them? Am I wrong to desire the embrace of my own husband?"

"Our sympathy we give, but we cannot grant your request," said Caleb. "You know the law passed by the Galactic Senate. Ariyo is property of the Basanti Empire and cannot marry until his bond years have been served."

"We could fake Ariyo's death. Then he and I can live in secret. I could still correspond with Frank's team, helping with creating new models."

"You are asking us to break galactic laws, knowing it is against our Code." Eyes stern, Caleb stepped from behind his pedestal and move within a yard of the teenager. "Over the past weeks, we have debated if you are really Layla Rangan or just an anthology of memories which a bewildered teen interprets as an entity. You just answered that for us. The real Layla would never ask us to endanger Essence Institute by breaking laws which would bring the wrath of the Galactic Senate upon us if the truth was leaked."

"This is for the betterment of everyone."

"No, only for yourself. You dare demand to be placed higher than the Code which the real Layla helped write? Dare to claim laws should be tossed aside for your happiness?"

"I am the real Layla. I apologize for not living up to your saintly expectations, but I was never perfect. Long ago I was once a bored, lonely teenager who decided to break the known laws of genetics simply because I wanted to see if it was possible. If I had not decided to be rebellious then, none of you would exist today. You lie to yourself, claiming I am just a phantom in a girl's imagination, because it's an easier reality to deal with when you have me killed. But I am real."

"It is you who is not facing truth." Caleb looked at her with cold eyes. "We are responsible for governing nearly four million quintessences. If we aided you in breaking the law, what message do we send to our brethren who have waited patiently through their bond years? Is Ariyo, a beta, greater than all others, even his birthmates?"

"I am not claiming he or I are better than anyone else. But we are a special case. A husband and wife reborn from the dead. The Code was never written to deal with that. There is such a thing as mercy."

"If you wanted mercy, you should have written it into the bylaws a hundred and fifty years ago." Caleb's eyes softened slightly. "As director, I must enforce the Code. Your petition is officially rejected."

The abrupt ending caught Layla by surprise. She wanted to continue debating until she had proved her case. She glanced at Jacob, pleading with her eyes for help, but he remained silent like his brothers. "If nothing else, would you at least grant my request to not execute Alexander, please."

Caleb glanced at each of his brothers, seeking their opinion. They each gave a brief nod. "His life will be spared for now. But a repeat offense will lead to serious retributions."

Chapter Twenty

Thump. Thump. Ariyo's feet pounded against the forest path. After leaving Layla at the Recreation Center, he had headed pass the living quarters and training grounds with their obstacle courses. Beyond lay thousands of acres of thick forests crisscrossed with hiking trails and streams. Eventually Essence's property merged with a national park which claimed the nearby mountain range. Trees and bushes whisked pass. A startled bird burst from a thicket, barely missing the quintessence. Ariyo did not slow. Nor did he pause when his sides began to ache, warning of the need for rest.

Faster he ran.

But he could not outrun his guilt. How many times had a quintessence stood before him in the Chamber of Five, accused of the same crime he had almost committed? Perhaps four dozen times in a century and a half. Some had fallen in love and had not, for various reasons, waited unto the bond years were completed to consummate the relationship. Alexander had felt sympathy for them but ordered their execution. Then there were a few quintessences, already freed from bondage, who had turned into vile monsters who either took mates by force or by using the epulo to change the memory and emotions of women so they gave themselves away willingly. Alexander felt no qualms about ordering those to be gassed and their names not honored on the Day of Remembrance. Yet just half an hour ago he had almost become one.

Onward he ran, heading off the path, moving through thick brush, jumping over fallen trees, ducking under branches. He followed a small stream until it became too curvy then leaped across, pushing his way through a tangle of vines. Briars ripped across his skin, drawing blood. *I deserve worse, far worse.*

He had almost taken Layla, still desired her. He had a lifetime of memories of being her lover, knew the feel of her body against his. The longing was acute after so many years of being separated from her. Then suddenly she was in his arms again, offering herself freely. A wife to her husband, she claimed. But both knew it was not true. It was Yashana's lips he had kissed and Yashana's body that he had almost taken without the teenager's consent. If he had done so, he would have become that which he hated, an atrocious monster that as director it would had been his duty to eradicate. Long ago, young Layla had almost been raped by Mason, the first of the quintessences who had probed too deeply into the mind of villains and almost became one. That event sparked the creation of the Code, which was far stricter than the regulations the Galactic Senate had passed dealing with their warrior products. Young quintessences learning the Code were told it was a guideline for their behavior which protected the outside world from the darkness every quintessence was capable of.

Darkness which I desire to do.

Right now, Layla only thought about herself, and not the teenager whose body she inhabited. Alexander placed no blame on her, but himself. Nearly two centuries ago she had created him, but now he was the one who had recreated her, forcing his lover to be reborn when she had not asked for immortally. He had not done so on purpose, but that did not remove his responsibility. When the Synod had voted to have her put to death if she lost control of herself, he had, without hesitation, volunteered for the task, secretly knowing he would ask for his own death after he took her life. It was only fitting.

Aching sides finally forced Ariyo to slow down to a fast walk. Panting hard, he moved through the undergrowth, barely noticing his environment, a lifetime of memories with Layla replaying in his mind. The first time their minds linked, the first kiss in the abandoned courtyard, their wedding among joyful friends and family, their honeymoon at a beach resort. A lifetime of work overseeing Essence while being public figures appointed by the Emperor to sway his citizens that quintessences were an important peacekeeping force. Few, if any, in the universe were bound as tightly as Alexander and Layla. Creation and creator. Husband and wife. Lovers. Soulmates. Then old age claimed Layla, the one force Ariyo could not protect her from.

She had semi-retired in her early seventies, and Alexander became director of Essence in all but name, while she focused on creating new models. Eventually her mind slowed too much and her Research Department began rejecting her designs. For nearly a decade she had wrestled with depression, facing one's own mortality, realizing that no matter how much you achieved in life, eventually your body and mind wear down, betraying its owner.

She finally found new purpose through religion after embracing the faith shared by her friend Rosetta. Shortly after she turned one hundred and five, the Galactic Senate had tried to double the bond years of quintessences. Body feeble and mind abated, Layla still gave them a powerful fight. Working with Roobaroo, she had pulled all her resources, using contacts made from decades of being a public figure for the pervious Emperor. Now she used that same power to turn citizens against the new proposal, and the Senate backed down.

Five years later they tried to change the bylaws of Essence Institute to allow the Senate to handpick a new director instead of the Synod choosing. Believing that quintessences should govern themselves instead of being bossed by an outsider whose main concern would be pleasing the Senate, Layla gave a rousing speech in front of the Senate and media. Frail and weak, she had rose from her wheelchair and spoke from her heart, gripping the podium tightly to keep upright. And again she had won.

It was the last time she had appeared in public and the last time she had stood under her own effort. For the final decade of her life, she had been tended by nurses and Alexander, dying peacefully in her sleep at the age of one hundred and twenty. In the end, she had accepted her mortality, but Alexander could not. His inability to let go of his wife had led him to accidently discover how to make ziphema and rebirth her.

Into insanity. Ariyo's footsteps faltered for a moment, but he kept walking through the bushes.

Humans valued individuality too much. Now she faced a war in which two entities battled for the same body. The blending had been easy for him for quintessences were comfortable with being a clone race. What did it matter if ten thousand shared your same face? Or one thousand came up with the same idea as you? They were a collective society where the group was more important than the individual. There was no conflict between Alexander and Ariyo, not even on a subconscious level. Alexander was used to being in charge, Ariyo trained to obey. Their worldview was shaped by the Code. Their life's purpose was the continuation of their species with Yashana and Layla placed as their highest priority in achieving that goal. Ariyo had never loved Yashana but had grown to feel a friendship with her despite his annoyance with her immaturity. Alexander's wisdom allowed Ariyo to understand Yashana better, leading to fondness, and the knowledge that she deserved the respect of her body not being taken without her consent.

Breathing having returned to normal, Ariyo began running again. From thick undergrowth, shots fired. Instinctively Ariyo dodged, but a stun bolt hit his left leg. Muscles locked up, causing him to fall. He lay face down, listening to approaching footsteps, his hand slowly reaching for his own gun attached to his belt. Someone knelt down and began to turn Ariyo's body face up. Without waiting, the quintessence pointed his gun in the general direction of his attacker and fired. A thump announced his success.

Ariyo sat up to see who had attacked him. A quintessence youth lay beside him, still alert, but Ariyo's stun blast had caused him to lose control of his right arm. A gun lay near the youth's limp fingers. The seven-year-old reached over with his other hand, grabbing the weapon. Youth and adult both raised their guns, aiming at the other's face, but neither fired.

"Why do you attack me?" asked Ariyo.

"You are a hostile target in enemy territory. Identify your rank and serial number." The young C2 model looked like a seventeen year old Caucasian human.

Ariyo relaxed and lowered his gun. "There has been a mistake." He read the youngster's nametag. "Robert, I was out jogging and did not realize a training exercise was taking place."

"Your story holds falsehoods." The youth kept his gun pointed. "There are no paths near here and the area is clearly marked off limits to civilians. I have already signaled my comrades who will be here momentary. If you do not tell me the truth, we will be forced to take that information from you."

The older quintessence gave an ironic laugh, causing the youth's eyes to narrow. "You do not recognize me from the Recreation Center?"

"My unit has little time for games now. We are soon to graduate. And why would you be in the Recreation Center? All non-quintessences are forbidden."

"Because I am quintessence." Seeing the other's doubtful stare, Ariyo explained, "You have at least heard of beta model AS1?"

"Yes, but you cannot be quintessence. You just laughed. Quintessences do not laugh. Neither are you in uniform."

"I'm off duty at the moment. And we both know quintessences do laugh, just usually not out loud. I would bite you to prove my identity, but I cannot walk at the moment, and your clearance level is not high enough to probe me." Ariyo opened his mouth and lifted his tongue, waving the tip of his epulo appendage.

Satisfied, Robert began to lower his gun but suddenly held it back up. "This is still part of the test. You want to catch me off guard. You will be taken as a prisoner to our headquarters."

Ariyo sighed. The C models were excellent in combat, often stationed on battlefronts, but had a far too serious outlook on life. Perhaps that was caused from having the highest death rate of any model. During times of long wars, only half of some generations lived to reach the end of their bond years. When this youth graduated next month, he had fifty years of slavery to look forward to, serving in some of the most intense and inhospitable environments known. Life was no game but a serious of deadly missions, any which could be his last.

A snapping twig caused Ariyo to look up. Three more C models appeared, each pointing a gun at Ariyo. "As I have stated, I am off duty. I apologize for the misunderstanding. It would be a waste of my time and yours if you take me prisoner." And very embarrassing for him. His birthmates would find it an amusing tale to repeat for years to come.

The youths glanced at each other. Standing up, Robert said, "You will still come with us. Our commander will decide your fate."

Ariyo's e-band beeped, announcing an incoming message. He glanced at the name of the sender. "I have to take this. It is from Jacob."

"Of the Five?" The youngsters looked at him then each other uneasily. What would an elder want with this strange beta model?

"It says I must meet with him immediately." Ariyo held out his hand so Robert could read the message. "As I am currently in the midst of a war zone, I commission you four to help me reach neutral territory where I may meet with our supreme commander."

Robert and his comrades saluted, recognizing Ariyo's authority. They helped him stand, but it was several minutes before the stun bolt's effect wore off enough for him to walk. Then they spread out protectively around him, guiding him through the forest. Several minutes later they encountered a patrol from a different unit. Robert and his brothers ducked down and crawled unseen through the underbrush. Ariyo tried to move as quietly as the C2's, but the patrol heard his approach and opened fire. Ariyo ducked behind a tree, stun blasts hitting the bark near his head. Robert's group used the diversion to surprise their attackers, taking down all six.

As the youths looked over their victims, brief smiles flirted across their lips, reminding Ariyo of both his childhoods when he trained with his birthmates who shared pride in accomplishments or disappointment in failures. The strong bond of birthmates was lifelong, forged in childhood, hardened in battle as each one's life depended on the others. A death of a birthmate was a tragic event felt acutely by his brothers. As director, Alexander had dealt with cases were C models where so crushed when the majority of their birthmates had died in warfare that they went on wild killing sprees, refusing to give mercy to enemies who surrendered. According to the Code, the crime was punishable by death. Deciding the fate of grieving brethren was one of the things Alexander hated about being a Five.

After cuffing their opponents, Robert sent a message to his unit, informing them of the prisoners. Then Ariyo continued with the youths through the forest. Soon they reached a path and followed it to a dirt road cutting through the thick forest. They walked along the road for half a mile, keeping an eye out for attackers. When they reached a board, paved road, they stopped and Ariyo sent a message. A few minutes later, a hover jeep pulled up and Jacob got out. As the elder walked nearer, the seven-year-olds held themselves rigidly at attention, but quick glances they shared gave away their excitement to be so near a Five. Later they would proudly share this memory with their other birthmates.

Ariyo saluted Jacob. "Reporting in, sir, with the help of comrades who took out a patrol to get me here safely."

The elder saluted the youths. "Good work, soldiers. Your quick response is to be commended. You may report back to your unit."

Robert and his brothers headed back into the forests, sly smiles ruining the stoic expressions they tried to keep. Jacob waited until the youths disappeared then strolled along the paved road with Ariyo.

Once they were out of hearing of the jeep driver, Jacob said, "Mighty far run for a jog."

"I needed time to think."

"And what conclusions have you reached, brother?"

"Quintessences should always be on guard, even when off duty. Dangers can come anytime, even in the Recreation Center." Ariyo looked at the gray-haired face of Jacob which had once been identical to his own. "I made a mistake and kissed Layla."

"We know. She came to us immediately afterwards and asked to take the blame." Seeing Ariyo's alarmed expression, Jacob soothed, "Relax. We are not killing her or you today, but we do believe the two of you should keep apart for a while. We recognize that the circumstance you both are going through is taxing, outside the normal realm of anything we have dealt with before. Still, you must keep to the Code. We expect you to act honorable. Being our brother will not protect you again if this happens." The elder looked sternly at his now younger sibling. "Do not put us in that position."

"I have no plans to do so. Yashana is soon to graduate. She will be working here and I can take missions off planet, occasionally eating meals together when I am here for review. I promise we will contain ourselves, obeying the Code."

Seeing the sincerity of his brother, Jacob nodded. "There is another unpleasant topic I need to speak with you about. You must understand that my wife wishes for Yashana's healing, but her professional diagnosis is that the split-personality disorder grows worse. If the time comes that Yashana must be silenced, can you really do it?"

Ariyo stopped walking, his fists clenched. He forced himself to relax before answering, "Yes. The confusion that traps Yashana and Layla is of my making. Therefore, it is my responsibility to end it."

"The emotional toll it will cost you will be harsh. We do not wish to lose you too."

"I am aware of the toll and will pay it that very day."

"What do you mean?"

"The day I kill her, I will voluntarily show up at the gas chamber."

Jacob took a step back in shock. "You cannot do that, brother. Your life is not yours to take. We live for the whole."

"As I will die for the whole. No quintessence can bear the weight of killing his creator. None of us. I rebirth Layla. Therefore, it is I, and no other, who will take her life. I am willing to pay this cost."

The elder shook his head in denial. "You are needed now, more than ever. The Synod grows older. Sooner or later we must be replaced by a younger generation."

"I feel that I have little wisdom to offer, brother, especially today. I am now just a beta and only my birthmates will mourn my passing. This deed must be done by me. That is all the wisdom I have left to give."

"We will honor your wish. For all our sakes, I hope my wife is wrong."

"So do I."

Chapter Twenty-one

Layla held herself together as she left the Chamber of Five, ignored the taunts of Yashana as she walked to the monorail station and rode back to Luncaster. When she reached her doom room, she was grateful Gauge was out. She tried reading a textbook to forget about the rejection of the Five, about kissing Ariyo, his touch on her skin. Yashana's teasing voice became harsher, more mocking. Layla sat on her bed with knees pulled up against her chest.

Your own creations have abandoned you. They said you are not real, gloated Yashana. *An anthology of memories. An arrogant phantom who believes she is better than everyone else, greater than even the real Layla. Look at me. I'm the great Layla Ragan reborn. Bow before me and do my bidding. Break the Code and interplanetary laws so I may be with my lover.*

Leave me alone. Layla raked tense hands through her long hair covering her face. *Give me peace for just a little while.*

Your precious Five gave you no mercy. Why should I? You care about no one but yourself. Even tried to give my virginity away. That is not yours to offer. You are a monster. A soulless anthology. Bits of data downloaded in my mind. Ethan might find that amusing if he would ever talk to me again. Perhaps he could upload you to Rover. How fitting for you to be a dog. You're already a bitch.

Shut up. I have a soul.

Oh, yeah. You got religious a few years before you died. If you faith is authentic, then your soul went on to some paradise, leaving you behind. You have been forsaken even by God. Perhaps that explains why you morphed from the exalted creator of life to a possessive demon without a conscience, destroying all who come near you.

I saved Alexander today, the old woman pointed out.

And put him in danger. What type of example are you setting for me, oh saintly creator? How many shrines and museums should we build for you?

I said shut up. Angrily Layla grabbed the nearest object and threw it. Her e-tablet smashed into the mirrored door of her closet, breaking glass.

Now you have done it. My dissertation was on that, fussed Yashana.

Layla walked over to the broken mirror and picked up the e-tablet. The screen was cracked. *Just like my life.* She sat down on the floor and stared at warped versions of herself reflected back in the cracked mirror.

Everything was on that. Class notes, projects, textbooks. Now we are never going to graduate, said Yashana.

Probably not. Even if we did, what does it matter? What quality of life is this? Hell is what I call it.

We finally agree on something.

Both the old woman and teen laughed, an emotion neither had felt in a long time. The hatred that both had fed on for so long briefly melted away.

One of us must die for there to be peace, said Yashana. *As you have already lived your life, I volunteer you. I want my body back and my friends.*

My instinct to survive is as strong as yours. Alexander needs me. The Research Department needs me. There is so much which needs to be done.

If our war keeps going on much longer, I warn you now that I will commit suicide, either by my own hand or opening my mouth about quintessence secrets. It will be easy. One night while you sleep I will regain control and slit my own wrist. We cannot keep going on like this.

I know. The old woman sighed. *But if you commit suicide, image how much it would hurt Gauge and Ethan. Affect your family. Or if Ariyo is the one who must kill us, then we are also his destroyer.*

There is no way out but death, said the weary teen.

Perhaps not, but what if our death was not physical but mental. We both willingly die so we may be reborn.

Why does this sound like religious mumble jumble?

Tiah said we must blend. We cannot do so as long as we both fight for control. Instead we must each lay down our egos, our desire to do things only our way. Compromise.

I thought you hated Tiah as much as I did. Ouch. We have already been in agreement about something. For the sake of my friends and family, not you, I will give it a try. How about favorite color? Mine is green.

Blue. To compromise, I guess we should pick another. Red will be our new color. Favorite food? Mine is idly.

Sushi. Maybe pizza can become our favorite.

But which type of pizza?

Among the shattered glass the two voices blathered back and forth, slowly, unconsciously becoming one entity which peered into the memories of two people, taking and rejecting ideas from both. Hours later when Gauge walked in, a smiling teenager embraced her.

"I missed you so much."

"We ate breakfast together," said the puzzled zonner. "What happened to your mirror?"

"I broke it. And my e-tablet." The teen laughed. "But all is well with my soul. Finally I am whole."

The next morning, the new mortal who thought of herself as Lashana hunted down Ethan. He had been avoiding her since the big blowup. She finally spied him in a study room of the library with a group of tech majors drilling each other for an exam. Staying out of view behind bookshelves, she waited until the study session ended. Then she quickly slid into the room, passing the other students leaving.

"Ethan, I need to talk with you."

The youth only glanced at her while tucking his e-tablet into his backpack. "I think we already covered everything the last time we spoke."

"No, we didn't. This semester I have been selfish and cruel, taking you for granted. You were there when I was sick, supportive when I acted crazy, quick to offer help. My best friend for four years. I don't want to lose that. Do you?"

"What about your pet leech?"

"Ariyo is my friend too, and that is all he can be for a very long time. I cannot…will not marry any but him. But friends I still need, desperately. Will you forgive me for being such a jerk? Please?" Lashana made an exaggerated, pleading face.

Ethan tried to remain solemn but Lashana's silly face caused him to chuckle. "I have missed you too."

Lashana laughed joyfully. "We can be as we were, before the accident. My brilliant geek hero."

"Are you kissing up to me because you need something fixed again?"

"Yes, but that doesn't make my apology any less genuine. You don't know the depth of my despair when I believed I lost you forever. I was so upset that I threw my e-tablet against a door." Lashana pulled her computer out of her backpack and showed him the cracked screen.

"You threw your e-tablet? Are you crazy?"

"I was but I'm much better now. If you don't want to repair it, I will understand."

Ethan took the device and closely examined it. "The hard drive is still intact. You're lucky that they have a motion detector built in that detects falls then braces for impact."

"Can you fix it?"

"Sure, just needs a screen replaced. Yashana, the next time you become mad at me, please don't take it out on a defenseless computer."

"You should see my mirror. It's in far worst shape."

Chapter Twenty-two

Deep within the Fetus Department surrounded by five thousand unborn, Ariyo peered closely at a thin placenta in a glass canister. The backlighting revealed nothing, but according to the computer monitoring the canister, a microscopic egg had successfully attached to the artificial placenta and begun growing. If all went well, six months from now the AS1's will no longer be the only beta model at Essence. Ariyo glanced at the forty-nine other canisters holding AF1's.

Welcome, brethren, he thought silently. *You are the end results of over a century of research and the work of dozens of scientists. The dream of my wife. She is already proud of you though she has yet to see you.*

Ariyo looked at his e-band. Still no messages. The graduation would begin soon and still he had received no invitation. Pushing his worries away, Ariyo reminded himself that they were supposed to be seeing little of each other for a while. Still, it was her graduation and she had no family in attendance. With two older sisters graduating the same week on Mansoor, her parents had no time to fly to Xi'an. She had her friends Gauge and Ethan with her, but he should be there also. It was only proper since he was her handler for three years.

A brief stab of jealousy pushed at Ariyo, but he brushed it away. What had he to fear? He had seen the memory of Ethan confessing his love for Yashana and the teenager's silently reciprocating the emotion. But that was only puppy love, a frail but powerful emotion of youths that usually faded into sentimental memories in adulthood. Nothing compared to the deep connection between him and Layla. Still, it was Ethan who shared meals with Lashana, told jokes to make her laugh, and saw her face every day.

He had not seen her since the closet incident. They avoided each other when she occasionally came to Essence for sessions with Tiah. With her community service and the dissertation completed, she had no other need to visit the institute. Still, they kept up with each other through messages. He had read her text at least a dozen times claiming a blending had finally happened, daring him to believe his greatest fear would now never need to be faced. A few days later the Five had examined her and confirmed that indeed the blending was real. He knew when she finished writing the dissertation and when the panel approved it. She had spent the final weeks of school constantly studying, desperate to make up her slacking grades. After each final exam, she happily sent her high grade to him.

She had shared much of her everyday life with him through text, yet never did she mention the graduation. Ariyo glanced again at his e-band. The ceremony had already started. He had supervised many such events at Essence for eight-year-olds ready to begin their military phrase. What did it matter if his secret fiancé refrained from inviting him to hers? They had many decades to look forward to together.

Ariyo looked back at the invisible AF growing in the nutrients. *The world that awaits you is full of wonders, but also of great dangers. May you find your place without it destroying you.*

He walked along the aisle between hundreds of glass canisters. The newest generation of his brethren. He was no longer director, but he still felt the heavy weight of responsibly for their welfare. He did not envy his brother Caleb or the Synod. In some ways, it was a relief to be an underling who only had to focus on one assignment at a time. The higher the promotion, the greater the responsibility. The Synod bore the heaviest burden of all—the continuation of their species. Too many missteps could bring the wrath of the Galactic Senate upon them. The relationship between the government and its slave warriors had been strained from the very beginning, with some fractions supporting the quintessences while others wished their extinction. Over the centuries, Alexander had led his brothers in a delicate dance to appease the politicians, keep public support, and protect the interest of his species. That meant sending thousands of new graduates to commanders who saw quintessences as sacrificial pawns to die in place of real soldiers on dangerous battlefronts. Who cared when a clone died? There were thousands more just like them.

But it was not easy to kill a quintessence, as their enemies soon found out. The quintessence ability to survive impossible odds became legendary. The Synod had used that to their advantage. First came the congress of Xi'an asking for freed quintessences to form a protective military force for the planet, all expenses paid by the planetary government. Usually only the most powerful civilizations had standing armies separate from the Basanti Empire. The Synod agreed, giving the condition that Essence would become a new district represented at the planetary congress, giving freed quintessences the ability to vote one of their own into office. Then came private pleas for help from organizations and small colonies dealing with problems that the Galactic Senate felt were too insignificant to consider. The Synod began sending freed quintessences on these missions, asking for monetary payment in return. The funds were used for salaries and to purchase battleships. Over many decades, the Synod had developed a formidable fleet, though not nearly as large as the one under the control of the Ediethean High Council. Resentment built among the ediethean rulers and other powerful cultures who believed that the clone race's place was to be the lapdog of the Galactic Senate and nothing more. How dare the dogs sit at their master's table and ask to be treated as equals. Opponents had joined together and wrote the bill to double the bond years of the quintessences. That bill and several others had been defeated by allies of the quintessences, but the Synod knew if they slacked in their diligence, their species could lose the frail independence they fought so hard to gain.

Ariyo stopped at the door and looked back over the vast chamber housing thousands of artificial wombs. How many of these unborn would die in the line of duty and never know the taste of freedom? Never have the self-worth of receiving a salary for hard work or experience the fun of buying their first vehicle? Or knowing the pleasure of wooing a lover?

His melancholy mood could not be shaken as Ariyo practiced bōjutsu or played basketball with several birthmates. Mid-afternoon he received a summons to Jacob's penthouse at the top of Richton Tower. Ariyo was instantly wary as it was not a place betas were usually invited. The walk was tougher than Ariyo expected. To reach Jacob's apartment, he had to pass the huge indoor garden where he had often strolled in late evenings with Layla. Then there was his own penthouse. Since his death he had only entered it once in order to grab the keys to his hover car to pick up Yashana for the first time. He paused beside its arched door, remembering his life as a husband and director. The Five had left the apartment untouched, not assigning it to anyone else. Ariyo hoped to claim it again one day as his own, sharing it with his wife.

He reached Jacob's penthouse. Tiah opened the door when he buzzed. Her greeting was friendly, but Ariyo detected pity in her eyes. She escorted him into an elegant living room highlighted with houseplants. She brought refreshments then disappeared, leaving Ariyo alone with his aged brother.

"How are things today, Alexander?" said Jacob sipping spicy tea imported from Tiah's home planet.

"The same." The huge couch they rested on was of neodite design, a combination of grace and bright colors.

As they snacked on pepper cakes, the conversation stayed light. Ariyo sensed something heavy pressing on his brother, but he waited patiently. Finally Jacob arose and they walked out onto the balcony. Flowering plants bloomed from decorative pots. A splendid view of both Essence and New Hope lay before the brothers.

Jacob studied the skyline. "You and Layla achieved so much together. Your marriage laid the framework of all quintessence marriages which came afterwards, thanks to the Canon. Every time one of us seeks a mate, we seek a connection that is sacred, a union between two kindred souls, a bond which will last a lifetime. But your tale is the epic one. A love so strong that not even death could keep you apart."

"You are in a strange mood this evening."

"Cannot a quintessence speak of romance? Are we warriors only?"

"Why did you call me here?"

The elder continued to study the landscape far below. "I remind you of the depth of your feeling for Layla because you will need those memories in the coming years. Hang tightly to them. If death cannot conquer your love, neither can several decades apart."

"You still doubt our resolution? We will not give in to temptation again."

"I doubt not your sincerity. But Layla or Lashana, as she prefers to be called now, doubts herself." Jacob turned to his brother. "She has decided not to work at Essence until your bondage is completed."

Ariyo stared a full minute, the words slow to sink in. "Where will she go?"

"Far away. She asked that you do not seek her out until you are free. I have the entire conversation for you when you are ready for the memory."

It was Ariyo's turn to study the skyline silently. Finally he turned his back to his brother. The prick then the link with his brother's mind. Ariyo found himself emerged in a personal memory of Tiah. Similar to watching a movie, all he could do was let it play out as it happened in real life.

Tiah sat at her desk reading through files. There was a knock then an Indian teenager entered. "Good morning, Layla," said the psychologist, standing up. "You have never been early for one of our sessions."

"I wanted to get this over with as soon as possible." The teenager and psychologist settled in thickly padded chairs across from each other. "You will be happy to know that a blending has finally taken place within me."

"I have hoped for this, but are you certain this is a real blending?"

"After this conversation has finished, you may have a mind probe done on me. I just ask that it not be Ariyo. The blending is as complete as it can be, but different than how it worked for Ariyo and Alexander. Both Layla and Yashana had to willingly die."

Tiah moved forward in her chair. "If both are dead, who are you?"

"I guess you can call me Lashana. I am made from both of them and have all their memories, but I am the living compromise that was birthed at their expense. It is a bit difficult to explain."

"Take as much time as you need," soothed Tiah. "That is why I am here."

The teenager paused to gather her thoughts. "Both were too strong-willed, neither would give quarter to the other. For the sake of survival, they agreed to lay down their separate consciousnesses, creating me."

"How does that make you feel?"

"Strange. In some ways I am a newborn, yet I also feel ancient. I am both of them yet not either. I feel Layla's passions for the quintessences, but I understand Yashana's frustration of being forced down the same path as her predecessor. I must compromise their conflicting ideas, finding my own path. Alexander's love in the one thing that Layla refused to bend on. She…I plan to marry him when his bond years are completed. That is if he will still have me."

"I am certain he will." Tiah's skin was deep blue as she sat on the edge of her chair. "He above all others understands the challenges of sharing personalities."

The teenager took a deep breath before continuing. "I have something I need your help with. A secret I need kept from Alexander until it is too late for him to do anything about it."

"What is that?"

"I have decided not to work at Essence while Ariyo is bonded. I have already accepted a job on a small planet on the outer realm of the galaxy."

"You cannot run away from your problems, Lashana. They will follow you. By staying here, you will have professionals like me to help you work through them."

"Thank you for the offer, but I do not leave to escape. I am keeping to the Code, placing the welfare of others above myself. If I stay here, I will destroy Alexander. My desire for him is quite strong. Sooner or later I will catch him at a weak moment then I will be meeting with your husband in a trial to condemn Alexander."

"Surely it will not come to that, Lashana. We can work together to overcome your difficulties."

"Tiah, I actually like you, unlike both Layla and Yashana who despised you. See, I am different from them." The teenager laughed, but the humor was fleeting. "You speak for the Synod whose purpose is to keep me here. Yashana desires to escape, and Layla wishes to protect Alexander. The conclusion is that I must leave. Twenty years is too long to stay near my soulmate yet be celibate. If you think it is a problem easily fixed with counseling, I suggest you go a year without sleeping with your husband, then come back and tell me how to deal with my emotions."

"I did not mean to offend you."

"No, of course not. You are sincere in wanting to help me, but no one here can. Long ago as Layla, I had to endure a year of being secretly in love with Alexander, but we had to hide our feeling from everyone, including each other. Passing in hallways, pretending all was normal, but I was broken, so broken inside. We thought it was impossible for us to be together because he was a product. Eventually the Emperor bought the quintessences and added the citizenship clause into the contract. Of all the up and downs of both my lives, that one year is still the worst period of my existence. At least this time I have hope. Twenty years. I can endure that for his sake."

Tiah looked away, wiping a tear off her cheek. Her skin had turned a dull bluish-gray. "Your love story would make a beautiful ballad on my world."

"Thanks, I think."

The psychologist forced a smile. "When Jacob began dating me, he shared parts of the Canon with me, including how Alexander stood by you in old age. I had doubts at that time of marrying someone over a century older than me. Later as a wife and psychologist I came to realize that the dynamics of the love between you and Alexander had become the core of every quintessence marriage. The two of you married three decades before any of the others and they looked to you as an example. Since your courtship is a centerpiece in the Canon, all other quintessences, in their own way, attempt to copy your pattern, seeking soulmates they can share a lifetime with. That was why Jacob sought me as a wife, when I was only a naïve girl fresh out of college. He saw a kindred spirit who cared strongly about the welfare of quintessences. He also believed in my potential of what I could become."

"I didn't realize that I...Layla...affected others that way. I made so many mistakes, including being really rude to you. Sorry about that."

"It's alright. Comes with the territory of being a psychologist. You may have only seen me as a shrink, but I have looked at you like a heroine who walked out a legend then became lost in the real world. I cannot describe to you how deeply concerned I have been, wishing a happy ending for you but fearing a tragedy. In a few decades you will be reunited with your love, while I must watch mine slowly die of old age. The story of Layla Rangan's death has given me the courage to face that time."

Feeling comradeship with the psychologist, Lashana reached over and squeezed Tiah's hand. "I look forward to having a true friend here when I return. We can swap stories about our husbands. We wives must stick together." Both women laughed. Then Lashana said, "I know you will pass the memory of this conversation on to your husband. When you do, I would like a message delivered to Alexander."

"Sure," said Tiah, drying her eyes.

The teen looked at Tiah, but she spoke to her soulmate. "Alexander, I ask that you forgive me for the danger I have put you in and for what I am about to do. I love you, even if I am a different person now. You understand how that is better than anyone. Please don't come looking for me, not until you are free. It is better for both of us this way."

The memory ended. Ariyo found himself back on the balcony overlooking Essence. For a long time he reminded silent, battling to control his conflicted emotions. Finally he turned to Jacob. "Why did she keep her plan of leaving from me?"

"Because she feared you might try to stop her and she would be too weak to prevent you. She asked me not to tell you until after her shuttle left orbit."

Ariyo tightly clutched the railing of the balcony, telling himself nothing had really changed. They would have been separated anyway, just the distance would now be further. After Layla had died, he had grieved for her fifty years, believing her gone forever. He could be patient twenty years. But he would not know her daily life, her ups and downs. Nor could he rush to her side to protect against danger. Much could happen in two decades.

Part III

"How all this will terminate I know not; but I had rather die than return shamefully—my purpose unfulfilled. Yet I fear such will be my fate; the men, unsupported by ideas of glory and honor, can never willingly continue to endure their present hardship."

—From *Frankenstein* by Mary Shelley

Chapter Twenty-three

From space, Volodymyr appeared an inhospitable, barren rock. Lashana stared out of a dirty window of the small cargo ship which was dropping into orbit around the massive planet circling close to a red dwarf star, far too close in Lashana's opinion. The entire planet was owned by Trisha Research Foundation which kept an outpost near the equator. From the brochure Lashana had read when job hunting, she had learned that TRF's purpose was developing high-yield crops for extreme environments. The low-budget organization was only fifteen years old and had yet to produce a product which passed the strict requirements of the Basanti Food Administration. Located on the outer-rim of the galaxy far away from the heavy populated core planets, TRF offered little to attract prominent scientists—the perfect place for Lashana to live unrecognized.

"Better buckle in tight," said a crewmember, a rough-dressed rockancher, sitting down beside the teenager. "It's always a bumpy ride. Not many pilots will fly to tidally locked planets. Don't worry, the captain's done this many times."

Lashana knew little about his reptilian species but noticed that they made up three-fourths of the crew of this cargo ship. She could not help comparing them to zonners. Rockanchers were more humanoid shaped and tailless. When standing upright they only reached four feet and walked scooped over. Often they dropped to the floor and scooted about on all four limbs, swift and nimble.

After fastening her belt, Lashana peered back out the window. "Tidally locked? I don't see any oceans."

The reptile laughed. "There are none. Just one giant ball of volcanoes, rock, and dust. Few red dwarfs produce planets with stable atmospheres. Too much radiation and stellar winds. The ones that do are usually tidally locked, meaning one side of the planet always faces the sun leading to steady breezes as heated air rushes to the dark, cooler side. On some such planets, the average wind speed is far greater than any hurricane you might have experienced on your cushy home world."

"How then can plants grow?"

The brown-skin rockancher gave a toothy grin. "Haven't you noticed Volodymyr's size? I bet my kid's shell that it is at least ten times larger than the planet you came from. Wind speeds near the surface are usually between fifteen and twenty-five knots on clear days." Seeing the teenager's blank look, the reptile added, "That's up to twenty-eight miles per hour. Perhaps a nice day on the beach for you? It's the jet streams we have to be wary off. Can rip a ship apart."

The rockancher grinned, propped his feet up on the seat in front of him, and put headphones over his earspots. He hummed along to blaring doom metal music. The craft jerked and Lashana gasped, clutching her armrest. Looking out the window, she saw that the descent had begun. As the planet loomed closer, all she could make out was dull brownish orange splotched with dark patches of mountains and canyons. Fiery vapors blocked the view as the ship crossed through the stratosphere. The view cleared once they reached the troposphere, but then the shaking began. The craft tossed back and forth, racks fastened to walls around Lashana made terrible screeching sounds. Sudden drops caused her to wish she had skipped breakfast.

"First time flying," asked the rockancher between songs.

"No, but definitely the worst."

Lashana closed her eyes and clung tightly to her armrests. As a public speaker for Emperor Kalyuga, Layla had visited countless planets, but all had been heavily trafficked places tamed eons ago. Never had she experienced a ride as wild as this one. More than once she was certain the ship must be spinning out of control and about to crash against the rocky ground far below. Yet the shaking eventually did stop, and the ride smoothed out for the final few minutes before landing at the bottom of a steep canyon. As the crew rose to begin unloading cargo, Lashana remained in her seat, trying to gather her wits.

A few minutes later a female rockancher wearing a patched jumpsuit greeted the teenager. "You must be the new arrival. I'm Vistula, assistant manager. Welcome to your new home. Hopefully your long journey was not too tedious."

"No, I was traveling with a friend most of the time." With no direct shipping route to Volodymyr, Lashana had been traveling for nearly a month, taking a dozen connections with stopovers sometimes lasting for days. The trip had provided a last outing with Gauge whose home planet was located in the same sector as Lashana's new job. During layovers, they explored shops and sampled exotic cuisine. Long conversations kept Lashana's mind off leaving both Alexander and Ethan, while Gauge bubbled over in excitement to finally be returning home. Their paths had split two days ago when Lashana had boarded this cargo ship.

"I will show you to your living quarters. Don't expect anything fancy. We keep things to the bare minimal just to survive here."

"That's fine. I don't need much."

Lashana grabbed her bags from an overhead rack and followed Vistula to the open cargo bay where workers placed crates on a forklift. The teenager only made it halfway across the bay before she was panting from lack of breath.

"Oh, I forgot," said the rockancher. "The oxygen level is lower than what you're used to. Wait here."

The teenager leaned against a stack of crates, feeling weak and shaky. Vistula soon returned with a mask attached to a small air tank. "This will help. We keep them at the entrance of most buildings for visitors like you. Look for red cabinets where we keep first-aid. They're refilled regularly."

"Thanks." Lashana placed the mask over her mouth, breathing deeply the stale, metallic tainted oxygen.

"You'll be fine in the main complex as it is connected to our greenhouses. Beware when heading out into the field though. Perhaps over time you will grow used to the air and won't need the tanks much."

A loaded forklift passed them, and they followed it down the ramp and onto the landing pad. Lashana studied her new home as Vistula led her across the dusty canyon floor towards a wide metal door built into the face of the cliff wall. Here and there outbuildings sheltered vehicles. Dull reddish-green plants protruded from cracks among boulders and crags. A warm, steady breeze played with Lashana's hair as she looked up at the dark purplish-orange sky. The high cliff wall blocked the view of the nearby red dwarf sun.

"Is it morning or evening?"

"Neither. We're in the twilight region between the light and dark hemispheres. There are no sunsets on Volodymyr."

"I mean time wise."

"Ah. It's mid-afternoon. Supper will be served in the mess hall in a few hours."

Reaching the blast door, they entered a pressure chamber large enough to hold them and the forklift. The heavy door slid down and the room hummed as air was vented in. Lashana removed her mask, grateful to breathe the thicker air. Another metal door slid up and the forklift moved into a large cavern created years ago by machines. Workers, mainly rockanchers, began unloading crates brought in by the forklift, glancing curiously at the newbie.

A tall, gaunt human separated from the group and walked over. "Vistula, who is she?" The fortyish man scowled in the teenager's direction, his brown hair cut short.

"The new researcher you hired."

"I didn't hire anyone, especially a child."

Lashana answered for herself. "I am seventeen. Yashana Kalkar, Ph.D. in genetics."

The man crossed his arms and glared at her. "Well, Yashana, I'm Seth Lanneret, founder and manager of TRF. I'm so glad to have you visit. Now turn your tail around and get back on that ship, taking your fancy degree with you."

"You hired me." Lashana placed hands on hips, refusing to back down.

"No, I don't hire children. This company does dangerous, hands-on work, not sitting around in fancy, air-conditioned labs all day. Vistula, send her back."

The rockancher tilted her snout. "Sir, you did sign the form I showed you two months ago. She had the highest qualifications for the job—and the only one who applied. We need Takean's position filled."

"I thought she was older." The man looked away, troubled. "I have enough deaths already on my conscience. She leaves now."

"Takean's death was not your fault." The reptile stepped forward, her voice gentle.

Seth responded with anger. "Of course, none of the deaths are. Volodymyr kills. We warn them before they come. States it clearly in their contracts. But I will not have a child here. You know that."

"My children work here."

"Your family is different. Rockanchers could be hit by flying pumice and you would just shake it off and keep going. She's human. You know how fragile they are."

"You're human, and that has not stopped you." Lashana was tired of being talking about in third person. "Just because I'm young doesn't mean I cannot handle the job. I'm used to hard work. You accepted my signed contract. If you send me away now, I will sue you for breaching it." The teenager crossed her arms, mimicking his stance. "Besides, I spent all my money getting here and have no place to go."

The lanky man studied her. "Your death is on your own hands. Give her a room."

Vistula led Lashana down a dimly illuminated hallway cut into the bedrock to the sleeping quarters which was nothing more than a large chamber divided into small rooms by thin panels. Lashana's area was barely big enough for a cot and a dingy dresser. The teenager stared, desperately missing her cozy dorm room.

"We rockanchers sleep on mats, but I salvaged Takean's bed. Rockanchers burn most personal items of our deceased, but I thought Takean wouldn't mind it passing to you."

"So Takean was a rockancher?" Lashana opened a suitcase and began unpacking.

"No, human, but he lived so long among us that he felt like one of us, just like Seth."

"How did he die?"

"I don't wish to frighten you off the first day here."

"I'm not leaving, really. But it would be helpful to know how he died so I can avoid the same fate."

The rockancher tilted her head, studying the newcomer. "Takean and my lifemate Wabash were taking samples of gas emissions when the crust covering a new eruption collapsed. My lifemate leaped to safety. Takean fell. Seth took his death especially hard, as they were college buddies. When Seth decided to create TRF, Takean used part of his inheritance to help fund construction. He came for regular visits then eventually stayed after his wife died, becoming our chief field researcher."

"I'll remember to avoid active volcanoes. Not a problem." Seeing the reptile frown, Lashana added, "I won't be actually working near one, will I?"

"Fireberries grow best near high levels of calcium and sulfate. They're one of the three dozen plants we're testing here."

"Oh." The brochure's line about developing high-yield crops for extreme environments began taking on a whole new meaning.

"We'll try to ease you in gently. Start with lab work for a while before moving into the field."

Vistula left and Lashana finished unpacking. Then she sat on the recycled cot, wondering if she was still insane. Did she really have to seek out the most remote, isolated post? Eyes closed, she thought of Ariyo's face, his lips, his hands touching her. Her eyes jerked open. Yep, she needed half a galaxy between them to prevent her from running back when cravings threatened to overwhelm her.

"Twenty years to wait. Can't be as hard as dealing with the Senate. I can handle this." That is, if she could avoid falling into volcanoes and whatever other dangers awaited on Volodymyr.

She navigated the passageways to the mess hall, taking a few wrong turns. Following her nose, she found a rough-cut chamber where several dozen rockanchers and a few other species were eating bland meals. She grabbed a bowl of brown soup and a salad made from leafy plants she did not recognize. Unsure where to sit, she settled for a table where several rockanchers and a tall zonner ate. Their conversation stopped as she sat down.

Lashana stirred her steaming soup and took a bite. Spicy—the extreme heat vainly attempting to cover up the lack of other favors. As she had twice grown up on Indian cuisine, she was used to dishes with a kick. The others at the table continue to watch her, not speaking.

Trying to form friendships, Lashana spoke to the tall, bulky reptile across from her, "One of my best friends from college is a zonner, Gauge of the Blackrock Tribe."

The upper lip on his scarred face curled in a snarl. "The Firecloud Tribe are mortal enemies with the Blackrock."

"I thought you put wars aside for the betterment of your species."

"Just because we no longer kill each other in combat does not mean our rivalry is over. Why else would I be here on this forsaken netherworld? I will bring the ambrosia of the gods back, earning my tribe's place in immortality."

"I did not mean to offend. I like all zonners, not just one tribe."

"What do you know of us, warm-blooder? We have seen too many of your kind who pretend to be our allies only to use us. Do you wish for slave labors or subjects to write mocking articles about?"

"Neither, I'm just here as a plant geneticist."

The zonner's clawed hands curled into fists. Vistula walked up from behind. "Is there a problem, Rook?" Her full height only reached the nose of the zonner sitting down.

"No, just chatting with the newest ghost-to-be."

A rockancher sitting by Rook said, "You missed us taking bets on how long the newbie will last. I placed fifty on her death within the week."

"I'll match that." Vistula turned to a rockancher sitting beside Lashana. "Jazzt, fifty on she will still be alive a year from now."

Jazzt grinned and pulled out a datapad. "Fifty on alive in a year. I give you long odds."

Vistula glared back at Rook. "Killing her disqualifies your bet."

The zonner stood up, towering over all. "It is not me you have to worry about. I have engine filters to change."

Lashana felt relief to watch him walk away. "What did I do to make him so angry?"

"Nothing. You are warm-blooded. That's enough. In this isolated sector of the galaxy, all dominating sentients are reptiles. But when we began running into mammals, the outcome rarely worked in our favor. We have a long, bloody history. Rook has suffered more than most. When he was a youth, the cargo ship he worked on was captured by pirates. He and his nestmates were taken as slaves. He was the only one who survived. He feels that until he can win honor, he cannot return home."

"I'm sorry to hear that." Lashana glanced across the room and saw Seth watching her. He turned and began stacking dirty dishes. "Does your distrust of warm-blooders extend to your manager?"

"Seth has more than earned our respect. He grew up on a mining colony where humans and reptiles worked together and died together. He has shared our suffering and understands us. Trisha is not just a research company for human crops, but for reptiles too."

Lashana glanced at a dozen rockanchers listening closely to the conversation. How many of them had already placed bets on the date of her death? "Jazzt, put me down for a hundred."

The bookie began eagerly tapping in data. "For which date?"

"Twenty years. I will still be alive and working here twenty years from now."

"Extremely long odds. You will make a small fortune if you win."

"I intend to."

The next morning Lashana was introduced to the experiments of Trisha. A large chamber cut into the bedrock served as a greenhouse dimly illuminated with artificial light mimicking the twilight outdoors. Sections of different plants were separated from each other by clear plastic walls. Most of the plants were young, waiting to be transplanted outdoors. Carefully tended mature plants were kept for reproduction. Vistula led Lashana down the rows of bizarre plants and fungi, explaining the properties of each.

As they entered the mature plant section, Lashana asked, "Are there any green plants like I would see on my home world?"

"No, we are designing for planets with far less sunlight. Several of our specimens don't even use photosynthesis for energy at all, but have found other unique ways to adapt." Vistula gestured to pale, swollen blobs giving off a faint glow. In their centers a few stinted leaves grew in a rosette pattern. "Glowrocks. Called that because their bodies are extremely hard. Can be grind up as a flour substitute. Problem is they grow too slow. We need to find a way to speed up their growth rate."

They turned a corner and found Seth tending tall, slender plants whose stalks twisted in corkscrews. Among the black stems were clusters of crimson berries giving off a faint red glow.

Curious, Lashana moved closer. "Are they dead?"

"No, a fireberry plant can live for decades," explained Vistula. "They are one of our primary focuses here."

"Hardy plants, if you can call them a plant." Seth plucked a cluster of glowing orbs from a black stalk. He tossed one to Lashana then plopped another in his mouth. There was a faint popping sound and his cheeks briefly puffed outward. "Fireberries aren't really fruit. They're pods where special bacteria feed on natural chemicals made by the plant. Try one."

Lashana studied the smooth, inch wide orb where glowing gases swirled among red juices. She placed the orb in her mouth and bit down. An explosion of fiery spice with a faint tang of rotten egg ripped through her mouth, glowing gas escaping between her stunned lips. Lashana coughed and her eyes watered from the heat.

"It's an acquired taste for humans but a favorite for rockanchers and zonners. Fireberries grow best near thermal vents, hot springs, and fresh volcanoes. They break down calcium, iron, potassium, and other materials into edible forms. Enough to keep you alive during emergencies."

"Delightful plant," sputtered Lashana, wondering if fire was leaping from her ears.

Seth ate another one. "Samples will be brought in from our various fields. You will need to analyze their chemical composites. We're attempting to grow a faster, more nutritious version which will win approval from Basanti Food Administration. Rockanchers have been growing them for centuries, but until fireberries pass BFA standards, they can't be sold on the open market."

178

Lashana imagined Ethan eating a salad where fireberries replaced cherry tomatoes, he stabbing a glowing berry with his fork, his entire salad suddenly blowing up, lettuce flying everywhere. "I'm not sure fireberries will be so popular on the core worlds."

"Of course not. Our purpose is to allow colonies on hostile planets to gain some independence by growing their own produce and not be completely reliant on supply ships. When those ships don't arrive, people starve to death—and I don't mean the phrase figuratively." Seth spoke with dark intensity.

"I will do my best."

Vistula said, "Chemical analyze has been my primary responsibility. I'm glad to share the load."

"What about genetic engineering? Editing the DNA of plants."

Seth frowned. "We don't have the money for the fancy equipment which would be needed. We keep it old school here. We plant, harvest, and save the best for the next generation."

"No wonder you haven't made much progress in fifteen years."

The forty-three year old man stepped forward, eyes meeting the challenge of the teenager. "When you get tired of being indoors, I will show you where the real work takes place. The purpose why you were hired."

Chapter Twenty-four

Grayish dirt and rocks blurred pass just a few hundred feet below the shuttle. Lashana held tightly to her armrest, wishing they flew higher up. Without warning a deep canyon suddenly appeared below them and the shuttle tilted, beginning its descent. Feeling dizzy from vertigo, Lashana looked away from the window, hoping she could keep her breakfast down. Several rockanchers strapped into seats nearby laughed at her expression. Lashana tried to ignore their jives at her expense.

Four months. That was how long she had made it, passing Rook's deadline for her. Many had expected her to take the next cargo ship off-world, but she had remained, throwing herself into her work. Within weeks she had memorized the names and properties of the thirty experimental plants grown at Volodymyr and mastered the process of running chemical analyze on each. Then she became bored. There was no creativity involved in dropping bits of plants into machines which actually preformed the tests. All she had to do was record the results. Seth and his upper staff used the information in deciding which subjects would be used for the next planting.

Nor had she earned respect or friendship. While most of her co-workers were not outright rude, neither did they try to befriend her. Vistula was the closest she had for a friend as they worked daily side-by-side in the lab, but their conversations stayed professional. Nobody at TRF knew much about Lashana or cared to know. At first, that was how Lashana wanted it, to disappear into her work for several decades then emerge to take her rightful place at Essence. But the tasks she had been given were not challenging enough to keep loneness at bay. Some nights she cried herself to sleep, hoping her neighbors could not hear through the thin dividers serving as walls. She had been director of the largest, most powerful research institute in the galaxy. Influential leaders of the empire had regularly came to her, asking for more soldiers to fix their problems. Now she was a nobody living underground in an isolated planet which knew no sunrise.

She had a combined total of one hundred and thirty-seven years of living experience, but it was more curse than blessing. It was too easy to become trapped in self-pity, mourning her lost lives. But she also had wisdom, at least some. To earn respect of co-workers she had to step outside the safety of the caverns and endure the hardships they went through. So she finally volunteered for harvesting duty.

Her first day out happened to fall on her eighteenth birthday, but she told no one. It did not matter that she was now a legal adult—at least how it was defined by law on the core worlds for humans. Co-workers were only concerned if she could hold her own when outdoors, or would she become a liability which needed babysitting. She saw those questions in Seth's eyes as he had went over last minute details right before boarding the shuttle.

"Did you fill your oxygen tank and its backup?" Seth had drilled her like an army sergeant.

"Check."

"Which pocket is your radiation shield in?"

Lashana had tapped the left pocket of the heavy military-style jacket she wore. "If I hear a beep on my watch, I have sixty seconds to put it on or I fry." Lashana spoke like an overconfident teenager to hide the fear she felt. "Though somehow plants and lizards are immune to radiation."

"Not immune, just hardier." Seth looked at her sternly. "If you don't take solar flares seriously, you will die a very slow, painful death. Red dwarfs are nothing like the tame yellow suns you are used to. The UV light and stellar winds they create can strip a planet of its atmosphere. Fortunately our star has matured somewhat, with solar flares only happening every two or three days. If you were on the light side of this planet when one hits, you would die instantly. In the twilight zone, part of the radiation is deflected, but it is still high enough to poison a human—a death I do not wish on anyone."

"I will be careful."

The shuttle landed at the bottom of the deep canyon which stretched half a mile across. Lashana barely had time to put on her oxygen mask before the back door opened. A strong netting separated the cargo bay from passenger seating. This was only a brief stop to drop off a few supplies to several field researchers. Vistula's lifemate Wabash led several comrades in unloading two crates. Seth gestured for Lashana to step out. She unbuckled and walked around her seatmates, two half grown rockanchers who were the offspring of Vistula and Wabash. They were too busy playing a handheld video game against each other to pay her any notice.

181

"I thought you should see what gingerfans looked like in the wild." Two small oxygen tanks were attached to his belt, but Seth kept his face bare. He had no need for extra oxygen unless doing strenuous work.

He led Lashana pass a tent into a field several acres in size covered in huge, fluffy stems which waved about in the steady breeze. Lashana knew the plants were edible, but she did not care for their ginger favor. In the lab, the gingerfans were dull, limp stalks. Here each stalk danced in the wind, its fluffy surface vibrant with tiny white flowers.

"Pollination season." Seth reached out and stroked a stalk taller than himself. He held up his fingers, now covered in yellow powder. "They use wind to carry the pollen. There are no insects—or any animals—on Volodymyr to do the job."

"They're beautiful."

"Glad you can appreciate something outside a lab."

Supplies unloaded, Rook cranked up the engine of the shuttle. Lashana hurried back to her seat and buckled in. Soon the researchers' campsite and the field of dancing gingerfans faded away as the zonner flew the shuttle out of the canyon. Grey, rocky ground whizzed pass again. They skirted around a dark cloud of volcanic ash. Lashana stared at red lava spewing several hundred feet into the sky.

Tula, the half-grown rockancher beside Lashana, looked up from her game long enough to say, "Mount Mickan is active again."

"Maybe it will give us a second crop of fireberries this year," said her brother Bash. "I just burnt one of your farms."

"You warm-blooder! My army will raze your town as soon as I smash your gate to bits."

"You won't keep your army together long enough for that. I hired a mercenary army of mortis elixir as reinforcements."

Surprised, Lashana glanced at Tula's screen. "Do you mean quintessences are in your game?"

"Of course," said the girl who looked identical to her brother except for a lack of a ridgeline on her head. "Can't have a realistic land war without energy leeches, now can we? But they're expensive. How many did you hire, Bash?"

"Like I'm going to tell you. Come and see for yourself."

Lashana felt surreal. Her quintessences who risked their lives every day for the empire had become pawns in kid games who cared not how many virtual people died, as long as their side won. The shuttle hit air turbulence and she gripped the armrest tightly. The children continued to play, unworried. Adult rockanchers chatted and joked.

Rook landed the shuttle near a deep, dark crack running across a plateau. Everyone but Rook and the children exited. Unsure what to do, Lashana stood to the side, watching rockanchers securing one end of ropes then tossing the other end over the side into the canyon. The shuttle lifted up, made a loop, and then flew to the bottom of the narrow canyon. With buckets firmly attached to jumpsuits, the rockanchers climbed over the lip of the cliff and began harvesting airspikes. Two rockanchers would remain at the top to oversee the ropes. Lashana knelt down and looked over the edge. Dizziness hit as she watched the shuttle landing two hundred feet below.

"Not backing out, are you?" Seth walked up with a harness in hand.

Pale-faced, Lashana moved away from the edge. "No. Like I said, I've done this before. Just been a few years."

Closer to ninety years actually, back when she and Alexander had spent a year on a long publicity tour for the Emperor. After Alexander had finally been reunited with his brothers, they celebrated by propelling down a thousand foot cliff, a popular landmark for mountain climbers on Xi'an. Somehow, Yashana had been talked into coming. While she had awkwardly climbed downward, fighting bouts of panic, Alexander's four brothers had quickly reached the bottom, climbed back up, then enjoyed the descent again. Alexander had stayed by his wife's side, talking reassuringly, giving directions when she froze up. She was three fourths down before she had finally relaxed and enjoyed the last moments before her feet touched level ground.

This time there would be no Alexander with his calming presence. Only Seth judging if she would ever be allowed out of the cave again. She had to prove herself a confident co-worker.

"You don't have to do this." Seth kept a blank face, but worry was in his voice. "There are easier harvests."

"But it is the only harvest taking place this week. I'm ready. I just need a refresher course in mountain climbing." If she wanted to earn respect, picking rows of glowrocks or gingerfans would not cut it.

Lashana put on the harness, and Seth attached the ropes. She double checked that her oxygen mask was on tightly and the bucket firmly attached to her belt. Then she stepped over the edge of the cliff. For a moment she felt panic, but she pushed it away as her feet found footholds.

"Careful not to injure the airspikes." Seth's voice was muffled through the oxygen mask he now wore. He climbed down beside her and begun picking large purple berries from the plants which grew among the crags at the top half of the cliff.

The teenager moved gingerly, trying to be constantly aware where her hands and feet were. The cliff wall was thick with the dark green plants whose small leaves were protected by sharp spikes. Lashana tried to avoid the thorns as she picked the juicy berries which grew in clusters. Seth kept near Lashana at first, but when he felt she had time to adjust, he soon outpaced her, descended downward while picking berries. The rockanchers quickly reached the bottom of their rows which ended about halfway down the cliff where the airspikes stopped growing due to lack of light. The rockanchers moved over to a new area and began climbing upward, picking berries as they went. The reptiles only used the ropes for lowering full buckets to the ground. Rook and the two children poured the berries into plastic crates then hosted the empty buckets back up. When rockanchers needed a break, they briefly rested on narrow ledges.

While the rockanchers made harvesting cliff berries look easy, Lashana struggled with every move she made. Much mental effort was required. Concentrate on location of hands, feet, and body. Avoid thorns. Ignore pain from cuts and scratches. Find solid footholds. Is each berry ripe enough to pick or should be skipped? Bucket full, must lower down. New, empty bucket must be attached to belt. Above all else, the plants must not be harmed.

By the time Lashana reached the bottom of her row, she was exhausted. She laid her head against the cliff wall, resting for so long that Rook called up to her to see if she needed rescuing. She ignored him as she moved over a yard to begin the ascent. Then her rope had to be readjusted carefully to avoid harming the plants. She was required to hold tightly to sheer rock while workers at the top and bottom of the cliff carefully moved the rope over. Lashana had barely begun climbing before her bucket slipped from her belt and crashed downward.

"Watch it, warm-blooder!" yelled Tula from below, now covered in crushed berries.

Nearby, her brother laughed. "She couldn't have had more perfect aim."

"Sorry," called Lashana, disappointed that half an hour of hard labor now lay wasted on the ground and on the angry youth.

Once her bucket was hauled back up by rope, Lashana slowly moved upward. Muscles ached, body trembled. Thirty feet from the top, her body gave out. Resting on a ledge too narrow to support her entire feet, she leaned against the cliff face, wondering if she passed out would the harness hold her or would she plummet to her death. *What do you expect after spending most of your entire life in classrooms or labs? Thought you would look spectacular berry picking on the side of a cliff?*

Alexander would have seen this as just another adventure, not even consider it dangerous. The worst case of homesickness Lashana had yet experienced stuck hard. Seth and the other berry pickers had long ago moved out of sight. Occasionally she caught faint phrases of their conversation. She was alone. No Alexander would come to her rescue, telling her she was doing fine. She was an inconvenience to the others.

Far below she could hear the children discussing her.

"Do you think she finally died?" asked Bash hopefully. "I put down four months."

"She better not yet," said his sister. "I gave her six months. She owes me, hitting me with those berries."

Despite her weariness, Lashana laughed at the absurdity of her situation. *Berry picking on a cliff for my eighteenth birthday. Alexander will get a kick out of this story when I tell him.* And she would tell him face to face. Lashana forced herself to move again, one foothold at a time. She paused to pick more berries, but knew she was overlooking many ripe ones. All she wanted was to reach the top. Twenty-five feet. Twenty.

Exhaustion caused her to be slow in recognizing the beeping. Panic hit when she finally did. How many seconds did she have left before the solar flare hit? Hands trembled as she opened her left pocket and pulled out a thin metal cloth. Her entire body needed to be under it. While holding onto the rope with one hand, she covered her head and body with it but that left her legs poking out. She tried to pull her legs upward, but a foot slipped on a rock and she lost her balance. Instinctively she grabbed the cliff face with her free hand for balance, accidently letting go of the shielding. Horrified she watched it fluttered downward, riding on the warm breeze.

With it fell her hopes of seeing Ariyo again. Or ever seeing her beautiful Essence. How long would it take to die from radiation poisoning? A few days? Perhaps a week? Even if she could send a message telling what had happened, he would not be able to reach her side before she died, alone, away from all who cared about her. Lashana closed her eyes, fighting against tears. She had let him down. She had promised her body to him once he was free, but now all he would get was her cold copse.

The beeping continued. Lashana opened her eyes and stared at her watch. The beeping was not coming from it, but from her oxygen tank. She laughed, shaking with relief. There had been no solar flare. She changed the hook up for her mask to the second tank.

From below came Tula's annoyed voice. "Spice weevils, who is throwing clothing at me?"

"Hey, isn't that the warm-blooder's shield? Maybe she fell off the cliff."

"We would have heard the crash."

"Oh. Maybe she died in harness. This could be my lucky day to make some money."

Lashana began climbing again, ignoring the berries. If a solar flare did hit, she would be defenseless unless she could reach the shuttle which was shielded. Fifteen feet. Ten. Wait, the ship was at the bottom of the canyon. She should be going down instead of up.

Suddenly Seth's face appeared over the rim of the cliff. "You made the tank transfer. Good. You're missing some berries to your right."

Not wanting her fear to show, Lashana paused and picked the berries. As she reached the top of the cliff, Seth pulled her up and unbuckled her. There was still more berries to pick, but both knew she had had enough.

"Is that your radiation shield that Tula is complaining about?"

"Uh, yeah. I kind of dropped it when I heard the beeping of my tank." She gave no more details, but Seth's expression told her he guessed the rest.

"We'll be finished soon." Seth yelled over the edge of the cliff, "Tula, attach that shield to the rope so I can pull it up."

Within a few minutes Lashana had the metal cloth folded neatly back in her pocket. She sat on the hard ground, resting until the harvest was finished. Her fingers hurt from countless jabbing of thorns, scratches covered her arms and legs. Rockanchers reached the cliff top and joked with comrades as they moved to a new spot and disappeared over the side again. Pulling sunshades out of her pocket, Lashana looked up at the sky. The enormous red star filled much of the eastern horizon, its fiery surface a boiling cauldron. Bizarre to be so near a star and not burn up. The warm breeze, the key to life existing on Volodymyr, played with the teenager's hair.

After the last berries were lowered down, Rook flew the shuttle up to the top of the cliff. Lashana watched, useless, as ropes were hauled up and equipment packed. Then everyone buckled in as the ship headed back to base camp. Lashana ignored the bickering of the children, now absorbed back into their video game. In the co-pilot seat, Seth looked over data on an e-tablet, occasionally talking with Rook. An instrument beeped on a panel.

Seth looked backwards over his seat. "Yashana, took a look out your window. You'll see your first solar flare."

As the teenager stared at the red dwarf, it suddenly turned electric blue, the sky a bright white. The effect lasted several minutes then the star was back to its bloody crimson. Lashana felt both awe and dread. If that had hit an hour earlier, she might now be on her way to her own funeral. *Forget trying to look noble. I'm keeping to harvests that don't involve cliffs or volcanoes for now on.*

The ship landed at base camp, and the crates of berries were unloaded. Lashana collected a basket of samples to run a chemical analyze on. Entering the lab, she sat the berries on a table.

Vistula looked up from her work. "Glad to see you survived your first harvest. Did my children behave?"

"Your son was disappointed I didn't die so he could win the bet on my life."

"I told him he shouldn't bet against you. Kids don't always listen."

The intercom interrupted, "Cargo ship has arrived. All personal to bay."

Vistula tossed down her stylus. "That includes us. Maybe the new clothes I ordered will be in. My kids can barely fit into theirs now."

Lashana followed Vistula to the large entrance cavern always cluttered with crates and equipment. Already it was bustling with excited activity. The arrival of a cargo ship meant fresh, imported food, mail from distant friends, and delivery of items ordered months before. Lashana waited until new crates were opened then carried supplies to the locations she was instructed.

Out of one crate, Rook held up a refrigerated metal box. "Yashana, you got a package."

"From who? I didn't order anything."

The zonner glanced at the address, his scarred snout curling in distaste. "From Gauge of Blackrock." Lashana reached out to take the small freezer, but Rook held onto it. "Too heavy for you, human." He carried the unit to a nearby table by the rocky wall. Then he went back to unpacking crates.

Curious what Gauge had sent her, Lashana opened the attached envelope and began scanning the letter. She had only made it to the second paragraph before Tula and Bash drifted over and began prodding the unit.

"Expensive to send a cryofreezer all the way from Zon." Tula touched its cold metal surface.

"Maybe it's a rare delicacy. I heard humans eat cream made from ice." Bash hit a button on the side.

"Don't open that yet," Lashana called out too late.

187

There was a hiss as cold, foggy air escaped. Bash pulled the door completely open, and all three peered in. It was empty except for a small, brownish lump about an inch high surrounded by limp leaves.

"You were sent a dead plant? What a waste of money," complained Tula.

Bash reached out to touch it.

"Don't touch!" The boy's hand was batted away by Rook who had come up from behind. "The ziker must wake naturally from hibernation."

The boy looked up at the six foot zonner towering over him. "What's a ziker?"

"Pets we keep on Zon. One of several plant-animal species native to our planet."

"There's no such thing as a creature that's both plant and animal."

"Yes, there is," cut in Lashana. "They are rare but I have studied several examples. There is even a slug on the human home world which can produce energy through photosynthesis after it eats its first bite of algae."

Rook gave a brief growl. "Our plant-animals are far more complex than slugs. Some are cunning predators who eat slow-witted hatchlings for lunch." He gave Bash a stern glance. "Do not touch the ziker. Is that clear?"

"Yes, sir," said Bash and Tulo together.

Lashana went back to reading Guage's letter which contained instructions of how to raise and train the pet. The children were called away by their father to carry supplies to their mother's lab. The ziker had partly thawed out when Rook returned with a habitat he had put together for it. In a large, shallow pan, he had placed rocks of various sizes. Using foil, he had created a tiny pond. Gingerly with his clawed hands he picked up the brown lump and sat it among the rocks, carefully spreading out the limp leaves.

"It would be best to keep her in the greenhouse, away from heavy traffic." He picked up the pan.

Lashana followed behind him, surprised by his attention. He had not spoken to her since the veiled death threat the first day she had arrived. "Thanks for your help. How do you know it's a girl?"

"From the patterns on her body. No gray patches. When she is fully awake, she will be hungry. Give her a few tiny pieces of meat. Don't use your hands, not until she knows you."

Some of the information he told her was in Gauge's letter, but Lashana did not interrupt. "Did you have a ziker when you were young?"

Rook paused, the dark look in his eyes telling Lashana she had treaded into an area of his life he wished not to talk about. "Avoid loud noises or you may wake up on the floor. In the wild they hunt by sound, paralyzing their prey with darts—which they also use for defense."

They reached the greenhouse, and Rook placed the habitat in an unused corner. Several hours later the ziker looked like an ordinary, brownish-green plant, its body and tentacled roots hidden by leaves. Under Rook's supervision, Lashana held out metal tweezers with a bit of meat. The two rockancher children gathered close.

"Make the sound," instructed Rook.

Feeling foolish, Lashana tried to squeak like a rodent, the natural prey of the ziker.

"You're not doing it right." Rook bent his six foot body down till his snout was near the tweezers. He squeaked. Immediately a tiny brown tentacle shot out and curled around the meat. It drew the piece under its leaves.

"That is the coolest plant ever!" said Bash. "I want to feed it next."

"No, I was first hatched. I go next," argued his sister.

"Only by five minutes."

"Quiet, you two." Rook crossed his arms, glaring at the youngsters. "The ziker may be an infant but her darts are still potent."

Lashana held the tweezers out to Bash. "You can both feed her if you promise not to fight."

The children had no problems mimicking the squeaks. Rook limited the feeding to only three tidbits. Fascinated by the ziker, the kids hung about, soon arguing over a name for her. Lashana grabbed a basket of berries to analyze but ran into Vistula and Seth coming in to look at the creature.

Vistula greeted her. "My children love your new pet. It's all they have talked about since it arrived."

Seth looked down the aisles of plants towards the excited children arguing. "Perhaps it will keep them out of trouble for a while."

Lashana sat the basket on a counter. "At least Bash is no longer wishing for my death. Your daughter wants me to live another two months. Then they can inherit the ziker."

"Don't be offended by their speech. It reflects our culture. Bash, behave!" Vistula yelled at her son trying to stab his sister with the tweezers. The boy looked startled but obeyed. "Our home world's environment is extreme. Death comes daily in the clans. You are considered an elder if you see twenty-five. We developed a nonchalant attitude as a way to cope. It's nothing personal when my kind bet on your death date."

"I thought you were in your thirties."

"I am. Away from our home world we have prospered, many living into our eighties."

Seth frowned at the kids deep in argument. "Rockanchers are highly adaptable. They never developed their own technology, but when a mammal race called Tiglic invaded their home world and took some as slaves to work in mines, they easily learned to use the equipment of their masters."

"Our history is of death and suffering. Before we were enslaved, we were barely more than animals, focused only on the daily struggles to survival. With longer lives we began thinking deeper thoughts, even learning to read for the first time. By then, our kind had been shipped to dozens of outposts and a few major worlds. On some colonies we pushed for independence, declaring ourselves their equals. Some warm-blooders agreed with us; some did not. Rebellions broke out here and there. We always lost. Then the Basanti Empire reached even this isolated sector. The Tiglics fought hard but even they had to bow before imperial power. My species allied themselves with the Empire and we were granted freedom when the Tiglic government collapsed. Other sentients came to this sector, including humans. In many areas tension is still strong between reptiles and mammals, but on some planets there has been peace for many generations."

"Like Greytomb where I grew up." Seth's eyes looked faraway into the past. "A small mining colony founded after the war by both humans and rockanchers. Our species depended on each other for survival."

"How do zonners fit into your history?" wondered Lashana.

"They don't, really," said Vistula. "No one knew about their existence until a little over a hundred years ago when a salvage vessel ran into one of their primitive ships. We rockanchers took an immediate liking to them as they were reptilian like us. We created a trade alliance."

The argument of the children became louder as each shouted the name they wanted to give the ziker. Suddenly Bash yelled, "Ouch!" and rubbed his neck. His body began to sway. His sister looked puzzled then rubbed her shoulder. Both children slowly dropped to the stone floor, asleep.

Rook shook his head. "Hatchlings think they know everything. I warned them Starbelle does not like loud noise."

"Least now we know how to quiet them when they're acting up." Lashana spoke then worried she might have offended their mother.

Instead Vistula and Seth laughed. Rook looked amused. Lashana relaxed, feeling for the first time since she arrived at Volodymyr that she belonged. *Thanks, Gauge. Your birthday present has helped me far more than you know.*

Chapter Twenty-five

"Starbelle has grown another centimeter," said Bash, holding up a ruler next to the creature. His sister wrote the information into a chart.

Lashana paused in her pruning of a glowrock. "Good. Rook said she may be tame enough now to feed by hand. Who wants to try first?"

Both kids raised their hands then glared at each other. They had learned after several more dartings not to argue near the ziker, so they resorted to silently sticking their tongues out at each other.

"Tula, you first today."

The sister grinned and put a piece of meat on her finger. She held it near the ziker who had a few twisted roots dipped into the tiny pool. Tula made a mix of rodent squeaks and clicks with her tongue. They had been conditioning Starbelle to feed by new sounds. A brown tentacle shot out and explored Tula's finger, at first unsure what to grab. Then it curled around the meat and dragged it under the leaves. Tula laughed in delight. Bash frowned, wishing she had been bitten.

Over the intercom came, "Cargo ship has arrived. All personal to bay."

The hatchlings cheered excitedly, hoping a video game they had ordered was in. Starbelle's leaves wiggled dangerously as the creature considered if she should shoot more darts. Lashana was as eager as the kids, wondering if the items she requested had also arrived. That is if Ariyo did not hold a grudge for her leaving without saying goodbye. Lashana and the kids headed through the passageways to the cargo bay where rockanchers were already unpacking. In one corner Vistula was arguing with Jazzt over a bet.

"It has been one year since she arrived. I win."

"But she bet twenty years. There can be only one winner. If she defaults before nineteen more years, then you win."

Lashana butted in. "Jazzt, it's possible for more than one to win the same pool."

"I pay only one winner. Perhaps that will be you, warm-blooder. Perhaps not. Can you really endure nineteen more years or will you run back to your kind?" The reptile titled his head, studying her. "Surely you must be lonely. Do you not wish to find a mate?"

"I am perfectly fine. Sorry, Vistula, but I plan to win this bet."

"I wish you well." Vistula turned back to the bookie, not ready to let go of the fight. "Jazzt, I still believe you owe me."

Seth walked up, looking puzzled. "Yashana, what did you order that takes up three entire crates?"

The teenager beamed. "He sent them. I knew he wouldn't let me down."

Lashana bounded to the crates, eager for them to be opened. Seth pried open a lid and she began rummaging through, excitedly waving boxes of glass slides and chemicals. When the second crate was opened, she squealed as she hugged a large electrical molecular microscope.

"Your worse than the hatchlings," complained Seth. "What is this stuff?"

"Your future. It's about time you made it into the twenty-second century."

Seth crossed his arms, looking wary. "What are you babbling about?"

Vistula walked up and stared at the open crates. "Is that an EMM?"

"Yes, and I have a NDB." Seeing Seth's scowl, she added. "It's a small nanotech DNA builder, but it will get the job done."

"A nano builder?" Seth could barely contain his shock. "Those are vastly expanse. We have no need for one here."

"Yes, we do. All this equipment is old and has been sitting around in storage at Essence for decades. I did an internship there while at college. I wrote a co-worker, asking for donations for a good cause, and he sent it."

"Just like that?"

"All it was doing was collecting dust. We have several mechanics here that can repair them when they break, which might be often."

"What do you plan to do with them?" Vistula picked up a box of Petri dishes.

"Speed up our research considerable. I will map the genome of each plant species, find the chromosomes for the traits we like, and design them into one plant. We can produce clones of the best plants and sell their seeds."

"You're talking about genetic engineering." Seth spoke the words with distain.

"That is what I have a Ph.D. in. It's not a new branch of science. Most major crops have been engineered for centuries. There are thousands of variations of just corn, thanks to genetics."

"And many of those versions came about using the same techniques we use here. The safer methods. Some genetically altered food has led to disease and cancer."

"I have studied those issues. The BFA is very careful in endorsing only safe food. That's why we need this. Your fireberries have been rejected two times because of high levels of magnesium during their tests, but some of the plants we grow here contain low levels. What if I could create a version that always has the perfect balance of chemicals? Without the sulfur flavor. I could save us decades of random field work hoping someday we stumble on the perfect combination."

"Engineering genes is the work of major corporations with huge budgets and hundreds of staff. None of them are interested in working with our plants. They want crops that produce the highest yield per acre and can be sold for a profit. No outpost will be able to grow enough airspikes for export but they can have fresh berries on a planet that normally cannot grow fruit."

"We don't need the help of an outside company. I can do all the work myself. If Vistula wishes, I can train her, perhaps taking on her kids as apprentices. Trust me. This is what I do. I am good. Very good. The best geneticist the galaxy has ever seen."

Seth glanced at Vistula, unimpressed with Lashana's boast. "What do you think? Will her pet project get in our way?"

"There's extra room in the lab. While the chemical analysis is taking place, we often have spare time. I'm interesting in learning her way. Perhaps it will be helpful."

The man took a deep breath before turning back to Lashana. "You may play with your experiments, but you can't cause us to fall behind in our work. And I have the final say if any of your toys get planted."

The eighteen-year-old smiled. "You will be amazed at what I can do."

This was the challenge that Lashana had been waiting for. The most content years of Layla Rangan's long life had been the times she could completely concentrate on research without bearing the vast weight of being Essence's director. Old habits came back easily. Lashana threw herself into the project, some days spending fourteen hours straight in the lab, sending the hatchlings to bring her meals. Anything new excited Tula and Bash. They eagerly embraced their apprenticeship, working beside their mother in learning how to map genomes and edit DNA. When the newness of the job wore off, Lashana began paying the children a small hourly salary from her own income to keep their interested. Besides keeping up with the normal workload Seth expected, she volunteered regularly for harvests, avoiding the more dangerous ones.

Weeks faded into months. During the day Lashana was content with her busy life. Often she worked in the lab until she could barely keep her eyes open then fall asleep as soon as she lay down. The nights when sleep was elusive, loneness haunted her, the absence of Alexander piercing her heart. Still, there were many pleasant events like when she showed Seth the first engineered spouts of glowrocks which she bragged would grow a third faster. He had looked doubtfully at the tiny plants. Months later when field tests confirmed she had been right, he had stared at the data charts in disbelief, while Lashana and Vistula vainly tried to hide giggles. After that Seth began taking her genetic engineering more seriously.

Lashana moved to a new gingerfan and rubbed her hand down its thick, fluffy stalk, seeds falling into the bucket she held under it. Other long stalks brushed against her in the steady breeze. Several rows over, Tulu and Bash competed to see who could fill their buckets the fastest. Her own bucket full, Lashana walked back to the shuttle and stood in line behind Rook who was pouring his seeds into a collection bin. Hearing a beep announcing an incoming message, he walked to the cockpit. Lashana dumped her seeds and started to walk back outside.

"Harvest is over," Rook called out as he put down his headphones. "A storm is coming."

"I thought it doesn't rain on Volodymyr."

"Doesn't. This is an ashstorm. Highly dangerous and moving fast."

The zonner walked outside and began yelling for the others to pack up. At the mention of the word *storm*, the jesting of the rockanchers ceased. Within minutes everything was packed. Wabash and Rook whispered urgently to each other. Walking pass, Lashana caught the phases *only an hour* and *camp three*. As Lashana moved to her customary seat, Wabash stopped her.

"If you don't mind, I would like to be by my children. Take the co-pilot seat."

Normally that was Seth's spot but he was missing today. Lashana moved up to the front, feeling awkward. "Where is Seth? He never misses a harvest."

"This is his day off." Rook revived up the engine.

"Since when did he start taking days off?"

Rook pulled back on the wheel. "He does so this day every year. Keep an eye on that screen there, human. Tell me if it turns red."

Lashana doubted he needed her to stare at meaningless numbers on a dial. He wanted her quiet so he could focus on flying. The ground seemed to drop away as Rook aimed the ship out of the broad canyon. The view north was of plateaus crisscrossed with canyons and several smoking volcanoes. Rook turned the shuttle northwest, facing the red dwarf.

"I thought base camp was due north."

"It is. We have to pick up several field researchers."

"Is an ashstorm like a desert sandstorm?"

"Worse by far." The shuttle shook as Rook climbed to a higher altitude and increased speed. "It is a mix of both old ash from the ground and new ash from active volcanoes. Highly electric, the ash abrasive. Nothing can fly in it. Nothing survives. Now no more questions. Keep watching the dial."

Lashana watched the green numbers then glanced at the rockanchers behind her. All the adults were tense, the ones near window seats stared nervously at the sky. Wabash sat between his children who silently leaned against him, their eyes fearful. Then Lashana noticed the fading light. A vast, black wall of darkness had begun blotting out the massive red dwarf.

"The numbers, what color are they." Rook's voice was urgent.

"Uh…red. Thirty-five knots."

The reptile banged on the steering wheel then glanced back at his tense co-workers. "Wind speed is too high. If I try to land, we may crash. If I do not, I sentence those researchers to death."

Lashana gripped her armrest, fighting fear, unable to think of anything to say.

"I cannot leave them, even if we die." The zonner looked at her, his eyes pleading for her to understand. "I did so once, years ago. I can never forget what their bodies looked like. The skin scoured off."

Lashana knew too well the weight of bearing the fate of others. It was what she hated most about being Essence's director. "Do what you think is right."

Rook pushed down on the wheel, directing the shuttle into a canyon. As they dropped below ground level, the wind speed dropped off.

"It's green again. Twenty-five knots." Lashana let out the breath she had been holding.

The zonner struggled to land the shuttle, overshooting the camp by a hundred yards. As soon as he touched down, the two field researchers scurried to the ship on all four limbs. They sat beside their bags in the cargo hold for there were no more seats available in the passenger section. Rook closed the cargo door and lifted the ship off the ground. They flew upwards out of the canyon. Wind slammed against the ship when they rose above the plateau. Rook fought to keep control as he turned the ship northeast.

Rook raced the ashstorm which loomed closer. Lashana stared in horror out the window as the planet which knew no sunset was plunged into darkness. The storm did not cover the whole planet, but its path effected thousands of kilometers. Lightning flashed among the boiling clouds of ash. As Rook pushed the shuttle to its max speed, the ship trembled with sickening jerks. Tula cried out and buried her head in her father's jacket. Bash covered his eyes with his hands. The researchers they had picked up were smacked by baskets and other loose equipment. Lashana silently prayed as she watched the red numbers climb higher and higher on the dial.

"We're almost there. What's the knots?"

"Fifty-two. What happens if we can't land?"

"Then we die. Are you prepared, human?"

"No, I have a lot left to accomplish. If you kill us, my ghost will haunt you for eternity."

Rook laughed, relaxing slightly. "You are tougher than you appear, warm-blooder."

"Thanks. Can't we just fly above the clouds? Climb into low orbit?"

"Wrong shuttle. This one can't handle space flight. Neither would we have enough fuel to land later."

He pushed downward on the control stick, beginning the descent into the canyon where their base camp was located. Crosswinds tried to slam them against the edge of the canyon. Lashana closed her eyes, certain they would crash. Somehow Rook avoided the rocks. Below the plateau the winds slowed, dropping into the green zone. The shuttle shook and bounced about, but Rook brought it to a stop on a landing pad.

Panting, Lashana stared at black ash flying past the window. She could barely make out the outline of the equipment sheds. The base camp entrance was invisible.

Rook punched the button to open the hatch. "You get to save your haunting for another time, human. Better put on your mask."

She slipped on her oxygen mask then joined the other passengers. The rockanchers ran on all four while she bent over, fighting the wind to the large door which led into the caverns. Once the door of the pressure chamber sealed behind them, they all sighed with relief. In the cargo bay, the rockanchers spread out to hunt friends, eager to recount their near death experience.

Lashana touched Rook's arm, causing him to pause. "I just wanted to tell you that you're the best pilot I have ever met. Thanks for saving our lives."

The zonner looked surprised. "I see why the Blackrock likes you."

Wabash and his children were already deep into telling the story to Vistula when Lashana reached the lab. Trying not to disturb the family, Lashana left to hunt for supplies. She moved through the maze of passages, entering a small chamber where boxes of chemicals were stacked on shelves. As she reached for a bottle, she heard a thump from behind the shelf. Curious, she stepped around the shelf and found Seth sitting on the floor in the dim light, his back against an old crate.

Surprised, Lashana blurted out, "What are you doing here?"

"It's my day of remembrance." Seth saluted her with a flask then drink from it.

"You're sitting around getting drunk on your day off? We almost died."

"What do you mean?" The gaunt man leaned forward, suddenly alert.

"Did you even know there was an ashstorm?"

"Did everyone make it back?"

"Yes, no thanks to you."

"Are you sure everyone is all right?"

"Yes. Everyone, even those two researchers from that other campsite."

"Good." Seth visibly relaxed and leaned back against the crate.

On any other day, Lashana would have left Seth alone, but the stress and fear of the flight bubbled out of her. "We almost crashed. Even Rook was upset. He didn't know if he should risk picking up the other two. Your place was to be with us, not hiding in this hole. I thought you banned alcohol here."

"This is the day I break the rules."

"Leaders lead by example. While we risk our lives, you get drunk."

Seth stood up, anger flashing in his eyes. "By the time I was your age, I had faced more risks than you could ever image, suffered deeper than you have ever known. You are in no position to judge, core dweller. Leave me. Now!"

Lashana began to turn away, disgusted.

Raising the flask high, Seth said, "To Trisha." He drank deeply.

"You dishonor your own company." Lashana shot back.

"If you say another word to me I'll have you fired." Seth glared at her, daring the nineteen-year-old to speak. "Trisha is not my company. She was my wife."

"Your wife?" Lashana felt her own anger melt away as understanding hit. "You named your company after her. What happened?"

"Didn't I say not another word?"

"I'm your only geneticist. You're not going to fire me. What happened to her?"

"You have trained Vistula and her offspring. What do I need you for?"

"Perhaps companionship. I am the only other human here." Lashana sat on the floor, her back to the supply shelf. Seth glared at her silently. "I'm not leaving so you might as well tell me your story. I know this shrink that keeps insisting on talking about your troubles instead of burying them."

Seth sighed, letting his tall, lanky body settle back against the crate. He took another sip from the flask then passed it to her. Lashana sniffed it cautiously and wrinkled her nose. Her alcohol experience had been limited to wine when dining with dignitaries. She took a tiny sip and began coughing, her throat on fire.

"Dragon breathe whiskey. Low on alcohol, high on pain. I drink it not to escape but to remember. Their pain, their deaths. You say you want to know my past? How can you even begin to understand? To you, the universe is civilized. When food is low you go to the grocery store. If someone treats you wrongly, you take them to court. The government is a safety net to bail you out when life becomes too rough. But not here on the outer rim."

"I have lived here over two years. I know a few things about hardship and suffering."

The middle-age man studied her for a long time. "That you do. You have lasted much longer that I expected."

"What bet did you place on me?"

"I don't bet on lives." Seth drank again. "Six hatchlings, fourteen adult rockanchers. Four children, two teens, and twenty-six adult humans. That is how many died at Greytomb when the cargo ships stopped running for a year. Had something to do with a conflict among several groups of pirates and the home world of Tiglic. It became unsafe for lone ships to travel to outposts. The Tiglics eventually pleaded to the Emperor who sent one of his fancy warships, letting his energy leeches root out the pirates. By the time peace was restored, I had lost everything that mattered to me."

Lashana flinched at the mention of her creations, but the light was too dim for Seth to notice. "I'm sorry the quintessences did not come quicker."

"The Emperor has little interest in this sector." Seth's eyes drifted to the past, deep grief marring his face. "My dad died in a mining accident when I was twelve. At fifteen I married Trisha."

"That's young for marriage."

"Few humans make it pass forty at Greytomb. You do as much living as possible in the short time you're given. When the first supply ships didn't show up, we didn't think too much about it. It's a regular problem on tiny colonies such as ours. Everyone was put on rations. Then Trisha discovered she was pregnant. We were happy. I built a nursery for her. But the ships still didn't come. Food began running out. My mom and I started skipping meals, giving our food to Trisha. It wasn't enough. I begged Trisha to have an abortion. Save herself. There would be other children later when the ships returned. But she wouldn't. She was determined to have the child. Disease broke out and my mother died along with many others. After that, things became really bad. I had to compete with lifelong friends for every scrap of food I could find. Trisha gave birth, but she could not produce the milk our son needed. She sat there, holding him for hours and hours until he eventually died. She followed him the next day. She was only seventeen."

For a long time Seth remained quiet, grief too strong for words. Lashana said nothing. She had never experienced such horrors, knew no words which could comfort such pain.

"I wanted to die after that. Thought I would. But a few friends kept me alive, forcing me to eat. Fireberries planted by some rockanchers had finally ripened, and it saved what was left of the colony. When the ships eventually returned, I couldn't stay at Greytomb. Too many painful memories. I took odd jobs. A deckhand, ditch digger, harvester. Traveled for three years, never staying on any planet long. Finally a man named Brandon Mckay took me under his wing. He was a wealthy farmer and I just another of his hired hands. But he saw something in me, encouraged me to go to college, helped me with the paperwork and loans. Having nothing better to do, I majored in agriculture. I started out with no purpose, but finally something clicked in my head. If colonies on harsh planets could grow their own food, famines like what we experienced at Greytomb could be prevented. I graduated with a B.A. then got a job at a large seed company. I tried to get my bosses interested in developing crops for extreme climate planets, but they didn't see the profit in that. So I struck out on my own, creating Trisha Research Foundation. I managed to win a few grants. Brandon, Takean, and some other wealthy friends I had donated money. So here I am, running a company that has always operated in the red and may never see a day of profit. But it has never been about the money. Never."

Lashana brushed a tear away from her cheek, reflecting on both her lives. She had originally created quintessences because she was a bored youth looking for a challenge, not understanding the huge ramifications which would come later. Seth labored from his heart, Lashana from her head. She had thought life hard when fighting to control herself, worrying about classes, her future career, and possible lovers. Over the many decades of Layla's life, she had watched friends die from sickness and old age, but never from starvation. Lashana could think of no worse horror than to be trapped, helplessly watching everyone you care about slowly die from lack of food.

"You are a better person than I."

Seth gave a bitter laugh. "Surviving a famine doesn't make you a better person. It leaves you haunted with questions. Why did I live? Others were more deserving. If there is a God, is this a punishment or his way of amusing himself?"

"It is not a punishment of a deity, but the results of political greed. You said so earlier. As for the reason you are alive? You're sitting in it. You survived so you may help others."

They sat in silence for a while, each lost in their own thoughts. Seth finally fixed his eyes on the teenager. "Occasionally there have been others like you who came then left after they have had their fill of this place. The ones who stay either believe in the cause like Takean or have no place to go like Rook. Why are you still here?"

With the conversation turned upon her, Lashana became uncomfortable. "I just am."

"You gave me the line about the shrink and spilling your guts."

"Back home, my shrink heard an earful. When I came here, I left everything behind. End of story."

"Then why do you cry at night?"

Lashana looked at him, startled. "I...don't cry."

"My room is adjacent to yours and the walls are very thin. You wept every night when you first came. Not as much now. I may not be a shrink, but I say you didn't leave everything behind. You're running from something."

The teenager looked away, clenching a fist. She had prodded him, getting him to share his past, but she could not do the same. "Let's just say love and lost. Leave it at that."

"Fair enough." Seth saluted her with the flask. "It must be an impressive story for you to flee halfway across the galaxy."

The next few weeks Lashana stayed busy helping with replanting. The ashstorm had wiped out most of the crops, though a few hidden in the deeper, narrow canyons managed to survive like the airspikes. Seth had been through this several times before and had an ample stock of seeds and cuttings. As Lashana worked beside her co-workers, she found herself always aware of Seth's location. When he talked to her, his voice took on a gentle tone that had not been there before.

Something had changed the day he had shared his grief with her. Before he was simply her boss, rough cut, sometimes rude. Now she saw his actions in a different light. He had tried to send her away that first day because he really had been concerned about protecting her, as he felt about all in his staff. To him, TRF was not a company but a surrogate family. He labored beside the others in the field, discussed difficult problems with staff before making decisions, joined late night card games, and held his own during the rockanchers' jibing contests. But behind every action he did, remained a deep, unhealed scar that Lashana could now see. It drove him, sending him into exile from his own species so he may, in turn, be able to prevent the suffering of others, no matter their race.

Being the director of Essence had allowed Lashana to meet many living legends, some like Roobaroo had impacted their cultures in major ways. Then there were quintessences who would, without hesitation, jump in front of a bullet to protect a friend or stranger. But how heroic was that when they knew, because of their ability to quickly heal, they had a high chance of surviving? Seth had no superhuman abilities. He was simply a man who had turn pain into purpose. As Lashana went about her everyday tasks, her mind wandered to Seth more than it should. Then Seth began invading her dreams. Among images of Alexander, Ariyo, and occasional Ethan intruded Seth. The morning she woke up with a fading dream of kissing Seth, Lashana knew she was in trouble.

She was falling in love with him. If Alexander had been anywhere nearby, Lashana would never have given Seth a second thought, at least not romantically. But she still had eighteen years of self-imposed isolation to look forward to. Eighteen years without being kissed or held or loved, the penalty for coming back from the dead. Sometimes she felt anger towards Alexander for forcing her into this situation. Other times she silently raged at the latest emperor or contemplated murderous thoughts against the Galactic Senate. Her dreams of Seth were becoming more vivid. It mattered not to Lashana that he was twenty-six years older than her. She remembered being a centenarian for two decades, body so weak she could no longer walk or feed herself. At forty-five, Seth was still strong and healthy. Occasionally the thought whispered through Lashana's mind that if she married Seth, he might be on his death bed by the time Ariyo was free. Guilty, she pushed such thoughts away, telling herself she was a terrible person to harbor such ideas.

Lashana rose early after another restless night, if you could call it night on Volodymyr with its eternal twilight. It was still several hours before breakfast. Lashana wandered about the greenhouse, trying to forget yet another dream of Seth. When she finally met Ariyo again, he would probe her mind, discovering her temptations. She knew from personal experience that secrets could not be kept long from a quintessence husband.

Starbelle rested on top of the highest rock in her habitat. Lashana clicked her tongue and held out a finger. The ziker sent out a tentacle, searching for food. Finding nothing, the creature reached out with more tentacles, gently exploring the human's hand.

Lashana's mind drifted back to when Alexander and her were first courting so long ago. They had kept the relationship secret from all but his brothers. Then Anthony, their military trainer, had found out and put a stop to it. During the painful break-up argument, Alexander had told her to forget him and marry someone who could give her children. Back then, all she had wanted was Alexander. Then there was that last day of her life over ninety years later. Alexander had asked her if she had any regrets in marrying him. When she claimed she had none, he pointed out that in the secret depth of her heart, she missed not having kids.

The tentacles had pulled Lashana's hand into the leaves, but the creature did not try to eat her fingers. Starbelle was tame enough now to enjoy being petted. Carefully Lashana stroked the ziker's small body, leaves wriggling contently. What would it be like to create a child, not in a lab, but the old fashion way? To feel life grow inside one's womb? The desire for children overwhelmed Lashana. Had not Alexander given her permission so long ago to marry another? But that had been another lifetime when he had thought marriage impossible between them. She had promised Ariyo she would wait for his freedom. How could she think of betraying him?

Withdrawing her hand from Starbelle, Lashana continued her wanderings about the greenhouse. She turned a corner and saw Seth examining a fireberry stalk, stroking the black, twisted plant, while his eyes looked into the far past. Warmth filled Lashana's heart for she knew he thought of Trisha. She felt no jealousy for his dead wife but understanding. She too knew the agony of being separated from one's soulmate. Seth would never stop loving Trisha. Lashana wanted it no other way.

Seth looked up as Lashana approached. "You're up early."

"Couldn't sleep." Lashana noted his wiry body and rough hands, scarred from a life of hard labor. He gave so much of himself to others, asking little in return. He deserved real happiness. She could give that to him, but in return she would have to betray her soulmate. Conflict rent her heart.

"What's wrong?" Seth stepped closer, concerned. "Are you sick?"

"Yes, in a way." She trembled, heart and mind fighting. To be loved now, to heal the scar of a man who had known such suffering, to give him a child to replace the one he had lost, she a real mother after a lifetime of barrenness. *Alexander, forgive me for what I am about to do.*

The teenager spanned the distance between her and Seth. She wrapped her arms around his neck, pulling him downward. He looked puzzled, perhaps thinking she was sick and about to faint. Then she kissed him firmly on the lips. He pulled back, startled.

"Yashana, I….uh…"

Lashana kept her arms around his neck. "It's time for you to remarry. I know you will always love Trisha. I don't ask to replace her, but for you to find room for me also."

"I'm an old man."

"You have no idea what old really is." She noticed he had not completely pulled away from her. "You said you believe in doing as much living as possible in the short time you're given. I'm doing the same. Marry me."

Seth looked into her eyes, uncertainty on his face, but his arms had wrapped around her back. "At night you cry for someone else."

"There will be no more tears except for joy when I give you a child. As long as you let me, I will stay by your side, raising your children—and designing the most miraculous plants the galaxy has ever seen."

He kissed her then, gently at first. Lashana pressed against his strong body and the kissing became passionate. When they finally pulled apart, Seth stroked her face with a finger, scrutinizing her eyes. Satisfied with what he saw, he smiled. "Rockanchers love wedding parties."

"Then let's not disappoint them."

Hand in hand, they walked down the aisle between the maturing plants.

Forgive me, Alexander, Lashana whispered in her mind, knowing someday he would see this memory. The day she stood in judgment, would he be understanding or kill her in rage?

Chapter Twenty-six

Children dashed cross a playground, chasing each other. Others climbed on jungle gyms or swung fearlessly from high bars. There was little laugher. Somber face, the children remained alert, reacting quickly to the actions of birthmates. The young quintessence looked four, but they were really only two. Each AF1 model was identical to the other, brown skin and curly black hair.

Ariyo watched the children play as he thought of Lashana, wishing she could see them. Her dream had become reality. There was now a model representing every major human race, strengthening the quintessences as a whole with new abilities and talents.

"Nice to not be the only betas."

Glancing over his shoulder, Ariyo saw his birthmate Rinji approaching. "How was your mission?"

"Exciting. A few close calls, shot in the leg, I killed one, arrested three. How about yours?"

"The opposite." Ariyo began walking with his brother towards their barracks. "I escorted some crown jewels between planets. No one thought them worth stealing."

"Maybe on your next mission you will finally see some action. Your downtime cannot last forever. Surely they know you are being wasted. After all, you have the highest kill record of any of us."

"Perhaps that is why I have been grounded. They prefer a higher arrest than kill record."

Ariyo refrained from mentioning the Five wanted to keep him nearby, safe, leaving Lashana alone. It irked him that they did not completely trust him. Lashana had made it clear she wanted to be left alone until he was free. How could they think he would violate her wish? With the experience of hundreds of missions, he should be given the most challenging, not the easiest.

They reached the huge crescent shaped building which housed adult bachelors who had chosen to work at Essence after completing their bond years. They passed through a lobby where several C3 models played chess on digital boards. A few IN2's watched news on a huge vid. A ME1 debated with a H5 about the properties of laser guns versus handguns. Ariyo glanced at the ME, feeling kinship since he was the same model that Alexander had been, but Ariyo could not publicly acknowledge that connection.

Rinji chatted about his mission as they walked down a long hallway to their dorm room which held twenty-five bunk beds, home for the AS1's when at Essence. While Rinji grabbed clothes for a shower, Ariyo unlocked his footlocker and pulled out an e-tablet. It was too bulky to carry on missions but served well when reading or writing needed to be done. He settled on his bunk and tapped in several passwords that he should not have clearance for. Soon he was scanning through the communication logs of Trisha Research Foundation. Lashana kept her infrequent messages very general, aware that the Synod may read anything she wrote. Still, Ariyo read each of her letters many times, looking for hidden meaning. He worried when she battled depression during her first year and could visualize her excited face when she opened the lab equipment he had sent. Then she had become lost in her work of splicing plant genes, becoming more like her old self.

Yet much was not told in her short letters. He resorted to hacking into the data stream to read the regular dispatches of TRF. From purchase orders, financial reports, and personal letters of co-workers, Ariyo pieced together what life was like on the harsh planet. The results worried him. There had been over a dozen accidental deaths since TRF was founded, all caused by the ruthless environment. Lashana, used to urban life, did not belong there. She could die before Ariyo even knew she had been in danger.

Ariyo finished scanning the subjects of each message. He randomly clicked on a few and peruse them. Several workers bragged to relatives about living through a close call with an ashstorm. He clicked on a marriage certificate, glancing at the names. Then his life ended, or so he felt. Yashana Kalkar had married Seth Lanneret three weeks ago. Ariyo read the certificate a dozen times, not believing his eyes. It had to be a mistake, or Seth had forced her.

Rinji came back, hair wet, suggesting it was time for lunch. Ariyo shook his head then went back to studying the logs. He reread Lashana's last letter, sent a month ago. All had seemed normal. She was excited about finishing mapping the genome for a gingerfan. Nothing hinted of trouble, no mention of the storm. He began reading letters of her co-workers, starting with the last ones sent. He found several references to an entertaining wedding party.

One named Vistula was pleased her boss had finally found love after so many years of sadness. Another called Jazzt sent his cousin an invitation to bet on when the first child would be born. There was no indication of forced marriage. If Lashana was in trouble, she would have sent a message knowing he would come immediately.

Instead there was only silence. A month of it.

Thoughts muddled, he was staring at the marriage license when Rinji came back from dinner with several brothers. Rinji tried to talk to him, but Ariyo brushed him off. Wishing to be alone, Ariyo hurried out of the room, leaving the e-tablet still opened to the marriage license. Rinji glanced at his departing brother then picked up the computer.

Emotions ablaze, Ariyo wandered about, little noticing where he went. Out of old habit, he found himself at a hanger which held the jetfighters used to train ME models. Ariyo entered the huge building using Alexander's security code then found the chief mechanic on duty.

"Which ones are ready for flight?"

"The two on the end." The HC2 model glanced curiously at Ariyo, wondering why he was there. The Hispanic models had a preference for working with technology. During their bond years, they usually served as technicians, mechanics, or weapon specialists.

Ariyo walked over to one and began climbing up to the cockpit.

"What are you doing?" yelled the mechanic, running over. "You don't have clearance to fly."

"Alpha hawk five eight two. Run the code. You will see I do have clearance." Ariyo began checking the instruments.

"But you are one of the beta's. You have had no flight training."

"Run the code."

Ariyo flipped on the engines, drowning out the mechanic's shouts. He eased the plane out of the hanger and onto the runway, turning off the radio. Without waiting for permission, he picked up speed and the plane lifted into the sky. Though it was Ariyo's first time as pilot, he felt the same confidence and excitement he had inherited from Alexander. Ariyo pointed the fighter west over the ocean. For a short time the thrill of flight blocked out Ariyo's problems. Speed. Freedom. Unbound horizon. Nothing else existed but himself and the purring jet which responded to his slightest motion.

The jet ran too smoothly, allowing Ariyo's mind to drift to Lashana. She had promised to wait. He had trusted her, never doubting, not even when Yashana had experienced fondness for Ethan. He had known Layla's love was stronger. After all, they had been married ninety-three years. In her first life, she had waited many years for his freedom. Why had she failed this time?

Ariyo's hand tightened on the control stick. He wanted an explanation from her. At least a letter admitting her betrayal. She had not even given him that much. Only silence. He turned the aircraft quickly to the right, feeling the G-forces pushing against his body. Had she forgotten him so quickly? No, their connection was too strong for her to. They had been through too much. She was for more than a wife, but his creator. Every breath he took, every thought he formed was because she formed him first.

Putting the fighter through its paces, Ariyo banked to the left then flipped the aircraft completely over. Perhaps he had placed too much faith in Lashana. She had claimed to be a compromise of her two selves, which meant she inherited both their desires and flaws. Had she so easily pushed aside memories of their many years of marriage, him tenderly caring for her as a feeble elder? He had believed her promise to wait for him. If the situation had been reversed, he would have waited forever for her. She had barely made it two years. Lashana's betrayal cut through him deeper than a blade, hurting worse than any battle wound.

The jet nosedived, heading for the ocean. Ariyo thought of Lashana allowing another to touch her, kiss her, sharing the other's bed. At the last minute, Ariyo pulled up, waves dancing in the wake of the jet's powerful engines as it skimmed near the ocean's surface. When Alexander had trained younger brethren, he had never allowed them to fly this reckless. Ariyo, though, did not care. He felt the anguish of betray, the rage of murder in his heart. If Seth had suddenly appeared in front of him, Ariyo would have killed him immediately and dealt with the consequences later.

Too bad the jetfighter could not handle space travel. He could have flown to Volodymyr, slain the interloper, and claimed Lashana as his prize. It would have also been his death sentence. The moment he went missing, the Five would alert the brethren to arrest him. If he did manage to evade capture, then the Death Force would be sent. The elite, highly trained soldiers' sole purpose was to hunt down and kill rare quintessences who went rogue. No prey had ever escaped them long. Alexander had commissioned the strike force years ago as a safety measure, never dreaming one day they might hunt him.

Two jets came up on each side of Ariyo. They flew close enough that he could see the ME pilots in the cockpits. One of them made the hand sign for *call.* Ariyo wanted to ignore him, but knew orders would be sent to shoot him down if he did not respond. He flipped on the radio.

"Flight one eight five, please respond," came a monotone voice.

"This is one eight five."

"You are ordered to return to Essence immediately."

"Yes, sir." Ariyo turned the jet back towards home, rage burning within him. As Alexander, he had taken many solo flights to clear his mind. Now he was being escorted back like a fugitive.

Ariyo landed and pulled into the hanger. Four IN models on guard duty met him, commanding him to follow. They brought him to the main office of the hanger where Jacob and Rinji waited. The guards remained outside as Ariyo walked in and saluted.

Jacob's face was expressionless. "Rinji, wait outside with the guards." Once they were alone, Jacob allowed anger to taint his voice. "What were you thinking? You know AS models have not been given flight training. Now we have to come up with a cover story for your joyride."

"Joy was not involved."

"I am sorry to hear about Lashana. Rinji was worried about you when he saw the marriage license and followed you. When he learned you had suddenly grown wings, he informed my wife."

"It was none of his business."

"Have you forgotten so quickly the rules you helped write? All strange activity is to be reported to a superior. Rinji followed protocol, which you are not doing. You cannot break rules just because you are upset."

"I needed time alone."

"Go jogging or swimming. Not stealing aircrafts." Jacob glanced at a video screen showing moving blimps of aircraft. "The way you were flying it, I was concerned you might not make it back alive."

"I am sorry if you feared the loss of a million credit jet."

"It is you I feared losing, brother. Once was enough." Jacob's e-band beeped, and he read the incoming message. "An emergency meeting of the Synod has been called because of your stunt."

"That was unnecessary."

The elder fixed Ariyo with stern eyes. "We take nothing lightly that evolves Lashana."

The four guards escorted Jacob, Ariyo, and Rinji to the Synod Chamber which was located on the fortieth floor of Richland Tower. Like the Chamber of Five, the room was circular but much larger. Amphitheater style seating for all fifty-five members plus a visitor section surrounded an open area for speakers. Barely half of the Synod had arrived. A least a dozen were off world tending to other matters. The guards stopped at the door, and Rinji hesitated until Jacob asked him to sit with Tiah in the visitors' area.

Caleb sat directly across from the entrance, Gabriel and Mason to his left, Jacob on his right. An empty seat was next, reserved for the fifth original quintessence. Though Ariyo contained Alexander's memories, the others did not consider him one of the Five. Instead, Ariyo stood in the center of the room, waiting judgment, remembering when he had sat as director watching nervous speakers defending themselves or petitioning for aid. Rarely did a sentient stand unfazed before fifty-five identical, somber faces of a full Synod. Ariyo felt no fear, only anger. If he had still been a ME model, he might have been able to calm himself enough to examine his emotions logically, forcing them under his control instead of them control him. Unfortunately, AS models were not so talented.

"Beta AS Zero Zero Four, you have taken an unauthorized flight using property of Essence Institute. How do you plead?" Caleb's voice boomed across the room.

"Guilty." Ariyo kept his face blank, despite his emotions.

"We the Synod have already decided your fate. You are hereby demoted, forbidden off world missions until further notice. You shall be a bōjutsu instructor for beginners. Do you have anything else to say?"

Ariyo met his brother's eyes. "Your judgment is sound, *director*." An understanding passed between the two. Despite his anger, Ariyo understood the logic of the decision and submitted to the wisdom of the others.

"Rinji, step forward," commanded Caleb.

The beta moved to his birthmate's side and looked up at the Five seated above him.

"You have done well bringing your brother's actions to our attention. You may have saved his life today, preventing him from further recklessness. As you have already figured out, he fell in love with Yashana. She had promised to marry him when his years of service were complete, but she has broken her vow. We will have need of your vigilant eyes in the coming weeks. Your mission until otherwise stated will be to guard Ariyo from himself. You will be his shadow, go wherever he goes, reporting directly to the Five any irregulars. Do you have questions?"

"No, sir. This mission will be successful."

Caleb looked down at Ariyo with pity in his eyes. "Dismissed."

As one, Ariyo and Rinji saluted then exited the chamber, their paces identical. Once out of earshot of the others, Rinji said, "I know you may be angry at me, but I had to report your behavior. You were very upset. I was concerned about what you might have done."

"My anger is not directed at you." Ariyo forced a smile as a peace offering to his birthmate. "I would have done the same thing if I was in your place. I do apologize that you now share my fate."

"I did not wish to have you demoted. When I talked with Tiah, she already knew about you and Yashana. Is that why you had been given only low-risk missions for a while?"

"Yes, they have not trusted me for some time. Now they have turned you into a spy for them."

"I hope, brother, you will give me no cause to report." Rinji led the way towards a small indoor courtyard with benches and flowers. "How is it you know how to fly jetfighters?"

"Special training I received when dealing with Yashana."

"You never mentioned it before." Rinji studied his birthmate, not accepting the answer. "Why would you need flight training to watch a teenager?"

"That is classified," said Jacob who had walked up behind them. The birthmates saluted. "Rinji, I need to talk with Ariyo. Then you may begin your guard duty."

The elderly quintessence led Ariyo across the tiny garden to a balcony overlooking Essence. Leaves of potted plants waved in the gentle breeze carrying the scent of salt. For a few minutes they studied the vista silently, watching sentients going about their daily lives far below them. Monorails rushed along tracks, and a distance V-shape formation of jetfighters flew over the ocean. Jacob leaned against the railing, his face showing more wrinkles than the last time Ariyo had seen him face-to-face two years ago.

"Perhaps you think our judgment cruel, but we had to protect you. We feel your grief deeply, brother."

"It is not grief I feel but rage as no quintessence has ever felt before."

"True we had never dealt with a case of adultery until now. Mind probes keep wives honest, and we, having waited fifty-seven years for the privilege to marry, treat our wives like precious jewels."

"Technically there is no adultery involved. This is Yashana's first marriage." Ariyo tried to keep his voice even, but his anger could not be hidden.

"Ah, when she spoke to us Five, she claimed to feel married to you. She has committed emotional adultery, if not physical."

Ariyo gripped the railing, white-knuckled. "If this is consoling me, you are doing a poor job."

"I leave consoling to my wife who is paid to do so. I offer understanding and perhaps hope. You may not want to hear this right now, but we believe Lashana still loves you. She chose a middle-age husband which means she still waits for your freedom."

"Getting married is not waiting. How can I look at her again without remembering her betrayal? I could never...touch her again."

"You have nearly two decades to learn how. Her profectus genes do not protect Lashana from human weaknesses. Perhaps in time you can forgive her."

"Forgive? She has tossed ninety-three years of marriage aside and taken another lover. Send me to a battlefront and you will need no others. My rage is enough to slay a regiment."

"Which is why we grounded you. Even when you were just Ariyo, you preferred violence over more peaceful solutions. A problem with all AS models. Alexander is a master strategist. The part of you that is him needs to be in control."

"Then you will remember that I know how to wait patiently, seeking the perfect time to strike down my enemies."

Chapter Twenty-seven

"I think we should use this DNA sequence to increase growth." Tula pointed at a computer monitor with a scaly hand.

"Did your mom forget to roll your egg? Too fast growth will destroy the flavor. We want fireberries to ripen to perfection." Bash had reached the height of his father. With two years training under Lashana, he had developed the reputation of a top researcher who other rockanchers came to with questions about plant genetics—except his sister who claimed she was the most talented scientist on the planet.

"We have the same mom. If she forgot to roll my egg, then she forgot yours too, which would explain why you are so dimwitted." Tula stood a few inches shorter than her brother. She lost most wrestling matches to him but held her own when it came to intellect. "Speed is more important than flavor. The point is to keep people alive."

"You're talking about the difference of two weeks. A perfect fireberry is worth the wait, putrid brain."

"Two weeks can mean life or death, shell smasher."

"Enough of the name calling," said Lashana, peering at the screen of the electrical microscope. "You're starting to make Starbelle nervous."

The siblings glanced warily at the six-inch ziker perched on the human's shoulder. Roots strongly grasped Lashana's shoulder while tentacles twined around her ear and clasped strains of her hair for balance. Lashana kept her movements slow when giving her pet a ride around the lab, an easy task to remember lately. Long ago she had learned the usefulness of Starbelle in quietening upset co-workers. Jazzt had been saved several times from beatings by those who lost money to him.

"How about a compromise? Tula, you design a version which is fast growing. Bash, you go for quality. Both versions may sell." Just a month ago the Basanti Food Administration had finally given their blessing on TRF's version of airspikes and already orders for seeds were coming from colonies in the sector and a few outside.

Carrying baskets of fireberries to be tested, Seth and Vistula walked into the lab. Seth sat his basket down then kissed his wife.

"How was the harvest today?" Lashana asked.

"A heavy harvest. The only injury was Wabash getting slightly scorched from being too close to a geyser that erupted suddenly."

"My lifemate takes too many risks," complained Vistula, placing a berry in a bin to begin a chemical analysis. "That's what attracted me to him in the first place."

Lashana suddenly winced, and Seth looked at her in concern. "Just a kick." She glided her husband's hand across her swollen belly to where the kick had been.

His face lit up. "He's very strong."

"*She* is eager to come out." They had been debating for months the sex of the child.

"Not much longer." Both excitement and worry highlighted the face of the forty-seven-year-old man. There were no doctors trained for dealing with human births on the nearest inhabited planets. Vistula had volunteered for the role of mid-wife. Both she and Seth had read all available literature on the topic, but it did little to relieve his fear of losing a second child.

Bash and Tula wrinkled their faces in disgust. The brother said, "How can mammals put up with their offspring growing like parasites inside them?"

"The gods played a cruel joke on them," answered his sister. "Instead of letting their young be kissed by the sun as they mature in their eggs, they must develop in darkness."

"I think it's a bit dark inside eggs too," said Lashana. Over the past months countless jests had been directed by rockanchers towards Lashana. She did not mind, for it was curiosity, not cruelty, behind their words.

"Dinner time." Seth carefully wiggled his fingers under Starbelle's roots. The ziker let go of Lashana's shoulder and gasped Seth's hand. He carried the ziker to her habitat, placing her beside the pool.

They headed down the corridors to the dining room where many were already eating. Seth kept near his wife, putting food on her plate and carrying her cup.

"You don't have to baby me," said Lashana for the hundredth time.

"Consider me babying the baby." Sitting across from Rook, Seth joined a conversation about the need of new satellites to increase their surveillance of Volodymyr's weather.

"We still have not replaced the satellite that went out six months ago," complained Rook. "Now we have longer blank spots where we cannot talk to teams in the field and larger areas were GPS's will not work.

"I'm trying to save enough to buy more, but the budget is pushed to its limit as it is."

"Perhaps you should gamble more often," suggested Jazzt, grinning at the idea.

"So you can win what little money I have left?"

Rook glanced at Lashana's huge stomach. "How much fatter can a human get?"

"Much more if carrying twins or triplets."

Jazzt became concerned. "Now you tell us it's possible to have multiples! I didn't include that as an option. If one is male and one female, there will be too many pool winners."

Lashana rolled her eyes. "Relax. I'm certain it's only one."

"Better be. It's bad enough that you told everyone the estimated due date before I closed the pool."

"They asked, I told. I'm not having a baby so you can make a profit. Perhaps that will teach you to stop betting on me."

The good-nature bickering continued through the meal. As Lashana stood to leave, Rook came up beside her and whispered so that only Seth, taking his wife's plate, could overhear.

"Your ziker will soon wish for a mate. Perhaps your Blackrock friend can send a male. I have been saving money and can pay for the shipment."

Lashana studied the zonner. Why was he reluctant for others not to hear his request? If he was ashamed to be asking aid from a member of another tribe, surely he could have contacted someone from his own tribe. "I'm sure Gauge would do so. I'll write her immediately."

Rook nodded and walked away. Seth and Lashana strolled back to their bedroom. Seth had taken down the partition that had separated their two tiny rooms, but the increased space was still smaller than the dorm room Lashana had at Luncaster. Instead of a cot, they slept on the floor just like the rockanchers, using a mattress stuffed with dried plant stalks. Not the most comfortable of beds, but Lashana had gotten used to it, except lately she complained about how difficult it was for her to rise with her heavy belly.

Before sleeping, she sat at the small desk and sent a message to Gauge with Rook's request. She turned to her husband sitting on the mattress. His lips were in a firm line as he studied the budget. "Is it that bad?"

"We need those satellites. Without early warnings, another ashstorm could wipe out everyone in the field. And even if we spotted the storm, we may not be able to warn them in time." He tossed his e-tablet on the blanket. "But the money isn't there, even with the sales of the airspikes."

Lashana slowly lowered herself onto the mattress. "We just put them on the market. We need to increase advertising then we will sell more. And we have two more products in the last stage at BFA. It is only a matter of time before they pass."

"We don't have the money for advertising. Word of mouth is all we have right now."

"Your reputation is very high, my gifted husband."

Lashana kissed Seth, hiding the guilt she felt. When she had been director of Essence she had a whole department who dealt with publicity, sponsored with a generous budget by the Emperor himself. She could have written to Essence asking for help but that would have brought up questions about Seth. Countless times in her mind she had pondered the words to explain her marriage, but she could not bring herself to face the Five—or Ariyo. She was certain he already knew for he had not sent a letter since her wedding. Better silence than facing his wrath.

"You're the gifted one. What you do with genes seems miraculous." Seth returned the kiss then placed a hand on her swollen stomach, smiling at the unborn child.

"Just logic applied correctly. Why does Rook believe he can't contact his tribe? It's not his fault he was enslaved."

"His is a hard case. Tribal honor is very important in their culture. Being forced into a servitude position is highly dishonorable. If he had managed to kill one or more of the pirates, he could have redeemed himself. Instead his nestmates died and he barely managed to escape himself. Until he does something grand which will bring honor to his tribe, he feels unworthy to return."

"He has saved many lives with his skillful piloting, including mine."

"Staying alive while flying is the goal of all pilots. Nothing extraordinary about that."

Lashana lay down. "Poor Rook. The opinions of others keeping him isolated from his own people." Her husband drifted asleep beside her, not knowing her comment's double meaning ate at her conscience.

Hours later she awoke, feeling a wetness. Pain stabbed through her abdomen. Gently she shook her husband awake.

"It's time."

"No harvest. Sleep longer," he mumbled.

"Baby time."

Seth sat up, sleepiness gone. "I'll get Vistula."

He returned quickly with his assistant manager. Out in the hallway peered the curious faces of Vistula's husband and children. Seth sent them off to find supplies then shut the wooden door. Lashana groaned as another wave of pain hit. Seth was instantly by her side, holding her hand.

Vistula tried to stay calm by repeating out loud the birth steps she had memorized. "Is the head coming first or the feet?"

"How am I supposed to know!" grunted Lashana, wishing now she had listened to her husband's plan of flying to a core planet, though the trip would have taken weeks and been costly. She had claimed there was too much work to be done here. Besides, there was the constant threat of pirates who occasionally looted cargo ships.

Seth moved to see. "It's too early to tell. Remember labor can last many hours."

The rockancher wrinkled her snout as Lashana groaned in pain. "Your god must hate humans to force such torture on you. It's so much easier for us."

"God does not hate us," panted Lashana. "It's just a punishment for eating a forbidden fruit."

"Some fruit."

"The price of human curiosity."

The door opened and Wabash brought in some towels. He took one look at sweaty Lashana and almost lost his dinner. Quickly he left. When Tula brought water, she wanted to stay but her mother ran her out. Each time the door opened, more faces could be seen as others gathered in the hall. Time dragged by. Lashana's groans became screams at the contractions came quicker. Seth and Vistula worked together, encouraging Lashana, timing contractions.

"A head! I see a head," said Seth. "Keep pushing."

"Is there supposed to be that much blood?" Vistula fought against nausea.

"It's normal. I've been through this before."

"How mammals have managed not to go extinct, I don't know."

Lashana screamed and pushed hard. Finally the baby dropped into Seth's waiting hands. Vistula handed him a towel which he wrapped around the bloody newborn. The reptilian looked away, disturbed, as Seth cut the umbilical cord. He then placed the infant in Lashana's waiting arms.

"We have a son."

"A son. I have born a son." Lashana gave a tired smile as she touched his tiny hands. "Nathan, I have waited for you longer than you will ever know."

Vistula began cleaning up. Then she stepped outside to announce Nathan's birth to those that had gathered—which was practically the entire population of the planet.

"What was the time?" came Jazzt's urgent voice. "Was it before or after midnight? I must know the exact minute."

"Jazzt never stops," said Lashana, drinking in the sight of Seth carefully washing their son. Seth handled the infant gingerly as if he was made of glass.

The father placed the clean baby in Lashana's arms. She held the infant to her breast to feed him, worrying if she was doing it correctly. When she felt the milk flowing, she relaxed and began humming a lullaby. As she finished the feeding, she noticed a strange expression on her husband's face and tears flowing down his cheek.

"What is wrong?"

"Nothing is wrong. All is right. For the first time."

Knowing he was thinking of Trisha and his unnamed firstborn, Lashana touched her husband's arm, drawing him to her. He sat beside her on the thin mattress and rocked their son to sleep.

Chapter Twenty-eight

A hundred young quintessences marched into a plaza. Their sober, identical faces turned to their instructor. The six-year-olds awaited their first bōjutsu lesson. The IN models reflected the physical traits of Native Americans but not of any particular tribe.

Portraying both confidence and sternness, Ariyo stood in front of the teenagers. "Hold the bō with two hands, dividing your staff into thirds."

The adolescences copied Ariyo's stance. Their faces remained blank except for their eyes revealing eagerness to learn. They have already had several years of hand-to-hand combat and gun training. Being IN models, they had a preference for specialized weapons training and a passion for sports. During free time it was common to see young IN's competing with each other in basketball, football, rugby, fencing, and a host of other physically heavy sports. IN's were an equal match with C models for combat, but because C models had been developed first, the Basanti Military preferred sending them to the battlefronts. IN's were usually assigned to military bases on planets suffering from political turmoil. As postings often lasted for years, they focused on mastering local customs, sports, and weaponry. When revolts threatened to break out, they became the peacemakers. After completing their years of bondage, many chose to keep their old jobs and marry locals, giving them the highest marriage rate of any of the models.

As Ariyo showed the youths basic stances, Rinji walked among them, giving advice as needed. Rinji enforced commands and re-demonstrating moves as the IN's practiced. It was the pattern they developed the first day Ariyo began his punishment. Rinji had been surprised at how easily his birthmate had taken to teaching. The first moment Ariyo stood in front of a class, he spoke with the authority of one who had years of experience, knowing exactly how to introduce each new move then combine it with what was already known.

When the hour ended, the youths lined up and marched away for target practice. A new group of a hundred entered, this time C3 models. As Ariyo repeated his previous lesson almost word for word, Rinji moved among the students, feeling unneeded. Ariyo was a master teacher, he only a shadow. Two years they had been doing this, and Ariyo remained aloof, sharing little of his inner thoughts with his birthmate, even when off duty. Rinji sensed a deep secrecy surrounding Ariyo. There were too many unsatisfied answers like Ariyo's claim of when he learned to fly. Rinji obeyed the commands of the Five, keeping close watch on Ariyo, wishing he could discuss his concerns with other birthmates.

The last class left, giving them free time for the rest of the evening. Using his e-band, Ariyo checked the schedule for the AF models. "They are having their first epulo lesson."

Rinji had once asked Ariyo why he closely monitored the AF's. His brother gave a vague response that Yashana had worked in the lab where they were created. Rinji felt there was more to the story. He kept silent but pondered deeply.

Ariyo and Rinji headed to the prison. They should not have clearance to enter, but when Ariyo punched in a code, the elevator took them to a sub-level where the fifty young betas watched their instructor cut his own hand then bite the upper neck of a prisoner. Quickly the instructor pulled away and held up his healed hand. The prisoner, who had been used many times before in such exercises, calmly walked back to his comrades standing in a line supervised by several guards. All the prisoners were volunteers who had chosen to take part in quintessence training exercises in exchange for shorter jail sentences.

A young AF walked up to his instructor who made a shallow cut across the boy's palm. The preteen winced but remained silent. He then bit a prisoner sitting in a chair in the middle of the room. Quickly he pulled back and held out his healed hand.

"Where you successful?" asked the teacher.

"Yes, sir. I completed what was needed." The words were a code, telling the tutor that the boy had found the memory he had been secretly instructed to seek. The prisoners, only knowing that the epulo was used for healing, remained unaware that their minds were being probed. The somber faced boy walked back to his birthmates and another took his place.

As the training continued, Ariyo became puzzled. After the prisoners and youths left, Ariyo spoke with the instructor, verifying that every AF had been successful today. Once they were back outside the prison, Rinji questioned his birthmate.

"Why were you surprised by their success? Is that not what we want?"

"This is their first attempt. Never has even half a group been triumphant the first time they seek a specific memory."

"How do you know no other group has had a perfect record?" Rinji felt irritated whenever Ariyo claimed special knowledge beyond what he should know.

"One of the areas I studied during my spare time when managing Yashana. Perhaps the AF models have stronger epulo talents than the rest of us."

"At least they lack our weakness of being too emotional."

"Showing emotions is not a weakness but a talent, as long as we remain in control of ourselves. Has it not allowed us to blend in many times with humans?"

"It has earned us the distrust of the Synod."

"Only I have their distrust." Ariyo turned to face his brother. "You and our other birthmates are highly regarded. Our model will be commissioned when our bond years are finished. I am certain of it."

"I hope you are right, brother." Their birthmates had privately discussed with Rinji their concern that Ariyo's behavior had jeopardized the Psychology Department's view of them. Punishing Ariyo may be the Syrod's forewarning that the AS line was to be discontinued.

When they arrived at their dorm room, Tadeo and several other birthmates greeted them. As Rinji listened to details of Tadeo's latest mission, he kept an eye on Ariyo quietly reading an e-tablet. Ariyo gestured him over and held out the device. Rinji glanced at the screen, concerned for Ariyo rarely shared what he read. It was a birth certificate for Nathan Lanneret, son of Yashana and Seth.

Keeping his voice low, Rinji asked, "You are not about to steal a jetfighter again, are you?"

"Not today. I feel no anger, just deep sadness." Ariyo glanced at their brothers several bunks away. "Let us walk."

Outside in the warm sunshine, Ariyo remained lost in thought for a long time. Rinji cautiously probed, hoping to find no danger to report to the Five.

"Why do you feel sad?"

"He has bested me. I would take a bullet for her, jump through fire, face a thousand foes. But I can never give her children."

"Many of our brethren have adopted children when their wives wished for offspring."

"It is not the same. We quintessences were cursed from the beginning of our creation. Designed only as males, we are the only sentient species in the entire galaxy who cannot produce biological offspring. We are products trained from birth to be weapons, never experiencing what it is like to have father or mother. There is nothing in our Canon to prepare us if we find ourselves in the position of being a parent. Roobaroo was right when she told me a race cannot be truly free until they can control their own reproduction."

"You met Ambassador Roobaroo, the one assassinated with Director Alexander?"

Ariyo paused, careful in answering. "Yes, once when Yashana was invited to a meeting with our director."

"A high honor, brother."

"How about a round of bōjutsu? I feel the need for action."

They headed to the huge gym where numerous matches were taking place. Both selected wooden bō's and stepped up to a platform with an empty mat. They sparred for several rounds, Ariyo quickly winning each bout.

Ariyo bowed, indicating the end of their match. "Do not be offended, brother, but I need a greater challenge."

Rinji watched Ariyo step down and put away his wooden staff. Ariyo headed across the huge chamber to the area where advanced fighters battled multiple opponents. After selecting a metal bō tipped with dull blades on each end, Ariyo stepped to a mat where four others waited to start a new bout. Worried, Rinji joined onlookers gathered around the platform. What was Ariyo thinking? To excel in bōjutsu took decades. All his opponents were freed quintessence over sixty years old, strong and agile. Teaching two years of beginner classes did not qualify Ariyo as a master.

The five rivals bowed to each other then the match began. Each twisted and dodged while trying to land blows against opponents. The metal staffs blurred as they twirled through the air with the force to break bones. Though the tips were dull, in the hands of an expert they were still lethal. Somehow Ariyo held his own, blocking and parrying, occasionally getting in a solid hit. Mesmerized Rinji watched until finally remembering his duty. On his e-band he sent a brief message to the Five informing them that Yashana had given birth and Ariyo was challenging bōjutsu experts.

Word quickly spread across the gym that a beta had entered a five person match, and a large crowd formed around the platform. Ariyo's feet were knocked out from under him. He rolled to dodge a blow then tripped a different rival. Before the other could recover, Ariyo had his iron tip pressed against the other's throat. A kill. The other retired from the game and Ariyo focused on another. One by one, each was defeated by the beta. Non-quintessences in the crowd cheered as the four losers bowed to Ariyo and he returned the gesture.

Rinji expected Ariyo to step down but his birthmate remained on the mat, ready for another match. Four new masters stepped forward, eager to face the youngster that dared to claim to be their equal. The bout was fast and brutal. No one held back. Blood flowed from cuts, and bones broke under crushing blows. Again Ariyo remained the last one standing. Blood trickled from a shoulder wound and he favored one leg. While his opponents sought volunteers to bite for healing, Ariyo remained on the platform, his face a stone mask.

The crowd watched him in awe. For some minutes no one dared meet his challenge. Messages had been sent to friends and new onlookers entered the gym, including several seasoned veterans. Seven masters stepped forward to accept Ariyo's challenge. A hush fell on the crowd. Never had a match included so many. Ariyo bowed to his opponents and then attacked the nearest one. Rinji watched in astonishment as his birthmate held against the others. How could anyone be that skilled? Was it anger or pride that kept Ariyo on his feet, despite his many injuries? Rinji stood near enough to hear bones break when a blow smashed against Ariyo's side. His brother fell but was quickly back up. Pain showed on his face but he would not surrender. One by one, the others were defeated and stepped down from the mat. Ariyo stood alone. Blood dripped from many cuts, and he could not put weight for long on his left leg. Still he remained on the mat, ready for another challenge.

The crowd had cheered at his victory, but when he remained for yet another round, many became mystified. He could not last another bout. Why did he not step down and heal? Did he have a death wish? Panting and grim face, he remained aloof, waiting. Silence fell on the gym and none stepped up to face him.

The back of the crowd began parting among whispers. Rinji stepped aside as Jacob, surrounded by six guards, reached the edge of the platform.

"Congratulation," said the elder. "We have been watching you on camera. I must say none have ever achieved three master-level victories back-to-back. You have earned the attention of the Synod who wish to meet with you immediately."

Ariyo stepped down among cheers from non-quintessences and admiring looks from his brethren. As he reached the floor, he wobbled. Immediately onlookers stepped forward, volunteering themselves for feeding. Ariyo bit several, careful not to drain any individual too much. Then he followed Jacob and the guards out of the gym. Rinji fell in step behind his birthmate, worried that the Synod saw Ariyo as deranged. Worse, he believed their judgment would be correct.

They entered the Synod Chamber. The meeting had been hastily called and only two thirds of the members were in attendance. In the visitor section was Tiah and several other wives of the elders. Neodites working in the publicity department controlled camera drones which flew about the room recording the meeting. Rinji turned to sit in the visitor area but Jacob waved him to the center of the room to stand beside his birthmate.

Caleb stood, gaining the attention of all. "Today we honor our brethren the AS models. They have served well in the field, saving many lives by putting themselves in countless dangers. We reward their hard work by promoting them out of beta stage and commissioning their model. From this day onward they bear all rights and duties of the brethren."

The Synod and visitors applauded. Rinji and Ariyo looked at each other in surprise, neither expecting this. No beta model had been commission while still completing their bond years.

"Step forward, Ariyo." Caleb stood before all, his wrinkled face stern. "Over the years you have earned several titles. You bear the record of highest kills for a non-war combatant. Now you have proven yourself a bōjutsu champion. You are a skilled teacher and expert warrior. My brothers and I are called the Five yet we are only four in number." Caleb gestured towards the empty seat beside Jacob. "It is time we amended that problem. Is there anyone who wishes to argue against my proposal?"

The director slowly looked around the room. None spoke. "Is it agreed that Ariyo shall be a Five?"

"It is agreed," said the Synod, speaking as one.

Shocked, Rinji looked at Ariyo, expecting to see surprise. Instead, there was calmness, almost as if his birthmate expected this.

Caleb addressed Ariyo. "As a Five, it is your duty to place your brethren above your own desires. Do you accept the heavy responsibilities of this office?"

"I do." Clothes bloody, Ariyo stood before all, quoting from the Code, "I will endeavor to always place the welfare of my brethren above myself. I will live an exemplary life, avoiding vices, protecting the weak. I will uphold our entire Code as I perform my duties." Ariyo walked up the stairs to the empty seat among the whirl of camera drones filming the historical event.

Unnoticed, Rinji moved to the visitor section. Something was wrong. Rinji felt not jealousy but shock. There were several million older quintessences more qualified to be a Five than Ariyo. A bonded quintessence should not be allowed on the council. Ariyo himself had said that the Synod distrusted him. They had held him back repeatedly, giving him low-level tasks for years. Why have they suddenly promoted him to the second highest position at Essence? And why had the AS models been commissioned so soon? The events had to be linked. Probably the beta status was removed to open the way for Ariyo's promotion. How could Ariyo be that important? Why would the Synod place a youngling in a position higher than most of them?

The meeting ended. As Ariyo stepped down to the floor, many came forward to congratulate him. Rinji watched from the shadows, disturbed.

Mason paused by Rinji and whispered, "There is a private meeting in the Chamber of Five in a few minutes. You are to be there." The elder moved away, not waiting for a reply.

Rinji became more perplexed. The Five usually summoned quintessences for either discipline measures or special assignments. He waited until most of the crowd cleared then walked behind Ariyo down the hallway to the chamber. Ariyo glanced at his birthmate but said nothing as they entered the circular room. Ariyo stood with the other Five beside the white computer pedestals. Rinji remained near the door, waiting until he was addressed.

As one, the Five turned their eyes on Rinji. Caleb said, "Step forward. You have served us well, but your duty is incomplete. You will continue to watch Ariyo, reporting any strange behavior to us."

Rinji glanced at his birthmate whose blank face revealed nothing. "Ariyo is a Five now. It would be unethical to spy on a supervisor."

"Not if Ariyo is aware you are observing him," said Gabriel. "By knowing his actions will be reported to the rest of us, he will refrain from doing anything rash."

"I wish not to argue against your wisdom, but I feel uncomfortable spying on my own birthmate. Perhaps it would be best for you to choose another."

Ariyo spoke for the first time. "Rinji should be told the whole story. He has sensed for a long time that something was amiss."

The Five met each other's eyes, silently agreeing.

Caleb explained, "My stubborn brother Alexander found a way to cheat death by passing all his memories as a mega ziphema to Ariyo. In essence, your birthmate is also our birthmate."

"How? When?" Flabbergasted, Rinji looked between Ariyo and Caleb. "After the explosion you passed out. Slept for days. But you were not anywhere near Alexander when he died."

Jacob answered, "Alexander stole his wife's memories as she died creating a mega ziphema. The memories were later passed to Yashana, almost killing her. Ariyo saved her, but at a heavy cost. Yashana is also Layla."

Rinji stood silently, fitting puzzle pieces together in his mind. Ariyo's sudden knowledge for flying planes, mastering bōjutsu, and knowing high-level passwords. After he recovered from his shock, he bowed to his birthmate. "I honor you, Ariyo, bearer of Alexander's legacy. I will serve you in any way you wish."

"Then fulfill my brothers' propose. You have seen my weaknesses. Serve as my shadow guard, keeping me balanced, protecting me from my darker self. I am capable of rage and revenge, going against the very Code I helped write. As a Five, I must think beyond myself, putting the continuation of our species above all else. I put away my own private anger and grief to serve the whole."

The other Fives nodded, accepting the pledge, welcoming their brother back as their equal.

Chapter Twenty-nine

Ariyo pushed open the double doors and entered the penthouse that had belonged to Alexander. His footsteps echoed through the airy living room. His brothers had left the suite untouched since their birthmate's death. Decorative shelves held heirlooms reflecting many cultures, each a gift to Layla or Alexander over their many decades as directors. An arched doorway opened to a balcony giving a splendid view of the ocean and Essence.

Rinji entered the room behind Ariyo. "A step up from our dorm."

"You have been assigned an apartment several floors below, much smaller than this one but large enough for a family if you wish to marry someday. You will not have much time to get used to it yet. We leave tomorrow for Bontinc. Have our few belongings brought up then you are dismissed for the night."

Rinji nodded then left, leaving Ariyo alone with haunting memories. Everywhere lingered the presence of Layla. One of the bedrooms had been turned into an office for her. Even after her death nearly sixty years later, nothing had been changed. At times Alexander had sat at her desk, reliving her memories. Tonight Ariyo was determined not to be trapped into sentimentality. Lashana had chosen to live without him.

He was a Five now, bonded in service to his race. Before he became overwhelmed with endless tasks which required his attention, he had requested leeway to investigate his own murder. The assassin had already been caught and mind probed. The perpetrator had placed the bomb on Roobaroo's ship before it arrived at Essence. He knew not his employer nor did he care. The ambassador had many enemies, any which could be responsible. The other Fives voted against Ariyo reopening the case, claiming there were no new leads. Perhaps they feared the topic would be too personal for their brother. Ariyo next asked to continue the inquiry to discover who had cloned Yashana and the other profectus. Again his brothers were reluctant. There were far worse crimes needing attention than cloning geniuses. Ariyo adamantly argued that since he had begun the investigation, he should be allowed to finish it. Eventually his brothers had agreed.

Ariyo sat on the plush sofa and turned on the huge vid. Using his new authority, he ordered a small space frigate owned by Essence Institute to prepare for departure tomorrow. A short time later Rinji arrived with several birthmates carrying Ariyo's footlocker which held all of his belongings. Bonded quintessences received no pay. The few possession they accumulated were either items assigned or given. Ariyo congratulated his brothers on their new status. They complimented his new job, but like Rinji, were hesitate, unsure why Ariyo had suddenly received such a high promotion. Still, they were proud to have a Five as a birthmate.

After they departed, Ariyo showered then slept on satin sheets in the large bed Alexander once shared with Layla. Used to narrow bunk beds with hard mattresses, Ariyo tossed and turned, half-awaking once in the night with arm outstretched, searching in vain for his lover. Angrily he pulled his hand back, drifting again into sleep where the innocent face of a youthful Layla smiled at him as she whispered the words, "I'll wait for you."

Rinji arrived early the next morning, eager to begin his first adventure as a Shadow Guard. As they flew up to the space frigate in a shuttle piloted by a ME model, Ariyo fought hard against his instinct to take over flying. There were already too many curious stares behind the courteous greetings of others. No more fodder needed to be given to the rumor mill. Ariyo must behave as an AS model, which meant not showing off his piloting skills unless absolutely necessary.

The cabin Ariyo was assigned consisted of a small bedroom and living room. After dropping off their luggage, Ariyo and Rinji toured the ship, greeting many crew members. The majority were ME birthmates who had been together their entire lives. The shipmates rotated chores of cleaning, cooking, and washing while each specialized in specific jobs such as weaponry and piloting. There were also twenty-five HC1 models who maintained the engines, shuttles, and computer systems onboard. The hive-like organization ran so smoothly than an outsider might believe the illusion that one superbeing's mind controlled dozens of identical drones.

Several days later *Dream Delusion* dropped into orbit around the core planet Bontinc. Ariyo and Rinji were shuttled down to the bustling Austin City Spaceport then rented a hover car. Zipping through thick traffic, Ariyo navigated the highways easily, pulling from memories of living in the city for several years. Leaving the metropolis, they headed north into a wild, underdeveloped landscape, eventually arriving at Bontinc Genetics Foundation. Ariyo parked the hover car near the main office building which was painted a drab brown like the many other structures across the ancient, sprawling complex.

"So this is where we began." Awe touched Rinji's voice as he stepped out of the vehicle. "I have seen it many times in our Canon, but it is different to be here. Like walking in a dream."

"It is just another cloning factory which specializes in creating bizarre animals—which we were classified as for a long time." Ariyo hardened his heart as he walked into the administration building, pretending that this was just another routine mission.

A secretary directed them to the human director who greeted them with handshakes, glancing uncertain between their identical Asian faces and military uniforms. "It has been several years since we have had visitors from Essence Institute. Are you quintessence?"

"Yes, AS1 models recently commissioned." Ariyo avoided mentioning he was a Five, wishing to evade the fanfare usually attached to visiting dignitaries. The last time Alexander had visited the planet was with Layla, gray-haired with age. Both the mayors of Austin City and the nearby town of Taylorville had given them parades and presented them with golden keys.

"Congratulation on your approved status. What can I do for you?" The director sat at the edge of his chair, studying his visitors.

"We would like complete access to your records to aid in an ongoing investigation."

"Of course. We were open and cooperative the last time your people were here. I believe they were looking into Doctor Larson who had retired a few years before."

"It is still the same investigation."

"Really? I doubt there is anything new to find. The investigators were very thorough last time."

"We will be the judge of that. Where are your archives kept?"

The director pulled up a map of the grounds on his e-tablet and pointed to an isolated building. "Here. A small warehouse which serves as storage."

Ariyo's lips pressed into a frown. "Storage? You could think of no better use for a building where two elite species were created?"

For a moment the director looked puzzled. "Ah. That's right. It used to be called the Advanced Department, but that was before I came here. BGF has long been out of experimental research. Now we keep to what is known. Best way to avoid lawsuits and investigations."

"If you wish to avoid investigations, I suggest increasing the rigidness of your hiring process." Ariyo stood, looking at an old picture on the wall of visiting Emperor Kalyuga standing with the department heads, Layla near the end of the line. "Perhaps you should open a new experimental department. BGF was once the cutting edge of genetic research. Age does not mean losing vision."

The director tilted his head, pondering. "We only hire the best and brightest, though we are competing with your Essence. Some of our employees have presented me with eccentric ideas for creating new animals which I did not want to bother the board with. Perhaps it is time to try something new."

Ariyo stood and shook the director's hand. "Good luck. Perhaps you will create the next synthetic pet to sweep the market."

"Thanks. I will call to let them know you are coming."

Ariyo drove across the campus and parked near the dull painted warehouse which once had been his home. A few skeletal bars of a swing set and the cracked concrete floor of a basketball court were the only remains of the outdoor play area once enjoyed by young quintessences. The warehouse was backdropped by a thick forest which had erased all visible traces of the military base that had existed here long before BGF bought the property. Perhaps hidden deep in the foliage still existed the ancient, overgrown garden where Alexander and Layla had met for trysts.

A sentimental wave hit Ariyo as he remembered racing his brothers through obstructs courses and along forest paths. Childhood had been full of adventure and exploring, the excitement of discovering new abilities, of pushing oneself to new limits. The universe filled with endless possibilities. Over the many decades, the Five had achieved more than they dared dreamed as kids. Still, Ariyo envied those days when dreams lacked responsibility— no, even then, when only children, they had been aware of the need to constantly prove their worth. The extinction of their species was a deep concern even for quintessence toddlers.

"Are you alright?" Rinji studied his brother's face.

"Yes. Just remembering my childhood—my first one."

They entered the building and walked down the narrow hallway to an office where several workers sat behind cluttered desks. For a moment Ariyo felt disoriented, remembering when the area served as the breakroom where the quintessences and caregivers shared meals at crowded tables.

"Can I help you?" said a fortyish woman looking up from her monitor. Her stern eyes flashed between their twin faces. "You must be the quintessence investigators. Your co-workers have already been here before to search our files."

"We want to see everything you have on Doctor Larson."

"We gave a digital copy of everything to the previous agents. There is nothing new. Perhaps it would help if you told us why he is under investigation."

"That is classified. The files, please."

The woman sighed. "Steph, show them what we have."

A friendly, heavy-set woman led them down the hall to a small room containing a table, a computer, and a few chairs. On the outdated monitor, she pulled up files of Larson. Then she left the room for a few minutes, returning with a folder filled with old printouts relating to the missing scientist.

"It is a great honor to meet quintessences for the first time." Steph looked nervous but awestruck. "Is there anything else I can help you with?"

Ariyo smiled politely as he glanced through the printouts which included the man's original job application and his retirement form. The previous investigators had visited the forwarding address provided which turned out to be an abandoned post office box. "You did not meet our brethren who came before?"

"I was out on maternity leave at the time."

"Are there newer pictures of Larson? The few you have date back nearly forty years to when he was first hired."

"We usually only take pictures for name badges. And sometimes for publicity."

"Did you ever meet him? Do you know who his friends were?"

The woman laughed. "I'm a recorder keeper, sir. Scientists rarely visit this building, let along care if we exist. We are invisible to them."

"What about at company picnics?"

Steph furrowed her brow in contemplation. "Perhaps. We do archive all photos of events after using a few in our newsletters." She moved to the computer and searched through databases, pulling up a directory for picnics snapshots. "Feel free to look, sir, but there are hundreds of photos taken by dozens of workers who voluntarily send us their favorites. I would not be able to recognize the doctor if we did have a photo of him."

"Then find someone who can recognize him. A co-worker from his department."

"I will see what I can do." Steph left the room.

Rinji leaned close to his brother. "The trail has grown cold. Even with a recent picture, it helps us little."

"I will follow any lead I can find, no matter how small." On the screen Ariyo flipped through photos showing jolly workers eating, competing in ball games, and socializing. He recognized the location as the training field where the Emperor had once came to watch Alexander and his brothers compete against the Imperial Guards. *At least one thing has remained the same after all this time*, thought Ariyo, glad the field was still is use.

Half an hour later, Steph returned with two elderly scientists from the Baby Department where eggs were fertilized with sperm that contained specific DNA ordered by parents. It took nearly another hour of searching through the photos before the co-workers spotted Larson in a group. Steph enlarged the photo then gave Ariyo a copy. The co-workers shared what they knew about Larson. He had been quiet, but friendly, becoming more aloof after his wife died from cancer, leaving him childless.

Ariyo thanked everyone then left. Back on the space frigate, he sent the photo to technicians at Essence, asking for a face match. With thousands of habited planets across the Empire containing trillions of citizens, finding someone keeping a low profile was extremely difficult. Several years ago Larson's fingerprints had been searched for in several databases but no match had been found. Ariyo pulled up the scientist's picture on his large screen in his private cabin and stared closely at the bearded face. Vaguely he felt as if he had seen the face before, but perhaps that feeling was caused by seeing photos of the younger version of Larson.

Feeling disappointment with no new leads to follow, Ariyo ordered *Dream Delusion* to return to the planet Xi'an. He had known the trip would probably be a waste of time, but he needed closure or perhaps the connection with Layla. At night her face drifted across his dreams, intertwined with memories of their shared lives.

The beeping of an incoming message awoke Ariyo. Hitting the intercom button, he heard the captain say, "We have arrived at Xi'an, sir."

"I'll take a shuttle down in the morning."

Ariyo lay in the darkness, trying to recall the dream he had been pulled from. Something to do with Layla—no Yashana. They had been walking hand in hand down a brightly lit hallway at Luncaster University, flirting. She smiled boldly as she pulled him into a corner to kiss him. Several teachers walked out of a classroom to scold them like children. Laughing, Yashana wrapped her arms around her lover, ignoring the professors. That was when beeping had awakened Ariyo. For a moment he held tightly to the vivid emotions of the dream, but they slipped away into the blackness till he was only left with the vague memory of her face and of the stern teachers over her shoulder.

Suddenly Ariyo bolted up. Why had he not noticed before? He called the technician doing the picture scan. "Run a search of every staff member at Luncaster University."

"What?" said the sleepy voice. "Are you sure, sir?"

"Yes, let me know as soon as you finish. Top priority."

Wide awake, Ariyo prowled about the room then preformed his routine morning exercises. After he judged it early enough to awake Rinji, a shuttle flew them down to Essence. Ariyo went to his suite where he restlessly read through mail. Mid-morning the technician called, confirming Ariyo's suspicions. An hour later, Ariyo and Rinji marched onto Luncaster University with a squad of C3 brethren. He went directly to the dean and gave her a list of professors who he demanded interviews with. Wellesz fussed that it would delay classes, but when Ariyo threatened to send the squad to personally seek out each professor, the dean gave in.

The one Ariyo sought was third on the list. The other names were a smoke screen to hide his real intentions. Using a small office as an integration room, Ariyo asked the first two teachers questions about their shopping habits and teaching methods then sent them on their way. Then an elderly man entered, partly scooped with age, using a cane for balance.

"Doctor Duken, take a seat," directed Ariyo.

"What is this about, soldier? I have students waiting for me." The old man settled in the nearest chair.

"Were you the advisor to Yashana Kalkar?" As he spoke, Ariyo slowly circled the seated man.

"Yes, along with several hundred other students over the years."

"I noticed that you began teaching here just a few years before Yashana attended, starting the same year when the first clone profectus arrived. And you were the advisor to every single one of them. Can you explain why?"

"Clone profectus? Here?" The wrinkled face of the man sagged. "What are you talking about?"

"Your guilt shows plainly, Doctor Larson. Shaving a beard does not change your identity. Who hired you to clone them?"

"No one hired me. You are mistaken about your facts."

Ariyo casually moved behind the man. "Who ordered you to clone the profectus?"

"No one. This is ridiculous. I have a class to teach." The man began to rise.

Quickly Ariyo grabbed the man from behind and bit, the epulo organ drilling into the professor's mind. The secrets of Larson easily unraveled before the quintessence, revealing far more than Ariyo had expected, leaving him shaken by their depth.

After Ariyo stepped away, the elderly man stared blankly for several minutes then dazingly looked around the room. "What was your last question?"

"I asked, 'What method do you use when dealing with rude freshman who believe they know more than their teachers?'"

"Ah, put the youngling in their places by throwing a lot of technical terms at them they wouldn't understand. Neither would you."

"Thank you. You have been most helpful. That will be all."

After the elderly professor shuffled out the door, Rinji entered. "Did you find what you sought?"

"Yes and no. He did clone Yashana and the others, and he did not act alone. There were others involved who kept close watch as the profectus grew, including Dean Wellesz. She made certain each was assigned Larson as an advisor. It is bigger, far bigger than we guessed." Ariyo looked away, troubled. "We will talk about this later. Send in the next one."

After the interviews were finished, Ariyo again met with the dean. Rudely polite, she demanded to be warned before the next interruption to her school. Rinji asked her questions while Ariyo pretended to be interested in a book on a shelf behind her. Then he turned suddenly and bit, searching her mind. Like Larson, she remembered nothing afterwards.

Back at Essence, Ariyo requested an immediate meeting with the Five. They gathered in their circular chamber, each standing beside a pedestal while Rinji kept guard near the door, listening but not speaking.

"I have found Doctor Larson's location." Ariyo touched his computer screen, and a hologram image of the elderly man appeared in the middle of the room. "He has been here, at Luncaster University, teaching right under our noses, advising the very profectus he helped create. Like we suspected, he did not act alone but was part of a network, a very powerful one, whose tentacles spread across many core planets." He glanced at each of his brother before saying, "The Coalition of Human Advancement."

For a long moment none spoke as each pondered the ramification of his words. The Coalition had been around in one form or another since humans first learned they were not alone in the universe. At first it had been only a philosophy that society's elite discussed among themselves. As centuries passed, devotees were drawn together, forming loose groups which debated ways to improve the human race. On some colonies, charismatic leaders drew many followers, shaping local policies and funding. Over the millenniums, various factions united into one vast, loosely organized movement that had branches located on every major planet that contained a sizeable human population. Many impressable college students joined local chapters, some for the elitism, others sought social connection, a few believing that humans were destined to evolve into higher beings. The chapters were as varied as the worlds they were located on. Several journalists published articles accusing certain members of being speciesists—discriminating against other sentient races. Other chapters where well known for charity research which aided local species.

The many branches had limited contact with each other until three centuries ago when several prominent leaders unified the factions with promises that geneticists had the capacity of evolving humans to the next level, if only galactic laws were changed. The movement built momentum, attracting top scientists, journalists, and politicians. Billions of humans across the core worlds voted into power key leaders who persuaded Emperor Anayasini to change genetic laws. For five short years it became legal for any sentient species to alter the DNA of themselves in any way they desired. A vast backlash rippled across the Empire from many species and among some humans who claimed religious or social outrage. After Anayasini died, his son's first act as Emperor was to pass the Sentient Purity Law, forbidding tampering with DNA belonging to sentients.

Those five years were enough time to allow the birth of five hundred profectus, including Layla. Because the quintessences were created by one of their own super humans, members of the Coalition of Human Advancement were quick to support Layla whenever she challenged bills of the Galactic Senate which affected her clone soldiers. Repeatedly the Coalition faced off against the powerful Ediethean High Council and their many allies, winning most battles. Deep resentment had built up between the elite on both sides, sometimes exploding into political warfare on the senate floor.

"Do you have any proof besides the mind probe?" asked Caleb.

"To arrest Larson, yes. But not any of the others—yet. I wish to learn how high the order came from. Even Larson and Wellesz do not know. I suspect hundreds may be involved. The dean was aware that several CEO's of prominent companies were deliberately offering jobs to graduating profectus. I seek permission to pursue these criminals. Grant me a warship."

Caleb took a deep breath before answering. "I applaud your success in locating the missing doctor. Now you will stand down and look to other issues which need tending to."

"There is still much which needs to be done. I must find how deeply the corruption runs before arresting Larson. We should not alert the others until we have proof."

"There will be no need for further investigation. Nor will Larson be arrested."

"Has age putrefied your mind?" Ariyo stared at his elderly brother. "Larson is a criminal. It is our responsibility to bring him and the others to justice."

"We are beseeched with requests to end genocides, restore planet-wide peace, save societies from collapse, evaluate colonies facing natural disasters, discover spies, and hunt mass murderers. Putting people on trial for creating life is not high on our priority lists."

Ariyo stepped out from behind his computer. "Since when did we begin ignoring criminal activity? That never happened while I was director."

Caleb moved into the center of the room near the hologram of the doctor. "You are too personally involved to see clearly. The Coalition has always been our biggest supporter. We cannot oppose them for a low level crime."

"Tell me, brother, when did we become the lapdogs of the Coalition? If there is one thing I believe in, it is that is no one is above the law. Not me, not you, and certainly not scientists or politicians who create the laws."

"Do we arrest everyone who commits a traffic violation? There are some laws more important than others. If the Coalition had not decided to push boundaries, Lashana would never have existed. Do you wish her erased from existence?" Caleb moved closer to Ariyo till only a few feet separated them. "Tell me, brother, is the real reason you wish to punish her creators is because you cannot punish her for the betrayal she tortures you with?"

Ariyo raised his hand to strike, his balled fist freezing only an inch from the wrinkled, unflinching face of his brother. "You know nothing about betrayal. Nor the hate I feel. Yet this is not about revenge but justice."

"You lie to yourself too well." Caleb's dark eyes held his brother captive. "Think beyond your own pain. Your rash actions will set off a chain reaction which will isolate us from our strongest allies, leaving us exposed to our enemies' plots. Do you wish to destroy all of us for your form of justice?"

"No, but we cannot turn a blind eye to injustice. To do so will make us conspirators."

Gabriel stepped forward. "Enough of this. Have you both forgotten that nothing will be done either way until we have voted?"

"I will support Alexander," said Jacob, moving to stand beside Ariyo. "We should trace this crime and hold accountable all who willingly broke the law. No one is above it."

"Normally, I would agree," said Gabriel, "but the ramifications are too great for a crime so small. We must look towards the welfare of our species first."

Four faces turned towards Mason, the only one who had remained standing by his pedestal. Mason studied both sides before saying, "Both arguments are valid. Our duty is to enforce laws even if we disagree with them. But sometimes mercy is needed. I, above all of you, know the value of that. What profit will be gained by placing teachers and scientists on trial for creating geniuses? It will rouse public anger, adding salt to an already raw wound between humans and edietheans."

"Should we end all trials then because the public might become upset?" said Ariyo. "That is not for us to decide but lawyers and judges."

Mason sighed. "Like Caleb, I believe revenge is part of your motivation. You are not honest enough with yourself to realize that. My vote is that we keep careful watch on the Coalition, but do not move against them without provocation."

"The whole Coalition is not guilty. I only seek those within it who are corrupt."

"Then watch from a distance but make no move to alert them. If their only crime was creating life, we leave them alone. If evidence arises of more serious misconduct, then we will pursue them."

Caleb caught the eye of each of his brothers. "Is it agreed?"

"It is agreed," said the others, Ariyo's voice slightly behind the others.

Chapter Thirty

Rockanchers scurried about, many on all four, hastily attempting to straighten the cluttered mess of Trisha Research Foundation, but their attempts helped little to hide the rough rock walls, half choked corridors, and endless stacks of crates. Dressed in her best outfit, Lashana stood in the middle of the cargo hold—which was the first room visitors saw—and yelled out directions at anyone within hearing. Wabash walked pass with a large, greasy axle balanced across one shoulder. Jazzt struggled with several co-workers to push a broken forklift out of the way.

"Mom, it's too late now. There is no way to hide this mess." Twelve-year-old Nabeela kneeled on the floor, shoving tools under a table. She had brown hair and eyes like her father.

"Why couldn't they have timed their visit until after the latest shipment? Half the boxes would have been gone." Lashana tried to force herself to relax, knowing her tension was putting others on edge.

"I thought the point was for them to see our daily operations." Nathan spread an old blanket over the table to act as a tablecloth. At fourteen, Nathan was tall and gangly, closely resembling his father. "We have nothing to hide."

"Except your dirty socks," giggled Yaira, nine years old, helping her older sister tuck items under the blanket. She, alone, reflected the strong Indian inheritance of her mom.

A loud bang announced the outer door of the airlock had slid into place. "Quick! Everyone to your places," yelled Lashana as rockanchers dashed about.

"We don't have official places," pointed out Vistula, walked up with her two grown offspring in tow.

"At least look official." Lashana placed her own three kids in a straight line, frowning at their patched clothing. "I told you to put on your best."

"And you told us to help with cleaning," said Nathan. "There wasn't time to do both."

The inner door of the airlock slowly slid open. Rockanchers, standing awkwardly at attention, stained to catch the first glimpse of the newcomers.

No visitors had ever drawn such preparations. Over the last decade TRF's reputation had grown as more products were approved, and orders had increased dramatically, allowing more staff to be hired. Some had only stayed a short time, while others now claimed Volodymyr as home. Seth had revoked the ban against children, and several half-grown younglings now stood beside parents. What little profit the company made was put back into research and buying new equipment.

Out of the airlock stepped Rook who had flown the shuttle to the visitor's space yacht. Seth was in deep conversation with a tall neodite, aged skin wrinkled and dull blue-grey. An elder stardancer, still slender and graceful, stood beside a long legged avian species whose piercing eyes scanned the chamber and its inhabitants. Three youthful neodites operated camera drones that flew into the room and began recording.

"They're all warm-blooded," complained Tula to her mother. "There's no way we will win. It's a set up from the beginning."

"Hush," said Vistula. "Only the best can become judges for the Zelzer." Still she tensed as the judges walked nearer.

"No humans," whispered Yaira. "Couldn't there have been at least one? Now I'll never get to see one."

"You are human, stupid," chided her sister.

"I meant someone besides us."

Lashana gave her children a warning look before smiling to the judges. As Layla, she had met many dignitaries, but never had she been more nervous. Winning the Zelzer would not only bring much needed publicity, but the million credit prize would go a long way in fixing up the place. Four other organizations had also received nominations—their research as important as Trisha. Memories of Layla accepting the award bombarded Lashana. She might still hold the record for youngest winner of the award, but the renowned contest had been rigged by the Emperor to gain support for his plans to build Essence. Over a century later, guilt still nagged at her. Though she had not been responsible for the cheating, once she found out, she continued to go along with it to protect her quintessences. This time was different. Seth's name topped the nomination, while hers was mixed in with a list of support staff who had been with Seth since the beginning. If they won, it would be because they earned it the hard way.

Seth met his wife's eyes and gave her a reassuring grin. "And this is Wabash, my field supervisor, and his lifemate Vistula who oversees the lab along with my beautiful wife Yashana."

The neodite bowed curtly. "I am Johaes Cepler."

"The Johaes Cepler?" Yaira gasped. "Who developed the Cepler Theory?"

"That would be me, child."

"Why did you have to make your theory so complex? I got a B on a test about it."

Seth quickly cut in. "This is Maria Curi, double Zelzer winner in physics and chemistry."

The sundancer formed a circle with her fingers. "May light always guide your path."

Little Yaira copied the gesture then looked at her older sister, wondering what it meant, but Nabeela only shrugged.

Without hesitation, Lashana walked forward and bowed her head, touching the circle. "Your brightness honors us."

"You know our ways." Dozens of hard spikes on Maria's head twirled slowly, showing she was pleased.

"I met sundancers when I interned at Essence Institute."

"Essence is a long ways off," said the last judge. The only clothing he wore was a fashionable cloak draped over his dark blue feathers. The talons on his feet were trimmed and painted a deep purple.

"I felt Seth's cause was worth leaving the safety of the Core worlds."

"Well said." The bright plume on his head fluffed double size. "I'm Xa Planck. We are keen to tour your facility."

"Right this way." Seth gestured towards the nearest hallway then addressed the dozens of staring rockanchers. "As you were."

Activity returned. Workers began packing shipping crates with seeds and bulbs. Without a word, Nathan climbed into a nearby forklift and expertly shifted its controls to pick up a heavy stack.

His sisters eagerly looked at their mom and whispered, "Nursery."

"Yes, but please spend more time supervising the hatchlings than playing with them."

"We will," promised the grinning girls as they hurried off.

Lashana caught up with her husband, letting him do most of the talking during the tour. The judges asked many questions while tapping notes into their e-tablets. Flying drones recorded video which would be reviewed by a large committee back home before the final decision was made. When they reached the arboretum, the judges peered closely at the plants, examining everything from the watering system to the compost bin.

Johaes frowned when he spotted a large glass cage sitting just off the floor. A dozen rodents ate and slept among the sand, rocks, and small pond of the habitation. "Pets for your children?"

"Uh, no." Seth glanced at his wife. "Food for our zikers."

Seeing the judges' puzzled looks, Lashana explained, "Zikers are plant-animals from Zon, a planet in this sector. They are raised as pets."

"Planimals as pets? Never heard of any species larger than a worm." Johaes scrutinized the habitation. "Where is it?"

"There in the corner."

All three judges peered through the glass at the bushy shrub about two feet high. Its reddish brown leaves streaked with green remained motionless.

"Looks like an ordinary plant that hasn't gotten enough sunlight," said Maria reaching over the glass to touch it.

"I would not do that if I were you," interrupted Lashana. "Their mating right now and become grumpy when disturbed."

"There's two?"

"The reddish leaves are Rocky, the male. The brown leaves belong to Starbelle. They will remain intertwined for weeks."

"Do they do anything besides sit there?"

"We feed them in the evening. You can watch later if you wish."

Seth cleared his throat. "This way, please, to our lab." As he passed his wife, he gave her an amused wink.

In the laboratory, the judges remained clinical as Vistula and Lashana explained their methods for improving plants. Tula and Bash demonstrated on a computer screen how genes where spliced. Seth passed out fireberries for the judges to munch on, but only Xa Planck found them tasteful. For dinner the judges and camera crew ate in the crowded mess hall. Seth boasted that most of the food was grown right on Volodymyr. The bland expressions of the judges showed the food was not up to their standards.

As dirty plates were being cleared away, Seth said, "Tomorrow we will fly you out to see several of our harvests. I hope you will not find your sleeping arrangements too uncomfortable. Unfortunately, we have no fancy guest rooms here."

"We want to experience what your lives are like," said Maria, "not just observe it. Our rooms will be fine. When can we see your zikers feed?"

"Uh, right now." Seth gestured Rook over who had been eating at a different table, keeping as far away from the judges as possible. "You met my chief pilot earlier when he flew you down. He is also our resident specialist in plant-animals who will answer all your questions."

The tall zonner looked uncomfortable. He only said, "This way," before leading the judges back to the arboretum. The bushy zikers had moved to the pond, letting some roots dangle in the water.

"They moved." Johaes was caught off guard.

"Zikers have a tendency to do that," said Rook, putting a small hunk of meat on a pair of long tweezers.

"I expected a plant to move much slower. That was a full six feet in just a few hours."

"They can travel fairly quickly when the need arises."

Rook reached over the glass wall and made a squeaking sound. A brown tentacle shot out from under the leaves and wrapped around the meat, pulling it away. The judges moved closer to the glass, impressed. Rook repeated the process, this time using a higher pitch squeak. A reddish tentacle pulled the meat under the leaves.

"Surely these are carnivorous plants," said Xa Planck. "We have a few on my home world."

Rook answered gruffly, "Do your plants react to sounds in different ways, recognizing between friend and foe? Do they use strategy when hunting? Can they remember and learn?"

"Then are they animals camouflage as plants?"

"No, they photosynthesis sunlight and draw water through roots, perfectly adapted to the harsh environment of my home world with its low direct sunlight and unstable water sources. To survive in the wild, all our species must actively seek out nourishment."

"There are other planimals on your planet?" Maria kneeled down to observe better.

"Several dozen species. Most are larger and far more ferocious, a few capable of killing adult zonners. Zikers were domesticated at the dawn of our race. Our hatchlings enjoy inventing games to play with them."

A furry rodent stopped on the other side of the glass from Maria and began nibbling a piece of fruit. "Why do you keep the rodents when you feed the zikers by hand?"

"Zikers will eat them sometimes, but the main purpose of zeasels is for reproduction. A mated pair of zikers will impregnate a paralyzed rodent with a bulboid which will grow inside the zeasel, eventually killing it. Then it will sprout from the body."

"A curious home world you have," said Johaes, "yet I have never heard of it."

"Zon lies near the edge of the galaxy and has not yet been nationalized by the Basanti Empire though we have requested several times." Bitterness laced Rook's words. "We are considered too primitive and backwards, having nothing to offer the Empire."

Maria stood up and formed a circle with her slender fingers. "May the unique light of your world be recognized soon."

Rook stared silently at her gesture for a moment then hesitantly said, "Thank you."

The judges took turns trying to feed the zikers, but the planimals only responded to Xa who could mimic Rook's calls exactly. Then Seth led them to their bedchambers where cots had been placed for them to sleep. For the next week the judges and camera crew were flown out to the fields to observe how crops were grown. Workers were interviewed and data complied. Despite busy schedules, every evening the judges visited the zikers.

When Starbelle finally accepted Johaes's food offering, the neodite's face lit up. "My grandchildren would love to have one of these."

"Forget the grandkids," said Xa. "I want one...no two...for myself."

"When their offspring are old enough, we could send you each one," Lashana offered, though she worried about the expense of shipping so far.

"Alas, we are forbidden gifts. Would look too much like a bribe."

Maria smiled as Rocky took her treat. "Perhaps after the contest is over, you might consider selling their offspring?"

Lashana glanced at Rook who would own half the offspring. "We'll think about that."

The next day the judges departed. For the next few weeks the rockanchers discussed the visit almost nonstop. Jazzt oversaw a betting pool for the selection of winners for all five categories of the Zelzer, with TRF getting short odds in science. Conversations with judges were analyzed, and the meaning of phrases hotly debated. Lashana's girls grilled their mom about the judges' home worlds. While working alongside his dad, Nathan never mentioned the contest. One quiet evening he confided in his mother he was worried about the deep disappointment his father would feel if his work was spurned by the committee.

Weeks turned into months, but there was only silence. Rockanchers became restless then angry, insulting the judges' ancestral bloodlines. Then one day an official message arrived. Close friends gathered around a monitor as Seth read the letter out loud. The first line was barely read before squeals of delight and back-poundings erupted.

Seth read further down. "They will send a yacht to pick us up. That will cut down dramatically on travel time. If we push it, we might make it back before the airspike harvest."

Lashana pulled up a map on the screen. "What about pirate attacks?"

"Do not worry," Rook frowned as several excited rockanchers pounded him with fists. "Their yacht was well armored with weapons. Pirates prefer picking on ships which cannot fight back."

"Forget pirates," complained Jazzt, switching the screen back to the letter. "Who are the other winners? How much money did I lose?"

"Only you would be upset we won," grinned Seth.

"I'm glad, really." Jazzt scanned the message till he found the winners' list. "I'll be out only two, three hundred credits. Perhaps I can regain it betting on a travel itinerary. Maybe pirates will delay you."

"You're going too, old friend."

"Me?" For a moment the bookie was speechless. "Rockanchers don't journey to core worlds. Too full of warm-blooders." He shivered at the mere thought.

"Since when did you start backing down from risks? I'll bet twenty credits you don't go."

Jazzt perked up. "I match your bet. You will lose, milk-drinker."

Seth patted the gambler on the back. "I hope so."

The following few weeks were filled with activity as Seth oversaw the preparation for the coming trip and the daily operation of TRF. He stressed about what would happen on Volodymyr during his month long absence. Lashana smoothed out arguments between rockanchers about who would be going on the voyage. Eventually Vistula, Wabash, Rook, Jazzt, and half a dozen others who had been with Seth since the beginning of TRF joined Lashana and her kids on the space yacht.

The trip went fairly quickly with the ship only stopping for occasional refueling. Being their first time in space, Nathan, Nabeela, and Yaira excitedly explored the yacht and pleaded at every fueling to visit the planets. By the time they reached the imperial city of Diamond on Basanti, they had several bags of souvenirs. Rook and the rockanchers were more cautious, rarely leaving the yacht, and only traveling in large groups when they did so.

Maria Curi greeted them at Diamond Spaceport and arranged for limousines to drive them to a five star hotel located near the palace. As the children oohed and aahed as they explored the luxurious suite, Lashana relaxed on the balcony overlooking the dazzling city, remembering when she had stood in almost the same spot over a hundred years ago, lonely for Alexander's companionship. An ache filled her. What would he be doing right now?

Seth walked up and wrapped his arms around her. "Some view. We don't get that on Volodymyr."

Lashana forced a smile. "Bet you never foresaw yourself visiting the Imperial Palace."

"I leave betting to Jazzt." For a while they stood in silence, watching the sun set, turning the dome roof of the palace into a glittering firestorm of colors. "Do you ever regret staying on Volodymyr?"

"Of course not. Why do you even ask me that?"

"I see a deep sadness in you at times, like right now. You are a brilliant, beautiful geneticist. I don't deserve you. Then there is the cost to our children, growing up completely away from their own species. We still don't know what impact that will have on them."

Lashana turned to her husband. "Listen to me, Seth Lanneret. I am honored to be your wife. Yes, my past makes me sad sometimes, but so does yours. We have each other, and that makes up for our loss. And we have done a fine job raising our children. They have had a good education and know much more about the real workings of the universe than kids growing up in fancy homes with everything given to them." She wrapped her arms around his neck. "I am so proud of you."

"How do you put up with an old man like me?"

"You're young to me." They kissed, lingering for a long moment.

"Hey, Mom," yelled Nabeela from indoors. "They have over two hundred channels, all live. Have you ever seen that before?"

"Yes, dear."

Seth held his wife tight as he called, "Don't get too use to it. We're only here a week."

Over the next several days, Maria and Johaes gave all the Zelzer winners a historical tour of the city. The rockanchers were as awed as the children by the ancient Tree of Serenity where the first Basanti Emperor united the planet under one government. The Science Museum staggered Rook as he tried to absorb the collected works of thousands of cultures far more advance than his own. In the Art Museum, the rockanchers crept silently on all fours under the watchful eyes of life-size statues. Little art existed in their own culture, and bright paintings attracted them. The children were fascinated by the simplest of things, a human pushing a baby stroller, a toddler holding a balloon, water bubbling from a fountain. After nearly two decades living on Volodymyr, Lashana felt almost as excited as her kids. Seth laughed with his children, enjoying their delight.

The night before the ceremony, they all went to a mall. The reptiles were flabbergasted by thousands of items which could be purchased so easily. Nabeela and Yaira dashed about, not knowing where to look first. At times Nathan walked near his parents, somber and thoughtful, other moments he became as merry as his sisters.

Back at the hotel as Lashana tucked in her daughters, Yaira started crying. "I don't want to go home. Please can't we stay? Please?"

"Yes, Mom." Nabeela sat up in bed. "This place is incredible."

Lashana struggled with guilt. Was she right to raise her kids so far away from human civilization? "I know there are many wonders here, but our home is Volodymyr."

"No trees. No flowers," sobbed Yaira. "Please, Mommy, I want to stay here. It's so beautiful. Why can't we?"

"Your father's life work is on Volodymyr. Remember, the crops we raise help many on other planets."

"What good is that when we don't get to visit those planets? I hate Volodymyr. I hate Trisha."

"Hush. That is enough. Do you want your father to hear you say that? It would hurt him."

"Sorry, Mommy. But I really want to stay."

"We must put the welfare of others before ourselves." Lashana kissed her daughters' foreheads. "In two days we head back. Now it's time to sleep."

The next morning the children were quiet and somber. After lunch, the winners had to endure several hours of interviews with media. Seth, always charismatic when talking about TRF, attracted reporters. Rook's nervousness showed with the swooshing of his broad tail whenever a reporter asked him questions. Most of the rockanchers preferred to not speak, letting Vistula answer for them. Limousines drove everyone to the Imperial Palace for the award ceremony. Distinguished celebrates and politicians greeted the winners, though the reptiles recognized few. Camera drones flew about. Seth's group was seated at several round tables, and waiters brought mouthwatering food which the rockanchers attacked happily.

Several renowned bands preformed, and the children stared wide-eyed, having never heard live music before. The host called up the technology winner who gave a long speech while pictures of his invention were displayed on the wall behind him.

The host retook the stage. "Our next category is science. This year's winner is an organization not well known among the core, but has made a major impact on outer words. Trisha Research Foundation."

The lights dimmed as the speaker left the stage among polite clapping. An image of Volodymyr appeared on the wall then was replaced with close-up clips of its rocky, volcanic surface. A narrator said, "Volodymyr, tidally locked to a red dwarf. Pounded by radiation and stellar winds. Life should not exist here at all." A close-up showed a ginger fan waving gently in the wind. "Let alone a garden."

A picture of Seth appeared. "Seth Lanneret created Trisha Research Foundation, named after his wife who starved to death along with their newborn child when famine struck Greytomb, the mining colony where he grew up." A photo of a teenager Seth and Trisha flashed on the wall.

Seth tensed, feeling uncomfortable with his life story playing out in front of a live audience on the giant screen. He had been told there would be a video but not what it contained. Lashana reached over and squeezed his hand. He relaxed and smiled at her.

The video explained the purpose of TRF. Action clips mixed with interviews showed rockanchers climbing cliffs to harvest airspikes, Wabash barely jumping out of the way of a geyser while picking fireberries, Vistula walking through the arboretum surrounded by plantings, a close-up of Rook feeding a ziker. Lashana grimaced when she saw sound bites of herself. Fortunately they were kept short, so the audience would not be bored with her technical jargon. Seth seemed everywhere, climbing cliffs, leaping among fresh lava spills, directing rockanchers, playing with hatchings alongside his giggling daughters, intensely studying data on a monitor with his wife, operating a forklift, moving heavy equipment with his son.

"The years of sacrifice have paid off," said the voice-over. "Not only has Volodymyr been transformed, but so too has Graytomb and many other outposts which can now grow enough food to support their populations."

An alien landscape appeared, orange sky backdropped by a smoking mountain range. Humans and rockanchers harvested a field of fireberries. The camera zoomed in on two children, one mammal, the other reptilian. Each pulled a berry off a plant, winked at each other, and then tossed the berries into their mouths. Grinning, they chewed as their cheeks puffed out. The scene changed to a field of gingerfans waving under a purple sky superimposed by an image of a smiling Trisha. The screen faded to black.

Drawn into the emotional story, the audience clapped enthusiastically as the lights came back on. The host called Seth's group to the stage and presented them with a gold Zelzer. The rockanchers pranced about, excited. Rook looked somberly over the cheering crowd, his tail twitching. Lashana grinned at her kids still sitting at the table. Seth handed the trophy to his wife and kissed her on the cheek.

He pulled notes out of his pocket. "We thank all those who have worked with us over the years, both our emotional and financial supporters. Without your help, none of this would have been possible. We honor our fallen comrades. The road to this place tonight has been costly in both sacrifices and lives." Seth choked up, glancing over his shoulder at the wall where Trisha's face had disappeared.

Lashana passed the trophy to Rook then stepped to the mike. "We thank the committee for selecting us. And we will continue our fight against famine."

As they moved to their seats, the crowd gave a standing ovation. When Seth drew near his children, Nathan rose from the table and embraced his crying father.

Nabeela leaned against her mother and whispered, "I understand why we must go back. It is the sacrifice we must pay."

Yaira waited until her father sat down then curled up in his lap, hugging him. "I love you, Daddy. And I love Trisha too."

The crowd settled down as the host introduced the next winner. Rook sat the heavy Zelzer in the middle of the table. Looking at Lashana, he said, "You have given me a great gift today, warm-blooder."

"And what is that?"

"For a brief moment, a zonner, the least of all sentients, stood at the center of the galaxy."

"You're welcome, cold-blooder." Lashana leaned against her husband. Surrounded by family and friends, she felt blissful.

Chapter Thirty-one

The screen paused on a close-up of father and son embracing, neither embarrassed by crying. Ariyo rewind the video and hit play. When Seth kissed Lashana, Ariyo's hand clenched into a fist. The one who had pledged her life to him stood before the galaxy as wife to another. Quintessences did not break vows, but profectus obviously did. It was anguishing watching the video, yet Ariyo could not stop himself. For eighteen years he had not seen or heard from her. Now with a touch of a button she became animated, walking and smiling—but not for him.

The video ended, and he replayed it again. Clips flashed of Seth overseeing his organization. Despite the human's age, the man was energetic, outgoing, family oriented, and well-loved by his workers. Jealousy burned in Ariyo. He lacked all those qualities except for energetic—a useful quality when mowing down your enemies. The video paused again on father and son embracing. Alexander bitterly stared. For two lifetimes he had oversaw the birth of several million quintessences and personally trained several generations. He was the closest father figure they had—yet never had he experienced the connection that Seth and Nathan had. Quintessences did not hug. And they definitely did not cry.

"How many times are you going to watch that?" spoke Rinji.

Ariyo turned, annoyed. "As many times as I wish. Why are you entering my office without knocking?"

"I'm a shadow who has no need to announce myself. How else can I see your true self if I must declare my arrival?"

"All others respect my office. Knock next time."

"I respect your position, brother. Please respect mine."

The birthmates locked eyes for a long moment. Ariyo looked away first. "Why are you here?"

"The Five sent me to remind you that the meeting started fifteen minutes ago."

Ariyo shot an irritated glare at Rinji and headed out the door. He paused outside the Chamber of Five to push his emotions into a far corner of his mind, allowing himself to become stoic. As he entered, his brothers shot him stares as reprimands for his tardiness. Rinji took his silent, customary post by the door. Ariyo moved to his computer pedestal and listened as Gabriel finished speaking about a petition sent from the losing side of a civil war on a distant planet. The Five voted unanimously to not provide aid. It would only lengthen the war whose outcome was inevitable, leading to more lives lost.

Other petitions followed. Eventually Caleb wrapped up. "Do we agree this measure should be brought before the Synod for a vote?"

"It is agreed," said the others in unison.

"Are there any other matters which need attending to tonight?"

"Yes." All eyes turned to Jacob. "There is one topic which I have pondered for a very long time. One which we avoid discussing because its impact is too terrifying. We ignore it, but it does not ignore us. It cannot be fought nor conquered."

The brothers glanced at each other, the deepest fears of each playing across their minds.

"I speak, of course, of old age. We are reaching the end of our lives."

"We are one hundred and eight-eight," said Mason. "Layla predicted our life expectance would be roughly two hundred."

"She also predicted that we would hit a stage of rapid aging in the last years. If we live to see two hundred, we shall be but shadows of ourselves now. Already the effects have begun. Can any of you deny that in the last decade your bodies have become weaker, your minds slower? What will we be like in five years? Ten? Will we know our own names or be invalids?"

Caleb asked, "Are you suggesting that it is time for us to begin choosing our successors?"

"If only our problem was that simple. Replacing one leader here, two there would be a smooth transfer of power. But because we are clones, we age together. The power of the Five will soon deteriorate to one—Alexander. Just a few years later the power of the Fifty will be zero, wiping out the entire Synod. Within a few decades every elder who lead our race since the beginning will be dead. Who will lead us then? Who can take our place? Alexander cannot bear the weight alone. The others only see him as Ariyo, a youngling barely out of beta stage. Without a strong central power, our youth will lose confidence and our enemies will jump at the opportunity to destroy us."

"Through the Canon we have passed our history and laws to our posterity," said Gabriel. "There are many excellent, middle-age brethren who can take our places."

"Static memories passed through ziphema are not enough. When dignitaries visit, will our successors know that this one will be offended by mentioning food during a meeting but another prefers snacks before beginning serous talks? A lifetime of hard earned lessons, tiny details which can mean success or failure for the continued existence of our vulnerable race will vanish with our passing. The mantle we pass to our successors may be a bane none can bear."

Caleb stepped from behind his pedestal. "You speak as if our deaths mean the end of our race. We have trained our heirs well. They will not fail us."

Refusing to back down, Jacob moved into the middle of the room. "They will fight wholeheartedly, but we have learned that the most potent weapons in politics are stealth, patience, and wisdom. What if I told you there was a way to pass our wisdom on by cheating death."

Mason moved beside Caleb, the wrinkles on his face deepening as he frowned. "Death is evitable. All must die sooner or later."

"Yet some are reborn." Jacob glanced at Ariyo. "It happened once. It can be done again."

The Five moved closer together in the middle of the room while each sought the eyes of his brothers, probing their private opinions.

Ariyo was the first to speak. "It is too dangerous. Yashana almost went insane, and I nearly lost myself."

Jacob said, "You were unprepared, exploring territory none had gone before. The next time, we will know what to expect. The process is too difficult for humans, their minds too fragile. But quintessences can handle it. If both host and giver are prepared, I believe the process will go smoothly. My faith is so strong that I volunteer myself to die first."

The others looked sharply at Jacob. "What of your wife?" asked Gabriel. "How can you wish grief on her?"

"Tiah and I have had many long discussions about this topic. We both believe this is the best opportunity to preserve our heritage. If I choose another ME model, she believes she can accept me in a new body, someone who has recently finished his bond years. After a short time of public grief, Tiah will remarry me."

Ariyo's fists clenched. "Do you think you can so easily toss aside bodies like cloaks? You are selfish, wanting this only so you may spend another lifetime with you wife. You think nothing of the host whose body you wish to steal."

"You think I would take a host by force? You know me better than that, brother." Jacob glared at Ariyo. "I will not lie that the idea of having a youthful body is appealing, but if that was the only gain from this experiment, I never would have brought it up. This is far bigger than myself or you. I have thought long about this, spending many late nights discussing it with Tiah, pondering its far-reaching impacts. I know there will be a cost to pay for immortality."

"You have no idea." Ariyo looked away, unwilling to share the anguish of his soul.

"If we can preserve our race, passing our complete knowledge to another generation, the cost is worth it. It has been the duty of us, the Five, to act as a buffer to the outside world, guiding the evolution of our race. Is it not also our duty to pass on our wisdom by shouldering the weight of immortality?"

"Where will it end?" asked Mason. "Will the Fifty also take hosts? Then every older generation as death nears? Will the evolution of our race lead to us becoming recyclers of bodies, only seeing the youth as potential hosts? They have labored fifty-seven years to become free, only to be stashed by their elders, never experiencing true freedom. Is this the legacy we will pass to them?"

"Your words are well-spoken," said Caleb. "There is great danger in such a path, leading to subversion and malevolence. If we decide to do this, it must be limited to no more than the Synod. And the secret must be guarded closely, even from our own kind."

"And who will watch you?" Rinji stepped away from the wall where he had been silently listening to the conversation. The Five turned to face him. "Forgive me for speaking, but your words disturb me. I have seen what Ariyo has endured and wish it on no other."

Caleb studied the AS model who dared interrupt his elders. "You have done well shadowing our brother and have earned our trust. Explain your concerns."

Rinji held himself rigidly. "Sirs, you speak lightly of becoming gods. I am no philosopher, but I know a bit about religions of other worlds. Many of their gods are believed to be powerful but care little for their worshippers. Perhaps they are all myths, but you will not be. Absolute power corrupts absolutely. If there is no balance, who will say when you are wrong or slipped into insanity from a faulty memory transfer? Who will be your judge?"

The Five glanced at each other before Caleb said, "What do you suggest?"

"Set limits. The Fifty should have knowledge of the memory transfer but not take part in it. Perhaps assign watchers like me who report directly to the entire Synod any eccentric behavior."

"Reluctantly I agree," said Ariyo. "I despise being watched, yet because I am, I keep my behavior in check. I may not have been here today without him." Ariyo looked directly at Rinji. "I owe you my life and my sanity."

Rinji gave a brief nod of acceptance, but kept his face impassive.

Ariyo continued, "Brothers, if you wish for immortality then the cost for you is to be shadowed the rest of your existence."

"May I question further?" asked Rinji, waiting until he was given a nod. "What if a situation arises in the future where you, in a rant of insanity, threaten to reveal secrets in public or turn violently on innocents? Will Shadow Guards have the authority to use force, even death, to enforce our laws against you? How much power will you really give us? Or are we only to be decorated bodyguards?"

The Five again shared eye contact, reading each other carefully. Then Caleb spoke for all of them. "You challenge us boldly, youngling. Will we share our authority or have you executed for opposing us? I propose that the Shadow Guard will be a secret third power who watches for corruption in both the Five and the Fifty. You will report infractions in hearings. If there is immediate danger, you have the authority to act, even if it means killing one of us. But you will then present your case before the others. If your actions are deemed wrong, you will pay the penalty of death."

Rinji bowed his head slightly. "It is well-spoken, director."

Caleb looked at his brothers. "Is it agreed that we take this plan to the Synod?"

"It is agreed," said the others.

A few days later, a closed session of the Synod met. No guests, reporters, or aides where allowed accept but Tiah and Rinji. Both Jacob and Caleb spoke of the plans then the floor was opened for debate which lasted for hours. Most embraced the idea of second life, but limiting it to only the Five aroused controversy. Had the others not also been there since near the beginning? Was it not their sweat, blood, and sacrifices which had turned Essence into a success? Their wisdom was as important for future generations as the Five.

Wearily of the debate, Ariyo stepped down from his seat and moved to the center of the room, gaining the attention of all. "Hear me, brothers, to what I have to say. Do you think that your essence is like water which can be poured into an empty jar? You forget about the one who owned the body first. He is still there. You will become a blend, never again existing exactly as you do now. A being that is both old and new, which may like and dislike simultaneously the same foods, friends, and lovers. At times you will be at war with yourself, even when the host's personality is similar to your own.

"You see immortality as a gift, but I tell you it is a curse. In hallways you will pass friends who only know you as a stranger. The secret of your identity will burn within you, but your silence is just the beginning of the cost you must pay. For those of you with adopted kids, you will have to watch them from afar, never again being their parent. Your status as an esteemed leader will be gone. Shadows will be your constant companions, watching for the slightest mistake.

"Do you think you are beyond temptation? Then heed my story. I, firstborn of all quintessences, trained you from childhood. You trusted my judgment, obeyed my commands. But what came of me? I was abandoned and betrayed, plunged into emotional chaos. Did you rejoice that I lived again? No, you stripped me of all power and assigned me a babysitter. I hold no anger towards you, for I would have done the same in your place. But it is still a bitter pill to swallow. There were times I wished for death, but you gave me responsibility instead. Your tight guardianship saved me from myself.

"The wisdom I gained from my experiences allows me to clearly say that a second life is a curse. Those who seek if for only themselves are malignant, and all measures should be taken to prevent them from succeeding. They will outlive birthmates and friends, doomed to loneness, becoming a hallow shell easily filled with bitterness. If given the choice, I would prefer to know the tranquility of death, rest from a lifetime of service. I do not believe in an afterlife, but some of our founders did including Rosetta and eventually Layla. I know that some of you also believe this way. Why would you wish to give up paradise to live in this universe again? Rest, brothers, from your labors and be at peace. Let the Five, as the first generation, bear the responsibility of all generations. Let us, alone, pay the heavy cost so others may enjoy happier lives."

Ariyo slowly scanned the chamber, looking each individual in the eyes. Some met him squarely, others looked away, shamed by the greed which had consumed them. Caleb asked for a vote. The measure passed unanimously.

Near midnight a month later Ariyo entered the large suite shared by Jacob and his wife. Elegant furniture, serene waterfalls, and robust houseplants reflected Tiah's decorating skills.

"Are you ready?" asked Ariyo to the three waiting for him.

Jacob's wrinkled hand held the strong, smooth hand of his wife. "Yes, we are."

Tiah forced a smile and squeezed her husband's fingers. "We are committed." Anxiety had faded her skin to a dull bluish-gray. Nearing middle-age, the neodite still had a gorgeous, curvy body and lush, lavender hair.

Ariyo turned his focus on Daryl, a respected air force captain barely sixty years old who had a long string of successful missions. But this was the one assignment he had almost refused. When Jacob had first asked Daryl to be a host, the ME model asked for a week to think about it, knowing that if he said no then all memories of the request would be erased from his mind. When the deadline ended, he asked for another three days. On the last day, he went to Tiah's office, seeking reassurance that a marriage was possible when they were currently strangers to each other. The psychology's words had soothed many of his concerns, but as he now faced Ariyo, his tension was palpable.

"The blend will go well, captain," said Ariyo. "You have been attentive to my instructions."

"Sir, I will do my best to not disappoint the Synod."

"Succeed or fail, the Synod is already proud of you. We understand this task is difficult, allowing another's life to become part of you."

"If it will strengthen our race, I am willing to do anything, even giving my life."

"I know, son. Come."

They walked into the bedroom. Jacob, dressed in pajamas, lay on the bed. Daryl sat beside him on the mattress. Tiah held her husband's hand tightly as Daryl bit. Unlike Alexander who had hastily, but sloppy done the first procedure, Daryl took his time, gingerly but forcefully ripping all of Jacob's memories, forming them into a super ziphema. Then he pulled it into his own mind. When Tiah felt Jacob's hand go limp, she tried vainly to stifle her cry of grief. Orange tinged her blue-gray skin.

Daryl pulled away and sat up. "It is done. The ziphema is intact."

"How do you feel?" asked Ariyo.

"Strange. Heavy. Very tired."

"That was expected. Now you should rest before you open it to begin the next stage. Rinji will meet you in the elevator and take you to a guest room where your Shadow Guard awaits."

After sending Rinji a message, Ariyo escorted Daryl to the hallway. Then he reentered the bedroom where Tiah still continued to hold her husband's hand.

Ariyo checked for a pulse. "He lives, but is unresponsive. A vegetable, like we predicted. Are you ready for the next part?"

"Give me to dawn. It will go better with our story." Tiah tucked her husband under the covers then sat on the bed beside him, studying the frail sleeper. "This is harder than I thought. He lies there, dead to me. It feels real, like I am really losing him. Perhaps I have. What if the blend does not work? Daryl may go insane, and you have to kill him. I will lose everything that is left of Jacob."

"Still you fears, doctor. Yashana was human. That was why she struggled. This blend will go well."

They sat in silence a long time, watching the rise and fall of Jacob's chest under the blanket. When dawn lightened the fringes of darkness, Tiah pulled a robe over her pajamas then buzzed the medical department. Paramedics quickly arrived, and Ariyo led them into the penthouse. With his apartment next door, no questions would be asked about why he had beaten the medical staff there.

Tiah stood near a wall, muttering, "He would not wake."

The paramedics examined Jacob. Seeing he was in a coma, they placed him on a stretcher and carried him down to the medical ward. Tiah and Ariyo followed, the neodite leaning on the quintessence for support. No acting was needed for her grief was real. Doctors labored over Jacob for a long time then placed him in an observation room. Tiah sat by her immobile husband, surrounded by monitoring machines which beeped and pinged. When several friends arrived to comfort Tiah, Ariyo slipped away.

He took an elevator up to the floor which held apartments for guests and mid-ranking officers. Rinji opened the door to Ariyo's knock, revealing a living room blandly furnished.

"How is Daryl?"

"Sleeping. He awoke long enough to say he was about to break the ziphema. Been out ever since."

Ariyo walked into the small bedroom. Tadeo quickly rose from the chair where he had been keeping watch and saluted. "Sir, he sleeps."

"We are birthmates. There is no need for saluting during informal greetings."

"Of course, sir." But Tadeo continued to stand at attention. It had been several weeks since he had been selected as a Shadow Guard, but he still wrestled with what that meant.

For quintessences there was no greater bond than that of birthmates, lovers coming in a close second. Yet Tadeo and Rinji no longer saw Ariyo as their birthmate but a reincarnation of a legendary hero.

The cost of immortality, thought Ariyo. *Never again can I share comradeship with you. If I show signs of unbalance, you may be the one required to kill me.* Grieved, Ariyo kept his dark musings to himself. After this business with Jacob was finished, he would ask Rinji not to select another AS model as a Shadow Guard, at least not from their generation.

"You may need to awaken him soon and force him to eat. Don't be concerned if he seems dazed or talks nonsense. It will pass."

"We remember what it was like when you went through it," said Rinji. "If we could handle you, dealing with him is not a problem."

"Of course. I will leave him in your capable hands." Ariyo hid his irritation at the distance that now separated him from Rinji and Tadeo.

Over the next few days, Ariyo visited Tiah early in the mornings and Daryl in the evening after the work shift was over. The tension across Essence Institute was evident, even among low-level staff. As Ariyo walked through the Grand Forum, conversations were kept quiet and groups formed around large vids showing local news. The quintessences were deeply affected as realization hit that their first generation was reaching the end of their lifecycle. It had only been hypothetical till now what dying of old age would be like. An elder warrior suddenly inflected by a coma had never been predicted. Would their lives also end this way?

On the fourth day, it was Daryl who greeted Ariyo when he knocked on the apartment door. "Good evening, brother."

"You are awake. How are you?"

"Quite well." The robust Middle Eastern model smiled. "The process was successful. Jacob and Daryl are one. How is my wife?"

"You are unmarried. *Jacob's* wife has not left his side day nor night."

"I now understand Yashana's claim that she felt married to you."

"That did not stop her from marrying another." Ariyo turned to the Shadow Guards. "How is he doing?"

"Impatient," reported Rinji. "A lot like you."

"I wish to see my wife…Tiah now," Daryl corrected himself.

"The plan was for you two to remain separated for a month. If she begins courting before you are even dead, it will raise dangerous questions, besides being highly inappropriate."

"A quick, private meeting is all I ask. She needs to see firsthand that I live. Only then can she let go. Please, brother."

Ariyo glanced at the Shadow Guards before saying, "A few minutes. That is all. Then you will keep to the plan."

"Of course. There will be no more contact between us until after the mourning period. I will keep my word."

When they reached the hospital ward, they had to wait for over an hour while other visitors ahead of them came and went. Finally a nurse announced that visitation was over. As the waiting room cleared of friends and co-workers from the psychology department, Ariyo and Daryl held back.

"You too," fussed the nurse. "Mrs. Vay needs rest."

Ariyo do not move. "I think Tiah Vay would wish to see me."

The nurse glanced at his nametag and paled. "Of course, sir. If I had known it was you, I would have let you in immediately." She looked to see Daryl's name, but he wore no tag.

"She needed to see her friends first." Ariyo offered no explanation of who Daryl was as they passed the nurse and walked into the hospital room.

Tiah sat in a chair near the bed. Her head was buried in her arms as she rested against the bed, long tresses of unbrushed hair spilled down her back. She half sat up as they entered but was too weary to glance at them. Ariyo locked the door as Daryl stepped close to the bed. For a long, quiet moment he stood beside Tiah, watching Jacob breathe as equipment collected data about the comatose patient.

"I am grateful you came." Tiah spoke in a monotone voice, not taking her eyes off her husband. Sickly orange highlighted her hands and face while the rest of her skin remained a dullish blue-gray.

"You need rest," said Daryl.

"I cannot rest while he lies this way."

"Then turn off the machines. Let him starve to death."

Tiah turned sharply towards him, the orange fading from her dull skin. "How dare you say such a thing to me!"

"I dare because I know he is but an empty shell. Let him go. Marry me instead."

"What?" She sputtered, seeking his nametag. Finding none, she peered into his eyes. "Jacob, is that you?"

"Who else would have the audacity to propose to you while your husband's heart still beats?"

She moved closer, searching for her husband in his face. "Your humor is tasteless as always. Why didn't you say who you were when you first came in?"

Daryl reached out and took her hands. "I love your color when angry. Indigo matches your hair so well."

"Is that why you like to provoke me so much? Am I nothing more than a chameleon you play with to watch its color change?" She leaned against him.

"That neodite trait always did fascinate me." Daryl wrapped his arms around her slender waist. They kissed. As their embrace became passionate, Tiah's entire body turned a rich magenta. Red highlights formed around her mouth and fingers, spreading down her throat and disappearing under her blouse.

Twice Ariyo loudly cleared his throat before the couple broke apart. "We need to go now."

"Not yet," Tiah grabbed Daryl's arm. "Stay a while."

Daryl stroked her cheek. "If it were my choice, I would stay forever. But my brother here insists we stick to the plan. We meet again a month after my funeral."

"I cannot wait that long."

Ariyo grew impatient. "I do not want to have to explain to the nurse why she is locked away from her patient. We must go."

Tiah clung to Daryl. "We could meet again, perhaps a week from now late at night. No one needs to know."

"I would and so will his Shadow Guard," grunted Ariyo. "Do not expect me to feel pity. You agreed to the plan. Now stick with it. You will follow a normal quintessence courtship. I should not have allowed this meeting. I will ensure that Tadeo will not let Daryl out of his sight again."

The red highlights faded on Tiah's skin as her voice took a professional tone. "Forgive us, Alexander. We are forgetting your loss. I spoke from four days of grief and little sleep."

"Apology accepted." The words came out harshly from Ariyo as raw anger filled him, rage not directed at Tiah but Lashana. He wrestled his emotions back under control. "Time to go."

As Daryl pulled away from Tiah, he whispered. "Feel no guilt when you order my death. That body is nothing but a husk. I am no longer there, beloved."

It took nearly a week for Jacob to die peacefully by terminal dehydration. His funeral was attended by tens of thousands who filled the parade ground. Hundreds of others across the campus gathered in front of huge vids to watch the event live. Ariyo sat on a platform with the other Five near the coffin. Each gave a short speech then Tiah spoke from her heart. Cameras zoomed in on her blue-gray face as she allowed a few tears to fall. When she stepped away from the podium, four low flying jets flew over in a V formation. As they neared Essence, the one in the middle pulled far ahead of the others, giving a traditional missing man salute. Afterwards Tiah retired to her apartment with close friends and family.

The mood over Essence remained somber for weeks. A historic turning point had occurred, marking the beginning of many deaths to come as the older generations died out. The mighty warriors who had cheated death many times with their talent of quick healing could not escape old age.

Ariyo jogged along a dirt path through the forest, Rinji ten paces behind him. Reaching a clearing, he slowed. Daryl and Tadeo stepped out from under a shade tree and joined them.

"You're late," noted Daryl, keeping pace with Ariyo.

"I had a few last minute calls to deal with. The business of the Five is unending."

"Until you die. I am enjoying this vacation quite well."

"Do not get too use to it. I do not enjoy the double work load."

"I carried your weight for you. Now is payback," Daryl challenged as he pulled ahead.

Ariyo increased his speed. The brothers raced along the path, each trying to outdo the other. Feet thumping, arms swinging, breath even. Rinji and Tadeo fell behind, sensing this was a contest they were not invited to join. The brothers turned off the main path onto a steep mountain trail which rapidly rose upward. Soon their breathing became uneven, but still they climbed, feeling the thrill of youthful bodies and pounding blood. The trail began following a winding creek. A cliff face rose up ahead of them from which tumbled a twenty foot waterfall. Without pausing, they climbed up the side of the mountain and pulled themselves up over the top, finally collapsing in a heap near the head of the falls. They waved at Rinji and Tadeo below them then enjoyed the view as their breathing returned to normal.

"I have missed this. We have not raced like this since our youth," said Jacob.

"Which youth?"

"Do not get sassy with me. I am now four years your senior."

"But I vastly outrank you, captain."

"And I out fly you. While you try to hide those joy flights you take occasionally, I had the privilege to fly at my own funeral. I was the missing man in the flyby."

"Strange, is it not, to attend one's own funeral?"

"I enjoyed the irony. Ah, how I have missed piloting—though I have been flying every week for the last forty years. What a fascinating paradox to be two beings simultaneously. I am both the captain whose has led birthmates on countless exhilarating missions, yet I am also the elder banned from the cockpit due to slowed reflexes."

"You always find humor in strange places."

"It is good to laugh at one's self."

For a while they watched the clouds moving across the sky. As the sun peeked out from behind its fluffy covering, beams kissed spray kicked up by the waterfall, creating a colorful arch.

"I should bring Tiah up here once we are married. She will enjoy it. Perhaps while we are making love, I can turn her skin rainbow."

Ariyo looked away, his fist clenched.

"Sorry, I meant not to upset you. I do not wish to rub salt into your wounds."

"It is not your fault." Ariyo forced himself to relax. "I never could have gotten Layla this far from her laboratory. She was married to her work as much as she was to me. I always had to compete against it."

"Perhaps having kids has mellowed her."

"I avoid thinking about children."

"You must start soon. In two years your bondage will be completed. Will you wait for her to come to you or seek her out?"

"She has made her decision. My place is here."

"That does answer one of our concerns. At least we will not have to worry about charging you with murder."

"If I killed her husband, she would never forgive me."

"Waiting is the best choice, but it is the hardest. She will come to you when the time is right."

"Why would I want that? I cannot be a father to her children." Ariyo picked up a stone and threw it over the falls into the pool. After a small splash, it sunk out of sight. "Am I a dog to pant and bounce about because my mistress has returned? I have no need for her nor her for me. She has a family to attend to."

"You are justified to feel angry, but when the time comes, you must forgive her. The bond between you and her is too strong for death or wayward marriage to sever."

"You have been married too long to a psychiatrist."

Jacob looked wistful. "Not nearly long enough."

Chapter Thirty-two

Surrounding a large table, six half-grown rockanchers bent over their e-tablets, furiously manipulating algebraic equations. As the timer ran down, several muttered in frustration. One cursed as he erased his work for the fourth time. The only calm one was Yaira who had finished her work within half the allotted time, double checked her answers, and now waited patiently for the test to end. She could have moved on to another assignment, but she did not want to draw attention from the others that the task was so easy for her. She already had to deal with being called the teacher's favorite. It was an unfair accusation. Was it her or her siblings' fault that they flew through the lessons while the rockanchers struggled?

"Tablets down," said Lashana, glancing at the master e-tablet in her hand. "Top score is again Yaira. Lich, ten points off for copying one of her answers."

"How could you have seen that?" fussed the youth. "You were busy helping the hatchling."

"I was going on a hunch, but you just admitted your guilt."

The rockancher opened his snout to argue further but could think of nothing to say except, "That's not fair."

"You will find that life is often unfair. There is still half an hour till lunch. For those of you who failed the test, go back and do the enrichment activity. The others will move on to the next lesson. For all who do not finish, your homework is to complete the lesson by tomorrow. If there is any file sharing, the computer will warn me." Lashana shot a dark look at Lich, who looked away guilty.

As the students worked, Lashana wandered through the rocky chamber between workstations and tables where nearly thirty youth studied, each group clustered by age. The older ones required little attention. The more frisky ones had already completed the required basic courses and quit school, preferring working with their parents in the fields. The few who remained, along with her son Nathan, worked through advance material at their own speed.

A smack followed by a yelp came from the hatchling table. Lashana turned to deal with the problem, but her daughter Nabeela was quicker. Leaving her own peers, Nabeela comforted the whimpering hatchling, discovered the culprit, and sent him to timeout. The fourteen year old had a natural talent for nurturing, and from an early age took readily to tending younglings. Lashana had come to rely heavily on her daughter as a teacher aide, which sometime led to resentment among older students who were occasionally reprimanded by Nabeela. A proper teacher would never have allowed a pupil to have authority over both her peers and older students.

Lashana, though, was not a proper teacher, yet the responsibility fell logically to her. Concerned about her own children's education, she had ordered materials to teach them. As the population of TRF exploded over the years with its growing success, other parents began asking Lashana to also instruct their offspring. At first it had been easy for her kids were well behaved, fast learners. Not so for all rockanchers. They preferred active, hands-on lessons. Few had the patience to sit for hours staring at computer screens. Colorful graphics and educational games kept the attention of the younger ones, but many older ones grew impatient, preferring real-world activities. Few had the contemplation needed to become scientists or scholars. Or perhaps Lashana lacked the skills to teach them properly. Doubt and second guessing, Lashana had soon learned, was a common companion for educators, especially those as ill-prepared as herself.

"Mom, it's noon," said Nabeela, patting a happy hatchling on the back who had successfully completed writing the alphabet.

"Right. Off with you all. Don't forget homework."

The rockanchers sprung to life, jostling to be first to lunch. Lich leaped off a table over his nestmates' heads while many hatchlings dropped to all fours to dash between the legs of older youths. A few limbs were stepped on and Nabeela went to comfort the whimperers. Nathan began shutting down each workstation.

Yaira paused by her mother. "Why didn't you release the young ones first, like you usually do?

"It slipped my mind." Lashana began straightening the room. "Did you finish your class work?"

"I always do. And I went ahead and started my biology assignment. When can I begin working at my own pace instead of being held back by the others?"

"You already take many subjects beyond them, but I need you to do at least a few things with them because…"

"…you need me to be a peer tutor. I'm not Nabeela, Mom. I don't have her patience. If they are dumb enough to fail, then let them. Lich cheated not once, but four times today."

"Why didn't you say anything?"

"Because they already make fun of me."

"They're rockanchers. That is what they do. It's not…"

"…personal. I know. But sometimes I still get tired of it."

"Mom," cut in Nathan. "After lunch I'll put in the new batteries in those older tablets. Then I'm helping Dad with the airspike harvest."

"Can I help?" asked his sister eagerly.

"No," said Lashana. "You're too young to be rock-climbing."

"Rockanchers younger than me do it all the time, and without harnesses. I promise to be careful."

"I said no." The words came out harsher than Lashana had meant. "What if there is a solar flare? Putting on a shield while hanging off a cliff is dangerous. Your brother has had a lot of experience."

"How can I ever gain experience if you never let me go?"

"Yaira, I'm not in the mood for arguing today. That is my final word."

The eleven year old pouted as she walked away towards the cafeteria. Nabeela smiled at her sister. "You can help me with egg sitting. A clutch is scheduled to hatch soon."

"No thanks. Too boring. You may sit all day and nothing happen. I'll just keep to the arboretum. At least I can make plants grow, unless Mom thinks being around Starbelle is too dangerous."

Nathan lingered, stacking several boxes on top shelves as his mom wiped off tables. Finally he moved to her side. At sixteen, he stood taller than her, closely resembling his father. "Is there something wrong, Mom? You seem distracted today."

"Wrong? No, just a little under the weather. Thanks for helping with tiding up. Go ahead and join your sisters before all the food is gone."

Alone in the cluttered classroom, Lashana stood still for a long moment, then her hands began to shake. She settled into the nearest chair, wrestling with her emotions. So certain had she been that she could navigate today without anyone the wiser, but she could not hide the turbulence from her observant son. Her lack of attention had led to several minor injuries to hatchlings in the mad rush for lunch.

"Get it together," she chided herself. "He is half a galaxy away celebrating his Day of Commendation. His freedom. He is not here."

But would he come? In the following weeks would he suddenly appear, demanding she abandon her family for him? Or challenge Seth in a battle to the death? Logically, she told herself he would do no such thing. Alexander was too strategic for foolish outburst. But he now had Ariyo's less controlled emotions. He might do anything. She was certain that he must hate her. Part of her wanted to rush to him, begging for understanding. But she could not leave her family. They were her world now. Her hands began to shake again. What if he did come here, demanding answers she could not give? Alexander was her soulmate, but Seth was the father of her children. To love one meant betraying the other.

Lashana took deep breaths, thinking of tasks which needed doing. Focus only on the now. Forget possible futures, possible nightmares—like losing her family. She rose to her feet and slowly walked to the cafeteria, now half empty. She chose a salad of dark leaves and sat with her children. Yaira walked away immediately. Nathan and Nabeela tried to pull Lashana into their conversation, but she only followed a little of it.

Seth emerged from a side passage, deep in conversation with the tiglic couple who had only worked at TRF for one month. Both were tall, with thick fur, their nimble fingers nearly twice as long as a humans. The male's mane was long and dark while the female only had fluffy fur on the crest of her head. Their clothing was plain, suitable for hard labor.

Seth grabbed a bowl of spicy soup and sat down with his family. In his early sixties, Seth kept as busy as ever, refusing to slow down.

"Where is Yaira?"

"She's upset I won't let her mountain climb. The tiglics also seem upset—again."

"Jazzt began the traditional pool of taking bets on their deaths, but they felt it was a death threat." He sighed deeply before taking a bite of a roll made from glowrock flour.

"Did you tell them it's normal rockancher behavior?"

"Of course, but they still aren't reassured. I'm going to have to ask Jazzt and the others to curb their enthusiasm for the tiglic's demises. This ancient grudge must end. These tiglics didn't enslave their race."

"Rockanchers have long memories. You knew there would be problems when you hired the tiglics."

266

"I was hoping by them working together they could see past their differences. It worked for us, didn't it?"

Lashana smiled and squeezed his hand. "It is a good dream."

"At least you made a nice profit when you won Jazzt's bet about you. I'm glad you made it twenty years."

"I am too." She leaned over and kissed her husband on the lips.

After lunch, Lashana went to the laboratory where she spent most afternoons. Lashana settled in front of an electronic microscope and peered at DNA sequences. She still helped in research despite duties as mother and teacher taking up much of her time, but the main workload fell on Vistula and her two adult children.

Vistula marched pass, reprimanding a young assistant who had gotten numbers backwards in a formula. After sending him back to redo his experiment, she peered at Lashana's monitor. "Where's your lab partner today?"

"Moping. Your grandson Lich was cheating again."

"That egg roller. I will tell Tula. She suspects he will be like his father, great laborer, bad scholar. At least his nestmates are more studious."

After giving Yaira several hours to mellow, Lashana strolled through the arboretum, pausing here and there to examine plants. She finally spotted her daughter hiding under a table in a niche between clusters of young fireberry plantings. Lashana casually arranged pots above the spot then bent down.

"Ah, there you are. Enjoying your break?"

Yaira lay on her back against the wall, stroking a young ziker resting on her stomach. "Before you complain, know that I already checked the nutrient levels, swept the walkways, and tossed some dead plants. I do know how to do my job."

"I never said you didn't."

"Yes, you did." The eleven year old changed her voice to mock her mom. "Yaira, you're too young to handle solar flares. Be like your older sister, telling on your classmates when they cheat. Why can't you be more patient with them no matter how dumb they are?"

Lashana settled on the rocky floor by the plantings. "I know it's tough being the youngest. I was a third child too."

"And you fought with them a lot. I've heard all your stories, Mom. Do you ever get tired of everything being the same?"

"I find that life is constantly in motion."

"Not here. Harvesting and planting. A sky that never changes. I'm never as good as Nathan or Nabeela, no matter how hard I try."

"You're younger. Besides, you don't need to be like them. I love you just as you are."

"You don't act like it sometimes." Yaira clicked her tongue at the ziker, and it curled tiny tentacles around her fingers. "You get angry when I complain there are no flowers or trees. Is it wrong to wish for sunsets and rivers? To walk outdoors without wearing a mask? How can you understand my longings? You and Dad grew up on such worlds."

"It is not wrong to want those things, but I wish you could be happy without resenting that there are things we cannot give you. Like it or not, your home is here."

"One day I am going to leave. Find a world with rain and snow. I have studied how they form but never seen either with my own eyes."

"When you are older and ready for college, you may go. But that day is still a long ways off." Lashana stood up and brushed off her pants. "I have work which must be done. I would appreciate if my marvelous assistant would aid me in splicing a new hybrid. I heard she is especially talented in calibrating the math."

"She is. Far better than Lich." Yaira crawled out from under the table, cuddling the ziker in one hand. After pushing the pots back in place, she followed her mother to the lab.

Dinnertime brought more drama. Seth and Nathan, both dirty from hard labor, had barely settled at a table with the rest of the family before a fight broke out between the male tiglic and a rockancher named Aak. Trays of food were sent flying and a table overturned before the combats could be subdued. Jazzt held back Aak while Rook pinned the tiglic's hands.

Angrily, Seth stood between the fighters. "What's the meaning of this? There are families trying to eat."

"He called my wife an egg scrounger," said the tiglic, trying to free himself from Rook's vise-like grip. His flashed his four fangs, displaying his fury. "We have tried to put up with the insults but this is enough. No more."

Seth glared at Aak. "Why would you say such a thing?"

"I was only implying that tiglics carry the blood cost of our enslavement."

The tiglic stopped straining. "My wife and I have never done anything to you. The war was over generations ago."

"But your ancestors still stole our eggs. We will never forgive you, warm-blooder."

"Enough!" bellowed Seth. "These tiglics are not slavers. I invited them here. They are your co-workers. You will either respect them or take the next transport off Volodymyr. Now apologize to his wife."

Aak spat out, "Never. No rockancher will kneel before a warm-blooder again."

"Then you are fired. If you cause any more problems before the next transport, I will have you locked up. Now get out of my sight."

Jazzt released his hold, and Aak stalked away through the crowd. Seth looked around the cafeteria at the crowd staring at him. Wide-eyed hatchlings clung to parents. Sobbing, the female tiglic held onto her husband.

"I am a warm-blooder. Do I also bare a blood cost?"

"No," muttered several in the crowd. "You are one of us."

"As you trust me then trust our tiglic scientists. They came here to help both your people and their own. Do you think they made the decision to live among you lightly? They sought friendship and you treat them this way. The death pool is terminated."

Jazzt stepped forward. "We meant no harm by it. It is what we do for all newcomers."

"It is a horrible thing to bet on someone's death," sputtered the female.

"I apologize if we offended you. Like Seth said, you are one of us." Jazzt held out his hand to the male. The other hesitated for a moment then shook it.

Lashana let out a sigh of relief as normalcy returned. Rockanchers began eating again. The overturned table was picked up and spilled food cleaned up. Yet the anger and hurt remained in Seth's eyes for a while. All the staff at TRF were family to him. Rarely had he fired one.

After dinner the children finished their homework then headed to bed. As Lashana looked into the bedroom her daughters shared, the girls giggled on their floor mattress as they flipped though comics on an e-tablet. The resentment Yaira had felt earlier for her older sister had vanished.

"Good night, ladies." Lashana flipped off their light.

"Night, Mom," they said in unison, turning off the computer, but keeping it close to look at once she was gone.

Lashana next checked in on her son. He sat hunch over his tablet, absorbed in a novel. "Night, son."

"Night." He flipped off the screen. "Mom, is Dad alright? He really seemed upset. I've never seen him angry like that before."

"He hates when family fights. It hurt him to fire someone."

"Tell Dad I know he did the right thing."

Lashana swallowed, feeling pride. "You are your father's son."

She walked to her bedroom next door, separated by thin partitions from her son's room on the left and her daughters on the right. The close proximity allowed her to hear if they had nightmares or needed her. Seth sat on the stuffed mattress, spreading ointment over aching muscles. Lashana sat beside him and rubbed his bare back.

"Nathan believes you were in the right firing Aak."

"What do you think?"

"If an employee cannot respect a co-worker, he should go."

"He was more than simply an employee. They all are. Aak has two cousins, an aunt, and an uncle here. His parents died three years ago and his uncle had hoped to provide a home for him here. He is a bitter youth who will not learn comradeship by me kicking him out."

"But he will learn discipline. And, perhaps, in the long run respect. What you did was right." Lashana wrapped her arms around his wiry body. "You need a vacation. We could go camping away from everyone. Just you and me—and no responsibilities for a few days."

"There is always work needing to be done."

"And others to do it. Can not a wife wish for her husband all to herself for a short time?" She kissed him, drawing him downward.

"Perhaps between harvests." He heartedly returned the kiss. "That is, if you can get away from your lab projects and students."

"I would leave everything for you."

But too much needed doing and weeks passed. New fields to break, three crops ripening at the same time, a blight threatening another. With a foreboding feeling that time was running out, Lashana took matters into her own hands. While flying out to harvest gingerfans, Rook landed the shuttle in the middle of nowhere.

"Have we broken down?" asked Seth.

"Nope, just obeying your wife, boss."

Seth looked through the cargo section to see that Lashana had already opened the latch and was unloading supplies. He unstrapped and headed towards her, passing curious rockanchers still buckled in.

"What are you doing, Yashana? We have a harvest waiting."

"And laborers to do it." She tossed a tent onto the ground beside several heavy bags of compressed oxygen tanks. "You are taking a vacation with me, like it or not."

Seth laughed. "I'm being kidnapped by my own wife."

She smiled. "I will make your captivity an enjoyable experience."

Soon Rook lifted the shuttle skyward, leaving the couple behind. For the next three days they talked for hours, hiked across landscapes never treaded on before, and slept under the everlasting twilight sky. Several times a day they called TRF, keeping updated on weather patterns and checking on their kids. When Rook finally returned for them, both were revitalized, laughing over the silliest things.

Back at base camp as laborers unloaded laden baskets, Rock called the couple into the cockpit. "I must tell you good news which may sadden you. You gave me time to return to Zon, allowing me to connect with my tribe. Because of the honor of winning the Zelzer, I could go to them with tail held high. Then zoos and collectors began trying to order zikers from me, offering extremely high prices because this is the one product that cannot be found elsewhere in the galaxy. Several of my clansmen have asked to partner with me to create a shipping company. Zon finally has an export."

"You're leaving us, then?" said Seth. "I knew the time would come when you outgrew us."

"Part of my heart will always be here. But the other part of me belongs with my people. I must go. But as my company grows, perhaps we can ship your crops."

"Of course. It would be an honor to work with you, kinsman." Seth pounded the zonner on the back.

"You can finally win a mate," said Lashana. "And have some little pilots of your own."

Rook's board tail twitched. "I would like that very much."

Seth and Lashana grabbed bags and carried supplies across the canyon floor to TRF. The airlock had barely opened before Wabash rushed up to them.

"Got visitors. A ship is in obit asking for a shuttle to be sent up."

"We're not expecting anyone," said Seth. "When did they arrive?"

Lashana's face paled and she grabbed her husband's arm. "Who is it?"

"Just a few hours ago. A yacht, luxury class. Claims to have a reporter as a passenger."

Seth sighed. "Most have the decency to ask weeks in advance for a tour. I'll ask Rook if he is up to another flight. Are you alright, Yashana?"

"Of course. I'll go check on the children."

She walked away, forcing herself to breathe deeply. Hearing that one word *visitor* had threatened to tear apart the life she had created. She had to get over the paranoia Ariyo would come. She found Nathan in the classroom working by himself on an advanced class he was taking for college credit.

"Mom, you're back. The update for *Encyclopedia of Everything* you ordered finished downloading to the server yesterday. I ran a diagnostic to ensure its working."

"Thanks. Lich won't have an excuse to not finish his report this time."

"How was the trip?"

"Enjoyable. Where are your sisters?"

"They were here for a while. Try the nursery."

Lashana found her daughters cooing over newborns then she headed to the lab, losing herself in statistics. Several hours later, she did not even glance up when Seth entered, escorting a well-dressed man.

"Yashana, this is Alberto Fairbank, reporter for *Galactic Times*. Winner three times of the Peaberg Award in journalism. Alberto, my wife."

She pulled her attention from the monitor and stared at the tall, dark-haired visitor. "You're human."

"Yes, the last time I checked."

"Sorry, I don't mean to be rude." Lashana extended her hand in greeting. "It's a rarity for humans to visit."

"With the fame of winning the Zelzer, I would have thought you would have hundreds employed here."

"Solar radiation and a thin oxygen atmosphere is a big turn off for *Homo sapiens* when job hunting."

The reporter scrutinized her. "Yet you settled here."

"I found a husband who can turn a desert into a garden."

"A fine job he has done, though I believe you had something to do with that. If you have spare time later, can I interview you?"

"Sure, perhaps after dinner."

Lashana returned to her work, forgetting about the reporter. At dinner Alberto sat with her family, jesting comfortably with the rockanchers. The children quizzed him endlessly about life beyond Volodymyr. Jazzt bet him when the next solar flare would take place. The meal over, Lashana took Alberto to her husband's cluttered office.

The questions followed the normal pattern. What led you to become a geneticist? Why did you become involved in the Trisha project? How do you alter the plants? Lashana wrapped up explaining the concept of splicing genes from various plants to create a better, new product.

"Has being a profectus had an impact on the direction of your research?"

"It gives me higher intelligence to deal with certain problems such as DNA alterations, but its little help when your child is crying over a nightmare. They want comfort, not logic."

"How long have you been aware that you carry the profectus gene?"

"Excuse me?" Lashana blinked, now only becoming aware of the trap she had blindly walked into.

"From your last comment, you acknowledged awareness of your unique make-up. Perhaps with your specialty in genetics, you could explain this to me." Alberto pulled up two pictures on his e-tablet then turned them to face her. "The one to the right is you at the Zelzer ceremony. The other is of Layla Rangan accepting the same reward over a hundred and fifty years ago. Can you explain why you look identical to her?"

Lashana forced a laugh. "All Indians look alike to outsiders."

"I ran the pictures through three face recognition programs, each confirming it was the same person."

For a long moment, Lashana considered what to say. "What do you want, Mr. Fairbank?"

"The truth. That is all."

"Yet you used lies to come into my home, befriend my family, and try to manipulate me."

"I did not lie. I am writing a story about TRF to appear in an upcoming technology issue. But that is not the only story I am working on. I do know you are not the only clone. I am sure you are aware that an old classmate of yours, Ethan Covey, won a Zelzer just a few months ago for developing robotic animals for the handicapped."

"We have kept in touch. I am proud of his achievements which help others."

"Where you aware that he is also a profectus? In fact, a clone of Richard Cambridge, renown for being both a visionary programmer and humanitarian."

"Why would I know that?" Lashana tried to keep her breathing even, but the paleness of her face revealed too much.

"You are not on trial, Mrs. Lanneret. I applaud the accomplishments you and your husband have achieved. I regularly cover the Zelzer ceremonies and was there when your team won. While writing a sidebar comparing new winners to those who came before, I began noticing an unnatural number of parallels between you and Layla, besides the face. You both chose the same major, attended the same college, even were born on the same planet. And most strangely of all, you both came from enhanced embryos ordered from Bontinc Genetics Foundation. When my editor saw my research, she cut the sidebar, saying it was too hokey-pokey. But I knew differently. When Ethan won the Zelzer recently, I began probing again, finding similar patterns. Someone went through a lot of trouble to create you both. Why?"

"How am I supposed to know? Did I choose my own existence?"

"Ethan was caught completely unaware when I asked him about his genes. But I can tell that you know something."

Lashana swallowed. "You told Ethan? Why would you want to destroy his life like that?"

"Destroy? After he got over the shock, he was flattered. Even volunteered for a DNA test which confirmed my suspicions of cloning. Being established as one of the smartest humans our race has ever known enhanced his ego quite a bit."

"Sounds like him. Still, he wrote nothing about this to me."

"He is waiting till my article comes out before going public, even believes it will boost his stock prices. Before I publish, I would like to know who was behind your creation."

Lashana glanced at a photo of her family. "Kill the article."

"That I won't do. I have learned that you worked at Essence Institute after an arrest as a minor. I have asked to see those records but they are sealed. Ethan claims he is forbidden to talk about the incident, yet he did lead me to some interesting posts by a hacker named Prankster Brainster. Fascinating braggart. Did you really break into a maximum security prison?"

Lashana leaned forward. "I am not an article for you to win another award. I am a mom who will protect her family at any cost. Kill the article."

"Ethan is fine with it, but even if he was not, it is time for the universe to know the truth. You don't have the power to stop that."

"You might be surprised."

"Do you think I am the only reporter who noticed the photos? There could be dozens or hundreds of others who have not taken the time to fly to this netherworld for a friendly visit. At any moment any of a thousand publications may carry the story. How do you plan to stop us all? You can either help by telling your story or stand out of the way. Either way, the story will break."

Lashana sighed. "I can tell you nothing, but when you arrive home, call Essence for an interview."

"I tried that before. They refused."

"They won't this time. I guarantee it."

Chapter Thirty-three

Ariyo stared at the encrypted message on his screen. "Urgent. Open immediately." For eighteen years she had sent him nothing. Now just a few weeks after his commencement, she suddenly had broken the silence. Ariyo held his finger over the subject line but did not open it. What if it was a demand he should never see her again? Or perhaps an invitation to visit? Both possibilities sent his emotions into chaos. No use just staring at the title. He click it.

"*Galactic Times* reporter Alberto Fairbank visited. Asking dangerous questions about cloning. I'm sending him to you. Silence him."

That was it. No "Congratulation for finishing your bond years" or "Sorry I broke my vows to you." Anger and grief washed over him, but he pushed them back. Now was not the time. Lashana would not have sent the message unless she truly believed the reporter was a threat. The last line had a double meaning. Did she want him to pressure the reporter to be quiet, wipe his memory, or kill him? Layla had been no murderer, yet she had ordered the executions of wayward quintessences. Perhaps Lashana had changed for the worse.

Before Ariyo could choose a course of action, he needed to know more about this reporter. After an afternoon of investigating, he sent an open invitation to the man. A few days later Alberto accepted, though it was several weeks before the meeting took place.

Rinji let the reporter in then stood silently near a decorative bookcase as Ariyo greeted the man. Passing the couches surrounding the large vid, Ariyo led him to the marble desk and took a seat behind it. Refusing to show intimidation, Alberto sat across from him.

"Spacious office with a great view. More luxurious than most yachts I've booked. Being a Five must pay well."

"Being a bonded quintessence does not. I invited you here to discuss a mural acquaintance whom you seem to think is a clone."

"Don't believe in small talk first, I see. And I don't think, I know she is. Along with Ethan Covey who voluntarily provided samples for a DNA analysis. I have the hard data to prove my claims."

"Unfortunately for you, the galaxy will never see that proof."

Alberto leaned forward, eyes challenging. "Are you planning to kill me? Is that the military's answer for everything? Shoot me if you like, but the article has already been written. If I don't show back up at work, my publisher will print it tomorrow."

"You came prepared."

"I didn't win three Peaberg Awards by being a pansy. Someone powerful has to be behind the cloning. Yashana knew something, but she wouldn't talk."

"She is under a silence gag by my orders."

"Ah, so we come closer to the heart of the matter. Huge facility you have here. Said to be the largest and most avant-garde in the universe. Plenty of labs where any experiment could be done. Such as, say, cloning profectus."

"Nice guess, but you are wrong. We were not aware of Yashana's existence until her mid-teens."

"That would be when she and Ethan broke into your prison?"

"That is classified, along with all information you have discovered." Ariyo picked up an official folder off his desk and passed it to Alberto. "You will notice the imperial seal. This is an executive order for an oncoming investigation. You are commanded to turn over all evidence you have discovered. You will publish nothing about this topic nor speak to anyone else about it."

For the first time, Alberto's confidence wavered as he broke the seal and scanned the documents. "And what happens if I refuse?"

"I will kill you," Ariyo said matter-of-factly. "I must obey Emperor Sereyasi's orders. After all, he pays for my spacious office."

The reporter stared at the documents then leaned back in his leather chair. He glanced at Rinji standing against a wall, noticing his belted gun. "My ex-wife always said I was too ambitious and would one day bite off more than I could handle. She left me for a baker. Now she has five kids and a mortgage. Claims to be happy." Alberto gave a bitter laugh. "I never could back down from a challenge. Told her that even if it killed me, I would always win."

"I will ensure that your death is quick and painless."

"Polite even in murder." He tossed the folder back on the desk. "I have fought corruption all my life. I have taken down major CEO's, politicians, even a pop star. That actually was the one that got me the most death threats. Now it seems I must face off against a despotic emperor. Kill me but you cannot kill my story. I have many backups sent to numerous comrades. This story will see the light of day."

Ariyo allowed a smile to play across his face. "Congratulations. You passed my test. Few do."

"A test?" The reporter frowned, expecting a gun or knife to suddenly appear. When nothing happened, he relaxed slightly. "The executive order was fake?"

"No, it is quite real. And if you do attempt to publish while our investigation is ongoing, I will kill you."

"Then how is this a win for me?"

"I said *while* the investigation is ongoing. It will end. Hopefully soon with your help. Then you have a story which tops anything that has appeared in media for over a century, guaranteeing another Peaberg."

Alberto leaned forward cautiously. "And what, I pray tell, would make the story of the century?"

"Reporting on corruption rotting the center of the Coalition of Human Advancement."

"The Coalition? They're behind the cloning? A least a third of our humans politicians are members. Along with many of our top scientists, philosophers, businessmen, and reporters. Damn, I was president of my college chapter."

"I know. I did some investigating of my own about you. I had to be certain you were not sent by them. I have need of a man with integrity. With you contacts and influence, you can get in deep, find names of the top culprits who ordered the cloning."

"Sounds like my kind of story. But if I am to help you, then you must tell me everything you know. Agreed?"

"Agreed." Ariyo pulled up pictures of the other cloned profectus on his computer screen, enjoying watching the reporter mouth hang speechless.

Finally Alberto sputtered, "This is bigger, much bigger than I thought."

Ariyo gave Alberto a list of names to focus on.

Once the reporter left, only then did Rinji step into the middle of the room to challenge his birthmate. "The Five commanded you to investigate from a distance."

"This meets their requirements. We remain in the background while my mole digs out the truth."

"If he finds what you seek, you will force our hand against the Coalition for cloning, yet as a clone race, we see this as trivial criminal activity. All you will do is hurt Lashana and others while alienating us from our biggest political supporter."

"My intuition from two centuries of living tells me that there is more going on than a simple science experiment. I know much more about human nature than you, as I was married to one. They are prone to pride, delusions, and betrayal."

"Quintessences are not completely immune to those vices."

Ariyo turned back to his monitor and sent Lashana a short message, "Containment sealed." Most likely he would receive no thanks back.

Then the wait began. Weeks crawled by. Alberto sent occasional tidbits. Then one day gold. Ariyo called for a closed meeting with the Synod, not bothering to inform the Five of his purpose. He stood in the middle of the large, round chamber and introduced an audio recording.

"What you are about to hear is a conversation secretly taped by investigator reporter Alberto Fairbanks dinning at a lounge with Norm Baldwick, a business CEO and president of a chapter of the Coalition." Ariyo moved to his seat and let the recording play.

For several minutes there was small talk about family, stock prices, and sports. Tinkling of ice could be heard as the men drank, along with background noises of other diners.

Then Alberto strong voice said, "Too bad things are not like it was in the older days, when we had profectus calling the shots. I remember a particular one which made a killing predicating the stock markets. Was he ever wrong?"

Norm laughed, "Rarely. My great-grandfather was a true genus. It's a shame that the profectus gene is recessive."

"So your blood runs with the gene but it does you no good. How messed up is that?"

"I got an excellent deal from it. Inherited his company and his good looks." Both men laughed then Norm's voice dropped down to a whisper. "I'll tell you a secret. I have arranged my daughter's marriage to another profectus carrier. Who knows, my grandchildren might be the bona fide thing."

Ice clang as Norm sat his glass down. "Isn't she only ten?"

"Yes, and her husband is eight. It will be some time before there are grandkids, of course, but some of us are tired of waiting for a profectus to be born naturally. We have to take matters into our own hands."

"Who am I to judge? Arranged marriages are normal in many societies. I wish your daughter all the best. Still, with the gene being recessive, the chance of her birthing a profectus is, what, twenty-five percent? Odds I wouldn't bet on. Surely there is an easier way than marrying off a child who might rebel as a teenager."

"She knows her duty." Norm sat his glass down heavily on the table. "There are others who have tried a different method. Crude in its randomness, but it is working."

Alberto's voice dropped. "What do you mean?"

"New profectus, or perhaps I should say, recycling the old ones. We cloned some of them then sent them unprepared off into the galaxy. With the first generation, we told them about their destiny and they rose to embrace it, altering almost every institution of our society. But with this batch, they were told nothing. Some of us believed because they are profectus they would automatically rise to greatness. But what have we achieved? Robotic dogs for the blind, hybrid crops, a pop star, and a serial killer awaiting execution."

"Besides the murderer, are not the other jobs honorable? Even singers can touch lives."

"If it was just human lives affected, I would not complain. Those crops are being used mainly by reptiles, allowing them to build up their societies. We have enough talking fish and birds to compete with, the least we need are well fed lizards. We've been working for some time to keep them out of the Galactic Senate. The first generation of profectus knew their place, giving us super weapons, advance technology, stretching our knowledge of the sciences. Some built cities, others societies. Our top achiever gave us a splendid prize—a warrior race created just for us, completely at our command. The populace's terror of them allows us to control the entire galaxy."

"Not to sound pessimistic, but I thought the quintessences were commanded by the Galactic Senate and the Emperor."

"We and our allies hold the majority vote. There is nothing those arrogant Edietheans can do about it. They once held the power, but after we turned Emperor Anayasini to our cause and he allowed the first generation to be born, the Edietheans have been sliding into oblivion ever since. They smell their own blood, and are becoming desperate."

"You sound more like a politician than a businessman."

Norm laughed. "We all have our place in the Great Plan. Mine is to make money—and natural born profectus. By guiding a super-genius from his first breath, anything could be achieved. Perhaps in a few generations, there will be a profectus controlling human destiny from the imperial throne."

"To dreams of grander." The men's glasses clanged together.

The recording ended. Ariyo wanted a few minutes for the impact of the words to sink in. Then he stood before his brethren. Looking Caleb directly in the eyes, he said, "I ask permission to launch a thorough investigation of the Coalition, using all means in our power."

Caleb stared back at his brother. He did not like being forced into this position, but the implications in the recording were far reaching. Political powers in the Galactic Senate could tilt too much one direction, leading to civil war. Caleb looked at his brethren waiting for his reaction. "I agree there should be further investigation. Is it agreed?"

As one, the Synod responded, "It is agreed."

Later that day Ariyo inspected the African models. The fifty quintessences stood at attention, faces impassive, muscles harden, eyes tracking his every moment. The AF models' effectiveness at mind probing exceeded elders far older than them. Ariyo had overseen their training, focusing on developing their talents. Each had been sent on low-level missions where blending in with humans was a requirement. They were the least emotional of all the models and found it difficult to pretend to be human. With practice, they were becoming better.

Ariyo slowly walked down the rows of youths. "Brethren, your last round of missions went well overall, but there is still room for improvement. To be successful as spies, you must be able to adapt quickly, change body language, and speak local dialects. It can be beneficial to smile and laugh occasionally. This helps your subject to relax, letting his guard down." He moved to the front of the group. "The Synod is pleased with your progress. And so am I. Currently we foresee no obstacle in having your model commissioned someday. When that happens, production will be kept limited, like my own model. There is power in great numbers, but there is also power in stealth, which is what we possess. A few of you I have selected to work in a special unit with me. Dubaku and Kunto step forward. The rest, dismissed."

As the others walked away, Dubaku and Kunto remained at attention with hands behind back, faces somber.

"Soldiers, you will work with me on one of the most critical investigations Essence has ever dealt with. Stealth is vital. I will be placing heavy responsibilities upon you. Do you think you can handle it or should I choose others?"

"We can handle it, sir," both said in unison, voices strong.

Their faces stayed stoic but their eyes showed pride. To work with a Five was a high honor, for it to be Ariyo, even better. He had been a beta like them, but was now a Five. Since their birth, he had guided them, becoming the closest thing they had to a father figure. Their greatest desire was to please him. Ariyo's influence was so strong that if he ever ordered them on a suicide mission, they would obey without hesitation.

Chapter Thirty-four

Waves lapped against white sand of a tropical island resort. Long-legged birds dashed through sea foam, snatching up crustaceans. The engine of a small space yacht raced, preparing for lift off. Another ship circled in the sky above, readying for landing. Staff carried luggage of guests down paved walkways to hut-styled bungalows. A gardener weeded in a flowerbed bordering a massage parlor. Long, shaggy hair half hid his eyes. His pants were stained with dirt. As his hands moved through the flowers, his eyes roved the landscape, watching sunbathers on the beach, children giggling under sprinklers, and waiters carrying drinks to relaxing guests.

Ariyo paused in his weeding to wipe sweat from his brow, and to make eye contact with Rinji, dressed as a waiter, carrying cocktails to a customer. Rinji's eyes shifted to the right, and Ariyo followed, seeing Dubaku walking up to a blond woman in a bikini. Reclining in a chair, she was engrossed in work on her e-tablet.

"Pretty lady, get a massage, right here. Twenty percent off just because I like your eyes. Tell them, Lucky sent you." Dubaku's accent, fake goatee, and long dreadlocks altered his appearance dramatic enough that if his birthmate had been standing beside him, no one would have noticed they were twins. "It's happy hour, so you'll get another ten percent off. Hurry now."

The woman took a drink from Rinji's tray. "I just might take you up on that." She went back to reading her e-tablet. After she finished the drink, she put her computer in sleep mode and walked into the massage parlor.

Ariyo worked his way gingerly through the flowerbeds so he was behind the building near an open window. He heard the woman exit the dressing room and lay on the table. She chatted to the masseur. Then several minutes of silence followed. In the room, he knew Kunto had bitten the woman, searching her mind for information. Then the youth would blend memories of other massages she had had, letting her think she had received one today. The woman sighed in pleasure and rose from the table.

"You have the hands of a god. If you are ever on my home world, look me up. My friends and I will keep you in business."

"You honor me, mistress."

"Keep the change. And my room number."

After the woman left, Ariyo stood up and casually leaned against the window sill. "Not enjoying yourself too much, I hope."

"Of course not, sir."

"Relax, I was joking. What did you learn?"

"She did not have the files on her, but I did get the security code. They are on her boss's laptop which has fingerprint security."

"Where is he now?"

"At one of the meetings, but he will be at the luau tonight."

"Good work. That gives us time to prepare."

Ariyo touched his earpiece and gave instructions to his team. Then he went back to weeding. Three months of investigating, visiting dozens of planets, popping in on leaders, probing their minds, then leaving them unaware of the intrusion had led to this final mission. The core leaders gathered once every three years for a conference, this time held at a popular resort. Ariyo's team had applied for jobs several weeks before the conference began, using the epulo bite to secure them positions which aided them best.

Once the sun set, bamboo torches illuminated the paths. Tourists drifted through restaurants, arcades, and clubs while hundreds of Coalition members headed to the beach for a private luau. Dancers performed fiery acrobatics to pounding drums. Jovial guests cheered and stuffed themselves on banquet food. Rinji moved through the crowd, serving drinks. He approached a table were a heavyset man joked with two gorgeous women.

"Your piña coladas. Sir, you have a private message at the bar."

"Thanks. Excuse me, ladies. Can't escape business, even here."

As the man walked away, Rinji began clearing off dirty dishes to place on a service cart. A plate slipped from his fingers, crashing to the ground. He bent and began cleaning up the mess—and casually slid a briefcase out from under the table and placed it on the bottom shelf of the cart, under a cloth. Behind him, Kunto, wearing a bright hat and a camera hanging from his neck, asked the women if he could take their picture. They smiled and moved closer together, paying no attention to Rinji wheeling the laptop away.

At the bar, Ariyo approached the heavy-set man. "Mr. Steen, this way please. Mr. Baldwick wishes a private word with you."

The man smiled and followed. "Of course. Is this about the building contract?"

"He did not tell me."

Ariyo led him out away from the luau towards a dimly lit grove of trees sheltering several picnic tables. As they passed restroom stalls, Dubaku moved out of the shadows and grabbed the man from behind, quickly pulling him into the darkness. He bit, and the struggling man relaxed and dropped into a deep sleep. Ariyo helped drag the man into the bushes. A few minutes later Kunto arrived with the briefcase. To unlock it, Dubaku punched in numbers he had just pulled from Steen's mind. He lifted out the laptop and placed the man's fingers over the keypad. Once the computer activated, he pulled up the files they sought and copied them onto an external hard drive. Then the laptop was placed back in the briefcase, and Kunto carried it back to the luau.

Dubaku bit the man again, altering his memories. Then the AF rose and disappeared into the darkness. Steen slowly sat up and looked around, dazed.

"Sir, are you alright?" asked Ariyo.

"No…I mean, yes. My doctor keeps telling me alcohol and heart meds don't mix, but I keep telling him that he's wrong. Guess he was right after all. I was on the way to the bathroom and passed out."

Ariyo held out a hand and helped the man up. "Do you need me to call for help?"

"No, it will pass in a minute. Don't want the ladies thinking I'm not man enough to handle a few drinks."

Steen headed back towards the beach and his table, passing Kunto who had just delivered dessert—and the briefcase. As Steen sat down, he said, "Just a boring acquaintance who wanted to network. Told him I had to get back to the most beautiful women on the island." The ladies giggled and moved closer to him.

Kunto cleared off a few more tables then quietly left the party. He navigated paths to the worker's quarters and entered a bungalow. The other three had already arrived and were in the process of uploading the captured files to their orbiting ship *Dream Delusion*.

"Good work, soldiers," said Ariyo, taking off his shaggy wig.

"Do we have enough hard evidence to begin the arrests?" asked Dubaku, removing his fake goatee and shaking a few twigs out of his dreadlocks. The exuberance he had projected earlier as Lucky had vanished when off duty. His face now showed as much emotion as a rock.

Ariyo and Rinji glanced at each other before the Five said, "It is not quite that easy. Evidence we have, but the Emperor may not agree to arrest the

Head. They are old friends. We must probe deeper, find something which will prod the Emperor's hand."

As the others headed to their rooms to sleep, Ariyo stood by a window in the darkness, watching moonlight reflecting like diamonds on the waves. He remembered being on his honeymoon with Layla. They had laughed and frolicked in the water. He had embraced her, aiming for a kiss. She had playfully pushed him away then slipped. He had tried to grab her, and they both fell into the surf. Her laughter echoed across the decades, filling him with longing. He savored the memories for a few minutes then buried them. There was work needing his attention.

Mid-afternoon the next day, Ariyo and Kunto put on new disguises, appearing well-dressed, with glasses and facial hair camouflaging their faces. They walked across the island to a large, isolated bungalow rented year around by Moyers, majority leader of the Galactic Senate. Several children played in the fenced yard, watched closely by both their mom and a security guard. A valet opened the door then led the quintessences to the study.

Broad-shoulder and athletic, Moyers greeted the visitors with firm handshakes. "Enjoying the conference, gentlemen?"

"It has been an eye opener, sir," said Ariyo. "When Professor Chayton recommended we meet you, I doubted a busy man like yourself could spare the time."

"I always have time for friends of Chayton. He is the professor which changed my life, patiently crushing a know-it-all youth then reforming me into a vessel whose destiny I could never had imagined. How is he doing now?"

"Enjoying retirement. We only meet occasionally now, teaching classes takes up much of my time. My colleague and I were honored when he asked us to represent our chapter here. Do you mind if I ask you some questions about concepts discussed in the workshops?" The quintessences had mind probed Chayton a few weeks ago, gaining the information needed for their backstory.

"Not at all." Attentive, Moyers sat in his chair behind a large desk.

"What exactly is the Great Plan?"

"Raising humankind to the next level. It's a long process centuries in the making which will continue long after you and I are dead."

"Have not we failed in this area?" Kunto pushed his glasses further up on his nose. "The profectus project earned a lot of public praise for the Coalition, but the profectus died out. How can we further our cause?"

"The most obvious is having the Sentient Purity Act repelled, but that's a tough battle we've been fighting for two centuries. If the profectus gene had been dominate, we would have had many of them born naturally by now, leading to a super-intelligent subspecies forming the crest of a wave bearing up our species above all others. But reality is the gene is recessive. When the first generation scattered across the galaxy, only a handful married their own kind, leading to just a few new profectus in the second generation. They, in turn, only married normal humans, nullifying our plans for a third generation."

"Then that is it? Can nothing be done?"

Moyers laughed. "Do you give up so easily? I thought you were professors of history. We are the Coalition. Our motto is 'Make the impossible possible.' Profectus do walk among us today."

"How?"

The senator grinned. "By pooling the sources of dedicated people like you. We each do our part for the good of humanity. Gentlemen, the dead do walk again. We have successfully cloned twenty-eight profectus, stretched out over two decades of intense, secretive work."

"I have not seen any in the news," said Ariyo.

"Yes, you have. You just do not know it. We have had two Zelzer winners and a pop star, among others." Moyers waved his hand towards a bookcase where images rotated in a digital photo frame. "Recognize any of them."

Kunto stood up and moved to the bookcase. "Several." A picture appeared of a gothic styled woman with blue hair. "Ice Babe is a profectus?"

"Well, this batch lacked the proper drive and ambition of the first generation. There have been disappointments, but they are our children. We must support them, and hope they find their way back to us."

"This is impressive," said Ariyo, "but in the end, have we really accomplished anything? I mean, they will die out, just like the ones before."

The senator leaned forward. "We are looking into several possibilities to fix that. I have high hopes of one day changing the law by…"

He was cut off by Kunto suddenly stepping forward and biting him. The senior's eyes glazed over as Kunto probed his mind. Then Kunto pulled back and returned to the bookshelf.

Moyers' eyes refocused. "…rebelling the act, of course. Others are trying to copy the method of our archenemy the Edietheans by using arranged marriages to breed geniuses."

"There was a mention of a Titan Project," said Kunto.

"Ah, yes. Some of us place high hopes on it. Several geneticists are attempting to create a new version of the profectus gene, but this one dominate. Unfortunately the work must be done in secret with much less funding than our first version. Progress is limited. I had high hopes that our child Yashana would have helped on the project, but she chased after plants, limiting her potential." He shook his head in disappointment. "That was a flaw found throughout this generation. They lacked direction, drifting, stumbling when they should have flown. But we parents do learn from our mistakes. The next generation will be raised differently. Currently we are considering two options. We will either place them in homes of Coalitions members who will train them with proper worldviews or raise them in isolation, controlling everything they see and do. Some believe isolation is the best method, giving us full control, but I see it as flawed. How can they become leaders of our race if they do not experience what it is like to be human? They need to feel that first love, the first kiss, laughter with friends, bonding with fellow humans."

"What happens when we succeed?" asked Kunto, sitting back down. "How will other species react when they discover what we have done?"

"Depends of the species. Some won't care, others will be jealous. We are not against other species, as long as they recognize their place, which is to be subservient to us. They need to bow to us for exports, technology, and guidance. In return, we will co-exist peacefully."

"I doubt the edietheans will bow to us," said Ariyo.

The senator nodded. "True. Their ancient race has been led by super-geniuses for millenniums, but their arrogance is their fatal flaw. By the time they realize we have created a self-sustaining genius caste equal to theirs, we will already be in position to wipe them out."

"Do you mean destroy their political power?"

"No, I mean the extermination of their upper castes."

"You speak of genocide."

"Not completely. We'll spare the lower castes and maybe the middle levels. Their IQ's are too low to be consequential. No other species in the galaxy will be able to match our profectus for intellect."

Ariyo frowned. "A great destiny you have planned for our race, but the Coalition is not known for violence."

"And we plan to keep it that way. Most of our members could not stomach it, but some of us must bare this weight if we are to succeed."

"And you think you are the man to do that?"

"I already have numerous times. How else do you think I earned the position as Head? A bomb here, a false arrest there. We must keep our enemies off guard, never allowing their focus to stay long in our direction."

Behind the beard, Kunto's eyes conveyed a deathly intensity, for he now knew the depth of depravity in the senator's mind. "Were you the one who ordered Ambassador Roobaroo's assassination?"

"Yes, that was my doing."

Ariyo's hands tightened on his armrest. "That explosion killed a Five."

"A casualty of war, which I regret. The bomb was set to go off after her ship had taken several trips to make it harder to catch our assassin. There was no way to predict it would have happened at Essence."

"Roobaroo was working against her own High Council. And she was preparing for a wedding. You could have killed many innocent guests who had rebelled against the council's breeding program."

The senator frowned at Ariyo's reaction. "She was an ediethean sending out spies to probe for information about our clones. We could not have that. And the High Council was naturally blamed for her murder. A perfect win-win."

It took all of Ariyo's self-control to say, "Perfectly played. Keep public distrust focused on the High Council, and everyone forgets about us."

A distant door slammed, and children's happy laughter rang down the hallway.

"Looks like it is about time for dinner. Gentlemen, I have enjoyed our conversation. After the conference is over, come back for another visit. We'll discuss your concerns more."

The valet showed Ariyo and Kunto out. They walked back to their bungalow, passing merry tourists of different species, unknowing that among them walked Coalition members who wished for their subjugation. Ariyo's emotions were in such chaos that when they reached the bungalow, he could not talk to the others. He walked outside and watched surfers attempting to ride waves. Most were amateurs who quickly lost their balance and fell into the rushing tide.

The door banged as Rinji walked outside and stopped beside his birthmate. "Kunto just told us Moyers is responsible for your murder. Are you alright?"

"I wanted to slay him right there, but to kill him without his sins becoming public would have made him a martyr for their cause."

"You handled yourself well, brother."

"He played us well. We Five have prided ourselves on our strategic skills, keeping several steps beyond our enemies. But we became blind, too self-absorbed to step back and see how the Coalition was using us. We are favored grandchildren to them because we were created by their offspring. They have always supported us, but in return we owe them our continued existence. It is we that they will one day order to commit genocide against the ediethean while they keep their hands clean. If we refuse, they can order our extinction."

"But that will not happen now. We know their plans."

For a brief moment, a surfer stood proudly on his board, arms spread out, a grin plastered on his face. Then he slipped and disappeared under a large wave.

"Perhaps. Perhaps not. As long as we cannot birth our own offspring, we are vulnerable to whoever controls the Senate. Currently that is the Coalition."

They went back inside, and Ariyo ordered a shuttle from *Dream Delusion* to pick them up. Once aboard the space frigate, he directed it to fly to Diamond, the imperial city. When he reached the palace, he was escorted deep inside to a secretive room to meet with Emperor Sereyasi and several key advisors. Ariyo explained in a logical, unemotional monologue what had been learned and played the audio recordings of both Alberto Fairbanks conversation with Baldwick and his own with Moyers. The advisors grilled him on details, but the Emperor remained silent. Eventually the ruler stood up and began pacing around the chamber, pausing occasionally to study portraits of his ancestors. As the advisors began a heated debate over what should be done, Ariyo left the group and moved beside Sereyasi.

For a few minutes neither spoke. Finally the Emperor said, "If I had died yesterday, I would have been a happy man. Why must you bring such news to break my heart? Moyers is like a brother to me."

"I am only doing my duty."

"Ah, the loyalty of the quintessences. You have served my family and the empire well for generations. Both my father and grandfather had complete trust in the Five. I wished I had reasons to doubt you, but you have given me none." He sighed and glanced at his bickering advisors. "You say by me putting one of my most trusted friends on trial, I will prevent future atrocities. Moyers and I grew up together. We share many traits. Both our fathers were busy politicians. We felt the same pressures growing up in the public eye. We spent many fun days of our childhood wandering the halls of this palace, annoying the maids with our pranks. Every year our families still vacation together."

"You are not Emperor of just humans, but thousands of sentient species, both weak and strong. Sooner or later, knowledge of the profectus clones will become known to the general public. You can claim you had no forewarning of it and let the Coalition continue to forge their Great Plan. Or you can make a stand against corruption now."

"The Coalition has been a powerful ally for me over the years. I cannot turn against them."

"Keep your attack focused on the culprits, not the organization. Your subjects will trust you if they believe you are a fair leader. If you show favoritism to the Coalition, the edietheans will turn against you. Sides will be drawn and a war on a scale never seen before will rip your realm apart. Perhaps not doing your lifetime, but in your children's children."

"You're a pessimistic."

"I am a realistic who has lived too long, and seen firsthand this mistrust between the species. The peace which holds your realm together is fragile. Some worlds still resent imperial rule. The coals of rebellion smolder, waiting for fuel to burst forth in open flame. Put aside your personal feelings and think like an emperor."

A few days later, Ariyo led a squad of ME1's into the mansion Moyers owned in the imperial city. A butler tried to stop their entry, but Ariyo flashed his warrant. He found Moyers sitting by the pool, watching his kids playing in the water. The senator's wife rose angrily, demanding the soldiers leave her home immediately, but her husband calmly scrutinized the intruders.

Ariyo ignored the irate wife. "Senator Moyers, you are under arrest for the murders of eleven citizens of Basanti including Ambassador Roobaroo and Director Alexander Rangan. Also, for breaking the Sentient Purity Act, among other crimes. You will come with me."

"I know you," said the senator, resting his arms on the patio table. "You look better without the glasses and goatee. I presume Professor Chayton did not send you this time. Are you aware that I can sue you for false charges and harassment? I have powerful friends who can make your life miserable."

"Are you aware, Senator, that my name is Ariyo of the Five?"

Moyers's confidence faltered briefly. "A quintessence? I have never seen your model before."

"You should keep up more with your offsprings' inventions. Now come with me."

The man stood, but refused to move. Two wet kids climbed out of the pool and ran to him. The younger one wrapped her arms around her dad, sobbing, while the older stood by her mom, glaring angrily at the squad in her backyard. The wife began cursing, but Moyers silenced her.

"They cannot touch me, Ann. I will be out in just a few hours. Emperor Sereyasi will see to that."

"Not this time." Ariyo held out the warrant. "He personally signed it. You will find he does not support those who plan genocide against his own citizens."

Chapter Thirty-five

Lashana's world collapsed with just one e-mail. "Basanti Empire Subpoena. You are hereby commanded, in the name of Emperor Sereyasi, to appear before the Galactic Senate to give evidence of what you know relating to the criminal investigation of Senator Moyers charged with murder, misconduct, and illegally cloning. Due to concerns of security, a military transport ship will provide you passage."

She stared at the subpoena for nearly half an hour, body shaking, mind panicked. The past had finally caught up with her. What would her family think when they learned she was but a copy of another person? With Volodymyr isolated from the core planets, the inevitable media circus might not be noticed here, except she would be forced to explain her suddenly disappearance to her family and co-workers. Would the transport ship have quintessences aboard? What if one was Ariyo?

For what few days she had left being plain Yashana, she pretended all was well. Except instead of working in the lab in the afternoons, she rounded up her children and played board games with them. After dinner Seth joined the fun. It was not until the fifth night, with her husband lying half-asleep beside her, that she finally spoke her fear.

"Do you love me?"

"Of course."

"How much? Would you still love me if I was more than what I appear to be? Say unhuman?"

"My best friends are reptiles. If you spouted a tail and claws, I would still love you. Though I would wonder what had been slipped into my drink."

"I'm being serious."

Seth kissed his wife. "What has upset you?"

"My past. It comes for me. I have tried so hard to escape it. I feel trapped in a nightmare where you run and run but get nowhere. Always you are being chased. It is so close I can feel his breath."

"You have never spoken like this before." Seth was wide awake now. "What do you really fear?"

"Losing you and the children."

"We're not going anywhere. Yashana, you are my wife. I will love you no matter what."

"Even if I am a shadow of another?"

"Yes. Look, I have known from the beginning that something happened in your past that hurt you so much you fled here. I always thought it was a lover's quarrel. Perhaps you fell in love with a married man. I accepted that you wish to not speak about that part of your life."

"I am a clone."

"A clone?" He sat up, looking at her strangely. "That's all?"

"That's enough."

"You mean by clone..."

"That I'm a perfect DNA replica of someone else. Someone not completely human."

Silence followed. Finally in a tense voice, Seth said, "Our children, are they human?"

"Yes, but they carry my gene. I'm a *Homo sapiens profectus.*"

"A profectus." Seth laughed shakily. "I already knew I was married to a genius. Who are you a clone of?"

"Layla Rangan."

"The Layla Rangan? The scientist that made those clone soldiers?"

"Yes."

"Why would you be ashamed of this?"

"Because from the moment I found out I was the shadow of Layla, I have sought to escape her legacy. At Essence, they wanted me to be like her, continuing her work. Instead, I ran as far away as I could. I was determined to live my life differently than hers. And I have. There is you and our children. I have offspring from my own flesh. A wonderful miracle."

"Children are miracles." Sadness flirted across Seth's face as he thought about his dead firstborn. "I am proud to have three of them with you. Yashana, you didn't have to bear this secret alone all these years. I love you no matter your genes."

"I wanted you to see me, not Layla. There is more I must tell you. I have been subpoenaed to testify at the Galactic Senate. They finally found who ordered my creation."

Seth took a deep breath before saying, "Well, the children have been hankering to go off world. They'll enjoy the trip."

Lashana smiled and drew her husband close. "I love you."

The next day Seth and Lashana sat their kids down for a talk. Nathan, Nabeela, and Yaira barely reacted when told their mother was a clone, but when the upcoming trip was mentioned, they became animated. Soon the girls were writing out a list of the places they wanted to go, parks and shopping being a priority. Nathan wondered if they could be granted a tour of a farm to see how crops were grown on a core planet.

Barely a week later, the ship *Dream Delusion* dropped into orbit above Volodymyr. Seth was going to have a rockancher fly a shuttle up, but the *Dream Delusion* insisted they had experienced pilots who could handle the turbulence. Shortly later, a sleek craft landed in front of TRF. The children oohed through their oxygen masks as they boarded. A quintessence pilot greeted the family. Lashana felt a suddenly rush of fear and anticipation because he had the face of Alexander, but so too did thousands of other ME1 models. After making sure everyone was strapped in, the pilot lifted the shuttle skyward. There was more aahing from the kids as the armored space frigate came into view.

Once the shuttle docked, the family stepped out. The kids watched in fascination as HC models serviced the craft, swept the floor, or studied computer screens.

"They're all the same," said Yaira in awe.

"Mom said they would be." Nabeela tried to sound cultured, but her voice betrayed her own excitement. "There are several clutches of birthmates on the same ship. They have worked together their entire lives."

The pilot of the shuttle studied the children. "Looks like your mom has been teaching you well. Can you name which models are on our ship and their roles?"

Nabeela stood straight, "The models are named after the human races they mimic. On this ship the mechanical and technical work is done by HS models which stands for Hispanic. The pilots are like you, ME models which stand for Middle Eastern. You might also have C models which usually serve as infantry. C stands for Caucasian."

Wanting to show she knew something too, Yaira said, "There is also the IN models which stands for Indigenous."

The pilot of the shuttle nodded in approval, "We do not have C or IN aboard. I do have eighty-nine birthmates here. Several of my brothers died in the line of service. Others moved on to other projects, like Daryl who is now a Five."

"We were sorry to hear about Jacob's death," said Lashana. The news had been slow in reaching TRF. It had been nearly six months after his death before she had read about it in a class report of one of her students who had written about Essence. Unlike the core planets where news was constantly updated on supercomputers which provided data for entire planets, isolated outposts relied on downloads to their small servers, usually by purchasing data packets relating to areas that interests the colonists. Lashana had thought the Five would have had the courteous to at least send her a private message of the death, but from Essence there had only been silence.

The pilot nodded. "His lost grieves us, but having a Five as a birthmate gives us pride. Your luggage will be carried to your cabins. The commander would like to meet you."

The family was led to a conference room. Lashana had expected the commander to be another ME1, but when she entered the room, her heart began pounding. Two AS1 models stood by a window. Behind them loomed the huge orange planet Volodymyr. As they drew near, Lashana automatically searched for names on their clothing. She recognized the name Rinji but the other was a stranger to her.

The pilot said, "This is our commander Aik and his aide Rinji."

Aik's eyes swept across the family, taking in details. "We are honored to have the clone of Layla onboard. If there is anything you need, please let us know."

"Thank you. We will try to stay out of your way as much as possible."

Yaira bumped her father and made a low whine.

Seth said, "Our children would like a tour of the ship, if that is allowed."

"Of course. Some areas are restricted, but there is still much we can show them." Seeing the three youths' eager faces, he turned to the pilot. "Please show them around."

The craft was much smaller than a cruiser, but the kids were highly impressed. The gym held the equipment for popular sport games and combat practice. The game room mesmerized all three youths, and the lounge allowed the family to sit and watch the stars zoom pass. Dinner was served in a mess hall were quintessences ate by shifts. The cooks serving the food were ME1's.

"Is there anyone onboard who is not quintessence?" asked Seth when they had set down.

Their guide said, "If this was an imperial ship, it would have had a mix crew or no quintessences at all, but this is a private frigate owned by Essence.

The crews of our ships are made from clutches of freed birthmates who have decided to continue to work and live together after gaining their freedom. Some of us marry and our wives travel with us. My brothers and I have only recently finished our bond years. So far only four have married, including our brother Daryl of the Five."

Nabeela grinned as she took a bite of apple cobbler. "The food is so much better than home. No offense, Dad."

Nathan added, "Can we create a sugar plant that can grow with little sunlight?"

"And coco trees," piped in Yaira, savoring a piece of chocolate cake.

"Talk to your mom. She's the genus here."

The family tried to keep out of the way of the busy crew over the following days, but they soon discovered the clones did not mind sharing their amenities with the family. The kids were invited to ballgames in the gym and shooting contests in the game room. Seth claimed he was far too old for such activities, but his kids talked him into playing video games with them. Lashana laughed at their antics, pretending all was well. Being around quintessences after several decades away, brought back potent memories from both her lives.

On the fifth day while her family was distracted, she sought out the AS models. Aik invited her into a small office where he and Rinji had been studying star charts.

"My brethren have enjoyed having your family aboard," said the commander. "They rarely have the opportunity to be around children and find yours fascinating."

Lashana sat across the desk from them. "My children enjoy the attention. They have only been off planet once before, and everything is still new to them. We live very isolated from mainstream culture and little filters to us. I wonder if you could share news about Essence. I have heard little since my internship was completed there."

The clones glanced at each other before Aik said, "The biggest events would be the instatement of Daryl and Jacy as Fives."

She tensed. "Jacy? Who did he replace?"

"Gabriel who died a year ago. Jacy is an IN model. The Synod is trying to represent all the models in choosing replacements for both the Fifty and the Five."

"Another gone?" Lashana turned away, trying to hide tears which threatened to spill. "I wasn't told. Not a word. Still they have not forgiven me."

Aik stood and began to walk to her, but Rinji held out his arm, stopping him.

Lashana did not notice as she fought for control of her emotions. "Losing your first generation. A tragedy. I had thought...read...they would live beyond two hundred."

"You were wrong," said Aik, his face a volatile mask.

Rinji stepped in front of Aik. "Would you like me to send for your husband to comfort you?"

"I...I'm fine. The news was just sudden." She stood up. "I probably should go." She turned to the door but wavered. "Rinji, how fares your birthmate Ariyo?"

"His duties as a Five keep him busy."

"I was proud to hear when he became a Five. He deserves it. When you see him next, tell him I said congratulations on his appointment."

"I will do that." Rinji glanced at Aik whose face had now hardened.

Lashana quickly walked to her cabin. Finally alone, she dropped to her knees and wept. She cried for the hole in her soul which belonged to Alexander. She cried for Jacob and Gabriel, for the lost opportunity of making amends. She had designed them then watched them grow up to become great leaders. None of the remaining Synod had even bothered to tell her of their deaths. As she had abandoned her creations, they had abandoned her.

When she heard children's laughter in the hallway, she dried her eyes and smiled when the door opened. Once the children were in bed, Seth sought to understand the source of her sadness, but she brushed him off. There were some things she could not tell him. Ever.

A few days later the frigate dropped into orbit around the planet Basanti. A pilot flew Lashana and her family down to Diamond, along with the two AS models and a squad of ME1's. Lashana thought the escort unnecessary, but Aik insisted it was a safety protocol. They landed on a launch pad near the Capitol. The military escort marched the family inside to a high security wing where other witnesses waited to testify.

Lashana's family entered a huge chamber where dozens of people milled about. Some sat on couches watching the trial on a large vid, others snacked or chatted in small groups. Children played games to pass the time. Several booths were set up in one corner where participates could talk with lawyers to prepare for testimonies or volunteer for tests. Lashana's breath caught as she scanned the faces. Many of the adults were profectus clones. This was her people, her race.

"Yashana, I was wondering when you would get here," came a familiar voice.

Lashana hugged a tall man with brown hair slightly out of place. "Ethan, you look…great. Very distinguished."

"It's the clothes. My wife insists I wear tailored suits when in public."

"You need to look the part of a CEO," said a gorgeous, blond woman, wrapping her arms around Ethan. "It is good to finally meet you, Yashana. My husband has spoken a lot about you over the years."

"And he of you." Seeing her children yearning to explore the large chamber, Lashana nodded, and they bolted away. "I don't think he would have ever gotten his robotic Handy-Dog into production without you."

Ethan beamed. "Are you kidding? I would still be in an office cubicle if not for her—and her grandmother. We had only been dating a few weeks when I visited her family and met her blind grandmother who just sat there day after day, depressed."

"My grandmother's Seeing Eye dog had recently died from old-age and she refused the training for a new one, claiming she was too old."

"Well, her grandmother reminded me of my own grandma who had passed away a few months before. I kept thinking about her all that week at work, wondering if Rover could be programmed as a replacement. Animals trained to help the handicapped must carry a lot of responsibility that most people are completely unaware of. Not only must they recognize dozens of verbal commands and gestures, but they have to anticipate their owners needs when responding, even if that means disobeying a command. For example, a blind person may walk into a street and not realize a car is not stopping at a light. The dog must realize the problem and pull their owner out of the way, disobeying the command to walk. Such high level thinking is difficult to achieve in robots. I went back to scratch, upgrading Rover's CPU, creating new programming, adding new sensors."

"You're getting too technical for them," said his wife. "They're eyes are glazing over."

"She's a profectus. She can handle it."

"But not a tech geek like me. Excuse my husband. Once he gets started, he has a hard time shutting up."

Lashana smiled. "You picked a good mate, Ethan."

"Of course I did. I followed your advice. Choose someone who could keep me in my place but believe in my potential."

The blond woman laughed. "Believe you me, it's been a hard job since he learned he is a profectus. Wanted to immediately use it in a slogan for our advertisements."

"At least with this trial, I can finally talk about it publicly."

A well-dress lawyer approached and invited Lashana to a private booth where they discussed her part in the upcoming proceedings. "You are to talk about how you discovered you were a profectus and why the decision was made to keep the information classified."

"Strange to talk about this after so many years of hiding."

"The hiding is over, Mrs. Lanneret. You and your race can finally heal after what has been done to you."

"Why would we need to heal? I've had a good life."

"Some of you have, but not all. We have been giving psychology tests to profectus and their families. While many of you went to college and found jobs that recognized your genius, others were not as fortunate. Some felt misunderstood their entire lives. That frustration led several to unhappy endings. One is on death row for multiple murderers, another committed suicide a few years back."

"I am sorry to hear that. I had believed by not knowing they were clones, they would live better lives."

"We hope this trial will give your race the recognition and understanding you deserve. When you have time, we would like to run some tests on your children. I assure you they're completely painless."

After Lashana exited the booth, she found her children mixing with a group of youth gathered around a blue-haired woman singing and dancing. The woman, dressed in black with her face covered in heavy make-up, relished the attention. When she finished, her audience rushed forward begging for autographs which she cheerfully signed. Lashana's kids hung back, having never heard of Ice Babe, but they were impressed. Lashana herself stared in astonishment. Underneath all that make-up was the face of Diana Richton, the architect of Essence. Diana had been known for her creativity but not for singing. Now her clone was a famous pop star.

Seeking her husband, Lashana moved through the crowd. Suddenly she saw a face which froze her in shock. "Janti? Janti!" She rushed forward and grabbed the person's arm.

The woman, in her mid-twenties, looked at her blankly. "No, I'm Henna Blackstock."

"You're the clone of Janti, my roommate in college…I mean, Layla's roommate."

"Never heard of Janti."

"Few have." Lashana swallowed, feeling a rush of warm emotions. "She died while in college when a virus jumped species. But that changed Layla forever. Janti's death drove her to create a being that could outperform all others. She created the quintessences because of you."

"Not me." Henna looked wary. "Who are you by the way?"

"Oh, Yashana, Layla's clone."

"So you feel close to your clone? There are others who have been researching theirs, but I haven't cared."

"But you should. She was brilliant."

"You said she died while in college. Not much time to be brilliant."

"She was going to be an astrophysicist. She loved the stars."

Henna frowned. "I considered that major before I got pregnant and dropped out of high school to get married. Now I have the glamorous job of being a check-out clerk at a grocery store. But I do have a wonderful family."

"I have three kids myself. They are over there by that blue singer."

"Ice Babe. My kids have all her albums. Maybe I'll bring them here tomorrow so they can meet her."

"You should go back to college. Get your degree."

"I have thought about it several times, but the money was never there."

"Doors will open now that it's out that you are a profectus. You can do anything you want. Maybe even figure out how to harness the power of black holes."

Henna laughed. "Harnessing black holes? I don't know if anyone has thought of that one before."

"Janti did."

The woman tilted her head, contemplating. "I'll think about that. It's good meeting you."

Soon afterwards, Lashana saw Seth exiting a testing booth. He greeted her with, "I feel like the dumbest kid in the room. My IQ is only a hundred and twenty."

"That is considered high by most standards."

"Not in this room. Can't wait to see what our kids score."

"I predict in the genius level, but still far below what we profectus reach."

Ethan and his wife invited Lashana's family to dinner which was served in an adjoining banquet hall. The kids enjoyed sampling new foods. Ethan spoke more about how he and his wife turned his robotic dogs for the handicap into a thriving business. Lashana and Seth talked about life on Volodymyr.

As the desserts arrived, Ethan leaned towards Lashana. "Why didn't you tell me, back in college, that we were profectus?"

"I wasn't coping well with it. I didn't want you to go through the same problems."

"If you had just told me, I could have helped you instead of you turning to that foeditas horribilis. We would have made it out together from that darkness you plunged into."

Lashana quickly glanced at Seth who was busy showing Yaira how to blow out her fiery ice cream. She whispered to Ethan. "If I did, we would never have married who we did. I think it worked out for the best for both of us."

Ethan grinned. "Yeah, you would never have put up with a house full of half-completed gizmos—which are not all made by me. My wife is pretty smart for a non-profectus." His wife heard the last line and punched him in the side as a reward.

A nearby five-star hotel served as home for the profectus and their families for nearly three weeks as different ones were called to testify. Each day many of the profectus and their families gathered in the wing set aside for them. Together they watched the trial on a large vid. Quintessences and other guards kept most of the media away from the families, but Alberto Fairbank had complete access as he was a star witness, which he used to his advantage as he sought information for new articles. Occasionally Lashana recognized Aik and Rinji in the crowd. Each time, she felt as if their eyes were scrutinizing her intensely, but she was too busy to think beyond that. It was surreal to Lashana when she watched her old professor Duken explain the procedure used in creating her and the profectus. For his testimony, he had been granted immunity.

Her own testimony before the Senate was nerve racking. In the huge chamber she sat before thousands of senators, visitors, and media. Camera drones swooped near her, projecting her face on gigantic screens so all could see. She answered questions as truthful as possible, feeling strange to share secrets she had kept buried deep within herself for so many years. Still, she spoke nothing about having the memories of Layla. That was one secret she planned to take to her grave. Her testimony over, she passed one of the large screens on the way out. The camera was focused on Moyers sitting calmly, surrounded by his lawyers. She froze, wondering who this placid man really was. He had ordered her creation, but his commands had also murdered two of her closest friends, including her soulmate. Behind his tranquil eyes was a mind which planned genocides. How dare he look so serene with the blood which stained his hands.

Days later when he finally testified, Lashana watched along with the other profectus in their private chamber. Seth sat beside her, holding her tense hand.

Moyers looked at the camera and showed no remorse as he spoke in a firm voice addressing his peers. "The edietheans have manipulated the many species of this galaxy for millenniums. If you do not believe so, you have not been paying attention to your lessons in grammar school. My colleagues and I decided to stand up against their bulling by creating their intellectual equals. My predecessors were considered heroes in designing the first generation of profectus. Many of you have reaped the benefits of their glorious achievements. Can you deny that medicine which keeps you alive, the technology you use, the arts that you enjoy have all been dramatically impacted by the profectus in the last two centuries? Your very safety is ensured because of clone warriors who die far away on the battlefield so you may sleep peacefully at night. Was I wrong to create another generation? Your verdict if I am guilty or innocent is irrelevant. It is history, not you, who will ultimately decide if I was right."

Several ediethean senators and their allies began shouting him down, but other sections of the audience remained quiet—too quiet. How many supporters did the Coalition have?

"I am merely a figure head of an idea. Chop off the head of a person and he dies. Chop off the head of an idea, and it spouts ten new ones. Hate me if you wish, but one day your children's children will honor me."

Lashana looked away from the screen, disturbed. She was not the only one. Many of the profectus and their families became restless, muttering angrily at the senator's words. But others sat mesmerized, soaking in everything their creator said.

Alberto Fairbank, on the front row, said loudly. "Found the headline for my next article. 'Senator suffers from messiah complex.' Then again, I shouldn't give his lawyers any ideas. They might try to get him off with an insanity plea."

Finally the proceedings wound down. The vote was close, but Moyers was removed from office. A new trial, this time in a criminal court, would take place, but the profectus were no longer needed. As the profectus prepared to head to their various planets, they exchanged contact information. The opportunity to bond with one's own race had deeply impacted many.

Back at the hotel, the kids finally fell asleep. Exhausted from the three week ordeal, Seth and Lashana sat on the couch, cuddling.

"Too much excitement for my old bones."

"You're not old to me."

"How many times have I heard you use that line?"

"Not enough." Through the window she watched an aircraft zooming across the sky. "I do miss the quietness of Volodymyr."

"No, you don't. I see the glint in your eyes which you try to hide from me. You miss living on a core planet as much as the girls want to."

"I would miss you worse. Volodymyr is our home."

"That senator who created you, I know I should abhor him for his speciesism's views, but he gave me you."

Lashana snuggled closer. "I will never forget he is a murderer. Those were my friends who died. He may have ordered my creation, but I choose my life. I owe him nothing."

"Have I told you how much I love you?"

"Not enough."

Chapter Thirty-six

Lashana knew this day would come, but no matter how many times she tried to mentally prepare, it hit like an ashstorm. She was in the lab when the call came that she was needed in the cargo hold. When she arrived, there was a large group of workers in a loose circle. Expecting to find yet another employee hurt, she slowed as she neared. Seeing her, the rockanchers and tiglics parted, revealing Seth lying limp on the floor, her son bent over his father.

"Mom, he's gone." Tears streamed down his cheeks. "We were harvesting airspikes, and he fell behind. I didn't think to see why. I was competing with Lich to see who could harvest the most. Then when we had finished, Dad had not climbed up." The nineteen-year-old's voice quivered.

Wabash squatted on the floor beside his boss. "He died in harness, still working. Always working. We have been telling him to rest. Let others do the work. But he said he must always lead by example."

Lashana's hands shook as she sat beside her son and held him. "He died as he lived. Laboring always to help others."

Nathan's body shook as sobs overcame him. One of the rockanchers began to keen. The lament was quickly picked up by those nearby. The keening brought others into the chamber to see who had died and soon their voices joined till the rocky walls vibrated with their grief. When Nabeela and Yaira arrived, they threw themselves on their father, weeping loudly. Seeing the whole facility brought to a standstill, Lashana deadened her own emotions and began directing others.

She moved her kids to a smaller room and offered what comfort she could. Then she left to prepare for the funeral. The dead were not allowed to tarry long in the caverns. Lashana asked Wabash to find a crate to serve as a coffin. She almost lost control of herself when she saw Seth lying in the makeshift sarcophagus, his hair gray with age, his wrinkled skin sagging, his lanky body worn out from a lifetime of hard work. With effort she kept her emotions in check as she directed his coffin to be carried to a shuttle. After the craft took off, her family stood with all the workers under the eternal twilight sky, watching. The rockanchers' voices united in a requiem.

Some minutes later, fourteen-year-old Yaira pointed to the sky. "There he is. Dad's a star now."

No one mentioned to the girl that the coffin, jettisoned in low orbit, would be nearly impossible to see from the planet's surface as it burnt up. She probably knew that but cared nothing about facts today.

For the rest of the evening, the rockanchers continued to lament, groups taking turns so the death song would not end till midnight. The tiglics hung in groups, whispering. Some sought out Lashana to see what they could do for her. She moved like a zombie, responding to questions, directing others as needed, feeling nothing herself. Nathan dragged his own bedroll into his sisters' room. For hours the children talked and wept, Lashana comforting.

When the kids had finally fallen asleep, Lashana went to her own bedroom. She stared at the empty bed. Just that morning she had lain there with her husband. His presence lingered everywhere. His dusty boots still by the dresser which held his clothes. His comb beside her brush. The Zelzer award on a shelf above her cluttered desk. Lashana curled into a ball on the mattress and cried herself asleep.

During the days which followed, Lashana keep busy trying to fulfill Seth's role as manager while being a mother, teacher, and scientist. She failed. The others were understanding. Wabash had been Seth's right hand for a long time, and he naturally took up the duties of Seth. His mate Vistula continued to oversee the laboratory and arboretum. Nabeela took over teaching whenever she saw her mother falter, which was often. Some days, Lashana did not show up to class at all. Yaira went through stages of clinging to her mom then times of isolation. Nathan tried to fill the gap left empty by his father. He attended every harvest and planting, letting his grades in the correspondence college courses he was taking slip.

Lashana struggled to keep together the life she had known for the last two decades, but from the moment she had seen Seth dead, guilt plagued her. She was free to return to Ariyo, but she could not walk away from her life. This was the only home her kids knew. Many responsibilities rested on her shoulders. Besides, Ariyo would probably turn her away. Why would he want to comfort a grieving widow after she had betrayed him? How could she explain Ariyo to her kids who still grieved for their father?

"You should rest now," said Vistula late one evening in the lab.

"I need to finish this." Lashana continued to peer into the microscope.

306

"It will be there tomorrow. Your kids need you now."

Lashana sighed and turned off the machine. "Sometimes I feel they are taking care of me instead of the other way around."

"We all worry about you. And your kids. Whatever happened to those plans of Nathan attending college last year?"

"Flying him to a core planet was expensive, and we kept having to push the date back. He has been understanding. And now that his dad is….gone…I need him here."

"How will he ever find a mate if you keep him here? Is not Nabeela also ready for college?" Both siblings had discussed attending the same university as their father.

Lashana shook her head, not wanting to think about it. "I'm not ready to let go of my kids."

"I don't understand all you ways, warm-blooder, but I do wonder if now is the time to send them off. When did you last see your parents or siblings? Your parents may not live much longer. We can run TRF without you."

"Are you trying to kick me out?"

"Never. You have done much for us, warm-blooder, but we are not your people. Perhaps it is time for you to go to them."

Lashana thought about her friend's words throughout the night. The next day she meet with her kids in a quiet room to talk about visiting their grandparents. They listened somberly.

"Then afterwards we can drop Nathan and Nabeela off at college."

"We can't leave you, Mom," said Nathan. "You need us here."

"I have not decided if I'm coming back here again. I have friends I haven't seen in years such as Ethan. Yaira and I can travel together. Trisha Foundation was your father's dream. It's time for you two to follow your own dreams. You both have spoken of attending college, being around humans—and dating."

Nabeela blushed, but Nathan frowned. "What if my dream is also Trisha?"

"Then finish college, perhaps find a wife, and come back. If that is what you wish, son."

"I do."

"Mom," said Yaira, looking uneasy. "What if I want to go to college too?"

"You can when you are older."

"How about now? Back when we went to Diamond, we all took IQ tests and did well, really well. I scored high enough that I was offered a scholarship to Luncaster University. Dad knew but told me I was too young to go off alone. So I dropped the idea…kind of. But I still want to go. Now that we're splitting apart, would not the timing be right?"

Lashana's face paled. Losing two kids was hard enough, but all three at once?

"Mom, if you don't want me to go, I won't. But it has, well, been my dream for the last three years. Didn't you go when only thirteen?"

"Yes, after fighting hard with my mom to do so." Lashana sighed. "Of course you may go." She forced a smile, but it was hollow like her heart. Everyone she cared about was slipping away.

They took a month to prepare, filling out college applications, messaging grandparents. Nathan finished his correspondence courses. A tiglic took charge of the one-room school. In the end, Lashana was no longer needed. Trisha could function without her—without Seth. It was a bittersweet parting as the workers gathered to say goodbye. Then a shuttle flew them up to a cargo ship which would take them to the edge of the core planets. From there, they would have to hopscotch from ship to ship.

The family watched from a window as their ship pulled away from fiery Volodymyr. Lashana knew she would never return. Neither would Nabeela nor Yaira. Their lives lay elsewhere. But Nathan was his father's son. Volodymyr still sung to him.

"Great view," said Gauge, entering the room. "I was delighted when Rook said he was taking you on as passengers."

The sight of the zonner immediately pulled Lashana out of her melancholy. "You have grown plumper, Senator, since having grand hatchlings."

Gauge beamed and her broad tail twitched. "It is an honor to serve my people as our first senator. We have fought far too long to be accepted into the Galactic Senate. My sons send you greetings."

"I apologize that the man who ordered my creation was the one blocking your people from statehood."

"You have no need to apologize for him. He has a life sentence for his crimes. Always will you be esteemed among my people."

The door slid open and Rook entered, followed by his recently won lifemate. "Like my ship, warm-blooder?"

"Little room for walking with all the cargo, cold-blooder," jested Lashana. "The zikers have more room to sleep than you do."

"What need have they to sleep when they hibernate? My pets have made me rich beyond decency. Your warm-blood kinsmen pay exorbitant amounts for them. I now own a fleet of six ships, and no pirate dares approach us with all our weaponry. You may sleep safe, if you can find the room."

The trip was pleasant, though lacking in amenities. The kids were subdued at first, but as they drew nearer to their grandparents' home planet, they became excited. Lashana thrived on their enthusiasm. At least her family was together for a while longer. Reconnecting with her own parents and siblings helped Lashana feel part of the human race again. Nabeela and Yaira spent every moment possible exploring Mansoor with their cousins. Nathan sometimes joined them, other times preferring to take long walks by himself.

When the beginning of the school term drew near, the family flew to the planet where Seth had attended college. Several of his old school friends welcomed them with open arms. They had donated money to TRF over the years and were delighted by his success. For a week Lashana's family stayed at a large farm where Seth used to work before attending college. Nathan felt a strong attachment to the family who had helped his father—and a strong attraction to one of the great grandkids who was soon to attend the same college as him. She and Nathan spent many hours roaming through the fields together.

Seeing her two oldest settled, Lashana flew with Yaira to Xi'an. It was still a few days before the term was to start. They stayed at a hotel in New Hope and explored the area. Everything excited Yaira. Neon signs, birds landing on statues, insects pollinating flowers. Walking down a street with her was slow as Yaira dashed here and there, a ball of tireless energy and endless questions. Lashana was worn out by the time they made it back to the hotel. Her daughter was not.

Yaira peered out a window, studying a distant wall rising up above the surrounding buildings. "When do we get to see Essence Institute?"

"They are very strict on allowing visitors."

"But you worked there. Surely they will let us in. Come on, Mom. You have taught us so much about the quintessence cloning process. Given us tests. We have to go."

"I'll ask, but don't expect anything. It's a busy place."

Keeping her word, Lashana sent a request for visitation. Her feelings were mixed. She desperately wanted to see Ariyo again but feared the encounter. Then again her request might be ignored completely. She deserved that after her long silence.

The next morning an invitation to Essence waited on Lashana's e-tablet. Yaira was ecstatic, talking nonstop on the monorail ride. They exited near Richton Tower, and Yaira gawked in amazement.

"It's so much taller than in the pictures. You can't see the top from here. And so huge. Is there a city inside?"

"Sort of, though limited on sleeping quarters. Most residential quintessences live with birthmates in fancy barracks which serve as self-supporting communities."

"Can we go anywhere?"

"No, much is restricted. We must wait for our guide."

"How long?"

"Until he finds us. We are tracked by the ID badges they gave us."

A few minutes later a C6 model approached. As one of the later Caucasian designs, he looked very human until one looked into his dark predatory eyes, which formed deep pools that seemed to pierce the watcher's soul. On the battlefield, it was the last thing many enemies saw.

"I am Marcus. Welcome back, Yashana. It has been a long time." He studied mother and daughter.

Where others would be intimated, Yaira grinned. "Can we see the fetuses? Do they look like eggs as there are no wombs?"

"You are a curious child."

"I'm not a child. I'm a curious teenager who is fourteen. And I'm about to be a student at Luncaster. They only allow geniuses in there."

Lashana cut in with an apologetic smile. "My daughter is used to living with rockanchers. She is still learning proper protocol for other cultures."

Marcus nodded. "There may be time for a tour later, but first there are old friends who wish to meet you."

He led them into Richton Tower, across the huge Grand Forum, and pass the food court. Yaira sulked at first, angry at being chastened by her mother, but she grew excited again as she drank in the sights and smells. Lashana felt butterflies churning in her stomach. Did he imply Ariyo waited for her?

They took an elevator up to the forty floor and enter a small meeting room with only one occupant. As the elder quintessence rose, Lashana felt a stab of disappoint. Ariyo was not here. Drawing near to the elder, she read his nametag. Caleb. She immediately gave a polite bow. Yaira copied her mother while peering curiously at the quintessence.

"It is an honor for Essence's director to meet with us."

"The honor is mine, Yashana. Your daughter almost looks like a clone of you."

Yaira giggled, but then sobered when her mother glanced sharply at her.

"I was grieved to hear about the deaths of Jacob and Gabriel. I had hoped to see them again."

"None can overcome aging, not even us. Are you aware that Mason died too? Just a month ago. His spot still remains open."

Lashana winced. "I had not heard. Then you are the last? I am deeply sorry you were not given more years. At least a decade more."

"Do not blame yourself. We are thankful for the time allotted to us. There are others waiting to meet you."

Caleb led them down the hall to the Synod Chamber. As they entered, Marcus closed the double doors behind them. The room was packed with the Fifty and their trainees. Shadow guards stood by the entrance and along walls. Tiah and other wives holding high ranking positions at the institution sat in the reserve selection. Lashana paused once they entered, not expecting the crowd. Caleb walked to the middle of the large room, and gestured for Lashana to come.

Yaira stared wide-eyed and started to follow her mother. Marcus gently stopped her. "This moment is for her, little one. She needs it."

Once Lashana reached the center of the chamber, everyone began clapping. There was no cheering, for that was not the quintessence way. Lashana opened her mouth but could not speak, tears rolling down her cheeks.

Finally she whispered above the din to Caleb, "I deserve no homage. I have wronged someone greatly."

"He is not here. You have not wronged the rest of us, Layla. Our bonds to you were never severed. We welcome you back home, creator."

When the clapping finally ended, Caleb led mother and daughter to the top floor of the tower where a large indoor garden grew under a domed glass ceiling. A reception was held as shadow guards served as waiters, carrying platters of food. Yaira barely had time to grab a hors d'oeuvre, before Marcus suggested now was a good time to give her a tour. Yaira was reluctant to leave the beautiful garden after just arriving, but when he mentioned the fetus chamber, she became eager. Each of the Fifty greeted Lashana and reminisce about old times. Caleb, along with Daryl and Jacy, always kept near her. It was difficult for Lashana to accept there were two new Fives. All of the apprentices who had been selected to replace the aging Fifty were also eager to chat with Lashana.

It was hours before Caleb finally pulled her away from the crowd. "There is yet one you have not seen. He refused to meet you in front of the others."

"I…I'm not sure I am ready. Has he forgiven me?"

"Only he can tell you that. Go to your old suite. He awaits you there."

Lashana left the garden and entered the hallway. She did not have to go far before finding her old apartment. Standing before the ornate door, her heart pounded in trepidation. Gathering her courage, she opened the door and stepped into the penthouse. She saw no one as she glanced about, but the furniture and decorations had barely been altered since the last time she had been here—on the day of her death. She walked further into the room near the couch. There was movement, and she quickly looked toward the arched doors leading to the balcony. There stood Ariyo, silently watching her.

Countless times she had gone over this meeting in her head, the words she would say. But now seeing her soulmate, no words came to her.

For a while neither spoke. Then Ariyo said, "You have aged."

"So have you."

"But it barely shows on me."

"Forty is not old for a human."

Silence again.

Lashana took several steps closer to him while glancing around the room. "You haven't changed it much."

"Decorating I always left for you."

"I'm sorry I wasn't here when Jacob, Gabriel, and Mason died. It grieves me very much that I left on such bad terms, that I can never make amends with them. And I am sorry for the pain I put you through."

"Are you sorry for having someone else's kids?"

Feeling as if he had slapped her, Lashana looked away. She visualized Seth's kind face. Why should she keep apologizing? "No, I'm not. I'm proud of my children. And of Seth. He was a good husband. An excellent one. He was there for me when you were not."

"Was that my fault?" Anger flashed in Ariyo's eyes as he stepped from the balcony into the room.

"No. The only thing I am sorry for is hurting you. Nothing else."

"You have no idea the depths of chaos and anger you plunged me into."

Lashana looked away, a hand shaking. "Can you forgive me?"

Ariyo remained silent.

312

"You...you will like my kids when you meet them. Well, only my youngest is here. I taught them to care about quintessences."

"I have met them before."

"How? When?"

"On board the *Dream Delusion* when you were going to Senator Moyer's trial."

Lashana's mouth dropped in astonishment. "Who were you?" She paused, thinking about the quintessences she had meet. "Aik?"

Ariyo gave a brief nod.

"But to disguise one's self as another is against the Code. It was the first law you wrote after almost killing Mason for pretending to be you."

"There is no Aik so I did not technical take another's place. The Five approved the plan. I was not to reveal myself to you. It would had been inappropriate since you were married. But I wanted to see you—and your family. To see if the man you married was worthy of you."

"Did you approve?"

"I did not kill him. That is the most approval I could give. Jacob wanted to come disguised too, but Tiah did not believe he could hide himself among his own birthmates."

"Jacob?" Lashana became puzzled. "Jacob had already died by the time I took that trip."

"He's not dead. As you and I can be reborn, so can others."

Lashana legs weaken and she grabbed the back of a couch to keep upright. "Not dead? Then he is?"

"Daryl, whom I believed you met at the reception. Gabriel is Jacy. And Mason is probably escorting your daughter someplace, at least according to the plan my brothers came up with."

"Marcus is Mason?" Lashana took several deep breaths. "Why did you not tell me? Do you know how much I have grieved? I cried in front of you and you said not a word. Nothing."

"If you had not chosen to live in isolation, we would have told you. It was you who sent not a word to us. Not even to mention your marriage or the birth of your kids. Your silence was the worst thing you could have done to me. You could have died, and I would not have known for months or years."

"I knew I had hurt you, and I tried to write. Many times. I still have a few of the letters, but I could never send them. I lacked the courage. I'm sorry, Alexander. Really I am."

313

"There were times I hated you. Hated Seth even more. Hated him because he could give you the one thing I never can—natural children. I was married to you for over ninety years, and would have gladly died a thousand times for you if needed. But I cannot give you children."

"I don't love you because of children. I love you because you are my soulmate. You have always understood me better than anyone else, including Seth. Forgive me for the pain I caused you."

She turned her back to him and pulled her long hair away from her neck, inviting him to bite. He hesitated only a moment before stepped up to her. Then he entered her mind. Quickly he swept through two decades of her memories. He felt her loneness and grief for his absence, her nights of weeping. She had deliberately left markers for him, silent conversations that one day she knew he would see. The day she had decided to marry Seth was especially pungent. *Forgive me, Alexander, for what I am about to do,* she thought just before kissing Seth. There was the joy and pain of childbirth. The thrills and worries of motherhood. The agony of widowhood.

Ariyo then showed her his life. Worries about her safety. The bitterness of betrayal. Hatred and loneness. Grief and rage. The love of brothers pulling him from the darkness. Heavy responsibilities of being a Five. Sometimes still reaching for her in the stillness of the night as he lay in the bed they once shared. His intense emotions as he watched her from afar at the trial. Her arms wrapped around her husband while he watched, an outsider.

When he finally broke contact with her mind, both were emotionally exhausted. He stood with his arms around her waist. She leaned against him, trembling. They held each other for a while, then she tilted her head up to him, inviting. He kissed her, letting decades of pent-up passions burst forth. All the universe was forgotten but each other. They tumbled onto a couch, still embracing tightly. Lashana's telecom rang three times before she finally pulled her mouth away from Ariyo long enough to answer it.

"Mom, it's dinner time, and we are at the food court. Are you coming to eat or not?"

"Um, eat." It was hard ignoring Ariyo nipping her ear. "Yes. Soon. Go ahead and start without me." She put down the telecom.

Ariyo gently ran his fingers through her long hair. "When do I get to officially meet my stepdaughter?"

Lashana sat up. "I'm not sure. How can I explain you?"

"Tell the truth. I'm an old acquaintance that you have feelings for."

"It's not that easy. Her father died barely three months ago. She is not ready to deal with a stepfather. Nor are my other two kids. We have to go about this slowly."

"I have waited long enough. Besides, quintessence courtships are notorious for being short."

"Not this short." Lashana stood up and headed for the door, but found it difficult because Ariyo kept stealing kisses. "I must go."

"We meet again tomorrow?"

"I don't know. I must think about Yaira."

"Tell her about me. No more hiding what we feel for each other. Tomorrow, marry me."

"Too soon, Alexander."

"No, it is not, beloved. We have waited long enough. Marry me."

Lashana escaped after one last kiss and hurried down to the food court. Her daughter and Marcus, deep in conversation, ate at a table under a flowering tree. Lashana paused, studying the burly C6 which held the essence of Mason, the only quintessence she had ever truly disliked. She had pardoned him for nearly raping her two centuries ago—but she had never forgotten.

Yaira looked up from her pizza. "Hey, Mom. Your party sure went long. Marcus said the reason they clapped for you was because it was their way of saying they want you to work here again."

Marcus added, "We place high value on Zelzer winners. Your mother has achieved much over the years, but it's time for her to return to her roots."

Lashana sat down beside her daughter. "I have made no promises either way."

"Why not?" prodded Yaira. "You'll be near me. We could explore the city every day after school. Aren't you eating?"

"I had food at the reception. Once classes start, you will have little free time. Luncaster is far harder than anything you have faced before. The job offer I will think about."

Marcus fixed her with his dark eyes. "Did you reunite with your old acquaintance?"

"We met. The uniting we will see about later."

On the trip back to the hotel, Yaira chatted nonstop about the areas she had toured. Even as they prepared for bed, she talked. "Thousands of toddlers in that giant room with enclosures dividing them. You can't tell any of them apart. But they are so well behaved. Nabeela would love working

315

here. But they wouldn't let me play with them. I had to watch through a window."

Lashana sat on the bed, only half listening, thinking of Ariyo. How would Yaira take her mother seeing another man? How long was the proper time to wait before remarrying? The only way to heal Ariyo's pain was to cause her children pain. She could not bear to do that to them.

"Mom, you're not listening."

"Of course I am."

"Then who is he?" Seeing her mom's blank look, Yaira added, "The old acquaintance Marcus mentioned."

"Just an old friend. Have you brushed your teeth?"

"Yes, while you were staring at the blank vid." Yaira threw herself on the bed. "What is it? Are you thinking about the job? I think you should take it. We'll be near each other."

Lashana sighed. "How would you feel if I started dating someone?"

Yaira cocked her head, studying her mom. "The old acquaintance?" Seeing her mother's nod, Yaira grinned. "Is he nice? Is he handsome like Dad?"

"How can you ask me that?"

"Dad would not mind. He would want you to be happy again, like how he married you after he lost Trisha. He said you pulled him out of darkness. I think you need someone to do that for you. Nathan, Nabeela, and I tried, but I don't think we succeeded. You are always so sad. Nathan almost withdrew from college twice because he was worried about leaving you, but Nabeela stopped him."

"He did not tell me that."

"We hide things from you sometimes to try to protect you." Yaira lay on her stomach and kicked her feet back and forth in the air.

"That is what parents do for their kids, not the other way around."

"Do you really like this guy? Can he help you?"

"He asked me to marry him."

"Wow." Her feet stopped kicking. "That was quick."

"We have known each other for a very long time."

"Did you say yes?"

"How can I remarry when your father just died?"

"I don't think Dad would mind if he is nice. I think you should do it. Then we will be neighbors for sure. And I can visit on the weekends, if you like, when I'm not studying. I'm sure Nathan and Nabeela would want you to. I'll ask them."

Before her mother could stop her, Yaira grabbed an e-tablet and sent a video message to her siblings, telling of the proposal. Throughout the night, Lashana worried about their responses. The next morning, Yaira was the first to grab the computer and play the reply.

Nathan and Nabeela sat close together near the screen. Nabeela spoke first. "Mom, heard you were proposed to already. Congrats. That is if you accept. We're behind you, whatever you choose."

"Don't worry about us," added Nathan. "You told us to follow our dreams. Now it's time for you to listen to your own advice. We love you."

Yaira beamed. "See, I told you. When do I get to meet him?"

Lashana choose the Grand Forum, hoping its friendly atmosphere would make their meeting less stressful. They waited near the museum, under the giant portrait of Layla.

Yaira studied the picture solemnly. "So that is what you will look like in another thirty years. Not too wrinkled."

"Thanks a lot for the reminder. Here he comes. Mind your manners."

Ariyo greeted them. "So you are Yashana's gifted daughter."

"My brother and sister are gifted to. They just didn't want to come to Luncaster. They went to Dad's college. Your name is familiar." Yaira pondered for only a moment. "Aren't you a Five? You, uh, run this place."

"That is my job."

Yaira grinned. "The others must do what you say, like with my Dad. He bossed people around a lot. But they didn't mind. We were a big family at Trisha's."

"We also are a big family here, much larger than what you are used too. When I marry your mom, that will make you part of this family too."

The teenager studied him. "You seem okay. But how powerful are you really? Can you get me in with the toddlers? I mean where I can play with them, and not just stare at them through a window."

Ariyo leaned closer and lowered his voice confidentially. "I can get you some toddler time, if you will be the sacred knot tier at my wedding."

Yaira turned to her mom. "He will do."

Chapter Thirty-seven

Across Essence hung a somber stillness. Tens of thousands of quintessences stood at attention on the parade ground. Inside each crescent-shaped barrack occupants gathered around large vids. Young quintessences stood with birthmates, as grave as the adults. Maintenance workers, scientists, cooks, custodians, gardeners, medical staff, and caregivers paused in their everyday work to listen to the speakers. The yearly Day of Remembrance had come.

On the dais at the parade ground Daryl read in a firm voice the names of the dead. Cameras broadcasted the event to the millions of quintessences observing the official holiday across the empire. "Tom, IN 15935, and Brock, IN 15936, died in a gas explosion while pursuing a suspect on Bentplane. We honor your sacrifice."

As one the listeners chanted, "Tom and Brock, we remember you."

"Stephen, ME G2-002, of the second generation, died from a fall while rescuing his grandchild who slipped during cliff climbing. His body cushioned the other's impact. For decades Stephen served as an officer for New Austin Police Department then as a member of our Synod. We honor your service."

Again the audience chanted, "Stephen, we remember you."

"Caleb, ME T2-A3, the third born of all quintessences, died from complications of old age. Served as a Five and was Director of Essence Institute for twenty-eight years. We honor your service."

"Caleb, we remember you."

Among the huge crowd gathered in the Grand Forum, a youth sighed in boredom. The college student whispered to his companion, "How much longer will this go on? We have been standing here for half an hour already."

Eighteen-year-old Yaira sighed, hoping those around her did not notice his poor manners. "It depends on how many died this year. Usually it's only a few hundred. In a bad year, sometimes it climbs into the thousands."

On the vid, Daryl stepped away from the podium, and Bill sighed in relief. "Finally, we can eat."

"It's just the changing of speakers. This will go for a long time yet."

"Then let's go ahead and eat. The food court is open."

"No, my stepfather speaks now."

"How can you tell? They all look the same to me."

"They announced his name." Yaira hid her irritation, reminding herself it was his first visit to Essence. "And you can read his nametag."

"You must read a tag before knowing who speaks? How annoying. There should be more variety. You can still see the vids from the tables. Come on, I'm starving." Bill took a step towards the dining area, but a quintessence in his path refused to move.

The C6 model glared at the young man's visitor badge. "Stranger, you should show more respect for our leaders."

Bill frowned. "I am being respectful. Please move aside, mortis elixir."

With a slight frown on his face, the tagless C6 scrutinized the youth then glanced at Yaira. "Where do you keep finding these, little one?"

Recognizing the catchphrase, Yaira smiled, knowing now that the C6 was Marcus. Like many of the Synod, he was prone to sometimes walk about Essence without uniform or nametag, an equal among brethren. How long had he been standing beside her without saying a word? "What can I say? I'm popular with the boys."

"Or perhaps it is your mother's fame that attracts them."

Bill glared at Marcus, not knowing he spoke to a Five. "You will keep out of my business, leech."

"You are my business, boy. You are dating the director's daughter."

"Don't you have some thief to arrest? Or perhaps you have been paid to overthrow yet another government?"

Yaira placed a warning hand on Bill's arm. "You should not talk to him like that."

Impassively Marcus locked eyes with Bill. "It is alright, Yaira. He is too insufficient for me to kill."

"Insufficient? I will have you know that I am the son of a prime minister, and my IQ is double, no, triple that of yours."

"Humbleness, though, you lack. Perhaps you will gain that with age…if you live long enough."

"I am not afraid of you, leech. My father has dealt with your kind. You are only slaves and mercenaries, created to obey the bidding of true leaders such as my father. Or myself. Remember your place, soldier."

A dangerous look came into Marcus's dark eyes. Yaira quickly intervened. "Bill, you should go now."

"It's about time."

"Without me. I will stay for the rest of the ceremony."

The youth looked uncertain for the first time. "I cannot leave you here."

"Have you forgotten this is my home? And you insult my family. It's time for you to go, now."

Bill frowned at her then angrily pushed his way out of the crowd in the direction of the monorail station. Yaira turned back to the giant vid and joined the chanting, feeling embarrassed by the disturbance her date had caused. For the next hour she stood with Marcus by her side, one among a sea of the dedicated remembering the dead. Only when the last name was chanted and the crowd began to thin did she turn to Marcus.

"I apologize for Bill's behavior. I would not have invited him if I had known he was going to be that rude."

"But you knew he disliked quintessences."

"I had thought that perhaps seeing our Day of Remembrance would change his mind."

"Our enemies do not belong here on this of all days."

"Again, I am sorry." She touched his hand. "Forgive me by dining with me. I'm starved."

They joined the long lines forming at the food court, speaking little as they purchased food. There were no tables left so they went outside to eat, finding a quiet courtyard.

"I missed your reading cause Bill took so long picking me up. I'll watch the recording later."

"You pick strange dates, Yaira. He is the second I have run off this year."

"Third actually, if you count the winter break. Can I not help it if my dates find being near your kind stressful."

"Sometimes I think you deliberately pick the same type just to watch them squirm."

The teenager kept her eyes downcast on her plate. "Why would I do that?"

"Why indeed? But you went too far bringing one to the Day of Remembrance."

"Again I apologize. I miscalculated." They finished the meal in silence. As they tossed their trash away, Yaira said, "I don't have a ride back to college. I came with Bill."

"There is the monorail."

"But then I have to take a taxi from the station to the college," her voice hinted slyly.

Marcus studied her for a moment. "I will drive you back."

Yaira smiled. "Thanks. To pay for your fuel, I will buy your ticket to the movie we will see."

"There was no mention of a movie."

"*The Battle of Lonsgrast* has great reviews. Bill and I were going to see it after the ceremony. Since you ran my date off, you owe me."

Marcus's dark eyes held her, giving the effect of peering into her mind.

The teenager refused to back down from his stare. "Even a Five must have fun occasionally. If you don't go with me, I must go by myself, walking home alone in the dark. Mom would not appreciate that."

Yaira knew she was being presumptuous inviting a Five to a movie. He had many matters to deal with and could easily order a subordinate to protect her. Yet he did not.

The epic war movie was nearly three hours long, and night had already fallen when they walked out of the theater. Without asking, Yaira turned away from the parking lot and strolled along the boardwalk bordering the ocean, Marcus by her side. Rich aromas of roasting meat drifted from a restaurant. Laughter and music came from a bar. Couples passed, hand in hand. Others sat on benches, kissing in the moonlight.

Yaira walked near Marcus. "So was the movie realistic enough for you?"

"The plot was not historical accurate at times, but at least the fighting looked real. The computerized quintessences reacted like real soldiers."

"Those were real quintessences. From what I read, there are several clutches of birthmates that make a good living portraying...well, themselves."

Shocked by such a concept, Marcus stopped walking. "Quintessence actors? We are real soldiers, not playthings for cinema."

"Don't be angry with them," the teenager teased. "You said yourself they did a good job in this movie. By portraying quintessences in a positive manner, they help your public image."

Yaira leaned against the railing separating the boardwalk from the beach. In the distance, lightning flashed across the sky from an approaching storm. "It is so beautiful, isn't it? Waves in the moonlight while a storm rages."

"I have seen it before."

"I never tire seeing the raw power of nature. So many take it for granted here. Back on Volodymyr we have ashstorms. Few who see that with their own eyes live to tell the tale." She shifted her body closer to Marcus. "You are fortunate to grow up on a planet where an approaching storm doesn't mean death."

"Fortunate am I?" He held still as her arm brushed his. "Storms I have fought in where death rained down from missiles, my birthmates dying around me, myself bleeding from multiple wounds."

"I am sorry they died. Their deaths we honor, their sacrifice we will not forget. That is why movies like *The Battle of Lonsgrast* are important."

Marcus turned away from the storm to look at her. "You have a way of finding something positive in everything."

Yaira's hand touched his. "I see miracles everywhere. A flower growing in a crack in the sidewalk, surviving despite trampling feet. A bird lifting itself into the air without need of an engine. Raindrops touching my skin. Fresh air in my lungs without the need to wear an oxygen mask. Perhaps you think I am silly to speak of such things which you experience every day."

"Silly does not come to my mind when I think of you."

The teenager stretched herself up and kissed him on the lips. Marcus did not respond, but neither did he pull away. Yaira was disappointed. "Sorry if I offended you."

"You have apologized much today, but your sincerity is lacking."

"I did not mean for Bill to disrupt the Day of Remembrance."

"But you did bring him to insult me."

"No, I…I…"

"Keep bringing fools by when we both know you are not interested in them. Your games to try to arouse jealousy in me need to stop."

"A game? Do you think I play a game with you?" Yaira began walking away, but turned after a few paces. "Maybe I am but a child to you, but I am older than my mom when she fell in love with Ariyo."

"I am forty-five years older than you, little one."

"Stop calling me that. Most quintessences choose wives much younger than themselves and still outlive them. Besides, I only look a few years younger than you. Maybe I haven't seen as much of the universe as you, but I can make up for that with loyalty, passion, and intelligence."

Marcus remained stoic. "We should walk back now."

Yaira refused to move. "I'm not the only one playing games. Since when has guard duty become a personal responsibility of the Five? Yet you have kept a close eye on me since I first came to Essence."

"I was asked to."

"Not after you became a Five. You seek me out when I'm at Essence on school breaks, listen to me prattling on about my life, and make sure I always get back to college safely. You went on a date with me tonight. If you don't care, you shouldn't act like you do."

"You are Yashana's child. It is my duty to care for you."

"Duty is all I am to you? Next time say 'no' when asked to dinner and a movie. Gives a girl the wrong impression."

Yaira walked away in a huff. Marcus easily caught up with her and marched silently by her side. They turned off the boardwalk towards the parking lot. As they passed an alleyway between several businesses, Marcus suddenly grabbed her, pulling her into the darkness behind a dumpster. Yaira barely had time to protest before he bit her, probing her mind. For a few minutes she was aware of nothing, but encouraged by what he found, he allowed her to become conscious of his search through her memories.

Conversations with her dad and siblings flashed by, laugher, frustrations, desires to be away from Volodymyr. The deep bond of mother and daughter. School friends. Countless embarrassing situations as she adapted to living in a culture she knew little about. Class assignments. Beginning her internship at Essence. Determination to prove she could be as talented a geneticist as her mom. Secret infatuation with Marcus. The budding of young love. Plots to win his attention.

Marcus then poured his own memories into her. A blur of battles and slaughtered foes. Villagers begging for help as they dug through rubble after an earthquake. His hands caked with mud and blood as he cleared debris with them. Sobbing thanks of a mom as he handed over a missing child. Politicians demanding war. More battles, new deaths. Bleeding bodies. Birthmates dying. Throbbing pain from wounds while he held a brother breathing his last. Deep grief. The pride of his commendation day as he walked across the platform and received his citizenship ID from Director Caleb. The achievement of being selected as a Five. His own infatuation with Yaira when he knew he should stay away. Yet she drew him like a moth to a flame.

The bite ended. Yaira leaned against his brawny body, her own slender one trembling as she tried to understand what she had experienced. "Mom never mentioned the epulo could do that."

"It is one of our most guarded secrets. We only tell our spouses."

"So is this the quintessence way of proposing?"

"You might say that."

The teenager turned in his arms to face him. "Then yes, I will marry you."

He kissed her then, and she melted against him. After several minutes he pulled away. "I must get you back before curfew."

"I'm in no hurry."

"What we can do with the epulo you must not speak about. It is a secret we kill to protect from outsiders. And our courtship should be kept quiet until your graduation three months from now."

"Alright. But once we are married, then can I speak about the epulo with my mom?"

"Yes, and with other spouses of my brethren."

Rain began falling. Yaira laughed, and tilted her head up, eyes closed, relishing the sensation of cold water running over her body. When she opened her eyes again, she found Marcus, with a rare smile, watching her. She grinned. Hand-in-hand they strolled out of the alley, lightening illumining their way.

Over the following months, Yaira kept her upcoming wedding quiet, too enticed in the wooing to question the secrecy. During the week, she stayed focus on her studies—most of the time. The days she had internship at Essence, Marcus was there when she got off the monorail. He always wore casual clothes and no nametag. They took their time going back to Luncaster, taking long walks or seeing movies, sometimes seeking secluded spots. As graduation drew near, Yaira became impatient. Her friends talked of upcoming changes in their lives as bright careers beckoned. They already knew that a job waited Yaira at Essence, but she could not share with them her joy for the upcoming marriage. She spoke several times to Marcus about announcing their engagement, but he kept asking her to wait, saying the timing was off.

Her patience wavered one day as she ate lunch with her mom in the food court. They chatted about work and ideas for new clones. Ariyo sometimes joined them for lunch, but the technical talk bored him. Today he was busy elsewhere when Lashana brought up the subject of apartments.

"Perhaps we could start looking for one tomorrow for you."

Yaira frowned. "I thought I would be living at Essence."

"Ariyo and I don't mind you staying in our penthouse during school breaks, but you are an adult now. You need your own place."

"There are apartments here at Essence."

"Yes, but they are reserved for quintessences and their families. There are many lovely apartments nearby in New Hope. I've already picked out a few which might interest you. If you like, I could call to set up some appointments."

"Mom, that's very considerate of you, but I...uh...plan to live here."

"If you really want to live in the penthouse, I do not mind."

"I was thinking along the lines of having my own penthouse."

Lashana paused, studying her daughter. "What are you implying?"

"That I'm engaged to a Five. We are to be married after I graduate."

"When did this take place?" Lashana's eyes narrowed. "They all are far too old for you."

"You married one who was much older than you."

"I was forty when I married him. Being the wife of a Five carries heavy responsibilities that you are not yet ready for. Who is it that asked you? Jacy?"

"Marcus. We are in love. I will learn to deal with the responsibilities of being his wife."

"Marcus? He hid from me that he was spending time with you." A dangerous tone came into the mother's voice. "You cannot marry him. I forbid it."

"Forbid it?" Yaira tossed her fork down. "Mom, you just said yourself that I'm an adult. I may marry who I please. You never said anything about any of those boys I kept bringing here."

"Those boys you were not serious about, and Marcus is no boy. Take your time. Date some scientists working here. Marry someone who shares your life dreams. Marcus is a harden warrior whose life is very different from your own."

"I know about his life." Yaira lowered her voice. "He showed it to me. Killing foes and saving civilians."

"Showed you, has he," Lashana's grim face become unreadable. "You have only seen glimpses of his life."

"And he will keep showing me more. The epulo is a wonderful tool, allowing couples to share their lives with each other."

Lashana attacked from a different angle. "Mason can never father children."

"So? I can adopt or have embryos made from my own DNA. You and your sisters were ordered from BGF."

325

"My sisters were created from egg and sperm of my parents. You will have a stranger father your offspring?"

"There are many women married to quintessences who do so all the time, and their children turn out fine."

"It is not the same as having a child from your own flesh fathered by someone you love."

Yaira glared at her mother. "I thought you would be happy for me. I don't understand why you are upset. You enjoy being married to Ariyo."

"There are some things you don't know. Trust me, do not marry Mason."

"Mason? We're talking about Marcus."

Lashana face paled as she realize her slip. "I meant Marcus."

"I am going to marry him. You cannot stop me."

Lashana held her daughter's gaze. "I'm sorry, dear, but I will prevent this wedding. It's for your own good." She rose from the table, tossed her trash away, and headed to the elevator.

Upset, Yaira sat for a while, pondering the conversation. Never had Yaira heard her mother once say a negative thing about quintessence marriage. Why the suddenly hostility? And that warning about stopping the wedding. Marcus was not bonded. He was free to live the life he wished. Her mom, as only a head of a lab within the research department, had no authority over Marcus. Deciding he should be warned, Yaira used her telecom to search for his whereabouts. Everyone could be tracked at Essence, but only those with high clearance could see anybody they choose. Birthmates, families, and friends had to seek permission to add each other to their buddy lists, which Yaira and Marcus did as soon as they had begun dating. With a few clicks, Yaira learned Marcus was walking into her parents' penthouse. Hurrying to the elevator, Yaira felt dread. What was her mother up to? Did she think being married to the director allowed her to boss around other Five?

Yaira walked into the penthouse without bothering to knock. In the middle of the airy living room her livid mother chided Marcus. Ariyo watched, but held his tongue.

"Why did not the Shadow Guards report that you were spending time with my daughter?"

"Contrary to what you may think, Essence no longer revolves around you. I have committed no crime. There was nothing for them to report." Marcus kept a calm, steady voice.

"But you never should have been alone with her. I will have you executed for this."

"On what charges? According to the Shadow Bylaws, a courting quintessence may ask for privacy. I asked and they kept their distance."

Lashana spat out, "Foeditas horribilis, that is when you should have been watched the closest. When were you planning to tell me you were dating my daughter? Once you were married?"

"That was my plan."

Yaira gasped, "I would never marry you without my mom knowing."

Marcus turned to her, a flicker of worry flashed in his eyes. "I had hoped, when the time came, you could be persuaded. That you would trust me."

"You knew my mom would disapprove of us?"

"I believed our love strong enough to overcome your mother's objections."

"But why the anger between you two?"

Lashana cut in, "There is much he has not told you. And much he never will. You should leave now."

"Leave? Mom, I'm still marrying him. You may not like him, but I love him."

Lashana glanced at her husband before facing her daughter again. "Marcus is deceitful and dangerous. You may marry any other quintessence but him."

"I am an adult, and may choose whoever I want. I will marry only Marcus. You cannot stop me."

A dark look came into Lashana's eyes. "Ariyo, take my daughter out of here."

"I'm not leaving, Mom, not without Marcus. If you are going to act so ridiculous about this, then I'm not inviting you to our wedding. And why should I keep waiting? We can wed tonight." Yaira held out a hand and Marcus began walking towards her.

"No!" Fury overcame Lashana. She stepped near her husband, grabbed his gun from its holster, and pointed it at Marcus.

"Mom, don't!" Yaira tried to run to her fiancé, but Ariyo grabbed her arm and held her back. She fought for release. "Have you gone crazy?"

Lashana flipped off the gun's safety and gestured for her husband to take Yaira out of the room.

"Let her stay," said Marcus, taking several steps towards Lashana. "Yaira should see what really lies behind that benevolent mask you so casually wear."

"You are the monster here. Why did you have to come after my daughter?"

"It is your daughter who came after me. We fell in love. Do you remember what that feels like? Perhaps not, since you have been too busy the last few decades betraying your soulmate."

"Brother, be careful how you speak to my wife," warned Ariyo, keeping a gentle but firm grip on Yaira.

"I have been careful for the last two hundred years. Constantly trying to redeem myself, hoping to receive just a glint of pity or sympathy from her. But I am the castoff, doomed to be despised by my creator."

"I pardoned you." Lashana glanced at her bewildered daughter, wishing Marcus would not speak about the past in front of her.

"Pardon is not the same as forgiveness. You have hated me ever since, though I have done everything you asked of me. Everything." Marcus stepped closer. "Now when I finally find hope in my desolation, you threaten to take her from me."

Lashana placed her finger on the trigger. "I will not allow you to hurt her."

"Hurt her? You still only see me as a monster after all these years. Rest your mind, your daughter is a virgin and will remain so till we marry. As I am too."

"That was almost not the case."

"I am weary of trying to earn your forgiveness, creator." Marcus kneeled on the carpet. "Kill me. Be done with this scorn. But raise your sight. Quintessences often live long enough after a chest wound to feed off their attacker. Head shots are the only sure way for a quick kill."

Lashana obliged by pointing the weapon at his head. Yaira screamed and fought against Ariyo's tight hold. Marcus looked coldly at the barrel, showing no fear, but Lashana's hand shook.

"Not so easy is it, creator, taking the life you designed." Marcus glanced as his brother. "Take your time. My brother will not stop you. None of my brethren will lift a finger against you when this is done. Absolute power is yours. Pull the trigger and become the monster you accuse me of being."

"Beloved," came Ariyo's soft voice, "As I forgave your betrayal against me, so you must forgive the offense against you."

"But he wants my daughter."

"If you kill him, you lose her forever."

"We can erase her memory, letting her think he died some other way."

"Mom," sobbed Yaira. "Please don't do this. I love him. Whatever he did, he is sorry. Please, Mom."

Lashana glanced at her daughter, her face softening. "You have no idea what he really is. What he is capable of."

"I...I don't care. You are the one pointing the gun, not him."

Lashana's hand trembled. Steadying the weapon with her other hand helped little. She lowered the gun and handed it back to her husband. As he took the weapon, he released Yaira who ran to Marcus and embraced him. Lashana turned her back to her daughter, trying to hide the vivid emotions she struggled with. No one spoke for a long time.

Still facing way, Lashana said, "There will be no wedding until after her graduation. Your courtship must remain proper until then."

"Of course, creator."

"And Marcus," Lashana turned and looked him in the eyes, "If you ever hurt her, no matter how many years go by, I will have you executed."

"I expect nothing less."

Marcus led Yaira out of the apartment and across the hall to his own penthouse. She wiped away the last of her tears as she surveyed for the first time his home with its dark, sober furniture. The few art pieces were repugnant, cryptic in meaning.

"We quintessences usually leave decorating to our wives. As I have never had one, you must forgive my choices." Marcus sat beside Yaira on a grey couch and searched her eyes for approval. "I have money saved up. Quite a bit actually, as I buy little. You may purchase whatever you like for our apartment."

Yaira looked around the room, gathering her thoughts, unable to speak.

"Are you alright? Would you like something to drink?"

"Drink? No. I don't understand anything that just happened. My mom tried to kill you, and you were just going to let her."

"I cannot harm your mom. None of my brethren will lift a finger against her."

"Why not? You outrank her." Seeing Marcus's grim expression, she added, "Don't you? She is only a head in the research department, yet you treat her like she is...is... What do you mean by calling her *creator*?"

"There is much I have to tell you, little one. Where do I start?"

"Show me." She turned her back, bushing away her long hair. "And stop calling me *little one*. You are not marrying a child."

He bit, sending images of his first life. Growing up with his four brothers, training upcoming generations. Top level missions. Decades of working for the Emperor, becoming his secret hand to investigate world leaders. Layla a distant observer, always waiting for him to make a fatal mistake. His grief at Layla's funeral, never having made peace with his creator. The rebirth of Layla and Alexander. Lashana's pleading for permission to marry Ariyo. His vote of no. Learning of her marriage to Seth and his brother's fall into darkness. Knowledge of his own upcoming death and choosing Marcus as his heir.

When he finished, Yaira sat silently for a long time in the stagnant room, sorting out the information. Marcus held her hand, his eyes noting each of her facial changes as she struggled through conflicting emotions.

"My mom is not just the clone of Layla. She is Layla. And you are both Mason and Marcus in one body."

"Yes, I am two in one."

"That makes you how old?"

"Collectively, over two hundred and fifty years."

The teenager spoke in a hollow voice, "I am but a caterpillar compared to you, an acorn next to a mighty oak. How can you love me?"

"How can I not? My life has been too long. What pleasure I once knew as a naïve youth was quickly lost. I made some mistakes, and have paid for those sins ever since. I have become harden and cynical, jaded by life. But to you the universe is new, everyday an adventure to enjoy. You see beauty and hope everywhere. Through you, I feel alive, perhaps for the first time since both my births."

"You make me sound much better than what I am. I'm compulsive and make stupid mistakes all the time. I am a *little one* next to you."

"Who has not erred? To love makes one vulnerable. My greatest fear is losing you."

Yaira turned sympathetic eyes towards him. "I'm not going anywhere. That is, as long as you want me around. I love you, Marcus…Mason. No matter which name you go by."

"You have not yet asked what sin I committed that your mother despises me for. And there are other dark deeds I have done. Before you are so quick to pledge your life to me, you should know all that I am."

The teenager swallowed. "Alright. Show me. But it won't change how I feel."

"This I will only tell. There are some things you should never see." Marcus rose from the couch and moved to study a large painting on the wall showing a swirling vortex of dark greys mixed with red splotches. "I had planned to never tell you about my first life, just as your mother never told your father. Makes things much simpler." He looked towards Yaira. "In our Canon, I am known as Mason, the Inquisitor. Before the creation of the AF models, none could equal my abilities of mind probing, not even my birthmates. My talent lies in the fact that I was unafraid to peer into the darkest depravity of minds, searching to understand hidden motives. Few others dared to go as deep as I. My brothers warned that I might become corrupted by what I saw. They were right.

"One day I disguised myself as Alexander and kissed Layla. When I tried to take it too far, she became frightened and ordered me to stop. Alexander found out, and we tried to kill each other. Layla intervened then pardoned me. Together we Five and her made the Code which all quintessences must live by. Many of those laws were made specifically to address my faults. Ironically, I become one of the enforcers of those laws, executing those who failed to live up to the standards I myself had failed. Eventually because of my talents, I was sent by several Emperors to investigate warlords who pledged fidelity to the Empire but ruled their own worlds with despotic fists. It was I who decided if keeping a malicious tyrant in power was better or worse than removing him, creating a power vacuum and possible civil war. Many sentients would die no matter which way I leaned. My choices were controversy, even among the Synod. I was the least popular of the Five and the most feared."

Marcus sat in a chair across from Yaira, his eyes haunted. "Alexander forgave my offenses against him long ago, but I was never able to regain Layla's trust, no matter how hard I tried. Thousands have died because of my decisions, but millions have benefited. Layla only remembers the harm and not the good I have done. I am not a murderer, but an arbitrator who has killed countless times. This is my job, and I will continue to do so." He looked his fiancé in the eyes. "Can you truly love me, knowing what I am?"

The teenager studied a small, ugly stature of a demon on the coffee table which separated her from Marcus. "You kissed my mom?"

"Long ago in another lifetime. Not for love but curiosity and lust. I was but an adolescent myself, acting on emotions and not logic. I have since matured. The only one I have ever loved is you."

"Loved?" Yaira glared at her fiancé. "You kissed my mom."

"Does this bother you worse than me being a hardened killer?"

"Yes! You don't go around kissing your girlfriend's mom."

"That was nearly two centuries before your birth. If you wish to break up with me, you have that right. It is what your mother wishes."

"I see why she wants that."

Marcus stood. "Then go. I will not stop you."

Yaira rose, glaring at him. Then her anger faded. "You can't get rid of me that easily. My promise to love you holds true."

"How can you love a monster like me?"

"Monsters don't feel guilt." Yaira stepped around the table. "I have seen my father make decisions which led to employees accidently dying. Guilt nearly destroyed him, but Mom was always there to comfort him."

"Easy for her to comfort when no crime was committed. I have sought absolution from her for two centuries and only known guilt and scorn."

Yaira wrapped her arms around Marcus. "I forgive you, my love, for everything. In time, when Mom sees you as a caring husband and father, she will too."

Marcus rested a hand on her cheek. "I do not deserve you."

"Remember that when I start throwing away all your furniture, starting with that ugly stature."

"Toss everything. You are the only thing I wish to hold on to."

After a kiss, Yaira smiled. "Stay put, I will be right back."

Yaira walked across the hallway and entered Lashana's penthouse. She found her mom and Ariyo talking on the balcony. When Yaira stepped outside, Ariyo gave a brief nod of greeting, but Lashana turned away, looking towards the ocean lying beyond Essence.

"Mom, Marcus...or should I say Mason...told me everything. It's kind of cool knowing you are Layla and my mom, though I am still trying to understand how the whole blending thing works." Yaira turned to her step-father. "And you're Alexander, firstborn of all quintessences. Pretty amazing. Both of you together when you are supposed to be dead. You hid your secrets so well that my father never knew."

"Your mother loved your father, never doubt that."

Yaira felt her throat tighten. "I know."

"Did Mason explain why your mother and him do not get along?"

"Yeah. He made a stupid mistake when he was my age. I make them all the time, and Mom forgives me."

Lashana spoke without turning around. "There is a big difference between attempted rape and not cleaning your room."

"Mom, he is very, very sorry. How long will you hold a grudge?"

"Forever if it involves you."

"I know you just want to protect me, but Marcus...Mason has not harmed me. Nor will he. He is not that foolish adolescent anymore. Mom, we will marry with or without your blessing, but I prefer with it." Yaira waited for a response as a sea breeze whipped strands of her mother's hair into twisted curls. The silence became deafening.

Ariyo reached over and touched his wife's hand. "Beloved, let not wrath divide you from love."

Lashana sighed and turned around. "I will support you and try to be open to him."

Yaira smiled. "Thanks, Mom."

"I said *try*. That doesn't mean I have to like him."

"That is a start. I'm thinking about going shopping tomorrow to purchase new furniture for his...our apartment. It's time to brighten up his life. Would you like to come with me?"

Lashana breathed deeply the fresh air. "Yes, I would like that."

Epilogue

Begin recording.

"Mema, it's on." An Indian child giggled as she made faces at a camera built into a computer monitor in Lashana's study.

From the living room came Lashana's voice, "Akari, have you picked up your toys yet? Your mother will be here soon."

"Mostly. Look at me." The child puckered her lips. "Fish face."

Lashana, dressed in an evening grown, walked into the study. "Clean up now, play later."

"Alright." The child reluctantly headed to the living room. Seeing her grandfather tossing the last of her toys into a bin, she grinned. "Papa, wanta make a video with me?"

Ariyo took his granddaughter's hand and allowed himself to be led to the computer. She sat on his lap and leaned near the lens, singing a song listing major bones of the body. "Mema, did you hear me sing?"

"Yes, dear. Excellent memory." Lashana peered into a mirror, putting on make-up.

"Do you know what I want to be when I grow up?"

"What is that?"

"Toy salesman. Can I do that?"

"If you wish. You can be anything you want to be."

"How about an ice cream maker?"

"If you wish."

"New flavors every day."

"Sounds delicious."

Akari giggled then turned in her grandfather's lap. Leaning near his ear, she loudly whispered, "I'm really going to be a geneticist like Mommy and Mema."

"Not a soldier like your father or me?"

The child tilted her head, thinking. "Maybe a geneticist soldier." Hearing the door of the penthouse open, the child beamed as she jumped to the floor. "Mommy! Daddy!"

Yaira, in her thirties, came into view. "Are you ready? The dinner party starts in an hour."

"But I don't get to go," pouted Akari. "Only you and Daddy. And Mema and Papa."

"It will be too boring for you. Remember, your Aunt Nabeela is visiting. You're going to play with your cousins while we're gone."

"Cousins! Cousins!" Arkari dashed out of the room, singing their names. "Papa, I can't reach my books."

After Ariyo left the study to fetch the items, Yaira leaned close to her mother. "I finished looking over the files for that special project we have been discussing."

"What did you think about them?" Lashana put on silver earrings.

"Perhaps your best work yet. Too bad no one else will ever see them."

"No one can predict the future. The possibility may open."

"At what cost? I fear only a great catastrophe will open such a path."

"Hope for the best, plan for the worst. That is the all we can do."

Arkari called from the living room, "Mommy, hurry up. Daddy says come now."

"Yes, dear." Yaira headed towards the door. "Was I that bossy when I was young?"

"Not as much as your sister."

Lashana brushed her hair. In the distance, the penthouse door slammed behind her granddaughter. Studying the brush, Lashana frowned as she held up a gray hair.

Ariyo, dressed in a tux, entered. "We're going to be late."

She held up the hair. "I'm getting old again."

"What does that matter? My love is not based on your hair color."

"I'm dyeing it this time."

"If you wish." He kissed her.

She pushed him away. "You're messing up my lipstick."

He caught her hands. "You can put it on again." He pulled her to him, kissing her firmly.

"We're late."

"They will not eat until we arrive."

Lashana sat the brush on the desk while her husband nibbled her neck, his arms wrapped around her waist. Seeing the light of the camera still on, she reached to turn it off.

End recording.

About the Author

Books have fascinated me since I was a small child sitting beside my mother, listening to her read books I had selected from the library. Soon I was reading on my own, and I never stopped. Over the years my interests have varied wildly from stories about animals to the classics to science fiction, and much in between.

In sixth grade my English teacher assigned us to write a short story. I got a tad carried away, writing a VERY long story about the adventures of a cat. Part of the way through the writing process, I realized this is what I wanted to do the rest of my life.

So I began writing short stories and eventually novels. I also became an English teacher because I wanted to share my love of literature with others. I later branched into teaching technology, another one of my passions.

The results you hold in your hands is from years of exploring my imagination and the intensive but exciting labor of writing.

I would appreciate, if you have a moment, giving my book a rating at Amazon, Goodreads, and other sites that interest you. In the limited free time I now have, the books I choose to read are usually recommended to me by friends, so I know the power of word-of-mouth.

I hope you enjoyed reading this book as much as I enjoyed writing it.

Sincerely,
Vista Townsend

Updates for new projects can be found at:
Website: vistatownsend.net
Facebook: Vista.townsend
Twitter: Vista_Townsend

www.ingramcontent.com/pod-product-compliance
Lightning Source LLC
Chambersburg PA
CBHW071048250626
47159CB00002B/400